# LORDS OF THE RIVERS

## Nancy Niblack Baxter

The Heartland Chronicles,
Book II

Art by Richard Day, Vincennes University

Guild Press of Indiana
6000 Sunset Lane
Indianapolis, IN
46208

ALSO BY NANCY BAXTER

BOOK ONE OF THE HEARTLAND CHRONICLES:
THE MOVERS, 1987

GALLANT FOURTEENTH:
THE STORY OF AN INDIANA CIVIL WAR REGIMENT, 1980

THE MIAMIS! (FOR CHILDREN) 1988

FROM GUILD PRESS OF INDIANA:

INDIANA HISTORY

WILDERNESS TO WASHINGTON BY ELEANOR RICE LONG

SONS OF THE WILDERNESS:
JOHN AND WILLIAM CONNER BY CHARLES N. THOMPSON

THE CONNERS OF CONNER PRAIRIE (FOR CHILDREN)
BY JANET HALE (1989)

MICHIGAN HISTORY

NOBLE MEMORIES: THE MEMOIRS OF PERCY NOBLE OF ELK
RAPIDS

Copyright 1988 by Guild Press of Indiana
Library of Congress Catalog Card Number 88-823-12
ISBN  0-9617367-7-1

# Acknowledgments

I am grateful to the historical editor of this book Tom Shaw, Assistant Site Manager for Ft. Snelling Historical Site in St. Paul, Minnesota; Dr. Ralph Gray, Professor of History at Indiana University, Indianapolis for reading and critiquing the manuscript as a southern Indiana native; Patsy Clark, of Leiter's Ford, Indiana, herself a native American descendent; and Shirley Willard, President of the Fulton County Historical Society for sharing their excellent material on the Trail of Death; Juanita Hunter of the Cass County Historical Society; Howard La Hurreau, Shup-She-wana, of Ft. Wayne, who is Chief of the Eagle Clan of the Potawatomi nation, for critiquing the Potawatomi material; Lora Siders of the Miami Nation of Indians of Indiana for help with the Miami section, and Frederick P. Griffin, Historian for Harrison County, for advice about Corydon.

I wish to thank the following New England libraries for documents on the Poore and Brooks families: Essex Institute, Salem, Massachusetts, and its researcher Prudence J. Backman for the two letters of John Poore from Pittsburgh reprinted in this book; the Lincoln Public Library, Lincoln, Massachusetts, for materials on the Brooks family; the Sons and Daughters of the First Settlers of Newbury, Massachusetts, for excellent materials on the Poores and their area. I wish to also thank the Indiana Division, Indiana State Library for Indiana materials.

I am indebted to the thesis "The Hidden Community: The Miami Indians of Indiana 1846-1940" by Stewart J. Rafert and to more than a hundred diaries, letters and accounts of Midwestern life written by the pioneers themselves.

## *Introduction*

In libraries and attics across the Middle West and America itself exists a treasure trove richer than Fort Knox.

It consists of the letters, journals and accounts of the pioneer generation who lived over a century before us. These documents tell of the hopes, aspirations, defeats, and triumphs of living people who settled a hostile country, meeting obstacles we can't even imagine today.

Taken together, these pioneer accounts weave a tapestry that is as varied and fascinating as any of today's television dramas. These were human beings who wrestled with the wilderness; and their tales of love, sin, and triumph are surprisingly modern. The tales are, of course, much more meaningful than some of those dramas, because they speak of courage under fire and endurance in the face of hardship. Just as importantly, they tell us of tragic mistakes made in the history of the Midwest, mistakes from which we all should learn lessons for today's social and political quandries.

Most of all, the documents of the pioneers reveal their love of the land: the rivers, the brown earth, the rolling hills in this Midwest, the same love we who live here feel today. There is in most of these letters and journals a quiet decency and an inspiring understanding of the meaning of America in its purest essence— opportunity and individual freedom for all.

The other great group this book is about, the tribal peoples of the Midwest, the woodland Indians, left few documents. Their story exists in tribal memory and in the heart of the land itself.

The people who tell their stories through their own documents in this book really existed. The Brookses lived in Massachusetts from the seventeenth century on, as described. Brooks Tavern may be seen in Minuteman National Park today. The three Brooks brothers did come west and form a transportation and mercantile empire much as described in the book.

Hannah Chute Poore and her family came to the Northwest from Massachusetts about as described, bearing grape hyacinths and roses. Her odyssey, representative as it is of the Great Migration, is a true one and the trial she faced really happened. Hindostan Falls was the largest town in Indiana in 1820, although its story has faded with the passing of the years.

Hannah's Christian devotion book, her pioneer tools including the toaster mentioned, *The Angel Visitant* book of Lewis Brooks, the McClure wool wheel, all exist today as prized family possessions. (The toaster is in the Indiana State Museum.) The *Walam Olum* was printed by the Indiana Historical Society in Indianapolis in 1954.

Finally, this is the 150th anniversary of the Potawatomi Trail of Death, which has recently and quite fittingly been re-christened the Trail of Courage. Paukooshuck, son of Aubenaubee and Menominee of Twin Lakes, lived the experiences detailed in this book.

Although most of the people in this book did exist and the occurences are a part of Midwestern history, this is a work of fiction.

The two original letters of John Poore have been left as originally penned, and other documents have been recreated in typical style and sometimes spelling to suggest the flavor of the times.

Nancy Baxter
Indianapolis, 1988

Poores

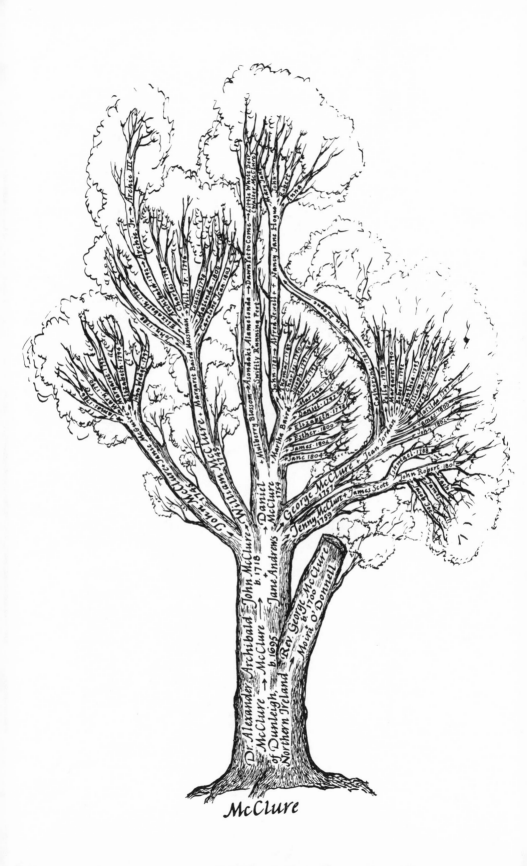

McClure

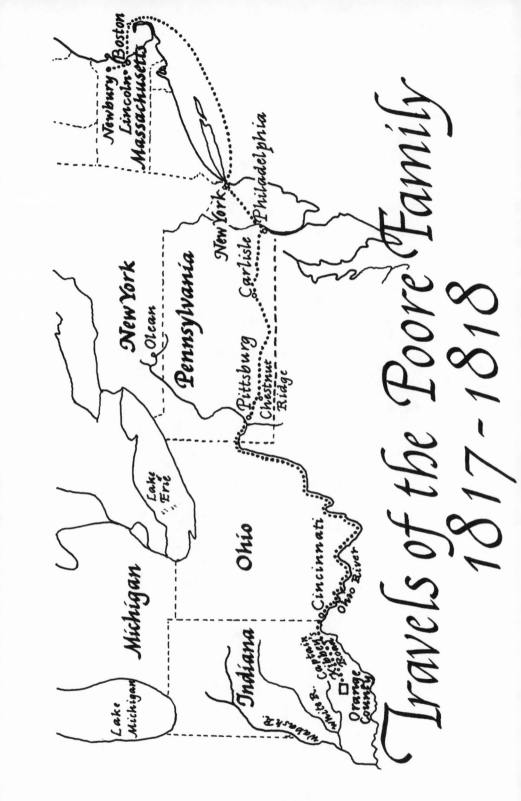

Travels of the Poore Family
1817-1818

Indiana in 1819

Cincinnati

Ohio River

Madison

Captain Kibbey's Rd.

Louisville

New Albany

E. Fork White River

Hindostan Falls

Paoli

The Buffalo Trace

Corydon

White River

Mt. Pleasant

Vincennes

New Harmony

Evansville

Wabash R.

Rd. to St. Louis

Duggerville

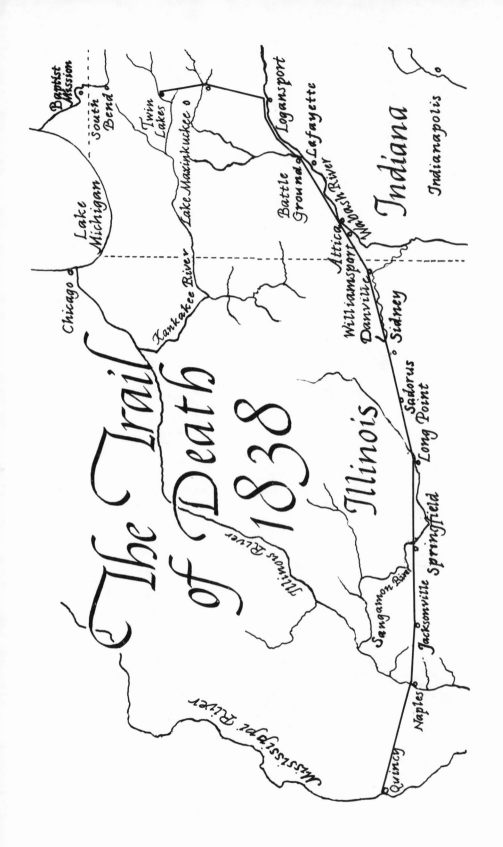

The Trail
of Death
of 1838

Indiana

Illinois

Baptist Mission
South Bend
Twin Lakes
Lake Maxinkuckee
Logansport
Lafayette
Indianapolis
Battle Ground
Attica
Williamsport
Wabash River
Danville
Sidney
Sadorus
Long Point
Springfield
Jacksonville
Naples
Quincy
Lake Michigan
Chicago
Kankakee River
Illinois River
Sangamon River
Mississippi River

*In the beginning, there was water over all the land*
*And the Great Spirit was there . . .*
*He made much land and sky . . . sun, moon and stars,*
*Creatures that die, souls and all*
*Then he made man, Grandfather man.*
*All men lived as friends, all were pleased,*
*All were at ease, all were happy . . .*
*This all happened very long ago, beyond the Great Sea*
*In the first land—The Walam Olum.*

"There is no alone, neighbor, especially in the wilderness."—
Sylvester Brown of the Society of Friends, Orange County Indiana, 1818.

Thomas Moore

Child of mine do you re-call, By O-hi-o's

shores    Wagons creak-ing o'er the trace,  And

might-y keel-boat's  oars

# 1818

(To the tune of an old Irish melody,
"Oft in the Stilly Night")

## The Song of the Immigrants

*Child of mine, do you recall, by Ohio's shores*
*Wagons creaking o'er the Trace, and mighty keelboat's*
*    oars?*
*The Great Migration emptied out New England's lands*
*    so drear,*
*From Caintuck, Virginny, too, they came, fifty thousand*
*    souls a year.*

*They left behind their kith and kin to take the wagon*
*    track.*
*They left the graves of children dear, they never would*
*    look back.*
*The men went with a joyful shout, to make their fresh*
*    new starts,*
*Tears were in the women's eyes, they left behind their*
*    hearts.*

# Chapter One

## The Account of Thomas Jefferson Brooks

Being a preacher's boy is the hardest of all the occupations of childhood, and believe me I have sampled them all, from snake-chopping to sister-teasing. At least it was difficult for me in those years around 1810, when the light of Pilgrim holiness was declining into a grim, gray sunset in the small New England village of Lincoln, Massachusetts.

The worst day was Sunday. To sit there in the frigid saltbox square of a pew, your feet turning to marble, your head yearning to flop down on the pew beside you—feeling the sun slant down without warmth on you through the huge arched windows, resorting to counting the dust motes to alleviate boredom—all of this was excruciating punishment for an active child.

Then there was the eternal progression of the service, the cry from the town clerk announcing the marriage banns, the singing of the Psalms of David, the reading out of Dr. Watts' hymns, the intoning of Galatians or Lamentations, "Thus endeth the reading of the ho-o-oly scriptures." Finally there was the long prayer that preceded the even longer sermon aimed at village sinners and miscreants. Oh, would it never end?

I can see the scene now, through the distance of all these years, as if I am looking through the small end of binoculars, the people far away and yet clear. I see my father leaning out of the pulpit like Moses, looking down on the sinners from Sinai, except Moses raged, and Father never raged. He gently reproved, he quietly expostulated, he shook his head sadly, especially at me.

At that time I was a boy of about ten. I can see all of my brothers and sisters, sitting like Prussian soldiers on the bench beside me in church, and I pass them by in the eye of my mind. There is Daniel, ten years older than I, slouching carelessly in the pew and picking at a glob of gravy on the sleeve of his handsome Napoleonic coat, which my mother hated. He was probably dreaming of a tavern maid in Concord.

And there are Tryphena and Lucy, aged sixteen and fourteen, immaculate in modestly-cut Josephine morning gowns they have made from French fashion plates. To their credit, they are attentive to the sermon.

Then Lewis, slight of build at thirteen and aloof, his aristocratic nose held high as he turns his head from the pulpit proceedings he has come to despise, little Becky, kicking her shoes beside me in time to the droning of the psalms, and Emily, at eleven nearest to me and a fairy girl, supple and dancing as a young aspen tree in a breeze. Emily, companion of my heart, Emily.

With some emotion I can see that younger self of mine, the frustrated ten-year-old, irritated with chilblains in that clammy church and ready to burst his bladder.

I remember that day well, though it has been over seventy years ago; a moment of such notoriety is not easy to forget. I gave a kick to the pushed-back seat in front of me, causing it to fall down with a crack like musket fire. Then I snickered in humiliation and wet my trousers, the little drops falling copiously out my drawers onto the wood floor.

Emily began to laugh uproariously, then, and my older brother Daniel attempted to cuff me. My father, momentarily distracted, paused in the sermon and began to stutter, as he sometimes did when he was nervous or bewildered, and people on the opposite benches craned their necks and nudged each other. On that Sunday in 1810 the eyes of one hundred twenty bond servants and aristocrats alike, not to mention those of my disapproving brothers and sisters, bored holes in the most miserable miscreant and sinner in all of Lincoln, Massachusetts and possibly the whole new nation of America.

High on a hill in Middlesex County, so the *Britisher's Guidebook to the Former American Colonies* used to say, stands the Lincoln Meeting House, 475 feet above the high-water mark in

Boston. From it, at that time in 1810, one could see Bunker Hill and turning the head, New Hampshire and Andover. Perhaps the very location of the town explains the lofty view Lincolners had of themselves. "Ahh, you're from Concord? How sad for you. Watertown? Oh, no, I'm sorry."

This in spite of the fact that the first Brooks originally set his Puritan feet on the soil of freedom at that very site of lowly Watertown in 1635. Thomas Brookes came in the ship *Susan and Ellen,* so those who write such things say, and became one of the founders of Concord. Those founding families burrowed into the hillsides and lived like squirrels in awful anguish that first January.

There at Concord the Brookses, who had somehow dropped their "e" like a too-hot biscuit, stayed on and vanquished both winter misery and poverty. They were soon known for running town meetings, apportioning land and breathing pious sanctity among the fens and hollows in the woodlands outside Concord. From his new mansion house, Hezekiah Brooks issued forth to help the elders deal with the Quaker menace; the meeting house records say the Quaker devils who talked of salvation for all felt the wrath of Hezekiah's rod on their naked backs.

And outside Concord another of my ancestors, Makepeace Brooks, found a witch near the old hill buryin' grounds and turned the wretch over to Reverend John Hale of Beverly, who could wring seven devils out of anyone.

Finally, in calmer days, under King George II, some of the Brookses and their fellow deacons decided it took too long to walk around Walden Pond to get to the meeting house, so they established a new town and meeting house at Lincoln.

Every second house is owned by the Brookses in Lincoln even to this day. I lie not to you, because you have asked me to tell you the true story of my life for your history of the State, and I am going to tell you all of it, letting you choose what you wish to finally use. There was the house from which Eleazar Brooks went to be a colonel for Washington and the Brooks Tavern, where Paul Revere was captured by the British before the shot heard round the world was fired nearby—these were part of the scene. But most of all there was Brooks Church (call it that even if others persist in saying Lincoln Meeting House). Joseph Brooks gave the bell that crowned the lofty tower and the vessels for communion.

Here my father Daniel, great-great grandson of the original Pilgrim Brookes, was christened in the prosperous years just before the Revolution. They said that he did not cry when water was sprinkled on him, but turned towards the congregation with a beatific smile. Perhaps the water from Brooks Pond had a soothing, sanctifying effect that day, and perhaps somehow it seeped into his bloodstream, making him ever after a pious, dedicated Christian.

Reverend Daniel Brooks was as bland as a poached egg. His round face beamed as peacefully as the countenance of one of the Papists saints he scorned whenever a housewife brought over scones or a pot of apple butter. He kept an hourglass on the pulpit so he would not offend the parishioners by over-sermonizing.

Well, he certainly wasn't like the rest of the Brookses. "A changeling, replaced by the gypsies," I once heard a lady whisper behind her poke-bonnet. "Why, one only needs to know any of that ornery, fire-and-Devil-thunderin' family to know that cussedness is the Brookses' stock in trade," the poke-bonnet lady said.

Alas, perhaps it was true. My father would not have been much good against the Quakers. But by this time the Quakers had become as settled and sleepy a Christian denomination as we former Pilgrims were. The witches were long since gone, and so was the fire of zealous faith that had pursued them, thank God.

In the place of the radical Quakers, however, had come the free-thinkers, saying that Congregationalism was too narrow and stilted, that what we needed was a universal God and universal salvation. My father kept his boat out of those stormy waters, holding the hands of the dying, speaking his gentle sermons and keeping his watchful eyes, full of sad reproof, ever on me. And I, the preacher's boy, learned little by little to keep out of the way of both deacons with collection baskets on long, poking sticks and ladies with apple butter, who frowned and tidied up your collar. I roved the hills with Emily and Rolf, our dog, and I did whatever mischief I wanted secretly, uncaring about either the eyes of the village or "the eyes of the Everlasting" that Mother and Sister Tryphena always talked about.

My mother's name was Bathsheba Dakin. She was called by that unusual appellation because early one morning her own mother had bathed in Brooks pond unclothed and the village idiot had come by and seen her and forced her to his lust. Twins were born of this obnoxious union and my grandfather, unbending in his condemnation of any woman who would expose her womanhood in this way, scornfully named them David and Bathsheba.

The boy twin, also half-witted, mercifully died. My mother, as bright in her wit as a copper saucepan, lived and flourished into a beautiful young woman. The suitors who clustered among the hollyhocks and foxgloves at the front stoop did not seem to notice that Bathsheba Dakin was a bit odd, that she wore different-colored hose and often looked into the trees as if she were listening for something.

Meanwhile, my father, Daniel Brooks, was also growing up in the town. When he was twelve, the Revolutionary War had begun in front of Brooks Tavern near his home on Brooks Road. He happened to be standing there as Paul Revere was captured by the British, when the patriot rode to alert the countryside. The British cut Revere's saddle girth and then released him. Meanwhile, Father's mother found her wandering boy in the midst of the excitement and gave him a dressing-down. Then she locked the door of the house.

Daniel, obeying some patriotic impulse that over-rode his usual caution, climbed down a heavy vine at the corner of the second story bedroom and went back to Brooks Tavern. Here the British marched by in full retreat, and just as they reached the tavern, the Minutemen attacked and killed eight of the redcoats. My father caught a stray bullet in the hand, which was soon pried out. This did not deter him from going to fight in New York with his Uncle, Colonel Eleazar, towards the end of the war. And when he returned to the village of Lincoln, exuding the aura of the god Mars from his very pores (although, really, he was more like a skeleton; the new nation could not afford to pay or feed the released soldiers), he attracted the beautiful hoyden, Bathsheba Dakin, and they were married.

Now she sat in church with all the rest of us, this woman who was still so beautiful even after all the childbearing, that strangers in the streets of the town stopped to stare at her chestnut curls and troubled, green eyes. She did not notice Daniel's glance straying across the aisle to the flowered bodice of Miss Otwell, or Emily's surreptitious paging through the psalter or even the strange tantrum of mine that had caused Father to pause momentarily. Mother was considering the sermon, filtering it through the odd sieve of her mind. The rest of us were watching the sands of the hourglass on Father's pulpit pass silently through the narrow neck, until, blessedly, they sat in a pristine little pile, all in the bottom.

If I turn my binoculars on any Sunday in those years, it would have been about the same: safe, predictable, and stale as third-day bread.

Except for the slight change that occurred about 1813. I remember a certain conversation well. It was held in the parlor of our house, after church. Here is how it went, to the best of my recollection:


Daniel, or "Brookie," as Mother called him: West. You've heard me right. I can't tolerate it here, you know.

Tryphena (aside): You mean the town can't tolerate you.

Daniel: What's that, dear sister?

Tryphena: Never mind.

Father: I had hoped I would enter my old age with all my children gathered about. What is the trouble with living in Lincoln?

Daniel: Dead. 'Tis dead as a fat hen with a wrung neck, I tell you. The land giving out, merchants loaded with stuff, can't sell enough of it.

Thomas Jefferson (me): The war did it—a merchandising glut.

Daniel: I don't care if it was John Q. Adams did it, 'tis done. Everybody poor as churchmice, living on credit—

Mother (turning her pained eyes to Father, whose salary of $600 and fifteen cords of wood had more wood than weight lately): Oh, dear, yes.

Tryphena (with a voice like a file on metal): Of course. Why, just think, necessities are sky-high. Olive velvet riding breeches you MUST have are $2 and boots are $3.50, best leather.

Daniel: My clothing doesn't have ary to do with this. None of you have ever appreciated my sensibilities, anyway.

Tryphena: Listen to the Down East *Belle Ame*. Reads in Papa's books all about Beau Brummel and thinks he's an English dandy. Straw in his pockets and road-dust on his shiny shoes.

Daniel: I'm a gentleman who desires to find his fortune. I'm going to Ohio, or maybe Indiana.

Father: The heathen wilderness?

Daniel: Not so heathen either, since Tip Harrison slaughtered the savages at Tippecanoe. Fine lands have opened up.

Lucy: And Miss Otwell? What about her? You have made tenders of affection I believe—

Daniel: Leave her out. She has nothing to do with the matter. I tendered, as you say, her nothing.

Tryphena (again, beneath her breath): Well, I certainly hope that is correct. It may take a few months to see that—

Daniel: Is it your affair, Miss?

Father: That is enough! A Christian family should not scold each other so!

Emily (unhappy about all the unpleasantness): I think Mr. Crowley brought over a watermelon from his patch. Shall we cut it on the porch and have some lemonade?

Daniel: As long as everybody accepts that I'm going. I shall start in a week so I can get to the Ohio before it drops too much. I must get into Indiana before leaves fall to outfit and set my cabin. I shall begin my road to fortune among the noble savages and stalwart sons of the soil in a humble way, perhaps grow grain, distill a few fine liquors.

Tryphena: How appropriate.

(A long silence, finally broken)

Father: Go from Massachusetts! I can't think why anybody who didn't have to would leave.

Mother (almost to herself): And I can't think why anybody who didn't have to would stay.


I had inserted the comment about merchandising in a firmly considered way; I was now apprenticed to a general store. As time passed and letters arrived from Daniel telling of the sweltering packet boat trip to Philadelphia, and from there by road and flatboat into the wilderness, of the final arrival in the rains of autumn at what he called the White River Country, I was measuring out my days in an atmosphere redolent of coffee, cloves, lamp oil, hemp and tobacco. I was toting heavy bags on my back, digging to the bottom of fish and pickle barrels, reaching for crockery on the rough top shelves of the store. And I was finding that for the first time in my life, I was strangely interested in something.

"I am discovering the secrets of trade," I would tell Emily as the two of us crouched in the corner of the summer kitchen, turning the spit that was jacked up over the coals in the fireplace. "Daniel said New England is poor because we have no specie for cash payment, and for once he is right."

Emily merely nodded, her large eyes wide at the extent of my knowledge. I might as well have been St. Paul dictating the Epistle to the Romans, as far as Emily was concerned.

"But I think that lack of ready cash can be an asset to the clever man, the one who waits by the road to profit when others foolishly rush down it."

"The hasty man will falter?"

"Yes, by his own foolhardiness. And yet in New England even the prudent man may fail. There is never enough money here—" We both looked about the whitewashed walls of the clapboard saltbox, I in sad scorn, she with love. "And we are not the only ones. All in the village pay accounts once a year and lately, with the slump after the war, they defer paying, ask for extensions. Many cannot pay and Mr. Tineton cannot help but extend their accounts."

"Their women and children could not eat if he did not," Emily protested earnestly. She had stopped turning the spit and looked me full in the face. I could feel her warm breath on my cheek. I was pleased to show off for her, this bright cheeked, pale-skinned sister of mine who thought I was king of the hill.

"Still," I went on, "there are ways to use what they owe over a year's time. A man could charge interest, demand and accept in-kind settlement, arrange for services. A clever man, that is."

"Clever man," she repeated with a smile, patting my knee and turning the spit over to me, "I think you will be a Yankee trader some day soon."

My father took me sometimes to the family home sites near Concord, and it was on one of these trips in my fifteenth year that he showed me the burial pits of our ancestors for the first time.

"The first winter they lived in a frozen wasteland," he said. He had told me the story before, passed down in front of the fireside for five generations now. It was of the carefully measured bushels of corn, the meat frozen in barrels with the prayer that the snow and ice not fail, the madness of hours, days, weeks spent without sight of neighbor or relative as snow hissed and spitted about the miserable shanties they called homes, really fox dens in the sides of cliffs. And finally the lung fever. He knew the details and recited them like a litany. Talking about the Brooks family loosed his usually-reserved tongue.

"Cemeteries are sacred," he said, "as sacred as churches and just as holy." He was looking at the sealing stones which marked the odd cairns in which the Puritan ancestor Brookses had deposited their dead of the lung fever that first year in the new land. "So cold it was, the ground all frozen and the women and men alike worn from it as threadbare as a carpet, it took all the energy they could muster to bear the departed to the animal stalls, hard against the hill. There the earth was kept warm by the breath of the few cows they kept, and they could hollow out niches to receive the remains of those they loved."

"How odd," I said, repelled by the morbidness, the faint odor in the remains of the animal stall and what were now just slipping stones with a carved marker, "to think of them there so near the manure. What an end for people proud and strong enough to leave England and brave the sea. To end up like that—"

"Like what?" my father asked sharply. "They aren't there. They live today." I looked up at him. It was true. He believed that.

He knew I was an indifferent Christian, so he was not surprised to hear me say, disdainfully, "Well, but perhaps not. What if they are only the jumbled bones that moles have picked through, and rotting skulls that lie, must lie, only a yard of dirt away from where we stand? James, Hannah, little Esther, two years old. Only skulls and thighbones left."

"No." His voice was more insistent, yet gentler, than I had ever heard it.

"You think not."

"I know not." I raised my eyebrows to him questioningly.

"If I did not have the Master's word and example, I have the voice of my own heart. I have proven the greater truth by the lesser every day of my life.''

In spite of the dullness of my heart, I could not help but be interested. We had talked, really talked, so very little through the years. I was curious about him and the faith that animated him. ''How?'' I wondered.

''When I prove that God directs and heals and saves day by day, I prove He holds our eternal souls and cares for us through endless eons. We live, we do not die.''

''If that were only so,'' I murmured. Feeling the unexplainable compulsion to mischief that still provoked me sometimes, I poked rather blasphemously at one of the stones banking the cairn and it loosened and fell to our feet.

My father did not comment, continuing to fix me with his eyes. ''It is so. Beyond all reason my heart tells me always that it is so as deeply as it tells I love your mother and this land. Faith in the immortality of man is the all of my life, just as it was the all of theirs,'' he gestured toward the cairns.

I stared into his sincere, urgent eyes, and I felt for just a moment that our hearts spoke. For a split second I experienced a surge of feeling, and I yearned towards this silent man who was so unlike me. It was as if he had reached out a hand in the dark. I leaned out towards understanding, yearning for it as one in a dream sea grabs for the lifeboat. Then suddenly a fragment of remembrance assaulted me and altered my mood, and I turned from him and the cairns and the moment passed.

And as we drove home, I thought of the fragment that had changed my mood. It was not the story of the first sainted Puritan Brookses, now rotting in glory in the cowpens, but of one of their collateral kin, a cousin once removed who went to preach to the Indians in the woods near the fens.

He had preached his missionary sermon, which lasted for some little time, and it was duly translated. The Indians standing in the circle listened and when it was completed, fell silent. Then one young man said he had some questions. ''Say on,'' said the Brooks preacher.

''If that which you say is true, and all are predestinated to heaven or hell, why must children suffer and die and go to hell, seeing they have not sinned?'' The Brooks minister had shaken his head sadly to indicate that the savage just did not understand, and the Indian had gone on, "And since the body sinned in many cases, why is the soul punished?" The Indian's voice had grown not louder, but more firm, "If a man repents in hell, why may he not be let loose by a just God?" The minister had raised his hand as if to forestall more, but the Indian would not be silenced, "And finally, oh minister, I ask you, why does not God kill this very bad Devil, seeing God has all the power?"

My relative did not reply, so the family story goes. But I think he should have tried, were he half the man and Christian the Brookses are supposed to be. More to the point, though, if someone could answer that Indian's questions for me and the larger one behind them, perhaps I could stand in the "glorious ranks of the Army of the Justified," instead of being the miserable camp follower that I always seem to be.

Some time soon after that, in 1815, which was the latter part of that fifteenth year of my life, a change occurred, as subtle and imperceptible as the day-by-day swelling of the budding trees in late March. My childhood companion, Emily, was growing into a beautiful young woman. As that happened, she pulled away from me, often seeking to be alone away from the house.

What was she thinking? What changed her? I did not know then, and I have never known. Perhaps the beautiful elements in her sensitive nature were a little unstable, like a crystalline compound a chemist mixes in a glass urn in a laboratory, which is ever trying to destabilize and escape from its confinement. Perhaps she merely reflected the malaise that affected New England in those days of economic and religious blight. All I know is that she wandered through the fields, sat on stone walls alone, mused at clouds.

Or so I thought. As the weeks of summer passed, she began to stay away longer and longer. We all did not speak of it, but the change in Emily hung over the house like a miasma, and even my mother began to mumble that Emily was too often gone and told her not to go out. Still my sister slipped away. The village began to chatter of it, and we came to know, the family being of course the last to hear, that Emily was visiting Brooks Pond, to see the freeman blacksmith who was a mulatto, son of a slave held by a shipmaster in Boston.

Within a week Mother and Father took her to Brooks relatives in Beverly and, a suitable older suitor having been found, she was married and sent on a honeymoon, like a pig trussed up and carried to market. Emily, my Emily, whose eyes had danced like sunlight on ash leaves!

The weeks passed. Tryphena was married and left the homestead; my unofficial apprenticeship among the hogsheads and lamp oil was ended, and I was named assistant clerk. Lewis, the sly, quiet one among us, apprenticed to a livery stable. Emily moved back to Lincoln with her middle-aged husband, a taciturn, witch-hunting Pilgrim with the imagination of a sweet potato. His thin lips drew together when he spoke to her; his small mouse eyes followed her every move with disapproval, as if she were eight years old and he were her father.

I went to see first the little boy, then the next year the tiny little girl that Emily produced after childbirths which were so difficult her life was despaired of. I did not visit her often. My life was busy, and we had gone down different lanes.

Daniel wrote, finally, of his new life in Orange County, Indiana. People were beginning to come into the wilderness. Although they were wary of the Delaware Indians who were about, cabins were beginning to dot the rough roads and watercourses. He had set up a horse mill to meet the settlers' demand for grain and operated a whisky still that ran night and day. These were his "fine liquors for gentlemanly tastes," no doubt, although it was difficult to imagine any gentleman among all those bramble bushes and hop-toads.

"The area is like a Chinese cracker exploding," he wrote, "and sparks of prosperity are flying about everywhere." He sent us a small gold piece and a whetstone, properly polished and cut, that had been found near his settlement, and said he was thinking of going in with other enterprising pioneers to produce whetstones and ship them on the Ohio.

My respect for him increased by one notch. Lewis, as silent as ever and bored with the livery business, read the letter, looked at the gold piece, picked up the stone and turned it over in his hand thoughtfully. The next day he bade us all goodbye and headed west.

One night six months later, March of 1818 it was, I slept the sleep of the dead in my drafty loft bed after a particularly busy day of hog-killing and pork-packing. The smell of lard still permeated my hair and skin and I dreamed of the huge, hot, stinking kettles. The clock chimed on the stair landing, and as it did I saw what my distressed senses took to be an apparition in the doorway, illumined by the flickering light of a candle.

It was my mother, her face and hair wild as a fensprite's. "I need you, Tom Jefferson. Emily has run off." I sat up, my mind awhirl. Run off? From what?

" 'Tis true. Perhaps she was out of her head. She'd had the fever last week." Mother's eyes showed she did not believe that. "They are searching with the dogs in the marshes."

And so I pulled on my boots and went out into the vapor-laden, pre-dawn air and tramped about, my heart in my throat, as dogs barked and the sound of the men's crisp, almost metallic cries issued about the bramble copses and soggy bottomlands. And when we had searched for the best part of a day and a half and no trace of my sister could be found, we had to admit the worst.

Emily had done the unthinkable, at least in our time and in that village or any of the other ones in New England: she had left a "decent" husband and two young children and gone off alone. She had not even run off with a lover who could at least protect her. Somehow she had found a way to save household pennies and had left. She was a woman on her own.

Sitting on the edge of my bed the next night, I hung my head in anguish. What future could she possibly have? Scorned by all society, unable to make a living at anything except the tainted trades of millinery, sewing or washing. It suddenly occurred to me that she could teach school. Such things were being done by women now, but without a husband, a son to protect her—

I did not sleep at all during the long watches of that night. Her haunting face as I had seen it of late, gaunt-eyed, unhappy, floated above the bed reproving me for not having taken more notice of the agony she must have been going through. I rose before dawn to light a candle and throw my few possessions into a valise.

At breakfast I told my family, "I go to find Emily. I will retrace her footsteps to Boston, where she must have gone. I shall ask at the packet boat dock, the stage line for anyone going south." My mother, her hair still uncombed, looked up over her cup of strong tea.

Father nodded. "It would be like her to flee to Aunt Ophelia." My mother's sister lived in Louisiana. "A long, hard row to hoe," he added, looking worn and old.

Yes, a long hard row it would be, with many rank and poisonous weeds along the way. It would have been better had she died in the bogs, I thought half-ashamed of myself, and yet I felt the truth of what I was thinking. Perhaps she had seen it that way too; since she did not have access to a large dose of laudanum or arsenic, she chose slow death. I turned from the family scene and, taking my valise, left. Goodbye, I thought to Brooks parsonage, Brooks Tavern, Brooks Pond and Brooks Road.


Before I left, I had it in my fancy, I do not know why, to visit the graves of the victims of the harsh 1630's winter, near Concord. With some difficulty I found the cairns there in the hillside and stood staring at their crumbling stones. I had the same odd impulse that had hit me before, when I had been here with Father, to dig through to the bones and irreverently disinter them.

"You in there," I shouted at the rocks, "you retched your way over the ocean to freeze and starve in your beds, and this is what it gets you. You are nothing but flayed shinbones and cracked skulls now, in spite of what Father said. I don't believe him, do you hear? And the free faith you prayed for is as dead as you in this dreary land you bequeathed to us all. All is compulsion and stifling tradition here!"

I began to weep, for the first time, I think, in my life. "Useless, all useless," I cried, as I turned to return to the road. I left Massachusetts with no regrets. "Emily, Emily," I cried out to the fast vanishing ruins of Brooks martyrdom, "I will find you if it takes me the rest of my life. And when I do we will go together to the Northwest, where my only prayer is that we may never hear the name of New England again. Emily, I shall not rest until I see your face!"

# Chapter Two

# The Poore Papers

To: Mehitable Chute Chambers, Newbury, Massachusetts
From: Hannah Chute Poore, Pittsburgh, Pennsylvania
August 10, 1817

My Dear Sister;

In God's name I salute you, my dearest Mehitable. It does not seem possible that I am here. Was it only six months since my family started from Newbury? It seems six years. We have bounced by cart to Boston, rolled on a coaster ship to New York (oh, dire journey and unrivalled difficulties in April gales), then jolted on by team and wagon from New York. We are an odd group of Israelites crossing the desert, "headin' to Indianney," as they say—a dour New England farmer, seven children, one mother who has just discovered she is in a delicate condition, and a tabby cat, beneath a Conestoga cover to Philadelphia.

The City of Brotherly Love seemed to me the end of civilization and in a way it was. On, ever on past Philadelphia, as seasons and miles wore on, to Carlisle and beyond, over rutted, weather-worn roads. Cold hail froze my dear husband's cheeks as he drove, and mountain streams poured over the road. But, praise be to God, we have finally arrived at the promised land of Pittsburgh.

My dear, I feel as though I myself have lived a travel volume. Town after village after settlement. How the Israelites must have felt journeying forty years! How far this odd Pennsylvania town is from Newbury, Massachusetts. How far from the fresh winds of the Atlantic, which I have loved above all else since childhood.

And yet I think we are right. West, west lies our destiny. And so I have borne with patience the never ending changes of scenery: Boston, New York, Philadelphia and over the mountains—because they are but the progress of the new pilgrims—I hope both Christian and faithful—as we go to new life in the West.

And, as our neighbor Old Stokes always says at Newburyport, "If ye want to catch the big fish, ye must put out to the far banks."

I shall attempt to tell you a bit about some of the last part of our journey—a lap along a steep ridge in the mountains of Pennsylvania, called the Chestnut Ridge. The wagon was continually jolting like a house in an earthquake, and we all had to get out and walk. Amanda was carrying little Harriet, and Susan was attempting to carry Betsy, while the others scrambled along as best they could on the stony ground which John constantly scanned for rattlesnakes. Flocks of wild turkeys crossed our paths and deer, which we rarely see in Massachusetts at Newbury, started as we creaked by.

As I told you in my other letter, we travel from sunrise to sundown. So far it has been in mostly civilized places. After we bought the wagon in New York, we stayed in it in farmer's lots, going only occasionally into an inn so we could conserve the dear-bought hoard John has managed to save.

But in Pennsylvania the road grew progressively wilder, and I did not know what to expect as we climbed the mountains. As the light was fading, we arrived at Entley's Inn, a very wild place on the Chestnut Ridge in the middle of a complete forest.

The owner and his wife, however, were congenial people who had built this large log structure almost without aid at the height of a wind-swept ridge. They welcomed us and regaled us with the tales of travellers—hundreds going by each day on this Pittsburgh Road, some coming from the Carolinas and Virginia to head west with those of us who had come from the East. Holes in the road that swallow axles, mud slides off the mountains, sudden hail storms that freeze good folk—the owners told us all the travellers had told them.

While we supped on bread and milk and cheese served with deer meat, a terrible ruckus sounded in the yard and John ran to see to the horses. What should he spy but a bear, large and black, disappearing into the woods carrying one of the landlord's best hogs. All over the walls were the skins of large rattlesnakes the landlord had killed in the last months. We slept but little that night as the November wind howled all about the poorly-chinked logs in the walls.

How very strange this wilderness is to one like me who carries the imprint of the neat homes and farmlots of Rowley and New-bury stencilled deep in her heart. Still, we are here in Pittsburgh and I do not regret the impulse that sent us west after that terrible summer, when snow and frost stood upon the nubbins of unripened corn in the pitiful shocks and the rusted, miserable wheat never ripened. The summer of 1816! I think never has such a calamity beset New England as last summer and I pray for you, Mehitable, for my dear parents and the Chute family, that you have had enough to eat without having to sell your prized posses-sions in this year of near-famine.

Surely our brothers James and Daniel Chute were right, at least I feel so, when they sought their fortunes in the Northwest, far from the pine flats and salt marshes north of Boston. I wonder how long it will be before we see them in Cincinnati! When God, who ordains all events according to His tender love, wills.

Now let me tell you something about this city of Pittsburgh. You descend from the mountain ridges and ranges I have described, from your tortuous, plodding, weary trip expecting to be in the promised land, an earthly heaven where you may rest body and soul. Instead, what you find is at first something like the place of Divine Retribution.

The banks along the river are of coal, and companies have formed digging-caves there. Sweating men with mules and carts throw the coal into boats. Limestone and iron ore are about, also, and the forges operate day and night belching their fumes to the skies and lighting the landscape by the Allegheny River like Plu-to's pits.

A sulphureous pall of smoke hangs over the city and filters its sediment over homes, waters, gardens. I think I may never be clean again, sometimes, working to pumice off that black grit from everything we own. Still, the landscape prospects are interesting and at times exalted. Here three rivers converge in a magnificently chiselled gorge, their waters yet clear, the hillsides beyond them at least still partially clad in trees which must be beautiful in summer.

One must pause to think that Pittsburgh is the beginning of a natural highway of river commerce that stretches 2,500 miles to the sea, that its hundreds of arks and ships and flatboats are carrying not only commerce but human trade, thousands of immigrants, into a new life along the riverbanks—it takes your breath. Surely, this vast tide of settlement west must be to the furthering of God's purpose, as we make this bright new land of America the envy of old Europe, the model for free men everywhere.

I find it no hardship to write so long, though my eyes squint in the candlelight in the poor shack we now call home. One of the most priceless gifts our dear mother gave us was the training in penmanship and spelling. Would John had it! But then the Poores were never much on parsing and conjugating, while our brothers went to Dartmouth, praise be to the Giver of All Good!

I pray not to take too much pride in our intellectual accomplishments, beseeching that I and the rest of the Chutes may not fall into the sins of the Pharisees. John has now gone to try to get the best price for our team. His scheme for catching the big fish that has eluded him all his life hinges upon our selling the horses and wagon with good gain.

We must be fed and housed here, and dear John, as ever trying like a frugal weaver to make two fraying ends of yarn meet and never quite knowing how to do it, rushes about attempting the impossible anyway. Fortune is always just around the bend for John; and here it will surely and truly be around the bend of the Ohio which we must take to soon. Naturally, I would be done with this place of smoke and new starts and would arrive in Cincinnati to have my new child.

My thoughts are ever with you, my dear sister. I believe that I have reconciled myself to the will of God and my husband in taking this family of seven, soon to be eight, children, most small and some yet in arms, into the hostile and savage wilderness, bringing with us only the clothing in our trunks and a few pieces of cherished furniture, and the supplies we buy along this road.

The memory of our last days in the old Chute homestead on the lovely lane between Byfield and Newbury cuts into my heart like a hot iron. I see myself standing there, looking at Father Chute's saltbox shrouded in trees up the hill behind me, the third house in which we lived as John moved us about constantly, always seeking to scrabble out a living in a county that is, as he says, strong on sons and weak on new, fertile land.

The garden is before my eyes, bathed in a breeze from off the ocean by Plum Island. I stand there, blinking at the brightness of the blue March sky, and I kneel to fill the corner of my traipsin' basket with the slips of the ground. They are just coming through the rocky soil, and so I must delve a bit. I poke for medicinal herbs among browning, wilted foliage. Rhubarb, its knobby red leaves just visible above the ground, for binding up the bowels, foxglove, the curled, tight fists of its leaves stark against the brown earth, for palpitations of the heart, pansy and lobelia for expectoration. So much for the practical; the rest of the herbs I could find in the woods of our new home.

But after I had carefully wrapped each root, being sure that soil clung to the roots and moistening all before I put them in oiled papers, my eyes fell on the fenced garden I had loved, now very much forlorn after that too-cool summer and the winter that followed it.

My dear Mehitable, you know I have thought beauty, above all qualities in life except holiness, is to be deeply cherished. Beauty, whether in the flowers of the earth or on the wing of the birds of the trees, uplifts. It takes the mark of the beast off the face of the human condition and fits it to see God. You and I have both seen the humblest cottage in our village made bright by a milk pitcher full of goldenrod and wild butter-and-eggs flowers.

And so I tenderly dug until my searching fingers clasped the bulbs of the grape hyacinths said by some to have come from England with the first Chutes all those years ago when Puritans lived, and strawberries, the first sweet promise of summer's coming felicity, and then finally, a shoot from the white rose bush that stood by the door. Pray God that all the plants and all of us, may live in the wilderness and flourish to praise God!

And so I do not go alone, I bring my family, my faith and, dear sister, the book of meditations you have given me. I shall read a page a day. I am looking now at its title: *The Joyous Christian: Piety The Only Foundation of True and Substantial Joy.* I see on its first page, "Men look only at the cross. They take their views from self-denial and the labors which do beset us. The Christian should be happy and cheerful. The lark is cheerful, as it mounts from its grassy nest and soars away to the heavens singing as it goes. Cheerful also is the summer morning, revealing its glad scenery. Nature in all this has a lesson for man." And so, dear sister, I shall be a happy Christian, which suits my nature anyway. Send regards to all our family. I remain always your dear sister,

Hannah Poore

To: Mr. Joseph Poore, Newbury, Massachusetts Post Office
From: John Poore, Pittsburgh, Pennsylvania

Feb 12, 1818

Dear Brother:

Possibly you may think it strange that I have not written you before this. But many pressing matters have occupied my time. On the whole we had a prosperous journey and have enjoyed our usual health since we have been hence—on our arrival however, we found the City full of Yankee Horses and chariots selling at auction through the streets. As my waggon would live without eating, I thought I had better let it stand by awhile than to give it to the crier for selling. But to my astonishment the emigrants continued to flock in from the northward in troups till about the first of January and kept the city gluted with horses and carriages. So you see I have been completely frustrated in my expectations of raising money from my team. And so we wait, using the small funds from the pattrimony I requested of Father, living in a squallid "stranger's cabin" occupied I think by Kentucky immigrants and countless types of vermin since the Revolutionary War.

Many of my friends and acquaintances thought me giddy to mount on the airey Castles of my own building—or intoxicated with visionary scenes of granduer—but their conceptions of the country—of me—and of my designs and expectations were alike silly, for surely no undertaking of my life was ever more premeditated or more evidently a point of duty, otherwise I should never had done violence to the finest feelings of human nature in breaking away from my old connections—but we thought it best to seek a new future away from the dead prospects and broken opportunities of the past. Nor have seen no cause to repent of it—but on the contrary have much cause of gratitude to the great disposer of all events who has preserved us thus far.

I often think of our Mother in her forlorne situation and of the care which falls upon you in consequence of it—and in particular upon my beloved sister—but I am satisfied that all is done for her which can be done—and have only to hope and pray that you both may be rewarded for your care in those durable riches that will never fade from God. Tell Father Chute I will write in a few days. With high consideration I remain as ever,

Your affectionate brother
John Poore

To: Mehitable Chambers, Newbury, Massachusetts
From: Hannah Chute Poore, Pittsburgh, Pennsylvania

May 1, 1818

Dear Sister:

I write to you today praying that you have the blessings of health. We are, at present, all well here. There has been an outbreak of lung fever of a particularly virulent nature but it has passed our domicile by. I have by God's grace been delivered of a son, born this past Saturday, here in Pittsburgh instead of at Cincinnati as we had hoped. We could not find the funds to go on, and so John has been making some few dollars at his trade—

cordwaining, making shoes for the citizens of this town as often as he can afford to buy leather.

The birth was long in coming, and so John went to look for the services of a physician. It being Saturday night and much of the coarser part of the town involved in indulging themselves in wantonness, there were few physicians to be located, although they are usually as thick as sandfleas on the shore. But either they were drinking themselves into besottedness or they were repairing the effects of that besottedness—swollen eyes, knife-gashed faces, and limbs broken in fights.

A so-called "Indian healer" from the mountain folk attended me. When this odd doctor appeared in his leather garb and hunting coat from another time, you can be sure I was somewhat disquieted, but never mind, it all turned out well, and the birthing progressed. This healer gave me tea of winter clover and cayenne, which seemed to increase the efficacy of the weak spasms that in the last few years have plagued me in childbirth and extended my labors interminably. He made me walk about constantly and did not once examine me, claiming that many are brought into childbed fever by the examinations of attending physicians who do not have clean hands. An odd idea.

Eventually the child, as yet unnamed, was born. When it seemed as if I might be losing more blood than would be thought safe, my herb physician administered tea of flowers of yarrow. This Indian doctor does not allow bleeding; in fact, it is anathema to him; he believes using leeches and cutting veins is stupidity. I think I have to agree with him. At any rate, I was well enough to cook dinner by evening.

I wonder if we will be blessed (I dare not say cursed) with more children out here. It is difficult enough to bring a new little one into a world where all is uncertainty as we prepare to trust our lives to the broad Ohio and cross the Buffalo track to the end of the road, then cut through five miles of dense forest.

You and I have often talked of the duty of a Christian wife to bear and bear again, and it is on my mind much these days. Yet Mehitable, I know you will pardon my personal confession for your eyes alone, that I wish I could bear no more, not ever. It is not only the childbirth, dangerous as it is to life, but the "other part" that I have never learned to like. You have agreed with me, when we have had our whispered sisterly talks over the tea table or crib that the wife's part in the "marriage responsibility" is not one to be looked forward to. "Put up with it, for it will be bearable. Men regularly turn into beasts when they get beneath the coverlets," Mother told us both on the eve of our marriages, and I have found no reason to think otherwise.

Surely most of the wives I know say that the only women who enjoy the marriage act are those whose natures are depraved in some way—enough of this. I will do what I must for my dearest John; surely one can never have too many children on the new homestead land, where all must be done from the ground up. John has finally sold the team for a reduced sum and we will take what we have left (a pittance) and what he has earned and board the flatboat tomorrow. I shall write more after we are on the broad bosom of the river.

Our tabby cat has run off to better pastures. Perhaps she knew a boat trip was in her future. The children are saddened; this tiger cat was their link with home, the past, and the friends they miss.

Hurriedly, on the flatboat *Egypt's Queen*

The babe cries, a rare thing for him, as the rocking motion of the waves is as gentle as a cradle and lulls him to sleep. I do miss Wendell and wonder if we have done the right thing in leaving our oldest apprenticed in Newbury. His eighteen-year-old arms and strong back would have been a great help in loading the kegs, hogsheads, furniture, and trunks we brought on board. Alvan does try, but then fourteen is not eighteen.

Susan, my good strong Susan, became a work horse and carried my trunks and traipsin' basket on board. Although she is really the third child, at sixteen she has taken on the responsibilities of eldest. I must rely on her older sister Amanda, flighty as she is, to take care of little Hannah and Harriet. Betsy and Mehitable (who sends her compliments to her aunt) are good for little else than peeling potatoes or kneading bread, when they are not scrambling about on this boat's three levels, looking on shore for Indians who aren't there and begging to get off the boat to romp on the river-bank. But then at nine and ten those two maidens are too young to worry about the trials that face us, so there are compensations in innocence.

Some days later: I now have leisure to pen some descriptions of the boat itself and the life we lead on it.

This is a queen of flatboats; we share it with one other complete family and still feel as if we walk the town square in Boston. I exaggerate only a little; still this boat is sixty-one feet long and fifteen feet wide. You will ask how in our straitened circumstances we are able to afford such luxury; more of that later. Suffice it to say that John has made arrangements and I have bit my tongue.

The flatboat is indeed a Noah's ark. Up on the roof of the cabin, in addition to our supplies and the crew's tent, are the milk cow and calf. John traded the last of his well-made shoes and leather for them in the country around Pittsburgh, and he also got a small pen of chickens, which we will use for our cooking pots on the trip.

At both ends outside the general cabin, which occupies most of the boat's length, are two little decks, bow and stern, where we women sit and peel potatoes and darn as if we were in our own keeping rooms.

Below, down two steps, is a spacious apartment with cupboards for dishes and shelving and pegs where we hang our gowns and shirts. There is a kind of a firepit, such as the Indians use, up against one of the walls. It has a circular chimbley running out of the boat; here we cook, suspending pots from a small crane. John has divided off the compartments for the two families with blankets and ropes.

Outside, on each side of the boat from deck to deck, fastened to the gunwale and projecting over the water are two "running boards" where the navigators and hands steer the boat through shoals and into the channel by laboriously poling it along.

We tie up for the night at river towns or small settlements, and the men get off to search for game, which is abundant in the woods. They never go far from the boat. Indians are about, although it is said they are friendly. When the moon is full, we sometimes run day and night, so intent is John to get to the land of opportunity, and so much does he press the captain and crew.

Our bible for the river is Mr. Cramer's *The Navigator*, one of the new Western traveler's guides. This marvel of a book describes every shoal and submerged sawyer tree in the stream and makes interesting comments on the towns. As the river is low, we must be constantly alert to "hanging up" on submerged trees; indeed, we have done so several times.

Last night, as we were running by moonlight, with the women and children sleeping below while the men manned watch and oars, I was thrown out of my bed by a terrific jolt. The flatboat had hit the trunk of a large oak which was just under the water and which the current had shifted directly into our path.

It was with real apprehension that we came on deck. In the last town we stopped, Lottsville, we had heard a story of the bottom of a craft being ripped out by a submerged tree and sinking in five minutes with the loss of an entire family from upstate New York. But all the men and even Alvan poled and grunted. John finally jumped into the water and heaved and tugged at the tree and we sprang free. Thank goodness!

I shall speak of Lottsville, the Ohio town I have just mentioned, where we tied up a night or two ago. If Mr. Cramer were writing about it in his typical enthusiastic promotional bill way, it would have sounded this way: "Lottsville is a pastoral village by the side of the flowing waters, a perfect heaven for Mr. Lotts who has built his manse on the hill, where he enjoys all joy and plenitude with his numerous family. Below, beginning new life with high anticipation and strong fortitude, are sturdy pioneers who have built rustic log homes in an idyllic environment."

If I wrote it I would say that the sturdy woodsmen spent a good deal of time standing in the streets spitting tobacco juice at each other's feet, talking of Andrew Jackson and taking umbrage at each other's comments. They continually bait each other, as a man baits a bear, and wait for an insult to develop into a fight.

These insults usually have to do with character or manhood in some form. "You ere a goldurned, dingratted liar," "You ere as dirty and disreputable as yesterday's sassafras tea and not half as strong," they shout with breath foul enough to fell a passerby.

Fighting is the perennial entertainment. All a man needs to do to start a fight is say, "I'm a better man than you." Or it may be that a man is wearing a shirt that has a few too many frills to suit the passel of men standing at every crossroads out here. There is a code of honor all along the river as definable as that of King Arthur and the Round Table. All fights must be "fit fa'r," no "unfa'r holts," and finally the loser must cry " 'nuff." During the space of fifteen minutes, one may view gouging, biting, hair-pulling, scratching, and even stamping on the poor victims.

I thought after a night on the shore by Lottsville, listening to the drunken shouts of men and dogs barking as they were tor-mented by swains who should have been home by the fireside, "Why, we have fallen off the edge of the earth." Not all our nights have passed in this manner, though. Sometimes the boat hands play mandolins and sing songs, or I read to the children from my meditation book or tell them stories of giants and wood elves.

Let me tell you about some of the other folk we are encounter-ing. I have been particularly taken by the family who are the other occupants of this boat, New Yorkers named Markle who have become our firm friends, perhaps only because of propinquity. They are talkative and decent folk with seven children who romp and tumble over everything, including the helmsman's oar and the cow's legs. They have brought nothing with them but beautiful gowns and velvet vests, chests of blue willow china and silver tablespoons and ladles and, folded up on the roof with our cow, a surrey carriage.

There is a mother like me who tries to keep up with her young children, a father who is a judge in Madison, Indiana, who is personally conveying his family to their new home there, three middling daughters named Effie, Emma Rose, and Evangeline, one stripling son of eight, and twin three-year-old-boys, James Madison and George Washington Markle. A new child is on the way. Probably the most interesting child is the oldest one, Auraleigh. She is nigh twenty, very spirited, and talks of nothing but politics. Her father has been out here for two years in the tiny new town called Madison and is making a name for himself as a lawyer and judge. Recently he was elected to the new State Assembly. Evidently because he had only girls for his older chil-dren, he brought Auraleigh up to know the difference between

Democratic-Republicans and Federalists, to talk of specie issues and canals and constitutions.

Judge Markle had gone back to the family's home in western New York state and brought them all in wagons to Olean Point, where the Allegheny River can be used for boat traffic. Then they all floated to Pittsburgh, where we met them on the quay.

Just two days ago, a touching incident occurred which shows how this immigration is rending families like ours, and how God sometimes re-unites in ways that give Him nothing but praise. "He sets the solitary in families," as it says in the Bible.

Mrs. Markle, Henrietta, as I am now familiarly calling her, has a sister in parts West whom she had not heard from in nearly a year due to the difficulties of communication with this Northwest and the constant travelling both families had done. Henrietta Markle knew only that her sister, Helena, had been passing through the southern part of Ohio, moving with her husband who was a travelling supplier of hardware goods. Henrietta had determined not to search for her sister as yet, but to settle herself and then write home to determine her sister's whereabouts.

What should be her surprise, then, when we got off to secure supplies at a little village set on high bluffs and, having gone into the general merchandising establishment to find some hempen twine, Henrietta should see her very own sister behind the counter slicing cheese?

The sister's face turned pale white. Crying out, she dropped her knife and threw her hands in the air, thus scattering cheese parings all about.

Both Henrietta and this younger sister wept unashamedly and hung onto each other as if they had met as on the golden shores of the new heaven we are promised in scripture.

Oddly, an unforeseen circumstance intervened, caused I suppose by Henrietta's generally casual way of bringing up her children. I cannot criticize; there are so many ways to "bring up a child in the way he should be taught."

Henrietta had allowed Emma Rose, the skittish ten-year-old, to go aboard another boat which was accompanying ours. For some reason they did not put ashore as we had expected them to do when they docked. In the afternoon it was realized that they were preparing to tie up downstream. Instead of being able to stay overnight or perhaps two days with the reunited sister, Henrietta was forced to re-board with all of us and continue downstream to find the lost child, which we did do without trouble. The sisters had a few hours' reunion, at any rate, and determined on a visit within two months' time which should give them as much time as they wished to catch up on marriages, illnesses, and funerals in their old, beloved New York neighborhood.

I have set my pen down to go converse with an odd tradesman out here—the travelling sutler—a floating mercantile. These purveyors of food goods come alongside, tie up, and sell at high prices whatever your palate desires. Henrietta Markle bought some lemons at four for a dollar to make a pie for our supper. I did not buy.

Now, I promised to tell you how poor folk such as we are, are travelling in such style. The answer, as you may have surmised, is that we have added more to our debt. John has been determined that his family will not travel in the pauper boats; it is a part of his plan for a new life. He sent ahead to our brother James and asked for a loan, which was generously granted. Am I worrying unnecessarily about the burden of several hundred dollars debt we are taking with us into the woodlands of Indiana? It seems a poor way to make a new start, but most out here do it that way.

Brother Daniel, still living with James and his family in Cincinnati, says the West makes all things new. He contends that the first year alone, raising corn and even wheat to supply the needs of new settlers before their crops are in, we will realize more than enough to pay back these obligations. I cannot but trust him and God. Each mile pushed beneath the bow of this ark takes me farther from the old securities of friends and family, the loved sites of village streets and the garden now awakening under the reluctant sun of a Massachusetts spring. Yet I share with you the Devotion of the Day from the little book you have sent:

> *Dearer, far dearer to my heart,*
> *Than all the joys that earth can give,*
> *From fame, from health, from friend I'd part,*
> *Beneath His countenance to live.*

Your Loving Sister,
Hannah

To: James Poore, Newbury, Massachusetts
From: John Poore, Cincinnati, Ohio

May 10, 1818

Dear Brother:

Yours by father Chute was duly received—our Mother it seems appears to be declining. It is truly remarkable that she has continued to live in such a state of dropsy but the ways of Divine Providence are unseerchable. I am under the necessity of disapointing your hope in regard to remmittance of the money of the loan. I had thought to make the first apropriation by now as you know I did a little cordwaining in Pittsburgh but the money went for supplies within a few weeks. You pay dearly for just eating beans and cornbread, and ham once a week and drinking watered-out cider in a city like Pittsburgh.

My distance from you has in no respect lesened my sence of obligation—and it is a source of much satisfaction that I find myself in a country where the law of industry is rewarded. I have reason to hope I shall rise from this eternal state of financial embarassement I have always known and partake of the comfort of life in common with my fellow creatures. My whole family, now settled in for what seems to be an extended visit at the home of Reverrend James Chute, my wife's brother's, send their love. You will recollect their names except for the one you have not seen and his name is John. A fine new boy for a fine new hope in this western land.

Your brother,
John Poore

To: Mehitable Chambers, Newbury, Massachusetts
From: Hannah Chute Poore, Cincinnati, Ohio

May 14, 1818

Dear Sister Mehitable:

Let me tell you about Cincinnati, the "Capital of the West." The city itself is somewhat of a marvel, said to contain thousands of acres of ground. There are, indeed several rows of superb brick buildings above the water line, four churches, two markets, a grist mill and manufactories for steam boats, glass and cotton.

The Markles will be moving soon down the river a bit to Madison; Judge Markle is a lawyer of some reputation, at least he was in the East, and he will be the Honorable Representative Markle when the new Assembly convenes. Madison is rather near to Corydon, which is the new state capital. Believe me there is plenty of business for the lawyers in this new Northwest. Many are unscrupulous, slinking about in taverns, keeping their shrewd eyes open for those who wish to bring suits about uncollected bills and drunken woundings.

The judge has already had a large, two-story home built at Madison, and Henrietta and Auraleigh have been bustling about ordering chiffonniers built to hang up their clothing in the large bedrooms. They have hired a teacher for the children and servants to serve the meals in their new dining room.

Henrietta had us over to the inn where they are staying here in Cincinnati and showed us the fine canopy bed and the samples of lace hangings she has ordered. Lace work in Cincinnati! It comes from France up from New Orleans! "Oh, my dear, you shall come visit us when you are settled on your place and we shall chat together about our adventures." This, as she summons her new hired girl with a little silver bell she brought from the East. They leave for Madison tomorrow.

What must it be like to have a ready supply of money? To have your shirts unmended, your shoes without holes? Lawyers always have money, but they are not the only ones here.

Walking about the new streets of Cincinnati are all sorts of people, genteel landowners and merchants, who are generally polite and grave, speculators who want to set up interests in salt and saltpeter pits north in Ohio, and quarry bosses who wish to get crewmen.

Then there are the rough, leather-clad men who wash once a month if they fall in the river. I blush to report there are also women of an unsavory nature in this town of Cincinnati who consort with the frontiersmen (and the "men of quality" I have to tell you, if I am going to tell the truth).

The other night there was a real hubbub as a sawmill hand from near Zane's Trace, considering himself ill-served in an impure place of the sort we have been discussing, set a torch to it. The women poured into the street with only bits of clothing or shawls to cover their nakedness. I begged our brother James to let me take in one poor wench with cheeks as painted as a bisque doll's.

Both Brother and my dear John begged me not to, but I sincerely plead Christian duty. Once she came into our two rooms, I did not know where to put her and grew frightened that she might have some loathsome disease. Still, I thought of Mary Magdalene and so must have Susan, for she came up and covered the poor shivering girl, who was yet in her shift, and put her on the floor beside her own pallet. In the morning we fed her mush and milk; her large eyes shed copious tears, and I gave her my Testament as she left. Haughty Amanda would have nothing to do with her.

John is apprehensive that we cannot go immediately to our claim because it seems that there is a dispute at the land office about it; someone else claims the fine piece of bottomland that we had contracted for with the land man in the East. Judge Markle is at work for us (fee in advance, even to friends).

Time passes. I am re-acquainting myself with our brothers. James is his usual pious self, a good minister of the gospel who talks of going north into Indiana Indian country soon. Our other brother Daniel is the same as he always was, as blithe and airy-talking as a young girl about to be betrothed. He assures us all is well. "All the land is good, never fear that you may lose this claim." And should we not be concerned that we are arriving too late to plant now, I ask? "Not at all, not at all, my dear sister," he says. From what he hears (although he has never been into the woods himself) all you need is sacks of cornmeal and flour; the land provides meat.

And—no, no, he cannot loan more than he has, many interests to pursue, tut tut. Does that not sound like the same Daniel who used to forget to lock the gate after the cows and you and I would have to follow the bells down the Dingletown Road halfway to Rowley?

Babe John is fretful; I fear the constant anxiety and novelty of our situation have unsettled him and may be drying up my milk. I may have to give him a leather bottle with a tin nipple and start him on porridge. Thanks be to God, the cow remains in health!

As soon as we got here, I took my plant slips out of the traipsin' basket. In spite of the best of my moistening and clipping, the rose and rhubarb shoots looked like spindly, failing, poor children. I stuck them out-of-doors in Brother James's garden, and now they are doing very well. Poor things! As soon as we can, we will put them in little pots and move them again, this time to their permanent home.

I should be asking about the health of your own brood, my dear Mehitable. Is Betty still teething? I suggest the salt biscuit as the best remedy. Did I understand you to say when you last wrote that Meg Coddington has married Old Man Bridgewater? A step up for her, and it may be as God wills.

I pray you make special condolence calls on Father Poore; it was hard for John and me to be so far away when his mother died, and the knowledge, coming in last week, hit him very hard, to know his father is alone in the house.

''Alone'' is a word John uses often these days, feeling our coming isolation and the jobs we must undertake without help. If I did not feel that ''Underneath are the Everlasting Arms,'' I do not think I could face it; with that faith I am serene about the future. We linger here, almost as waltzers at the midnight ball, longing to stay where music and comfort abound, but knowing that soon we must go out into the late-night, bitter cold air.

Your loving sister,
Hannah

To: Mehitable Chambers, Newbury, Massachusetts
From: Hannah Chute Poore, Cincinnati, Ohio

August 1, 1818


Dear Sister:

At long last our claim is finally settled on the land John bought for us in New England. We have not been awarded the land he claimed. An earlier claimant, a speculator from Virginia, won the suit.

We have therefore, sworn our intention to buy land that will cost more and is less desirable, although still decent. It is in Orange County, Indiana, near a town called Paoli in the hills forty miles from Madison. John is, of course, disappointed, but we are both resolved to accept the will of Providence, allow ourselves to feel the spirit of the new land, and go immediately to see our acres and prepare to take the children out to them by the end of the summer.

John and I will take the horse tomorrow and go by Captain Kibbey's road into the wilderness. Even the little stocking-up we have done has been so dear! Wheat flour—4 cents a pound, corn meal—50 cents a bushel, butter—31 cents a pound. It seems incredible that prices should be so high, and I pray nightly that God will supply the means to reduce this debt which mounts daily and is now an overstuffed pack upon our backs. But the closer we get, the more determined John grows to reel in this fish of prosperity he has struck out on an unknown sea to hook.

He says, "The strength of my own arms and hands is our fortune." I hope he is right. Oh, Mehitable, what in the world will the wilderness trail we are about to embark upon bring us? We are now the poorest of the poor, have had to sell most of our possessions and settle for less than half the acreage John had planned on, with land not as fertile.

God protect us! Still, I send you hope from *The Joyous Christian*: "Let the Christian, acting on the principle that 'godliness with contentment is great gain,' seek mainly the one thing needful, and his path will have the approbation of God and lead the soul to joys that are pure and unending."

I shall write you at some convenient point. Going forth for forty days and forty nights I am, with trepidation, Your sister

Hannah Chute Poore

To: Mehitable Chambers, Newbury, Massachusetts
From: Hannah Chute Poore, The Wilderness

August 15, 1818

Dearest Sister:

It is with sincere emotion that I sit down here in a clearing outside the little log settlement of Paoli, where I will mail this epistle, to write and tell you that I have been wrong, so wrong. The wilderness is not what I thought it was at all! It is not the place of squalor, danger and unremitting danger that our Massachusetts sages have dwelt upon without a shred of real knowledge. How can I depict what I have felt these two weeks as we have been borne on Brother's horses, first across Captain Kibbey's Trail and finally, the last few days, along a track that has brought us near our own land?

We have slept in a small marquee tent similar to what soldiers use (in fact it was our cousin's in the last war when he fought with the Ohio troops). We have eaten mush and molasses beside dashing cataracts in the knobby hills while cardinals and bobolinks called to us, and cooked wild deer and grouse John caught over open fires. I have turned the spit and smelled the game as smoke clouded about my face while John, himself exhilarated by new hope and new life, reached to pull a wisp of hair from my eyes and tenderly touch my face.

Never have I known such utter, sublime freedom! Without even an Indian track on the last leg of this trip, we have followed the stream beds and compass. The clear water, where fish dart ready for the spearing, the echoes off the hills behind us, the smell of earth and the beauty of flowers and moss enchant us. We are children of the land, digging for edible stew roots, guided by a book John bought. Last night we camped by a lost river, which issues out of the earth in great gushing torrents which splash into a large, beautiful pool. This river runs only a few miles, so the settlers in Paoli say, and then disappears into the earth again. It is only one of many wonders in this wilderness we are coming to know.

The nights are best of all. Snug in our tents with the flap secure against swarming insects, we lie and, as the campfire flickers, as its embers pulsate orange-red with the dying fire, we watch the stars clear and large and bright as distant candles in the night.

The smell of the earth is warm and musky, the night alive with humming. Alone! There is no human voice or ear within miles of us. Alone! Nature feeds our souls, and we are conscious of its goodness and grandeur as we have never been at home. In New England the voice of the elements is one of several presences, a low voice murmuring among the other voices of village activity and human commerce. Here Nature is the giant, a voice, booming through tall trees and down rushing rivers and high, forlorn, wind-swept hills. It is a power to be reckoned with.

My dear, dear sister, shall I tell you the rest, the secret truth that is making my heart sing? I have been wrong, wrong about something else, too, and I cannot believe that it has taken me nineteen years of married life and nine children to learn what my husband was really like.

Ah, it is true that I have known John as an intelligent, striving man, upright above all else and devoted to all of us through the adversities he has undergone in trying to make a living for us in a harsh land with little opportunity. Surely I have shared his frustration. Our relatives, without sufficient understanding, have upbraided him and even scorned him for so many attempts to "start over."

I hope I have brought him comfort; at times I have felt almost a mother to him as I have held his head against my shoulder after yet another failure. And I had known the tenderness of his solicitous love which was ever watchful of my happiness and health.

But here all is different. We have moved into a new life as if we have crossed an ocean, with all rules gone, all old associations altered. Whatever land we now have is ours alone, not fought over by three brothers. Whatever is to be made of it will be made by John and all of us alone, with few to comment, with no one to judge.

John looks at me with new eyes, eyes of pride as we see the good rich earth, the finely watered land that is ours. He takes my hand, looks into my eyes and he is almost a boy again. My mind goes without my asking it to the happy day when he took me as an eighteen-year-old as his bride, both of us choosing from love, not from parents' wishes or convenience.

And as we have lain beneath these starry western skies, breathing the air of freedom, I too have felt reborn. All is before us, the past turned and sewn under like a worn-out skirt. What joy! And as I have turned to him as a wife, something new and alive has awakened in me, and I have felt a love that I have never known flutter from its shell, bursting to be born and fly into the night. I would not have thought such feelings possible, and I have not been ashamed of them. I am awakened to a sense of love that has made me ponder, rejoice, and exult as John sleeps quietly by my side, while afar off a wolf cries.

To you only, my fondest friend of girlhood, could I write such things, and I know you will bind my letter to your heart alone. It pains and puzzles me that as I affirm my own new thoughts I may then be proving our mother's words so wrong, our own experience of many years so false. Is that so? I do not know.

Perhaps love is different for every woman, that at different times and under different circumstances it blooms in ways appropriate, responding to changes in soil and moisture like the rose bush I have brought. Still, perhaps this new awakening is only the subtle voice of the Devil, whispering his blandishing suggestions, trying to cast a shadow of sensuality over a marriage that has had so much of the spiritual in it.

Yet, does not the heart also have a voice? My own heart tells me my new love is pure. My husband is wondering, a little startled that I have presented this transformed love to him as a gift, the unasked-for token of so many years of faithful, shared experience. I shall pray God will confirm it to me as a good in marriage; He alone shall send the sign.

Tomorrow we take a surveyor from Paoli to survey the boundaries of our lands. We shall choose a home site and then return to

Cincinnati to confirm all and bring the children out before fall sets in too surely, and with it the rains and cold that will make our necessity of cabin-rearing difficult at best.

Your loving sister,
Hannah

To: Mehitable Chambers, Newbury, Massachusetts
From: Hannah Chute Poore, Cincinnati, Ohio
August 30, 1818

Dear Sister:

As we wait here again in Cincinnati the final disposing of the legal papers that will make this two hundred acres of land in Orange County, the new State of Indiana, ours, I will take the leisure to acquaint you with some of the people of the new locality where we will be living. The area around Paoli, as the nearest woodland settlement to our farm is called, is but sparsely settled. The nearest farm is five miles from us across rough terrain.

Most of the settlers have arrived in the last year or two, just since the land has been made safe from Delaware or Miami attack by the final purchase of a good part of this state from these Indians. Truly, it was a good for all of us that General Harrison won the Battle of Tippecanoe and that these United States won the recent war and sent both the Indians and their English allies packing.

But I can see as we come into this raw woodland area that it was not good for the Indians, and I am bewildered by what I see. We have been taught in Massachusetts to scorn rather than pity the few Indians we see, the frayed remnants of what was a fine human tapestry woven through all our New England lands. There are too few to even notice.

But here there are many Indians and they have about them the attitude of a dog who has just been beaten by a younger, smarter cur and must slink about. These Indiana Indians are indifferent, listless, casting their eyes on the ground so the conquerors will not see their humiliation. They are an obvious, degraded presence that will not go away, a reproach to all white men.

The Delaware, Miamis and Weas hereabouts have just begun to face the fact that they will no longer make their livelihoods from the forests, wandering before the herds of deer to the habitation of the beaver and fox. Government agents pay them annuities, making them come to central spots to collect paltry calico skirts and tin pots they have traded (unwillingly) for the life of free men in the woods. The Delaware live about here and particularly to the east on White River. Sometimes those settlers who venture upriver see them, silent during the morning hours as they visit the traders and attempt to sell the few furs they can still find, noisy of an evening as they forget their lost kingdom with cheap whisky, which they buy with the small monies the government sends them for their periodic annuities.

But the "camp" Delaware are not the only Indians about. In this county are also "Quaker" Indians, who have come with a cadre of religionists from the Carolinas to avoid persecution both of themselves and of their Indian friends. Quakers have always gone out to the red men in Christian charity. And while we have been taught that they have sometimes been fools about their Indian charity, casting the pearls of their families' safety before the feet of sometimes ungrateful tribes, I for one think the Quakers are right in defending these Indians of the Northwest.

The poor creatures are often ill with smallpox and loathsome diseases brought among them by the white man. They are dispirited and lonely, as if they are the last survivors of some sort of shipwreck, and whether they be Delaware or Miami up north, all are constantly swindled by the folk on shore who are supposed to be rescuing them—the white traders, the government and even their own kind.

The Quakers take their part, attempting to teach them the values of agriculture and baptizing them in the name of Christ, and I say good for them! Certainly not everyone around here agrees with that view. In a village not far from Cincinnati last year, when there was fear of an Indian uprising, there was a burning in effigy. The straw man set fire to in the center of town had dark clothing and a Friends' hat on its head.

John, like most of our old New Englanders, has learned to hate and distrust the Quakers and every other religious sect that is not descended from Winthrops and Bradfords. He is suspicious of the "Friends" and says they meddle too much in affairs not their own. Independent this husband of mine is, though strong of character.

As for the rest of the folk on the scattered farms, there are as many good and as many unreclaimed souls among them as in Massachusetts. But they are too busy and too tired from the awful exertions of land-clearing and simply surviving to worry much about theological disputations. If they get once a month to church services (which are usually Methodist or Presbyterian and held in someone's cabin, with smoke choking up the preacher during the sermon and dogs and cats chasing about his feet), it is thought they are candidates for sanctification.

Already among these scattered newcomers, industry is beginning. Whetstones as good as any in the country have been discovered thirty miles further west of our holdings and men have banded together to ship them down the Ohio and even to Philadelphia and New York. It amazes me that even while they are grubbing to put corn into the mouths of their hungry children, men will seek to "capitalize" and speculate. The urge to make a fortune must be deeply rooted in the very heart of our humanhood. I suspect Cain carried a Yankee peddler's pack on his back when he was sent into exile into the land of Nod, and probably his one great desire was to eventually appear in rich clothing, with fine livery at his parents' door and say "Look . . . I am a man of fortune."

One industry that repels me I will tell you about. It is the digging of a plant called ginseng which is common in this part of the Ohio valley. This plant is gathered in great bunches, dried, and sent to far China and the Orient, where it is greatly valued. It is thought to be a great aid to those old men who wish to marry young maidens. It enhances manhood, so they say.

Why any of us should grub in the ground to supply the needs of those who wish to nurture their baser natures, why my fellow pioneers should encourage vice in this way, I cannot fathom. Yet the pay is very good for a pound of ginseng dug with simple prongs in the woods. Still, I cannot conceive that any of us would be in such desperate straits that we would need to live off the depravity of our fellow creatures. Am I looking at this incorrectly?

Tell Goody Barnes I thank her for asking about me, and that the babe thrives and he enjoyed the porridge and cow's milk our sister-in-law fed him while we were gone to the land. We have named him John Henry Harrison Poore, in honor of the hero of the West, and my own hero, my dear love who so bravely has set his face against the past to make for us all a future by the sweat of his life.

When our brother Daniel, idly looking at a new chaise someone was driving down the street, asked if he could come with us to aid in the prodigious amount of work it will take to ready the land for winter survival, John said, "My thanks to you, but we will work our land, build our house—alone."

Your own sister,
Hannah

## The Journal of Hannah Poore

October 1, 1818. Today I begin a journal of our life here in Orange County, Indiana. I do this in the hopes that I may put some expression to the strong trials that are coming our way in this part of our earthly pilgrimage and, I would hope, triumph over these same trials.

"In this world you shall have tribulation, but be of good cheer. I have overcome the world," the Master tells us. Every fiber of me believes His words. There is need of this comfort for the past three weeks, as tribulations seem to cluster and grow as thickly as the nettle bushes I see everywhere in the woods about.

We knew that when we came finally to our lands, it would be necessary to cut a wagon road through to bring the ramshackled Conestoga and all our household possessions in to begin building our cabin. What we did not know, for no one told us, was the amount of time it would take to fell this hardwood out here. Four weeks! And each day the sun sets lower in the sky and the wind blows colder.

I do wish for Wendell, although I know he is rightly placed with the folks at home. Still Alvan does his best and, because at fourteen he is fairly straight and tall and has some of his man's growth, he tries to help with the prodigious amount of axe work that occupies us all day and night. Amanda helps take care of the younger ones (a great relief), so I may prepare food.

But it is Susan, my strong, tall and handsome Susan, who has astonished us all. We knew she had unusual qualities, but it was not until we saw her in this trying situation that we understood the metal with which she is formed.

Seeing her father and Alvan starting at dawn and applying the felling axes to huge sycamore trees and oak trees. sweating and tugging with ropes to fell them correctly, hauling trees out with the ox we spent our last money on, she evidently began considering the slowness of their advance through the forest and the rapidity of the advancing winter.

Truly it was a matter of grave concern and prayer with me too, but Susan decided to act on it. The third morning we were here at the land she rose at dawn and pinned that straw-colored hair of hers back in a bun. Then she donned some of her brothers' clothing and asked to be "relief man," stepping in with the felling axe whenever by necessity either her father or Alvan could go no further.

At first John looked at her severely, muttering that she had stepped far beyond her woman's station and should return to the campfire and children, but still she stood by his side, refusing to leave. Finally he gestured to her to pick up the axe. He was intending, I suppose, to show her how difficult, nay, impossible it would be for a sixteen-year-old girl to fell a tree with a three-foot circumference, let alone some of the enormous ones five-feet thick in this virgin woods.

"Pa, you are often right, but about this you are not right," she said.

Susan set her mouth in the firm line I have seen when someone's speech or actions do not suit her, picked up the axe and began to swing. I have seen her beat a wash on a board, beat twenty pounds of yeast dough in a dough box and beat a carpet, but I have underestimated the strength in those firm arms and shoulders. Susan was a competent axeman. It was obvious to all of us.

Her father's mouth flew open. Then he turned to look at me and he started laughing. He bellowed and guffawed and, wearily mopping his brow, gestured to the girl to continue the chopping. Giving her a few instructing words, he took up his position on the other side and then, expert judge by now of the way one of the huge brown and white trees they call sycamores will fall, stepped out of the way and let the tree go by the wayside. Thus was another ten feet of road gained, and by the help of a "female girl baby."

Even with Susan's constant help now, the work proceeds excruciatingly slowly and with real pain of effort. It has taken us weeks to move two miles, and we still have about a quarter of a mile to go before we reach creek and homesite. They may fell only five or six of the giant monsters on a good day, spending part of the time in clearing away what they have felled with the ox and moving through smaller trees.

Of course not all of the trees are huge oaks and sycamores; there are middling-sized sugar trees, walnuts, ash, hickory and poplar. And between them all are blackberry bushes with irritating brambles and the nettles I spoke of. Even in the clear spaces the thorn apple trees clutch and pull at the skin and gash the arms of Betsy and Mehitable, our little nine-and-ten-year-olds, who are supposed to be pulling the branches away after they have been cut down.

Clearly the "axemen" are in the most peril and continually exhausted. The gnats and autumn flies have been buzzing relentlessly about them. Mehitable is responsible for keeping a small, smoking fire burning constantly near the hewers of the trees to discourage the swarming pests, but this means that the axemen have reeking, acrid smoke constantly in their eyes and nostrils. Still, it is better than the irritation and dangerous distraction of having insects sting you, thus causing a mis-stroke.

Also, there is the danger of the axe flying off the handle, which does occur for each hewer at least once every two or three days.

Then a new handle must be fitted from nearby wood. We pray God that a limb will not be lost as the pair of choppers stands close together and the axe head flies. Already John's foot has been closely shaven in a mishap of this sort and he was lost to the work for a day, brooding and mumbling about debt and lost opportunity as he lay with his foot up in the wagon.

October 3. Food supplies are running low now. John has no energy to hunt in the woods, but falls each night on the ground after he has cut the last tree and lies there as if dead—through the noise of the children's play, the rain and even cold sleet.

I fear that we are not feeding the axemen adequately. Last night Susan took her father's gun. She asked for a few instructions and went to the woods and returned after quite a while with a fat raccoon. She was proud she had been able to bag something on her first time out. What sort of place is this where women must learn to shoot?

Still, there was meat on our tin plates. I had never tasted raccoon before, but I assure you it is palatable, barely. Truly the wise man has said that "there is no sauce like hunger." But John and Alvan could hardly eat; they go to their work and to their beds like wraiths.

Praise God, tomorrow we will be at the site. I wish to rush up to it, to abandon this horrible felling of trees and clearing of brush, but it will do no good to abandon the work and wagon and rush through to the homestead place. Our wagon and ox must come too, so we can build our shelter.

October 5. At last! Today we dragged the ox and wagon through the stumps to this swath of land which will be our home, above the rapidly flowing creek. Tomorrow at dawn we will begin putting up the cabin. Certainly it is time; the skies are glowering with October rain and a cool breeze tells us that soon winter will be here. I have need of my devotions book and will copy the verse that catches my eye and lifts my spirit: "The Christian is represented as a warrior, clothed in a panoply which is to be used for attack and for defense. Put on the whole armor of God, for you know not how the Devil will plan his next foray, from what flank he will assay your strength.''


October 7. How true that devotional passage was! John could not rise from his pallet under the tent today. He called me to him. "Hannah," he said, "I now wonder if indeed my course was proper to take you so far from family and friends to this uncertain quarter where we may certainly perish. I seem to have a boggy ague—I cannot move and all my bones ache." Alvan, too, was feverish. And so the Devil brings us to low pass. I have given Amanda full care of the babes, who cry from cold and may be coming down with agues too. Responsibility will have to develop in that flighty heart of hers! And my Susan has slipped away again into the woods. What a morning she picks to hunt, although certain it is that we can use meat.


Evening—About one o'clock John went out of his head with fever. Alvan was not much better. John wrestled with unseen enemies, tossing about on his pallet in the tent, and I did not have the strength to get him to come to the wagon, although Amanda and I actually wrestled with him and tried to pull him there. He ranted loudly, and finally, his forehead burning up and sweat pouring from him, began singing in a hoarse voice, frightening the children, "I must fight if I would reign, increase my courage, Lord."

I laid him back on the pallet and covered him with a blanket on sticks. I watched him there, helpless and dirt-streaked in the rain. Tears came to my eyes for the past month's sacrifice of his energy and health, for the utter independence of spirit that would not allow him to seek for help, even though I suppose my brothers would have come had he really implored.

I cried, then I set my shoulders. This would not do. I began singing, joining in his feverish refrain. Surely I have never sung a hymn in our Newbury Church with such fervor as I did the prayer "I must fight if I would reign—increase. . .''

Our crazy hymn was interrupted, and I started at a noise behind me. As I knelt on the ground I looked up to see two very tall men standing, with Susan behind them, silent and exultant. One of the men was dressed in Quaker black, the other in Indian winter wool and leather.

"Who—" I asked, bewildered. John's head cleared momentarily and he leaned up on one elbow.

"Who the Devil—"

"Not the Devil, my friend," said the Quaker calmly. "Let us hope it is the Lord. We have come to build thy house." John's look mingled hostility and surprise. The Quaker went on.

"But first I think we should build up thy body a bit. It appears to be in disrepair." Not waiting for an answer, he sent the Indian to the saddlebags on horses tethered to young trees. John began to protest, but weakness overcame him. He fell back on the pallet.

"Wanted to do it alone for them—" he mumbled.

"There is no alone, neighbor," the Quaker said as the Indian brought a flask and poured it into a pot above the sputtering tripod fire. "Especially in the wilderness. This is not thy New England or my North Carolina. Here we are as exposed babes in the woods. We must keep each other warm or we will die from the harshness of the forest."

John looked at him resignedly, then gratitude entered his gaze. Weakly he held out his hand to the Quaker, and I wept anew and had to be led away by Susan, who had found these angels of mercy and brought them to us in our extremity.


October 8. Praised be God, John is better today and watches as the Quaker and Indian build the shanty cabin. Alvan, now completely well, assists them with the ox. John has been finding out about the angel visitors who appeared in our time of need:

John: "What is your name, Quaker?"

Quaker: "Sylvester Brown, by thy leave, sir."

John: "And the redskin?"

Quaker: "A Delaware, christened by some of my fellow Quakers in my home state of Pennsylvania. Mark Ebenezer Highcreek is his name.

"The Delaware, original friends of our William Penn, have been driven from every state as the white man advances. Our particular congregation took the cases to court, hiring lawyers for

Delawares in Pennsylvania and New Jersey. There men rode by night to tar and feather some of our congregation who worked to get disputed land claims brought into court.

"They trumped up charges against our Indians. A group of us turned the work over to others and finally, for the sake of our Christian Indians, we left to come to North Carolina. We did not find freedom and peace on the frontier of the Carolinas. We found naught but trouble. Our Indians were not welcome, and finally, unable to live in the midst of the slavery we found there, we all came to Orange County."

John grunted and shook his head, more I think at the loquacious frankness of this Quaker than at the story itself. In New England men do not write their life's story on the brim of their hats and prattle it forth at the drop of a penny. Still, there is much to admire in the openness of this new West.

We women and children sit in the wagon. "This is man's work," the Quaker says, and although Susan protests that she wishes to help, he has set her to work stewing great pots of venison which will be salted down for winter. The Indian shot two deer this morning. As for me, my task is caring for the sick ones and I have delved into my herb basket for lemon balm, which I am steeping for tea. I shall apply a horseradish poultice to the aching joints. I put down my pen to do so now.

Back—all rest well. I shall describe what I have watched and what I now see before me of this rude ceremony called, "The throwing up of the cabin," so strange to my Yankee eyes used to seeing only frame houses carefully raised by master builders. Here, of course, we have no lumber, no brick, no lime for mortar, no nails. But the Quaker watched the sickness, now spread (though not dangerously) to Betsy, Amanda and little Harriet and scanned the skies for signs of coming winter. "We must put together whate're we can in a day," he said.

And so Mark Ebenezer the Indian has cut two forked posts and put them as high as he can reach. Between them he and Sylvester Brown, the Quaker, have put a cross timber, hewn flat on its face with a broadaxe. On either side of the timber they and Alvan are placing thick log poles to make a long slanting roof which reaches to two huge walnut logs on the ground.

Later—Now they have cut side logs and covered them with more logs, brush and mud brought from the creek. On the deep roof the Indian and the Quaker have laid more brush and mud to hold the roof down and keep us warm through the winter. Now they are going inside this "log pen" or three-walled cabin we will call home and putting down "wallpaper" of buffalo hides, and cat and wolf skins they brought with them. "We shall make thee a tamped dirt floor for this first winter," Sylvester mumbled almost to himself. He looked up and put the head of his axe against the dirt, tamping it to demonstrate how that floor would be done.

"On thy floor there will be more of these fur rugs. 'Tis an Indian dwelling, really," Sylvester Brown told me solemnly. I glanced up at his red friend, but Mark Ebenezer gave no sign that he had heard.

There is something almost comic about our new Quaker friend, dear man, at least it seems so. He has a large nose and a long face with pocks, not at all like the rotund, well-fed Quakers we saw on the streets of Philadelphia. Perhaps that is because he has no woman to cook for him; his wife died in North Carolina of her first childbed and the babe with her. Poor man, he devotes himself to his family of Indians. Twelve live with him, and more are scattered about in the several families, most of them named Lindley, who make up the Quaker settlement five miles up the road.

The rain has started. Sylvester Brown has quickly moved inside the leanto to cut out the hole for one window and cover it with— what? He has come to me, and I have searched for paper and found Mehitable's last letter. I have sewn the pages together. 'Tis all we have, and I must part with even that one last prized possession.

He listens to the hacking cough of little Harriet, lying beside her father in the back of this wagon. "We must get the sick ones into shelter and light a fire; the rain is turning to sleet."

Later—Susan has given us all dinner, venison and potato stew with corn bread the Indian made. John receiving his plate on his pallet, shouted out, "Quaker, we thank you for your charity but we will not be beholden to you. We have bags of cornmeal and wheat flour to get us through the winter."

Sylvester Brown told him, "Brother, that is well enough, but it is not bread thee will need but fat and meat. When the wind whistles through the chinks in this cabin, as it will, and thee cannot hunt because the storm abides, thee must have fat meat stored and hanging from thy roof to give thee strength."

My stomach churned. I had hardly been able to eat the raccoon. John asked, "And where are we to get fat meat. How salt it?" His voice sounded, well, not beaten, but certainly humbled.

It was obvious my brothers had not given good advice about the wilderness. "Do some hunting until the first crop comes in," they had said, and presented him with a fine Pennsylvania rifle. Dartmouth College did not prepare one well for the rigors of wilderness living, which is probably why these high-toned youths had chosen to live in Cincinnati instead of on buffalo robes in Orange County.

But Sylvester Brown had come with answers. "We shall salt the venison today, before we leave. And tomorrow and the next day, bring a porker for thy wife to pickle in salt brine and hams to smoke and salt."

John told him, "I can smoke hams. We do have meat in Massachusetts. But we have no money to pay you."

Sylvester Brown said, "No one has money or coin out here. Whoever has, does for whoever is short. We do not stand on ceremony at this time of year." The Indian glowered a little as if John had breached some sort of decorum.


Later—This day is coming to an end. The Quaker has just come to me and said, "Tonight we light a monstrous fire at the end of the hut. Tomorrow morning we will build the fireplace which will give permanent heat and light. At least thee will have shelter for this night, as the storm howls down. Now I must close the front opening next to the fire by clapping together some of these boards for a door before the light is gone—"

He turned, startled, as John clambered unsteadily out of the back of the wagon. "At least I can bind my own door together," he said walking towards the Quaker, "whilst you put up side pieces to hang it from. My friend, I thank you for the needed help." John held out his hand to the Friend, who clasped it warmly, but briefly, before they both went to work on the temporary door opening.

I wonder how much those words of gratitude cost my proud husband.


October 15. And so we are all in this large leanto, with camp beds along the walls. These little beds rest on poles stuck into the chinks and are bound with grapevine to the floor supports. Amanda, Susan, Alvan and Mehitable sleep on these field cots. John has put the best bedstead from Newbury up for us, with its trundle beneath, and that trundle does for Hannah, Betsy, and Harriet. I thank God all are reasonably well, though they do hack in the stillness of the night. Still, the fire does burn brightly in our mud and wattle fireplace along the sidewall, and it gives us cause for contentment, as a fire always does.

Each day now I spend my time outside with the Indian, who does not seem to mind returning through the woods on his horse to help us, though he must have other things to do. We dig roots he knows about in the woods and gather the odd fruits called papaws and persimmons. We dry the papaws and cook the persimmons with small crabapples and maple sugar into conserve.

He has shown me how to put the dried fruits and pots of mashed fruit, along with turnips Sylvester Brown keeps bringing us by the bag, into a potato hole as they call it, which we have dug out of the dirt floor and covered with a clapboard door. This vegetable hole will hold the things that will keep us from scurvy, so the Quaker says, through the winter.

We brought the Chute maple table and chairs along with the best bed into the leanto. How odd its slender legs and polished surface look in the middle of this low-roofed hut. The pallet beds, covered with the hairy skins of animals, are surprisingly comfortable and warm, Alvan and Susan say. Only Amanda complains, but then she complains of everything.

We have made some three-legged stools for the children to sit on as they pat slivers of wood and mud into the chinks between the sides and roof. From this odd, pitched roof John has just finished hanging the winter dry supplies: wild onions and many Indian herbs Mark Ebenezer the Indian is introducing me to, hemlock for dysentery, cattail for inflammation, mayapple to stimulate the bowels.

Then to purify the cabin I have hung herbs I have dried in the tin oven: bunches of sage, pennyroyal, summer savory, thyme. Truly I look forward to the stuffing I will make for the partridge and wild turkeys John is beginning to shoot.

The use of a gun is something new and strange to us—John had forsworn pleasure hunting in New England and game is scarce there anyway. But here you may see a deer look in your window any morning, and John is getting passing good at shooting. The Indian is teaching him to salt and jerk meat, and they have built a salt shed.

I can never stand to touch the gun. To take an instrument of death in your hands, ram home a charge, cock it and fire, thus depriving a beautiful doe or young buck of life—I could never do it. Alvan is trying to learn to shoot, but I think he has inherited the Chute eyes, poor at a distance. He may never be accurate enough to kill an animal for our pot.

Susan begs to perfect the art of hunting she has begun to learn, but I have need of her constant help in sewing deerskin moccasins as Sylvester Brown has shown me. Our Massachusetts shoes have worn to pieces on this rough ground and John does not have leather to even make shoes for his own family.

On his final trip for the fall, Sylvester Brown brought us buffalo robes from Michigan and told us to make winter garments for the men to wear during the bitter nights of January and February when they must feed the stock outside. They tell us our Eastern wool greatcoats will freeze stiff and solid in the freezing rain common in this climate.

John frets to get the stock shed finished so the ox, cow, and calf can winter warmly.


October 21. And so at last a day comes when we sit before our fire and feel ready for the winter. John and Alvan have finished the shed today and the ox and cow and calf are safe inside. I do not wish to criticize my children, but I could wish Alvan were more fothcoming in his helping. He holds back, uncertain, and his frail constitution and recent sickness make him have to sit and rest often while John, as always, shoulders the work, this time hoisting huge logs with handspikes up as high as he could get them for the cattle shed. All this week John has been doing back-breaking work. He has chopped out rings around trees to kill them so he can clear a field, and with the ox he pulled out stumps of trees he had already cut. Small wonder that at the end of a week like that, he was so weary he could hardly eat supper.

But tonight he sits and sips a cup of sassafras tea, the daily drink out here, and there is a look of contentment I have never seen in all my years with him. Little Betsy sits at his knee, her long hair braided around her head, looking up at him as he works on harness, and Hannah spins a top on the floor by the fire. He looks at his little girls and Baby John and is happy and proud.

Many new settlers come in groups. My husband did not choose to travel this way. Alone he left New England against all advice, alone he came into this wilderness to start again where all is free and a man is rewarded for labor, and when he could no longer do this alone, God sent the helpers that he needed. Still, the accomplishment was John Poore's.

"What do you think of?" I ask my love on this October night. I wonder if he is recalling the many fires of many evenings that have warmed our love together, the campfires of our recent trip, as I do.

But no. "Of winter. And of the debt we face the winter with. Six hundred dollars to Father and my brother James and your two brothers."

I look up at the lines of weariness in his face. "And yet spring will come after winter," I say, setting my mouth a little firmly so he will see I am not afraid.

"Yes, spring will come after winter," he nods, putting his hand on Betsy's shining hair. "And I will clear my fields and plant and pay the debt and these lands will be filled with harvest fruit that will pay for all these children's future. For here the land does not fight you with stones and salt and sand. Here it reaches up and clasps your plow as if it were clasping the hand of a friend." He sighs.

"In spite of it all, I am glad we came," he says and his eyes catch mine for a long moment.

Suddenly I think of the reality of the spring I have just spoken of, of the slips of my plants, carried so far, watered so often, put in the ground to grow in Cincinnati and pulled up again. Somehow, they are still alive! Just today I put the grape hyacinths in the ground and heeled in the rose cuttings and strawberries and other plants in the back of the new cowshed. "I too am glad," I said, thinking of a garden in the spring.

I have written long into the night. The candle burns low and we do not have many more. Devotion for the Day from my beloved book: "We are under obligations to imitate our Savior. But must we imitate him in his poverty? Must we cast away our pillows of down, or comfortable mansions that like Jesus we may 'not have where to lay our heads?' Christ meant what he said, 'You cannot serve God and Mammon.' And, dear pilgrim, recall that you cannot be poor while Christ is yours!"

So to bed.

October 22, 1818. At the end of this, the saddest day of my life, I set my pen to paper. In one day's time all is changed, changed so awfully. John awoke early with indigestion, so he said, and I rose to prepare him an infusion of dandelion leaves. He stayed in his bed complaining of increasing pain spreading down his left arm. Soon palpitations and heart pain began. Hurriedly and with a prayer I prepared foxglove infusions; my pen trembles to write this. Within four hours of taking sick my dear husband and love of these twenty years died on the Lord's Day, leaving me—

Alone! With the snows due to fall, no hunter here, in an Indian wigwam with so great a debt it will take years to retire. God forgive me for thinking of it. His last words ring in my brain. "I will not live to plant the spring fields."

Alone! With the Indians still about and no living soul for five miles. Alone! My love gone, gone when I had found him anew. Was all that new-pledged joy in my love from the Evil One? Is this, God forbid, the sign I called forth? I cannot think so, and yet I wonder and will the rest of my life.

Yet not alone, because this hut is filled with his children to look at me with his eyes, his smile, whenever I turn two paces about.

And not alone because in me is the new child, the last, whom I told him about as he lay clasping my hand to ease his pain.

Most of all I am not alone because I have my faith in eternal life for my loved one and us all, and because I know I will be strengthened through whatever trials—I cannot even think of them yet.

"The Lord giveth, and the Lord taketh away." I cannot say, "Blessed be the name of the Lord" as yet. Perhaps later.

# Chapter Three

## The McClure Papers

To: Jack McClure, Branham Tavern, Corydon, Indiana
From: His cousin, Catherine McClure Hogue, Vincennes, Indiana

June 5, 1818

Dear Jackie Dee,

I am sorry, I can't stop calling you that even though you've asked me to. Being your McClure cousin for thirty some years I should have some privileges, shouldn't I anyways? Wasn't I the one who used to keep Cousin Ish from beatin you half to death at McClure Station in the Caintuck days? When you put wood-roaches and rabbit pellets in his bed, remember, and then hid behind the door to see him come in and turn back the sheets Aunt Jenny had so carefully ironed for him?

And wasn't I the one who saved you in Caintuck when we were only fourteen, saved you from being tarred and feathered by half the county after the revival at Big Bend, when air-brained Johnny tole that you put calomel in the lemonade and made everone sick? And I made up a story how grace had come down on your head, and you had repented the next day and fell on your knees in my sight beggin forgiveness for ruining the testyfing for everybody including the preacher.

Elizabeth and Mary thought I was crazy for covering your tracks and said you were a disgrace of a cousin, but I couldn't stand to see you and Jim suffer. Well, after all I only had my fingers crossed a little bit. A squirrel's nest did fall on your head and you did screech out "For Lord's sake!" that day. So I figure you were calling on the Lord after all. I hope so, it certainly wouldn't hurt you a bit.

Anyways, I have never seen your ma so mad as she was that revival day, and I have seen her through a lifetime of getting mad.

I thought I'd write and tell you how folks and things are goin here in Vincennes. Things are jest the same for me and John, with the Old Farmer's Almanac our Bible and three little ones to look out for. I never was sure I'd cotton to being a mother, me being so independent and John almost having to tie me down and break my spirit to get me in a marryin mood. But I do love the babies, especially Nancy Jane. She is the spittin image of my mother, Jean McClure. Yet sometimes she is as strong-minded as Grandma Jane. She even laughs like her. Some folks in India believe people live again, but I guess that isn't Christian, is it?

Surely seems strange you and Jim aren't here. Things just aren't the same atall without you to crack your jokes and act like a boy even though everybody knows you're a respectable man and the father of two. I know Bessie writes to you there in the State Capital, but it isn't the same. I think I know you lots better than your own wife Bessie does, even though that's an odd thing to say. Oh, I forgot I have to call her Lizzie now. She thinks Bessie sounds too low.

I hope Jim is surviving being in the Assembly. Member of the "loyal opposition." Seems odd to think of it, a member of our family in state politics. It all happened so fast.

Seems jest yesterday his Pa Uncle John died there at the mansion house, not really very old, there before the Battle of Tippecanoe in '11.

Cousin, Jim was a different man after his pa's death. Why was that? I've never known. He seemed to me then to be bent on gobbling up life all at once, like a fat boy come late to the Sunday school picnic. Maybe he had twenty-five years of flim-flamming to make up for. Anyways, before we knew it, Jim was reading the law in Vincennes with General Washington Johnston. Then Harrison's party picked up on him.

And now, even though Harrison is gone to Congress (might as well be gone to the moon) and his enemies are in power in Indiana, Jim got himself elected to the State of Indiana Assembly. That's another thing that sounds funny. State of Indiana. Going on two years now.

A new state and a cousin of mine famous—well, a little bit anyways. And I still can't quite get used to it all.

Jackie, are you enjoying being in Corydon? Being aide de camp, Jim's secretary there for a while? I think I know better than anyone else how tiresome it has been for you on the farm. You are a good father, I say it not to flatter but because it is true, but I know how 'tis between Bessie, that is, Lizzie, and you.

So I hope you are finding yourself now and will find a promising future in politics or something else besides farming. I guess Tom and Charlie are seeing to your land, since your Pa still officially owns the "improvements." They seem to be readyin to plow for a good stand of wheat and corn. I saw your Pa last week when John and I drove the young ones down there after services at Upper Indiana. I think he misses you.

"Catherine, I shore do think of Jack a lot." And it seemed to me I could see a light in Uncle Dan'l McClure's eye, as he pictured you at the Battle of Tippecanoe in your big moment leading the charge at the final moment for the Parke Dragoons.

"Yes, Uncle Dan'l, I think of him too," I told him.

"Somethin will come along for him, I know it. He jest aint' got started," he said.

Naturally I didn't tell him our secret about Tippecanoe—that the horse got away from you when you spurred it and sort of chased the Indians alone, with you as a passenger. He's got enough on his mind, what with Charlie wounded in the war so bad he can't walk good and won't court or marry and Esther and Jane puny from the ague.

Write soon and tell me what it's like in the State Capital where all the big heads walk and talk as if they were real people. At least so we say in Vincennes.

Your Cousin Cat

To: Catherine McClure Hogue, Vincennes, Indiana
From: Jack McClure, Branham Tavern, Corydon, Indiana

August 15, 1818

Dear Cat:

Your letter has sat around a while on my bedside table, and I'm sorry for that, but as they say in God's Country better give the Cat her cream late than not at all.

Well, it is good to hear from my cousin in God's Country. The legislature holds forth, debating its momentous, earth-shaking problems, and our cousin Jim sits in the midst, Solon that he is, trying to keep the rabid Jennings-ites under control.

Give the Jennings people their rein and they'd have all playing the lottery every day and every dog, skunk and the President of the U.S. on an equality. They call us the "aristos" here but we're much more Republican than we used to be. Sure! Republicanism is where the wind blows in this here "era of good feeling" President Monroe has got us all into.

Why, you wouldn't recognize that Federalist Burr-lover Jim McClure now—he goes to raise log cabins with the best of the "simple folk" and he can talk Jeffersonian better'n Jefferson himself.

It's a dumb dog doesn't know what side of the fence his food dish sits on.

I sit here in the empty House chamber, with its brass chandelier and painted speaker's platform, its wide, classical windows and the polished walnut legislators' chairs, scratching out my letter to you. It is difficult to believe that in this room only an hour or two ago the delegates were sitting, some with their feet propped up on the desks, some smoking pipes. They were debating the subject of whether the new Indiana Constitution really does prohibit slavery—at least the holding of slaves that were in servitude when the state was admitted two years ago.

Naturally, we McClures have an interest in the matter and you know what it is. The McClures and their relatives now hold over one fourth of the slaves in the State of Indiana. 'Tisn't your fault.

Your pa, Uncle George, rants and raves about it and none of your branch of this corrupt tree has ever held a slave.

Neither has my pa. But Jim and his brothers and sisters and our other cousins have over a score of black people in ''ninety-nine year servitude.'' Who knows what the legislature will do to clean up the mess left by the Constitutional Convention. ''No slavery, but sometimes some slavery,'' it seems to say.

'Tis difficult, I reckon, to try to reconcile the pictures of our childhood, the Jim McClure whose hair stood up like a surprised woodpecker, who hid his pennies under a loose board in the loft of Grandmother Jane's house and snarled at us if we came near, the Jim who ran off to join Aaron Burr's treason trip and then quit before he even got on board—to reconcile that with the smooth-as-custard man who stands before the group in this elegant room and speaks of ''the necessity of internal improvements.''

I think it's the same man. He's just as frugal and sly and ready to take an opportunity as he was back then.

He's ''fer'' internal improvements. Especially if they can help line the pockets of the Vincennes cartel. Behind the scenes he's working on a big project that could make him very, very rich indeed. I shan't say beans about it yet, even to you, Cat.

You ask me what changed him from the carefree boy he was, and I have an idea on that. You mention Uncle John's dying—I can remember seeing him at that moment, lying there, his stomach et out, ulcerated inside with worry, lines all over his face. He was ''wore out'' as Pa says, plumb wore out.

He'd have to have been. Go back a piece. They had come all the way from Ireland, Uncle John then a boy of six, Uncle Will only two, Grandmother Jane (blessed memory) and the Grandfather John McClure we never knew, dead during the Indian wars in Pennsylvania.

'Twas the original Irish Grandfather John who bore the brunt of all the movin' on to better things, across the ocean in 1751 into Cumberland County, Pennsylvania, when it was only a few shanty cabins.

Soon he was dead though, and by the time of the Revolution or even before, our Uncle John, Jim's pa, had to take over, to get the other uncles out of trouble, to manage the money, to take the

whole kit and caboodle to Caintuck when only 5,000 people lived
in it and Indians lined every path.

Then later 'twas Uncle John, really, who brought near to a
hundred people across the swamps on the Buffalo Trace. Took
'em three months. Then Uncle John built and managed a huge
mansion and land holdings and slaves—he just wore out, plain
and simple and he wasn't all that old.

Uncle John died near to dawn. After it was over and Jim had
helped his ma from the room to her bed and the old man was bein'
laid out by the slaves, Jim said to me, "Jackie, I don't want to live
and die like that. I ain't gonna have my gut et up by giving to
others that don't give back. I'm goin' to be more sparin' of
myself, do somethin' else but farmin'."

"Sech as?" I asked.

"I got me a few ideas," he said. "Besides I've always felt like
I was nobody and something in me is saying it's time to be somebody. I've lived under the shadder of Pa and these McClure uncles
for twenty-five years. Now I'm going to see whether this horse'll
run or not."

So the week he got back from Tippecanoe he went to reading
law. He listened close to Harrison and the others who had power,
how they talked, what they read, and he imitated them. I was
doing something of the same kind right about then, trying to read
up a bit and improve myself. I hoped to get a little shine on the old
shoe, and I guess he did, too.

Jim always was quick to learn, and he shined up pretty good, I
guess. Some way this cousin of ours was in the right place when
William Henry Harrison left, when Indiana was about to become a
state, and he decided to go to Congress.

Harrison had a few favors to bestow on them that had done him
good through the years. Our Jimmo was about and became the fair
young man of the opposition to Harrison's enemy, Governor Jennings. And so here he is, here we are.

Cat, did I hear you were setting about making your own fortune? Lizzie writes me that you have ordered a silkworm factory
to be shipped to you from New York City. My cousin is going into
business. A woman with three children? What are we going to
hear about next, Lizzie wonders. If you won't tell anybody, I'll
tell you that I think it's just fine.

You always were the Queen of Caintuck and if you'd been born a man you'd be governor. So gather those mulberry leaves, stick em in the little boxes, and maybe soon we'll be wearing kimonos from Cat's caterpillars. Good luck.

Oh, one more thing. Not only has Representative James McClure got a new career in the legislature, he also has another novelty for him—a lady in his life. Someone who has just come west and moved into Madison a few weeks ago. Jim's in love.

Your Cousin Jack McClure

To: Judge Andrew Markle, Hill House, Walnut Street, Madison, Indiana
From: Representative James McClure, Branham Tavern, Corydon, Indiana

August 20, 1818

Dear Judge Markle:

I want to thank you for the nice reception you gave me and my secretary (cousin) Jack when we came to call the other day. Even though in the Indiana House both you and I are new dogs to the pack, as we say out here, you have the experience on me in this lawmaking business.

Your advice is of value to me. Particularly since you have been in the East and have had a chance to talk to people who know about this new Erie Canal that is going to be built and fine roads and improvements they have out there. Just what we're crying for in Indiana—backroads chicken crossing and hog waller that it is. But not for long.

I know I count on your discretion about the matter we talked of—the cartel. I represent some big guns back in Vincennes and they want to move.

Did you know I ran on the platform "Progress Means Growth?" There's nothing I believe in more.

I would like to pay my respects to your wife Henrietta and thank her for her cordial reception of us. It is a pleasure to see what the fruits of industry can bring to a local domicile: the silk hangings, the eagle wallpaper, the chiffonnier and venetian glasses in the dining room. It is hard to realize you floated down the river on a flatboat only this summer.

You have made your abode the light set on a hill in Madison. To think the town has been there only a few short years and you have supper parties for your own party members and even those of us in the "loyal opposition" that, I am sure, are equal to those in Washington city.

One last thing—please convey my respects to the lovely Auraleigh, the finest flower in the garden of children you have been blessed with. I have enjoyed her discourse on political subjects the last few evenings we visited your home. Although all do not share my viewpoint, I admire a woman whose intellect shines brightly.

My cousin Jack sends his solicitations and regards—

Yours, ever, etc. etc.
James McClure

To: Honorable James McClure, Branham Tavern, Corydon, Indiana
From: Auraleigh Markle, Madison, Indiana

August 21, 1818

My Dear Mr. McClure:

I have sent this letter by special courier because I wish it to be put directly into your hands. Yes, I, too, felt particularly stimulated by our conversations of the past two weeks. I was somewhat chagrined that we had to be at many points interrupted by the children about here—my mother lets them wander freely. She believes as I do that children must be given the chance to develop free, like the fawns and small rabbits of the field. Sometimes, though, rabbit jumping and squeaking gets tiresome, especially when you are trying to converse with a man of intellect and determination.

Yes, we are on different sides of the bench politically. That is nothing new to me. My father is a moderate and I am the most Democratic-Republican you could find. You may wonder where I have read so much. At home in northern New York, winters were often long and tedious. As the oldest child, with my next sister four years younger than I, I often sought to relieve the strain of long afternoons by reading Adam Smith, Rousseau, Paine, or Jefferson in my father's library. I grew conversant with all of them. Father indulged me and even taught me far beyond the level of most of my sex. I wonder if he now regrets it?

I suppose I am fearless, speaking out at church school classes and sewing bees beyond my "woman's place." I must admit to you, Mr. McClure, because you seem sympathetic and kind to me, that I would much rather discuss the details of admitting new states that wish to be slave states to our Union than I would the knitting of stockings and the curing of blistered feet. Can you understand that? Did I hear you say that your mother was a woman of independent spirit? That she had once entered a barn in the Revolutionary War to save horses after Tories had fired the premises?

I am eager for more conversations with you. Really, Corydon and its neighbor Madison are only log-cabin towns, pretending to be uppity because the assembly convenes in our area. Do not think I am snobbish if I say few around here have anything that is interesting to talk about.

I shall ask Father to invite you to dinner on Sunday and we will be able to have the gazebo above the river to ourselves so that we may debate our theories of political economy together. May I suggest for topic the social experiments of Robert Owen at his manufacturing town, New Lanark in Scotland?

Respectfully,
Auraleigh Markle

To: Daniel McClure, Esquire, Church Road, Vincennes,
Indiana
From: Jack McClure, Branham Tavern, Corydon, Indiana

August 25, 1818


Dear Pa:

Thank you for the letter about the harvest. It's thoughty of you to take me into the plans; I don't deserve it, really. You all are being patient with me as I stay away and live among the airy castles of politicsville.

I can read between your lines that you are wondering how Lizzie and I are getting along and whether I left her or no. I think I'd say I never was with her to start with, that's the way to express it.

You know that I buried my heart along with my first love Adahbelle Granger close to ten years ago, now. I never could get over how she died rather than have my baby. Only you knew the real truth and I think it has bound us together. Thank God Ma don't know.

Lizzie wanted me, that was it, and after all a man must marry, mustn't he? She was as good as any of the other pale imitations of Adahbelle that the rest of the women in the world seemed to be.

To tell the truth I think she's glad of a little respite from having to cope with me. All she wants to do is go to services at Upper Indiana, to talk to the women about the preacher and his wife, to organize the sugaring bees and the grape stomping sessions in the fall. She's never really 't home unless she's got women in the house and all their mouths open to full steam position.

Someday I'll come back, when I can hold my head up. I won't tell you what I mean by that, I don't even know what I mean myself, except I don't have anything in my life to be proud of. Everybody needs something. It sure wasn't the Battle of Tippecanoe. Nobody could be proud of that—I know you don't agree with me. They'll be re-fighting that battle around the tables and by the fires in the year 2,000. If they have tables and fires.

I am beholden to you for taking care of Little Alf. He's an odd little chap, ain't he? Like an old man before he's six years old. I'm glad he's taking to books already. I wish I'd been able to read better when I was a child, but I know we were all out in the woods and it took all we had to put a little mush and milk on the table in those days. I tried to make up for it later, but—

Jim's got me rushing about trying to find out everything any of the legislators know about Robert Owen. I read a little about Owen in the Philadelphia paper—has an "enlightened factory" in Scotland where workers are treated well, have churches and schools and decent pay. Can't imagine why Jimmo is interested in all that. But these times are odd and a lot of former Federalists are wearing strange disguises to be classified as supporters of the "people." My job as his secretary is to keep him informed with whatever he needs to know.

Wish I weren't so itchy all the time for something meaningful to do. I feel, always have felt, as if I were carrying around a pocket full of red ants. Don't know why, Pa, but 'tis so. At least I'm enjoying the New World Forensic and Debating Society; they talk about politics but also scientific discoveries. I'm still awfully interested in science.

Pa—one thing. Luke Dugger and son Jay Byrd have just arrived and are putting up at the Raccoon Head. They aren't saying, but my nose tells me they've come to influence legislators. I had lost track of them at Vincennes before I left and I'd like to have you tell me what they're up to back home.

Your mostly obedient son
Jack McClure

To: Jack McClure, Branham Tavern, Corydon, Indiana
From: Daniel McClure, Vincennes, Indiana

August 31, 1818

Dear Son Jack:

Vincennes is about the same. Your little sister Janie Lou is playing the piano and now and then she gets fretful and throws the music book on the floor. She's a tryin to play that Irish poet's music, sad and sweet it is, and she can't get the sweet part. Thomas Moore, I think the name is.

Ma would have chuckled to think we have a Mere Irish songbook in this here house. The Scotch Irish don't truck much with the Mere Irish, though she used to tell us about some good ones she knew all that long ago in Dunleigh. Oh yes, it slipped my mind I'm not supposed to be talkin about the old days in Ireland when times was hard and even the seed corn gone, and some of the folks in the village et grass.

Well, the Britishers druv all us Scotch Irish across the sea. And I don't think no more of the English than my ma did. Just a suppose I'm goin to shake hands and say thankee for the black-guards that burnt up the President's mansion and rent up the Injee-ans in the war not too long ago.

But I know you boys don't like George and me to talk about the Irish days, or the ones in Caintuck neither. Though I don't know why we shouldn't be proud of living through the Years of Blood of the Shawnees and Miamis with our scalps still on our heads. And survive to come acrost the trace to all this fortune God has been good enough to give us.

I know your Ma is proud of this here mansion house. I am too if truth be told. The new addition looks real good and the English garden (pah) with its labyr, labeer, well, maze, and little house in the middle is just dandy. Although I feel kinda silly sittin in that there little gazerbo as Martha calls it at tea time and having the hired gal bring us tea.

How your Grandma Jane would have loved it though. "Don't mind efn I do," she woulda said, and her violet eyes would just have beamed. Them little cakes, too, she woulda loved, had so precious little of that sorta thing. Sassafras tea she had and bohea, even bread crumbs browned and water when Injeean times was at their worst, but not much oolong like I can afford.

Thank God she lived long enough to see us all rich and all the trouble of sixty years, a lot of it travellin time, brought to fruit on farms of thousands of acres.

The hired gal has put a punkin pie on the sill to cool and I am smelling it here thinking of lots of times I et punkin pie. When I can first remember things, I recall Ma pickin punkins in the patch in Pennsylvania and storin them in the cellar hole for winter. Times we didn't have much else, she'd make punkin puddin with maple sweetnin and punkin and wild crabapples stewed. Sometimes we'd have nothin' but game and punkin for weeks on end in the winter.

Still, those weren't bad times. I think about us around the hearth there in Pennsylvania. Your Grandfather John making his barrels and sometimes fine beds or cupboards, your Uncle John tendin to the two horses, Uncle Will whittlin piles of scraps and Aunt Jenny, jest a tyke, throwin them onto the fire to see the fire flare up.

And acourse my brother George sawing away on his fiddle in the corner and talking like a swell head even though he warent seven years old yet.

I hear tell Harrisburg is quite a fine city now. Twarent even a town when I was born. And Lexington and Louisville are rich cities. When I knew those places they were two huts each with land shark wild boars and sows for their fancy residents. What a lot o livin your Uncle George and I have lived through. He is fine, still goin into his office with Badollet writin for the paper. He is happier since Harrison is gone. Never did like him, your Uncle George didn't, like the rest of us did. But Harrison was mighty good to us all. You know that acourse.

Glad Jim is making it good as a politician. I have give politics up for Lent. I had my fill when I was judge and we had to get Indiana ready for the Battle of Tippecanoe and all that. Corydon and the State Capital, or any of these places includin Washington city on the Potomac, seem to me to be like the crow tree outside your bedroom window. I'm a lookin at it now, all the crows peckin and jostlin and yelpin and flip floppin around on the branches without acomplishin a durn thing. They call it legislating.

Now about Luke Dugger. He and Delva and Jay Byrd have bought up a lot of land where White River flows into the Wabash. There, in the bottomland they got thousands a acres. Bought em from farmers who can't pay the government payments at foreclosure time. Sad. The Duggers have their own little town now, call it Duggerville. They are plannin to set up a way station for the corn and pig boats going down to the Mississippi. Then they hold 'em there to wait for pilots and rondeevoo groups. They have a inn and shippin service, too. Jay Byrd's runnin the shippin station and I spect it will see a lot of service, though why anyone would want to consort with the likes of them that man the flatboats, the Caintucky boatmen and river pirates—but to each his own poison.

But Luke is playing the reglar laird, as John used to call it. Has a porticoed place over there on a rise, biggern your Uncle John and Aunt Jane's old place. Little cabins all about for the slaves—pardon—the "nigger servants" as he calls em, now that we are a free state.

Says he can't run his plantation without the "niggers." Can't be having the governor and legislature tamper with the Constitution. Right now, the way most folks reads it, you can keep the slaves you had at the time of statehood and that's the way the Duggers want it. And I gotta admit that your cousins Archie and Johnny and Elizabeth are right with him. The Duggers got money behind 'em now, lots of it, and I'm not sure where it all come from.

I am glad you will be back for a visit with your fambly soon. Lizzie is a good gal and Little Alfred a rare crittur indeed.

Your loving Pa
Dan'l McClure

To: Miss Auraleigh Markle, Madison, Indiana
From: James McClure, Branham's Tavern, Corydon, Indiana
September 1, 1818

Dear Miss Markle (if I may be so bold),

I can't tell you how much I enjoyed our evening at the New World Forensic Society there in Madison. I was most interested in your paper on "New Lanark: a New Age for the Working Man." It was interesting to hear more about the model schools, the clean living quarters set up by Mr. Robert Owen, and the Sunday schools where the children learn the Bible, although I must admit I enjoyed even more hearing you talk about Mr. Owen with me in the gazebo the Sunday before. Am I being too forward?

I hope you didn't think I was impertinent at the meeting, asking why if Owen is an atheist, he has Sunday schools? And why he potters about being sure everyone is in good family quarters when he himself is a libertine? I thought you answered the questions very well.

Miss Markle, Auraleigh, as you have given me the great joy of asking me to call you, I have to confide that most of all I enjoyed the refreshment time under the full moon along the river. I hope you didn't think me too bold in taking your hand.

I shan't forget how you looked at me so straightforward and told me you admired some of my stands in the legislature. You say that I am a man on fire for the future of the land. 'Tis true I see this great new West above the Ohio as a proving ground for the future, even in the world's eyes. It does fire me to think of the land stretching on across the desert and the Stony Mountains to the ocean, and all of it for all of us and all our children.

I've always been that way. Some folks keep bringing up that I tried to go with Burr. 'Tis true, but the reason was I saw him getting Mexico for all of us, more land yet for America. Burr's empire in the Southwest would have been ours eventually; he could never have held it. But we could have had that, too, if we'd had the daring.

You shyly asked me whether I considered you much too bold, as other men do, because you talk politics and care about the issues of the legislature. At first I have to admit I was startled. Women I know sit about the fireside with their darning eggs and tatting hooks. But I considered that you had come from the East, where women are much more apt to think and talk about the world.

Besides, not all the women I know are melting sugar cookies. My own ma is as independent a woman in spirit as ever trod the soil of Indiana. She has been kept down, I think for a lot of reasons.

I don't blame my pa, I just think the Scotch-Irish weren't ready for my mother, for her feisty ideas, her breaking of customs, her managing ways. I think some women need to be given their heads, like horses running, and these are worth getting acquainted with. I'm not afraid of 'em like most men are.

I will be over to Madison in a short while and will stay some days. The scheme your pa and I have cooking is about to boil. We have put a good deal of work in on this, and it involves some mighty big interests. But say nothing of the matter outside the family—this stream has many shoals to pass before we are there.

Your sincere friend James

To: Honorable Judge Andrew Markle, Madison, Indiana
From: Representative James McClure, The Inn, Madison, Indiana

September 13, 1818

Dear Judge Markle:

I am settled in town now and can give my attention to our great investment plan. I hear you have been in touch with the Vincennes State Bank interests and that they have given a final nod to the loan arrangements. I am glad you understand why my name is not on the official papers. I am proud of this scheme, glad to own up to my part in it, but I do run for office from that neck of the woods. Let me be the silent partner as far as signing goes.

It is an enthralling project; I confess I am as eager to have it consummated as I've ever been in my life. As I understand it, Mr. Frederick Sholts will be there when I arrive at your home tomorrow. How fine it will be to welcome our chief investor! I shall have my secretary cousin there in the negotiations for the first time. We may have a place for him.

Yours etc<br>James McClure

To: Mrs. Catherine McClure Hogue, Vincennes, Indiana
From: Mr. Jack McClure, The Inn, Madison, Indiana

September 15, 1818

Dear Cat:

Well, I just had to write you about the speluncular things that your cousins are up to over here at the seats of power, as they call them. I don't dare write to Pa cause he'd probably not understand it all and go and copy something out of the Bible and send it to me. And I don't write about anything of substance to Lizzie. I don't owe her a letter anyways for three more weeks; I just saw her last week, didn't I? I don't want to spoil the lady.

Anyways, we were all over to Judge Markle's house. Pretty big place it is, with all the fancy carpets and brass chandeliers like Grouseland, the Harrison place. Or Luke Dugger's, as I hear tell lately.

Judge's children were all there, tumbling about. Mrs. Markle has new child-rearing ideas. Came from Rousseau in France she says. Let a child develop itself, free from the trammelling restraints of society. They were untrammelled enough, I tell you. The twins, James Madison and George Washington Markle, played under the dinner table and knocked our knees together while their ma ladled soup from a big tureen shaped like a fish.

Finally their sister Evangeline came and got 'em thank God and trammelled 'em up some, so we could eat our fish course untrammelled to some extent.

Well, a Mr. Frederick Sholts was there, a tall, sneaky-looking man with extra heavy sideburns, who smokes cigars like he was eating candy, one right after the other. He also stammers.

Cat, they got a real plan afoot. Jim hadn't taken me in on it till last night because he wanted it to be full blown and ready to put into operation. Sholts has taken options on a lot of speculation land at the falls of White River there about twenty-five miles from Vincennes in the wilderness. He's been selling land for about a year now.

He has thousands and thousands of acres. He is forming a combination to found a town there for all the Eastern immigration that's a pouring into this state now. Did you know they say that over 30,000 folk have come into Indiana this year? I knew there was a lot, but not that many.

He and Jim have got the Vincennes State Bank involved and they are loaning money for development, using the promise the land will return for security. Jim and Judge Markle have put their money in, too. They call this new wonder the Hindostan Land Company. It's big, Cat. They want it to become the Louisville of Indiana, bigger than that even, heading for the biggest town in the new Northwest. Their heads were so big, and their talk shocked even an old-time projector like me.

Jim wants me to represent him at the new town site; they start building immediately. The town should be a real spot on the map by this winter.

Back to the supper. After we had our sweet pudding, Jim and the oldest daughter of the family, Auraleigh, who sits in the midst of all and talks like a regular Cicero, walked in the garden amongst the boxwood.

They were gone such a long time that Mrs. Markle finally sent little Emma Rose out to find em and she came back in pulling on Jim's coattails and smirking like a pussycat. Guess they were kissing.

Sorry, Cat, that I didn't get to see you and that husband of yours John Hogue and the little ones when I was back home. I wanted to be with Alfred and his sister, little Jewell, and I do owe some time to Lizzie. Pa seems to be overseeing the farm, bless him. Ma came over to Sunday supper and just sat looking at me. Called me John, like she has been doing since Tippecanoe, after the old man in the Indian wars.

Tom and his wife were with her. That brother of mine is still doing everything right. The pork-packing on his farm is making him rich.

I leave that all to him, and I wander around the wilderness trying to find my life. I'm uncomfortable among my own kin these days. I feel like the naughty puppy that is supposed to be trained to stay in the house and he keeps making mistakes and has to be switched. Everybody's eyes are on me and they are big and sad, someway.

How are the silkworms? I keep waiting for my kimono.

Your cousin Jack

To: Jack McClure, New Town at Falls of White River,
Calcutta?
From: Catherine McClure Hogue, Vincennes, Indiana
October 1, 1818

Dear Jackie Dee:

I want you to talk to Jim about his ma. You know ever since
Uncle John died, Janie McClure has stayed to herself, seeing only
Mary and Sam Emison and their children. Margaret, Eliza and
John Wedge are married off now and moved into the New Pur-
chase lands in the upper part of the state.

It's good Sam'l and Mary live right near the old place, because
now it's just Aunt Janie and the slaves, colored servants. Aunt
Janie is acting strange, and I don't think Sam'l and Mary will
write because they don't want to disturb the great man in his civic
duty. Pother, I say.

Aunt Janie talks all the time about repenting. Says she has a lot
to answer for in her life. Yet she says she can't stand it up at
Upper Indiana Presbyterian and doesn't want to do her repenting
there.

Says there are too many McClures in there, they drip from the
eaves and hang from the rafters and they even get the best places
out in the cemetery lot. She opines that a lot of em are hypocrites
anyways at Upper Indiana. The elders voted last month to expel
Archie McClure for drinkin too much and lots of McClures voted
yes even though they love their share of corn liquor too. Aunt Jane
says Archie was picked on, but then he is the spittin image of
Uncle Will and Aunt Jane always did have a soft spot in her heart
for Uncle Will.

She keeps mumbling about renunciation, and she isn't even
takin care of all her horses any more. Some of the fields are going

fallow out there, and the brick kiln Uncle John worked so hard to build is falling to pieces. Both Mary and Sam'l are too gentle to do much, but I say 'tis time to take her in hand.

You asked about my silkworms. Well, little Nancy Jane and I spent a deal of time picking mulberry leaves and even planting slips along the creek. It all went pretty well until one day the baby got in and turned all the boxes upside down and the worms got out and crawled all over Knox County. But mark my word I'm going to get something to do and know I'm somebody that isn't just John Hogue's wife, much as I do happen to like that state of affairs.

Tell Jim his new love sounds like my sort of woman. I'm sending this by messenger to the new town on the falls of the East Fork because you said you and Jim would be over there for most of the fall. I keep forgetting the name—something about India.

Your Cousin Cat

November 15, 1818

Address Given by the Eminent Legislator from Daviess County, James McClure on the Dedication of the New Town at Hindostan Falls, Indiana

My Dear fellow citizens of the great State of Indiana: Forty-two years ago all across this land the bells of freedom rang to start the War of Independence. In towns like Philadelphia the bells rang. Their metallic voices blended with songs of jubilant colonists who had finally severed the ties with Great Britain.

In villages the bells rang, the ropes pulled not by the rich aristocrats but by farmers and shoemakers and coopers. In the hearts of each was a dream: the dream that one day every man would be free by the strength of his own strong arms to make of life what he would with his own land to own and till.

Those strong arms were soon called on to serve the cause of freedom, to carry guns across the frozen farmlands of New Jersey, to row boats across the Delaware, to drag cannons across mountains to win against the invincible redcoats at Saratoga.

My own father served at Brandywine using his strong arms to repair wagons and take care of horses. Your own fathers have records as proud and shining as the Stars and Stripes themselves.

And now the victory is won and the people of this fair new Union, living under the protection of the Constitution and our laws, have taken their strong arms into the wilderness to fight a new kind of battle. They are taming a new land, they are making of it another testing ground for the power of free men loosed to pursue their own destinies.

The land has need of those free arms. There are millions of trees to fell, millions of acres to bring under cultivation. Just as we all came out of our own mountain villages, seacoast towns and tiny hamlets to unite and tame the British, so we must now unite again to tame the land. An individual working alone can fell trees, drag them with his ox into positions and raise them into a cabin in two weeks. But a group of men called together for the cause can put up a home in a day.

We are the town builders. Ten cabins have been put up on this site, and they are the beginnings of a real city. We have come together, men from the eastern seacoast towns, the mountain villages of Virginia, and some of the great conclave of the Scotch Irish here in southern Indiana.

Here we will build the largest city of all in this Northwest, a town to rival Cincinnati, Louisville, St. Louis. Here with the waters of the great White River and Wabash at the front door and the great central traces of the Northwest at the back, we will be the hub of a wheel of industry, the focus of a center of commerce unrivalled in this wilderness.

I wish you to know what has happened in the two short months since Mr. Frederick Sholts has come to us from New York. Town lots have been drawn up in an orderly way, planned and squared off and surveyed, as Mr. Dupont did for Washington City. Vast tracts of land have been subscribed to. The town's organizers have donated land for a seminary and land for public offices. Most of all they are planning a stupendous mill with iron gears to grind grain, saw wood and even produce linseed oil.

They have been told it cannot be done—that White River here at the falls cannot be tamed because its currents are too swift. But these sagacious and fearless men, with the spirit of freedom and enterprise in their hearts, are determined to create a great mill and build the fortune of the town around it.

Today we mark the birth of a new town, a town of freedom and enterprise. With the arms of free men we will build a future that is limited only by our own imaginations. I can see this town in only two or three years, my friends, with flatboats on the tide, loaded with produce for New Orleans, with inns and fine homes over street after street, with stages going to all points of the compass.

Our new city's name suggests its purpose and future. Two hundred years ago a group of enterprising merchants in Holland and England formed companies to bring the riches of the East to the world. They taught all of Europe to know what vast promises and wealth lay in the Indies.

We are mining and developing the new Indies here in the new Northwest, in Indiana. It is fitting that we call our new town after the East India company and call it Hindostan—and may we all grow as prosperous as they did in the land of the rajahs. I want you to know that, as your representative in the legislature, I am doing all I can to make the road to prosperity here in Daviess County smooth. To that end, I must add, I would appreciate your vote when the time comes round for elections for state representative for these three counties. Thank you, and I would like to introduce to you the founder of the Hindostan Land Company and its senior proprietor, Mr. Frederick Sholts.


To: Auraleigh Markle, Madison, Indiana
From: Representative James McClure, The Inn, Madison, Indiana

November 17, 1818


My Dearest One,

All went well at Hindostan Falls. The town lot Sholts has arranged for me is being cleared. I must have you with me in this new life, or else it pales and has no more meaning than a sugar cream pie.

How I regret that your father cannot see you living in the wilderness, and has forbidden our wedding. There is more than that, of course. He has called me, ''hide and seek'' Federalist. It was not easy listening to him saying that I wear my fringed hunting shirt on the outside and under it a rich man's tailed coat. Odd that he should say that when he is such a man of means. I suppose it is because I so strongly support the Bank of Vincennes, and all the old Republicans hate established banks.

Your father and I must speak on business matters, because we are both incorporators and proprietors of Hindostan Falls. We are as joined as hip-twins in the scheme to build the town and to sell thousands of acres.

Well, we have quarrelled on these issues, but I suppose some day we shall make up. In the meantime, my dearest, I live for the sound of your voice, your footfall on the stair of what will, must soon be our own home. I will send this with Jack and he will put it in Letty Jo's hands at your back door. He will tell you the plans for this evening's ''escape.'' The minister awaits us downriver. You are of age and I certainly am. I cannot live another night without you.

How like you to agree so eagerly when I suggested this after the quarrel with your father last week. You have called me a ''man of principle,'' although my principles don't always agree with yours. I now call you a woman of spirit. I have waited a lifetime for a woman of spirit and now I want to spirit her away, if you will pardon the pun even on this serious occasion. I pray your spirit helps you down the hill and to the boat waiting on the Ohio in the moonlight tonight! May God speed our journey to a new life in the new Mecca of the West!

Your adoring
James

# Chapter Four

## The Account of Thomas Jefferson Brooks
### (Continued)

My search for Emily did not take me to Japan or the Ecuadorian jungles, but it might as well have. I searched in every city on the route between Boston and Natchez, Mississippi in the summer of 1818.

It was, of course, the search for a brooch fallen into the pigpen. I asked in the hospitals in New York (had she become a nurse in those desperate, dingy establishments?) I walked the streets of Philadelphia, looking for little shops of seamstresses. I scanned the pages of the *Enquirer* to see if any "Governesses with strict upbringing and knowledge of some Latin and literature" were running advertisements.

I looked into faces behind bonnets, I crossed streets on a gallop, only to have strangers turn and look inquiringly at the Yankee boy in the worn jacket who held onto their arms as if he wished to ask something, then turned and backed away.

I finally ran out of money in Pittsburgh. I had slept on straw in the stable of an inn on the riverfront for three nights and was down to my last, stale currant bun, when I saw a sign at a dock. "Keelboatmen wanted at Redstone."

Redstone was the keelboat port south of Pittsburgh. I tossed the crust of the currant bun into the Allegheny and began the walk to employment.

The keelboat dock was in need of paint, and my foot stuck between two broken planks. Many of the more genteel or astute shippers were beginning to patronize the steamboats. Still, the captain of the keelboat was putting on a jaunty air; his clasped arms were resting on the shelf made by his fat belly. He had stuck a chrysanthemum in his cap. No doubt he had got it from a woman in one of the ramshackle two-story log houses by the quay. The curtains fluttered in one of the windows directly behind us; perhaps "she" was watching.

Thank God I did not need to give even a passing moment's worry to Emily when I thought of those women who maintained "lodgings" near the docks of every river town. Emily's pride and stout heart would never allow anything but decent employment. No, she was probably with Aunt Ophelia downriver. Eliminate Boston, New York, Philadelphia and Pittsburgh and what did you have? Surely she was at our aunt's. I was feeling more reassured these days.

I approached the captain.

"Do you have a place for a polesman?" I asked, trying to look half as cocky as he did.

"'Sperienced?"

"No, but I have a strong arm and I can—"

"Where ha' ye worked?"

"Well, in the Lincoln Mercantile in Massachusetts."

"Store clerk?"

"Yes."

The captain whooped scornfully and called for a be-whiskered old cook and a tough-looking man with a patch over one eye to come over.

"This yere's a reg'lar fop, he is. Sold dimity lace and little slippers to the ladies. Thinks he can haul a boat over a sawyer at low water." He came up to me and his fat stomach intruded on my chest. He was taller than I. "Pickle-head, this yere work is for men, not namby-pamby butcher boys," he said.

The one-eyed man, who on closer inspection seemed to be only a few years older than I, edged up. "I bet you be a schoolmaster's or preacher's boy." He poked a finger at my eye. The nail was dirty and chipped and as long as a hawk's talon. He used it for fighting. His breath reeked with rum and he stank. I think it was the odor of this man, who seemed not to have washed since childhood that sent me into action. And after all, he was shorter than I and I had my wits about me.

But I would have to be quick, I knew that. "You need a bath,"

I said and tackled him as I would in a game of village football. He pitched backwards into the river.

Without even waiting for him to surface and his sputtering mouth to begin shouting its obscenities, I turned and, with a crooked smile, strode off.

In an hour or so, when tempers had all cooled, I returned and found the captain supervising the loading of butter and eggs, venison hams and pickled pork into the hold. I leaned over and tipped my cap respectfully.

"I will work for you for a dollar a week, no less. I will be up at dawn and will be the last one to go to my bunk at night. And I can put my shoulder to the pole as well as any man, and better than most."

The captain took a long look at me and finally gestured with his finger towards the cabin." 'Peers I'm agonna take this trip with more'n one soft shoulder," he said. "See that you do pull your oar like the rest."

I nodded and opened my little backpack of gear so I could stow it—clean shirt, two clean pairs of drawers I washed in streams, and silhouette miniatures of Father and Mother done in silk. Why I had brought them I never could explain to myself, except that they made me feel a sense of reality that I did not otherwise possess. Somewhere were people I knew. Somewhere was a village I had grown up in, a churchbell on a tall hill. No one for over a thousand miles cared whether I even existed. There is no lonelier feeling on earth.

I stared at the drawers. They had holes the size of silver dollars in them.

"Your personal linen could use a little attention, friend," said a piping voice behind me, my fellow poleman on the crew. I turned to see a small man with a large head, protruding forehead, prominent eyes and bright red hair.

"Dr. Donald Drake at your service, sir," said the man, bowing from the waist. He walked over and picked up the drawers. "I shall make you two new pairs of drawers from muslin I have in my pack."

"Are you a tailor?" I asked in astonishment.

"No, but where I grew up in the woods of eastern Ohio, a pig must learn to root for himself. I can dry apples and cherries, make bark concoctions for medicine, iron a shirt.''

''Were there no women in your home?''

''Alas, no. Ma died o' the milk sickness when I were twelve. I was the oldest branch on the family elm and since Pa had run off to Canada to follow the fur trade, I were ma and pa to the others.''

''How many?''

''Six boys. Now they are growed to manhood and I am off to make m' fortune.''

''You call yourself Dr. Drake—''

''A tooth drawer, sir. Pull teeth, make wooden dentures. Shore do. Latest in scientifical procedures. Headin' down this fair and elegant stream and payin' m' way as a keelboatman, as you are, so I can survey the fair domains to see where I might set up my permanent tooth sign.''

He had the oddest speech, a combination of rough frontier and *Elby's Grammar*. ''What was your education, sir?'' I asked. He had taken the muslin out of his pack and had found a pair of scissors and paper.

''I couldn't read nor write nary a tittle until I were fifteen. Then a old man in the village took me in at nights and learnt me to read. But all he had were Shakespeare's *Hamlet* and *Pilgrim's Progress* in the house. 'Twere out by Zanesville, 'twere.''

He had me stand up and held a copy of the *Pittsburgh Press* to my posterior as pattern. ''I were a fast learn, the old man said. Got the speeches right away. Then I went out and declaimed 'em on stumps. Like the one where Hamlet talks 'bout Polonius after he's a-killed 'im.'' He put down his scissors and pattern and stood up in the middle of the cabin. The man with the eye-patch had come down and was eyeing me hostilely as Drake began his speech:

'' 'Now Hamlet, Where's Polonius?' '' says the king,

'' 'At supper,' says Hamlet. 'Not where he eats, but where 'a is eaten. A certain convocation of polite worms are e'en at him. Your worm is your only emperor for diet. We fat all creatures else to fat us, and we fat ourselves for maggots.' '' Doctor Drake winked at me and came over and patted me familiarly on the shoulder. Then he went on declaiming.

As he proceeded with the robustly disgusting speech, I watched the eye-patch man, the steersman who Drake said was named

Goose Gatch. As syllable rolled after syllable, only moderately butchered, Goose's one eye lit up. Was it admiration? Yes, this illiterate rum-guzzler was impressed by my red-haired friend.

When it was finished, and Hamlet had told the king he could "nose Polonius up the stairs into the lobby," Goose walked towards me with an ugly look.

"Ah, Mr. Gatch," said Drake, "I see you have made the acquaintanceship of our fledgling seaman. I think we should let him help cook. He has bragged 'bout his culinary infalibilities. Says he can make a cherry cobbler better'n a woman and knows how to cobble up a ragout from India."

The stern steerer had clambered down and stood, his mouth open, looking at Drake. Goose Gatch shrugged and went on deck. Good God, what had Drake committed me to? Ragout from India. Well, he had better help me. Anyway, his ploy had worked. It appeared that I was to be tolerated, even though I was P.C.— Parson's child among the brute Philistines.

I thought it might prove to be an interesting trip.


And so it did. The routine did set in after we cast off and began the trip down the Ohio.

'Twas the life, indeed it was. To float down that beauty of rivers, the waters sloshing under you, the breeze above, the scenery flashing by. To aid in steering a bit by day, to watch that the cargo remains safe and does not re-settle. Faugh, 'tis the downriver part of life that is always easy. Then, at night to pull up to a river town. Aye, there's the rub. For conscience did not make cowards of any of us, except perhaps myself, at least for a while.

But I soon found I could down a tankard of hot rum, throw off a string of glasses of whisky and visit a dark-alley, backstairs flat as well as any of them. Unfortunately. But youth and wisdom, so they say, mix as ill as castor oil and orange juice.

I found I could also wield the spoon well before the fireplace in the galley on cook's day off—Sunday. With the little packet of curry powder Drake carried in his gear, and some cacklers we bought in a river village, I whipped up the best little chicken ragout this side of Bombay.

I have to admit that when our keelboat crew tied up, the good matrons of the Ohio River village closed their shutters and blew out the candles early, whisking young folks to bed. We danced jigs in the streets, we fought (I didn't, usually) until somebody bled or called "nuff," we sang the pirate's song at the top of our lungs, we let loose the animals from the pound and rode them about.

Why didn't we get put in the town jails? Because we also filled up the pockets of the tavern and store keepers and the staid old man who ran the inn. To say nothing of giving the revivalists and New Light preachers plenty to talk about, with the living examples of the Devil's work right before their eyes.

Dr. Drake didn't enhance our reputations. I found him a grand companion in all the carousing (he did not fight either). Clearly, though, he was eccentric. I thought my dear mother odd, our whole family including myself snipped from a different cut of cloth. But Doc Drake's eccentricity was a way of life.

A good deal of it was put on, a garment he clad himself in to mock the stodgy respectibility that permeated these raw, pretentious little river towns. He liked to spit in their eyes.

When everyone had finally gone to bed at night after one of our festive evenings ashore, about midnight, he would run through the town screaming like a vulture out of hell. He wore red flannel underwear all year long and he streaked through Maysville, or Madison, Indiana or even Louisville with only this underwear on.

He liked to go to the revivals and get converted. In one town he would become a no-dancin' Baptist, in the next town he was a jumpin', stompin' Methodist. Shaker, Campbellite, whatever was tentin' that week, he was willing to try. He could pray louder and longer than anyone I ever knew. But what he really liked to do was to leave town the next morning ironically unrepentent, swearing again at the top of his lungs.

Yet he was the most just man I ever knew. He believed that all men were equals, Negroes and all. And in a time when Indians were the most scorned, reviled race on the face of the earth, he was decent to them. "The Shawnees brought me and the little 'uns beans and corn in the starving winter. Saved our lives," he said. He believed we were earning the troubles we had with the tribes by our treatment of them. He spoke a little Shawnee, and he thought of Indians as human beings.

He also had come to know both Christian and non-Christian Delaware in his Ohio youth, and he knew their religion and taught me about it. It came to me, as I listened to him over a period of days and finally weeks that the wilderness seemed to have taught him a lesson, that we are all part of each other.

Let me tell you a tale to prove how he respected Indians. The flatboat came to the new little town of Batrand, Indiana. Doc and I took some time off to go hunting for a day, and in the hinterlands we shot a deer. We left most of it, and taking the hams with us, decided to spend the night at a log cabin we spied. We went to the door, and some womenfolk told us we could sleep under the roof if we promised a dollar in payment.

We cooked our venison over a fire outside, and as we slowly broiled and turned one of the hams, the men of the family came in. They had had a bit to drink themselves and were slapping each other on the back.

"We ben up to the Delaware Injeean graveyard," they said.

"That so?" Doc Drake asked, suddenly interested. He was especially fascinated by native burial beliefs.

"We jest been up to the grave of Big Benjamin, the chief," said the man who owned the cabin. His brother nodded.

"They buried him last Friday. Died of apoplexy." The man seemed to find it amusing. "Guess 'twas because the Delaware are fixin' to be shipped on out o'Indianney. 'Bout time. I couldn't sleep a night with them damned, smellin' savages living in the woods."

"I believe the Delaware were here before most of the whites," Doc said softly, eating bread and cheese before the fire.

"So? God never made a more squalid, vile animal than a Delaware Injeean," the owner's brother said. "Big Benjamin hung about all the time, trying to hunt on the land that's ours, talking to the government agent. I say good riddance 'bout him."

"They got him buried up there in a little log cabin," said the father of the family. "So the wolves won't get to him. Buried in a secret ceremony. No whites allowed."

"That's because they's jewry and gold work 'bout his neck I bet." This was the oldest son, a gawky lad of about fourteen.

"Now, I got it, men," said the uncle. "Let's us go dig him up and see the jewry."

Doc sat stiffly, taking in the scene.

"Righty-tighty, men," said the father. "That big buck don't deserve to rest in peace. Sleeping as if he were a Christian with a cross around his neck."

"I thunk he were a Christian," the scraggly wife put in. "Roman church."

"So much the worst. Let's dig the bastard up," said the father.

We ate our pone and venison and watched apprensively for dark to come. It came, as it usually does. The men, drunk as hogs by now, began searching for shovels. Doc had left the cabin just about sunset. When I went out to find the privy, he whispered to me from the brush. I found he had stripped, painted himself with walnut and charcoal and pinned his hair back. He had on a breech clout made out of some of the stuff in his travelling pack. "Come with me," he commanded. "We are going to interrupt this evil deeboch'ry."

He looked right in my eyes. "The play's the thing," he said. I nodded.

The night was as dark as a grave-digger's heart. Only by following the group from the cabin, slinking behind in the last flickers of the pine-chip torch they carried, could we find our way.

The Delaware chief's grave lay on a lonely strip of prairie, on a slight rise. To the south lay the clump of small ash and oak and haw trees which hid Doc and me.

We watched in that wierd, glaring light as they disassembled the small log pen which protected the grave and heaved the logs carelessly to the side. We could hear their voices. "Corpse prob'ly smellin' like bear grease—"

"He wouldn't dare ha'nt a white man." But I thought their laughter sounded nervous.

The sound of shovels hitting stones began. At that moment Doc leapt from the trees, yodelling the Indian scalp yell at the top of his lungs. The torchlight illumined his greased, shining body. I swear without any thought of contradiction that I thought for the briefest second, knowing differently, that he was the ghost of the dead Delaware chief.

Some such thought must have also come to the grave-diggers, because without disturbing another stone they took off down the path. We cleaned ourselves off in the creek and made our way to the cabin. We could hear disgruntled conversational noises come out the window holes, the buzzing of relatives talking to each other. Was it angry noise or just frightened? We pushed the door open, apprehensively.

"Watch out, strangers. Ha'nts are abroad tonight," one of the sons said, his eyes still wide. "We saw some strange things up on the hill. Threw some scummy dishwater in the shape of a cross over the path. That should hold 'em back." So superstition had protected us, after all. Still, I thought the youngun's father's eyes narrowed just a little as he watched Drake's small body settle in before the fire. If the man suspected anything, though, he was too ashamed to mention it.

That night we slept the sleep of the just on the floor of the house, troubled neither by ticks nor lice, although they were abundant enough for all that. Perhaps the Delawares' good Manittos blessed us. I rather think they did.

So, merrily down the Ohio to the Mississippi and then down the Father of Waters, steering skillfully through Devil's Chute, the Salt and Pepper Isles, and all the other trying parts of the Great River. Our captain, old Whisky-gut, was a pencil sharpened by years of keelboating. He could whistle his way through the eye of a needle, and I gave him credit for it and watched his ways. All life was a school to me that summer, the river my textbook. It took me many years to learn that the Father of Waters was a firm but fickle friend, but I began my acquaintance that keelboat summer.

The captain and Goose Gatch the steersman, the two other polemen and even the cook continued to abuse Doc and me. Practical jokes were the least of it, but annoying enough. If we went off, as we liked to do, to bathe in the Mississippi at sunset they called us "Polly Priss." Worse, they locked the hatch so we couldn't get in. The moment the sun drops on the Mississippi hordes of mosquitoes as big as luna moths descend. Our bodies swelled with their bites. There would be slop buckets sitting on the deck for us to trip over, steps oiled with fat—we vowed revenge and awaited our moment.

Now you are going to ask while all this was going on if I had forgotten my original quest. Forget Emily? Never. But after all, I had to get there. And I couldn't think of her night and day, anyway. You wouldn't have either, when you were eighteen.

When we passed Natchez, I was sorely tempted to jump ship and seek Emily directly. Aunt Ophelia lived in Feliciana, a settlement of English-descended aristocrats just south of Natchez. But much as Whisky-Gut had mistreated me, I could not leave—yet. So much I owed him.

Sometimes we were sent to check the cargo to be sure it wasn't shifting.

"Those hams don't smell top-notch," I said to Doc, after one of these trips belowdecks.

"The captain bought the tail end of last year's crop. They're spoiling," my friend told me, rolling his eyes about.

We came to New Orleans. There we sold the cargo and the captain took his share, divided with the steersman and took out the owner's share. We all were given paltry sums, which the other three took into the grog and apertif shops of the French Quarter.

I did not go into the city. My heart was low, and anyway something told me Emily would not be there.

I sat on the quay and talked to a Frenchman. He told me of the changes that American rule had brought to this sultry, steamy village. Government was more orderly but just as corrupt as it had been under the French and Spanish. The Creole families still ruled, holding their exotic masked festivals and eating their rich, spicy food. Men that he said were pirates lounged about the apertif shops, sipping liqueurs.

" 'Tis hard to believe there are pirates still left," I murmured. Jean Lafitte had helped Jackson in the recent war, but somehow the age of steamboats did not seem the place for the Jolly Roger and sword play.

"The real pirates now are on the Natchez Trace and the Mississippi," the Frenchman said.

"Ah? Where?" I asked, curious.

"All along. They can come out from shore and waylay slow-moving boats. Be sure when you are loaded with your pay now you do not lay up for the night without your pistols ready."

I promised him I would not. Later I thought our captain the worst pirate of them all; he delivered his spoiled pork and rotten flour as sound cargo, bought the best Jamaican rum, and celebrated by roaring drunken oaths in the cabin with Goose.

Doc stood outside the door listening to their drunken carousing and came back to report what he had picked up.

"More than one thing is rotten in the state of Denmark," mumured Doc. "We saw the captain buy part of the cargo himself up north, and that he delivers for full price spiled. Then t'other part, the consignments from farmers along the Ohio, he just sold and collected for. I heard him sayin' he's going to tell the farmers 'twas lost overboard. Nothin' to pay 'em for. So he wins all around."

We forgot our woes in the exotic mélange of the French Quarter. Doc was thoroughly at home. There were nearly as many eccentrics as he. My friend danced on the street with an organ grinder and his monkey; he put on odd masks and marched in a mummer's parade.

When we came back, I flopped on my back among the ropes in the bow of the boat. "What is it, m' friend?" he wanted to know. "Dost thou ail?"

There was tenderness in his voice. I nodded. Sleeping on the quay, walking among the noxious smells of the river bottom, rank with miasma, had made me feel light-headed and feverish.

I do not remember much for a couple of days after that; all I know is that Doc Drake nursed me and put cool compresses on my forehead and clucked and worried as if he were my mother.

I was very ill there in New Orleans; I do not know if it was yellow fever but I think it must have been, perhaps not a very bad case. Bad enough it was, and I was like a crying baby who had to be held down, starting and thrashing in an agony of pain and delirium. Somehow I always felt the presence of my friend, and I swear to this day that it was his awkward, heartfelt concern and tender nursing that pulled me through.

After I came to myself, it took two weeks for me to regain my strength; it came back remarkably fast, considering. The hurts and harms of youth knit fast, the old women say.

Soon we were ready to leave the luxuriance of New Orleans. We began the laborious poling job upstream. We unfurled the sail for the first two days out and made headway with a good southwest breeze—at least for short stretches. The rest of the time we poled: stuck our poles in the river and moved her up. Slowly we progressed upstream in what has to be the most aggravating, cursed labor known to the nineteenth century. My thoughts were on Emily; I planned to get off the boat at Natchez and go seek her. Drake said he might go with me; he had not found a city to his taste for tooth-drawing and might take the Trace home with me.

So we came into the wide area of the river near Natchez, cursing and poling in unusual heat. As the men's tempers brewed, they cast hateful eyes on us, the greenhorns. And as men will kick their curs when they are out of sorts, so they kicked us.

The other two polemen slammed Doc about in the confines of the cabin. Goose tripped me apurpose and twice they threw us in the river when they were particularly exasperated, saying we got in the way.

By the time we reached the Natchez strip, I was fuming to see justice done to the bastards who bossed me. Irritatedly, I ask myself why I had ever come on this jaunt. Sister or not, I have been through too much I told myself. I was not surprised that there was no justice in the world, but that some pip-squeak, fenbrained, ignoramuses should dictate the details of my life—I could hardly wait to jump ship and elude Destiny. I did not know it was waiting for me around a bend in the river, ready to change my life completely. Thus does Destiny ever travel, wearing the clothing of everyday life and hiding behind a tree. That way we do not recognize her for what she is.

*Chapter Five*

## The Account of Thomas Jefferson Brooks
**(Continued)**

We tied up early that evening in the early fall of 1818 on the Mississippi River. Our keelboat lay near a darkly forested shore. A huge piece of land jutted out across the river from us, almost forming a bay. A murky bywater lurked behind it.

"Hey you, Soft Shoulders," yelled the captain looking at me, "Go on land and take your gun. Shoot us some game for supper."

I did as I was told. The woods abounded with game; most of the shoreland was wild yet here, with none of the shacks and tumble-down sheds which marked the river villages further upstream. I had my Pennsylvania rifle and wanted to shoot a deer if I could find one.

I stalked into the woods, silently slipping through groves of oaks festooned with the repulsive gray moss that was everywhere. The land was spongy; mistletoe throttled whole tree trunks.

I heard a sound and thought I saw the flash of antlers through the limbs. I moved as fast as I could, concentrating every fiber on not making noise as I narrowed my eyes to see the deer—suddenly I was grabbed from behind by an arm and my mouth was covered. The deer I had been stalking crashed across in front of me and was brought down by a gunshot from off to the side.

"Waal, Maw, we bagged us a good 'un. Here's a squagnacious young buck efn evern I saw 'un." The speaker was a tall man with a mane of coal black hair that made him look like a cross between a Chocktaw and a lion.

"Shore thing, Captain Pete. And I think he may lead us to t' others in the herd." An enormous woman wearing huge dragoon boots and pants, a calico shirt that hung down over her stomach

and a broad-brimmed man's hat, came crashing through the saplings. She had evidently fired the shot.

"Tie his hands, Crawdad," she said, gesturing at a youth who
followed behind her, and who resembled more than anything else
a chicken.

Soon I was sitting, bound hand and foot before a smoky campfire designed to keep away the hordes of Mississippi bottomland
varmints that were already buzzing about in the sultry, late after-
oon air. I took stock. These were pirates and meaner than a Rus-
sian torturer.

I watched the one called Crawdad pare a plug from a huge
chunk of tobacco with a huge hunting knife so sharp it could cut a
hair in two. He tossed pieces of 'baccy to Captain Pete, who he
called "Brother." This brother Captain Pete was obviously the
son of some Chocktaw or Chickasaw and this awful woman.
There seemed to be some sort of odd rivalry between them based
on race. Once, when this half-breed brother spat too close to
Crawdad's leg, the white boy rose and ran to put the knife to
Captain Pete's throat.

"Ma Mavis, he's a-goin' for me," the half-breed half-brother
whined.

"Now, now, younguns," said Ma Mavis, indulgently. "You'll
get your share o' killin' soon 'nuf." She smiled a crooked smile at
me. She was going through my hunting pouch.

"Gol-drat the luck," she said. "This craphead ain't got nuthin'
but some pitchers and corn pone in yere." She was holding up the
miniatures of my parents.

"Keep your paws off those," I said, attempting to rise from my
confinement. Crawdad immediately whacked me full across the
face, knocking me almost into the fire.

"Let's shoot 'im in the head now for not having anything,"
Crawdad said.

"Naw, let's drown 'im after supper for defyin' us," Captain
Pete said and they both began to scuffle over how and why they
would kill me.

I began to laugh within myself rather hysterically, then said,
"Wait. You said something about my leading you to the herd—I
can do that. I'm part of the keelboat crew that is heading north
from New Orleans."

Ma Mavis looked up shrewedly.

"Waal, mebbe we'll jest make you tell us where your ship-mates are."

"And then you'll kill me." She did not answer. The huge breasts inside her calico shirt hung like two of the big ostrich eggs I used to see in my father's book on Africa. They seemed out of place. It was as if such a bestial creature did not deserve the title of woman.

"Mebbe we'll strike a deal. I'm in a sportin' frame o' mind." She winked up at Captain Pete. Tobacco juice drooled out of the corner of his mouth.

"Cut," she commanded, taking out a worn deck. I turned one of the grimy things face up and saw to my surprise the figure of a dark woman.

"Tarot deck," said Ma Mavis. She turned a card and displayed the figure of a hanging man. "You get a chance. Belladonna beats Doomed Man." She chuckled cynically to herself and then began outlining a plan. We would eat, wait for evening, then row silent-ly upstream above where the keelboat lay, hidden behind low-bent trees. I would show them where. They would spare me.

"And my friend, too," I said. Over the protests of Ma Mavis, the two men shook my hand and went to stir up supper.

And so at nine o'clock, we rowed through the murky, mildewed darkness towards the keelboat. My mind was flashing like a shoal beacon. I had contracted to betray my shipmates, but I was regret-ting it a bit. I ought to at least give them a chance to beat this pack of rodents in a fair fight. A rat fight was only interesting to watch if all the rats were equally matched. And Doc Drake was on watch in the stern, that I knew.

Ma Mavis and her boys did not look at me. I had a scrap of paper in my pocket and a pencil. We had now reached the tie-up point; we lurked beneath the keelboat's stern, behind a tree touch-ing the shore. I reached up in complete silence and felt for a rock. I plucked a string from my sailor's blouse.

I scribbled "Behind the arras" on a piece of paper, tied it to the rock, and lobbed this stone message through the darkness in the direction of the cabin. When it landed with a clunk and a little clatter on the part of someone on the deck, Crawdad muttered to himself that it was time to go. He may have suspected my warning; I could only hope it had reached the right hands.

They pushed me ahead of them onto the deck. The gun was at my head. "I'm with you," I said, "but I want my share."

"Done," said Crawdad. They had no time for me in a moment anyway. It was obvious my note has somehow done its work and that Doc had at least roused the crew from its sleeping quarters. I was just beginning to hear them running about, loading guns and swearing.

The element of almost complete surprise gave Ma Mavis's gang an edge even against the crew's numbers. As they wrestled, knived and shot each other in the dark, I found Doc. We scuttled below to the Captain's day cabin for the money. We would pay ourselves a fair wage and take the farmer's dues and the list of their names and sums so we could pay them, and get out of here as fast as we could.

This done, we slid over the side and into Ma Mavis's boat. As we went, we saw the captain lying dead, his head dripping blood onto the running board. Both our other polemen and Crawdad were wounded. Goose Gatch was cringing in the corner, miserable coward that he was. Only the tough old cook was holding his own.

Drake and I whistled and chortled ourselves up the river road and were heading south in Mississippi by morning.

"Let's walk in the woods when we can and lay low for a while," I said. "Some of that crew is going to survive and they'll pursue the money."

Still, we had to eat. And as we sat in a lonely log tavern about noon that day my prediction of pursuit came true, but it was not the crew who followed.

We were pulled from our chairs by the rough hands of Ma Mavis and her sons. They robbed and beat us and left us half dead. Doc's arm was broken. I guess they didn't kill us because there were people around. People on the Natchez Trace might keep on drinking ale and eating possum pie while men blacked each others' eyes and broke each others' arms, but they might raise an eyebrow at a killing. Or maybe Ma Mavis's boys had some sort of grudging respect for us. I don't know.

The last thing I heard was Crawdad's whining voice. "You wanted your share, so I come personal to deliver it. Hope ya like it," he said and gave one final kick to my head.

We dragged our beaten bodies through Mississippi, hardly knowing where we were. I set Doc's slightly fractured arm with a straight stick and the rags from one of my sleeves. We sipped at streams through swollen lips and finally we both grew feverish. Still we staggered on through at least three days and nights, collapsing by the side of the road for long intervals to sleep through our fever.

When I finally awoke to myself, I realized we had taken a wrong fork somewhere. The sun was behind us. We were going east and had been for quite a while.

No money, no Emily, no hope. Both Doc and I now began to be hungry, and as our bodies healed from the beating and fever, we became ravenous. I looked about at the wild countryside with a sigh.

"There's nothing for it but to throw ourselves on the mercy of some householder," Doc said.

"Yes, if we could find a house," I agreed.

This part of Mississippi was certainly not like gentile Feliciana. Pine trees marched up and down the hillside. The dirt was raw and red, like a sore.

Soon, however, we did see smoke curling down from a hillside ahead of us on the road. We came upon a farm, and a man with a craggy face and buckskin breeches approached. He had the dark, lanky hair of an Indian and for a split second I thought of Captain Pete and my heart sank.

But no. This was a full-blooded Chickasaw. What was he doing here?

"Hail, my friend," Doc said to the Indian. "Is the owner of this plantation to home?"

"You see him before you," said the Indian solemnly. Though Doc with his Jeffersonian ideas was probably not surprised, I was. An Indian owning land?

"Tottie, show these folks to the house and give them a cup o' water," he said, gesturing to what I had to believe was his slave.

The Chickasaw gentryman watched my surprise and perhaps enjoyed it. "Name is Charley Bad Wind. I have twenty slaves," he said. During the rest of the evening, dining with him at his decently-set table, we learned that he had been rewarded with land for his help during Andy Jackson's New Orleans campaign. He had then made a fortune in furs, which he had lost gambling. Now he was supplying pine products to the Navy. Turpentine was his principle crop.

And yes, he confided, after we had had a few glasses of apple-jack together, he could use a couple of good white hands. I smiled as I ran my finger around the rim of the cut glass brandy goblet.

We were hired. The slaves let us dog around after them to train us. We saw trees, thousands and thousands of them, shooting to the sky with branches far above human reach, supplying the raw material of turpentine. We saw spigots like maple syrup spigots on their bases and sap dripping into metal pots. And, in the yard a huge square, staved barrel that was the still, up on stilts.

And we began a few weeks' work that stretched out to almost five months. We learned to gather the pine sap, to bring it in the buckets to the still, to boil it down to separate the products it made. There was the gummy pitch that was the residue, the rosin that was left at the bottom of the boiling pot and finally the clear, distilled turpentine that passed out of the top of the barrel still as steam and dropped into the catching pans.

We fed the fires, we felt the heat that was almost hellish. Sometimes, if a tiny piece of hot pitch shot at us, we knew an awful, searing burn until we dunked the arm, or leg or whatever unfortunate member it was into the water bucket.

"They's Nancy and Harry and Jimmie and Bert, Millie and Fanny and Wilbur and Mert," sang an old slave still-master about the different grades of turpentine from dark brown to clear. "Named after the colors of slaves in Mississippi," he said with a grin that showed only two teeth.

Each night we ate at the table with the Indian plantation owner, Charley Bad Wind. We jested and drank a little and listened to the odd, alive darkness. There was and is a certain languorous contentment in being in the South. It is, indeed, the land of the lotus eaters.

The pay was good, and I had finally done what I should have

done in the first place: I wrote to Aunt Ophelia and found out that Emily was not there. Where to look next? I did not know; I would need to think about it. In the meantime, I was comfortable and earning good wages with a good friend by my side. He was grateful that I had set his arm when he could not do it himself. He liked me. It was a heady, comfortable feeling for me. I had been too stand-offish and too much Preacher's Child in Lincoln to have even one friend. Except, of course, for Emily.

And at night in one of the cabins in the slave quarters, I watched Doc practice dentistry at least two or three evenings a week. He would lay out the odd tools, the blood-catching cups and the pullions, funny little hook-shaped things that caught under the offending tooth and pulled it out.

I marveled at the gratitude in the eyes of slaves and even the master himself after we had held him down and pulled out the pain, blood spattering all over the cabin floor. I thought they looked on Doc as an angel, and truly I did too. He did not have to spend his nights giving relief to these poor souls at the end of the world. They loved him and I loved him too, with the love only a man who admires his friend as a good man can feel.

But, at other times, I had a hard time keeping up with his practical jokes. He would put on a sheet and pop up in the darkness outside a slave's cabin window and moan and groan like a ghost and claim he was the ha'nt of Swamp Grove. Or he would hide in the barrel Tottie, the cooper, was working on and sing out in a small voice, "Don't hit me, Mr. Man with the li'l hammer," until Tottie ran from the shed.

It came the time for the winter firing of the shed, the last firing of the season. We stacked the oak wood high, higher until the fire grew almost white hot. "More, more," the still man shouted. "She ain't a-comin'."

We sweated like steamboat stovers. It was a hot day for January, even in Mississippi. Tottie was working by our side, and the still master was checking all the tuns and bins to see how the distilling proceeded.

"Lay to, my friends," Doc shouted at us, his smile gleaming, the carrot hairs on his chest wet with perspiration. "You get more cordwood, I'll shove her in. We're goin' to get top grade stuff this time."

"Hotter! Hotter!" I heard that black man at the top of the still yell as Tottie and I ran into the woods for more wood. Then I was knocked flat by an explosion that rent the air.

"God, the still has blown!" I screamed in anguish and turned to see Doc running towards me, his body aflame and coated with flaming pitch. I remember the smell of his hair singeing, his flesh peeling off and him rolling, screaming piteously in the dust to rid himself of the indescribable pain of having his flesh burnt off by flaming pitch.

And I do remember, in my dreams late at night, the sight of the still man, blown miraculously free but staggering, coming up with a gun and shooting Doc in the back.

" 'Twere a mercy to him," said Tottie, coming up behind us. "Take him mebbe one, two weeks to die otherwise. Christ have mercy." He crossed himself and knelt to pray.

I felt sobs wrack my body as if someone else were experiencing them and heard my voice shout across the smoldering clearing, "You pray and call on Christ? Where was He when one of the best men I ever knew was broiled like a piece of charred meat?" I ran about the clearing stomping out the little fires until my own shoes burnt through. I did not know what else to do.

And the next day, without even trying to find Emily any more, I started for Indiana to join my brothers.

*Chapter Six*

## The Poore Papers
### The Journal of Hannah Poore
### (Continued)

October 23, 1818, Morning.

In some way I have lived through this night after my husband John Poore died. It is odd that when we consider death, we think of it always in exalted religious or philosophical terms. I found out yesterday that it was the practical problems that overwhelmed me. I was alone in a woods with the immediate need to bury a loved one, and I and my children were the only ones to do the tasks.

It is difficult enough to lose one you deeply love. But to have to face the burial chores without friends and neighbors, to cope with the necessities of washing that body, digging a hole, finding a coffin! Build one? Of what? Awful chores, the worst that life can give to one alone.

I should have remembered what the Quaker said. We are not alone. After Alvan and I had washed John's body and laid it out on the bed, I heard the door creak. In popped the head of Sylvester Brown. The children ran to him.

"Someway I knew to look in on you today," he said sadly, as he looked at the still form on the bed. And he did all the things that needed to be done. He organized the weeping children into work crews, put Susan and Amanda to cooking, went to hew slats to construct the coffin.

And so, with, "I am the Resurrection and the Life" read over him, we laid to rest John Poore on the twenty-second day of

October, 1818, on a rise above the creek, near fields he would never see heavy with grain.

My Quaker friend stayed through the night and now has left, the exhausted children are still asleep except for Susan and Alvan, and I sit before the fire. I have felt so much pain that something in me has shut down. I am as numb as if my entire body had lost circulation and "prickled" itself to sleep.

"How will we live?" I hear my own voice saying. Alvan starts to venture something and then hesitates, looking at me for guidance. But Susan goes to wash her tear-streaked face. She has set her mouth and reached for her father's gun.

"I shall oil this thing," she says. "I'm going out to hunt."


November 25. Affairs of the moment have kept me from writing daily or even weekly for this past month. I have decided to enter my thoughts less often now, but in greater fullness. Perhaps someday I will read these pages and remember how all of us triumphed to wear our crowns by carrying the cross.

There have been many crosses, but thanks to God and Sylvester and the Indian Mark Ebenezer's provisions before John died, we have ample food. Both Sylvester and Mark Ebenezer would be here often, if I let them have their way. But making this life work is our task, not theirs.

I must remind myself of that, when I would rather have them pull these stumps to clear the cornfield for next spring, instead of letting my children and me work with the ox, when I would have these convenient friends begin the new cabin that is supposed to replace the leanto. But I find there is healing and forgetfulness in bone-exhausting work.

Babe John gives me joy; he has recovered from his ague and thrives, pulling himself around the confines of this leanto. Harriet, two and a half now, plays with him constantly. She is a silent, sweet child and adores John. With Betsy or one of the other girls to supervise, Harriet can even pull him about over the cleared ground, on a sledge Alvan built.

That I am to have another child, and under such circumstances fills me with wonder. The new little one moved inside me for the first time yesterday. My heart is stabbed with the thought that

John cannot see his own child. But we must go forward with God's grace.

We have so few tools. When the meal supply runs low, we must grate corn on a tin pieplate with holes punched in it. The children's hands are bleeding and cut from hitting the punched holes. I have had Sylvester get salt with some of our precious money. Here are the prices from the store: salt—three dollars a pound, molasses—one dollar and fifty cents a gallon, sugar—twenty-five cents a pound, tea—two dollars a pound. Naturally, we do not drink tea now and we sweeten with the small amount of maple sugar the Indian has brought. But salt we cannot do without.

This month, indeed this winter, I am not even allowing myself to consider the debt, and yet it hangs on me like wet clothing. Still, I know spring will be a fitter time for solving that problem.

Susan sits before the fire melting lead for bullets by putting lead pieces in a ladle, laying them in a hole in a piece of wood and heaping coals about them till the lead melts and forms the proper shape. We have no bullet molds.


December 26.


So the birthday of the Savior has come and gone and we observed it as our Puritan ancestors did, by not observing. This was not by choice, and my heart was heavy that I did not have even the slightest small gifts to give my children.

But keeeping ourselves warm and fed has taken all my time and energy and that of the older children. Snow came on Christmas Eve, and we had to re-stack the wood to keep it dry. Our prayer is ever that the fire may not go out! We have no flint and no neighbor. Alvan would like to shoot the fire into being, but powder is like money here—in fact it is money. People use it as specie.


In spite of my best efforts, I was despondent last eve, thinking on past times in Newbury, with strings of cranberries on the tree and warm pudding and mince pie to eat and the kisses of arriving aunts and uncles. And for us these days, dried venison, turnips and the howls of wolves outside.

A letter has come from my brothers and sister-in-law in Cincinnati begging me to come there. It contained an offer to send money, a stern remonstrance that my children will suffer if I continue "John's petulant pride," but I will stay where John brought us.

Anyway, I did what I could for the children, toasted a few nuts and gave them each a piece of hoarhound candy Sylvester had brought from the Paoli store. And we read together, before the light of the fire and our one linseed lamp, the story of the heart-stopping miracle in that long-ago stable. That was all we had.

The leanto had seemed particularly confining this sacred night, and because I did not wish the children to see how I felt, I went out to the cow shed to see the animals.

I slipped in, with a sense of shame that I did not feel more gratitude for what we did have—a healthy cow and her calf, now a young bull, an ox to pull heavy loads and do the stumping, and now a horse the Quakers have loaned us. It was more than some had.

Yet seeing them there, I thought of the other Christmas stable and I began to weep, feeling all of the poverty of our situation. The tears fell on my hands, now so chapped they bled. The separation! The discouragement! Most of all my Love taken from me. Grief, hopelessness and a yearning for home filled me till I thought I would choke.

Then I chanced to glance at the back of the cow shed. In the light of the lantern I saw them: the slips of plants I had brought all the way from Massachusetts. I rose from my bed of grief and hurried to them: the ones which were still waiting for spring planting, the lilies, the strawberry roots. And then I saw it. My white rose shoot had managed to root itself in the manure, and in the small cracks of light between logs had leafed out in spindly, thin shoots. There at its top was a bud, just showing color. A white rose bud, a Christmas rose. Was it my Love sending me a message, or was it God? Or both? I do not know and it does not matter. What matters is that the great burden of grief that I bore began to fall away at that moment and I went from the shed to my children with a measure of joy again in my heart.

January 28, 1819. Winter plays with us like a coquette. Ice hangs on all the trees. The ground froze fast for almost two weeks, then there was a strange thaw with almost two weeks of spring-like weather. The meat supply has all spoiled. We have had nothing but pone and turnips for days.

Then yesterday Susan shot a large, wild hog and we roasted it outside. Manna from heaven! I have never in my life thought I could be so eager for fresh meat. As she turned it on the spit, I watched the bright, eager eyes of the children and fervently thanked God for fat hogs!

These hog giants occasionally root about in the acorn mast which piles high underneath the oaks. Their great-grandfathers probably graced some stockade along the Buffalo Trace. They have escaped to total but very risky freedom. As we have!

Tonight an ice storm about supper time turned the area outside into a magical dwarf's kingdom and kept us all inside this hut. I am at my wit's end at times like this to keep tempers calm. The baby sleeps only to be awakened by the younger children arguing. The mustiness, the offending smells of unclean clothing, the BOREDOM! Day after day after day. If only I could have one person speak to me about some adult topic.

A book, a book, my kingdom for a book!

Alvan and Mehitable slipped and slid to take care of the animals. I often set them together. Even though Mehitable is younger at ten, they seem to speak each other's language. The trees creak and groan outside from the weight of the ice, and adding to the feeling of strangeness is the sobbing cry of a panther in the woods nearby. May he not come down to jump on my children, as they go about their chores!

I wonder how we have gotten this far, and I know it is because of God's grace and the help of my children. Strong, willing to work, sensing what needs to be done without my asking. They have made it possible for us to live and for me to begin to heal.


Susan has found a way for us to get our corn ground. A man, Daniel Brooks by name, has opened a horse mill just beyond the Quaker settlement and grinds for them. He is from Massachusetts too, Susan says, the son of a minister. My heart leapt when I heard it!

But she says I may not find much to speak with him about. He spends as much time grinding grain for, and running, his liquor still as he does making cornmeal for bread. His brother Lewis is in Indiana also, running a fur-trading post near the Indian territory. The Quaker settlement is abuzz with the news that another brother will soon join this Daniel Brooks in the Promised Land.

My belly swells and, thank God, I am well, although my legs pain me always. The child will come with May flowers. Posthumous. An oddly cold Latin word for such an agonizing state of affairs.

February 13. It is again mild enough for all of us to be outside if bundled up much of the day. Sylvester says we shall begin to rear our cabin home in three weeks. I do not believe I could stand another month in the leanto. This last week we have had an infestation of bedbugs. I think some of our Indian visitors, who are frequent now that the earth is beginning to thaw and they can hunt again, brought them in. At first I did not know what was the matter; we woke often at night and little Hannah cried and whined in her sleep. Then I saw the huge, strawberry-sized splotches on all of our skins—on the baby's arms and buttocks. I have never seen such a thing in Newbury.

We have taken everything out of the hut and boiled all the skins and all of our clothing and hangings. Then we poured boiling water down the sides of the hut and put quicklime on the floor with a broom. Affairs are better, but the little vermin are still with us.

Mark Ebenezer, the Indian, does not often speak. But of late I have been coaxing him and his wife and relatives, who come to sit outside the door and smoke their pipes with us, to speak of themselves. I have learned to do this odd thing, to smoke the kinnick-i-nick herbs with them. Sometimes they speak of their people.

"The Delaware," they say, as the fragrant smoke fills the room, "are the proudest Indian peoples of all." Then Mark Ebenezer speaks a long time. The children, particularly the smaller ones like Betsy and Harriet, look intently into his eyes, trying to understand.

He tells about how these Lenni Lenape were living in peace in the East and how the English gave them the name of a nobleman, Lord Delaware. So they do not even have their own name. They warred over the beaver with Iroquois before the white men came. Then the white man in Pennsylvania treated these Delaware both fairly and unfairly—two sides of one face, as they call it.

"We were driven to Susquehanna, then to Allegheny, then beyond Ohio. My brothers live on White River north of here now, and we who are Christians stay with the Quakers. All are in Indiana, and we do not wish to move again." The night is dark. The fire blows its trail of smoke towards him, but he does not move.

"We are at our destined home," he says. His voice is a whisper and there is an edge of insistence to it that frightens the small ones listening. "So the sacred writings say," he says, his face inscrutable.

"He is son of the priest but not priest," his wife says, looking into the fire as if we did not exist. "The wide hats try to change that but they cannot."

"I am John Mark Ebenezer named for Gospel tale-teller," he says, and gets up, and the odd moment has passed.

During these last days of winter I have been dyeing goods. I have kept a urine pot by the corner of the leanto outhouse and so have a good supply to set the dye when I start. I have indigo and woven goods my sister-in-law has sent from Cincinnati and so we shall have good jeans for the summer. Half wool, half cotton—they should do till warmest weather.

February 20. I sit here writing in frustration when I should probably be better occupied, but there is nothing I can do today. The creek has begun to rise and I fear it may overshoot its banks.

10 a.m.—We all sit at the doorway of this leanto watching the creek, nay, river come over the small rise which holds our home and possessions. Alvan and Susan have gone to bring the stock up just in time. The river carried away their shed down the hill. Odd that I should decide to go with them into the cow shed and risk myself and the new babe to save the shoots and roses, but I did. We must hang on to beauty in the face of ugliness, for the one must blot out the other and ugliness is strong in life.

Several families in this Ohio valley have been swept away in the last two or three years, so they say. Should anyone find this journal and we be gone—nay, I will not send my thoughts this way. I commend us to the Giver of All Good.

ll a.m.—

The cattle low anxiously, the youngest children cry, the mustard waters come by the very foot of the leanto, carrying all in their midst. We must flee by the only side left to the higher hills—

l0 p.m.—

The awful, despicable waters. I have ever thought rivers lovely, full of meaning. Now I hate them. The flood washed over our only home, though it did not carry all away. In the ten short minutes we had, we were able to bear away clothing and the Poore furniture and our scanty remains of food. But the tools we have made, the rakes, the shovels, even the baby's cradle, the tables, the bedsteads, all gone. Are these waters God's wrath or simply the voice of raw, unbridled sin in the world? The latter, I think. Anyway I shake my fist, weakly it is true, around a belly now swollen with a six-months child. But still I shake this fist in the face of disaster.

It is now night-time, and I have found a candle and match. I do not know why I keep writing in this journal book. I think it is because my thoughts run to distraction, and this journal has become my friend, the only thing I have to talk to.

We have retreated to the wagon which Alvan providentially had taken, along with the horse and cattle, up the hill. As soon as the water subsides a bit, Susan will go for the Quaker and Indian. We have corn meal enough for mush, and even a small jug of maple syrup to put on it. And I have my shoots and the seed corn. So we have something to thank God for.


February 22. Susan returned from the Quaker village. The leader there, one Mr. Lindley, sent ample provisions. This society of Friends truly define the meaning of the word love! Sebastian and Mark Ebenezer sent word that as soon as the waters recede, we shall start our cabin in earnest.


March 1. The sun shines, the cabin's walls and roof are finished and we can enter a real home, a large room with a small leanto on the back. We can give thanks to God's grace and the generosity of the Quaker settlement. Several of these kind folk came over for a cabin raising and even sawed puncheon boards for the floor and made a cradle for the new child.

Johnnie took his first steps today, from the hands of Harriet to me. We have put away his nipple bottle and he now eats at table and jabbers away. He has a small baby doll he carries about that belonged to all the rest and Mehitable saved from the flood. Its stuffing is still wet.

How quickly our children go from being babes to playing babes. How soon sweet babyhood flies; it is as a buttlerfly winging over the lilac bushes. We try to touch its beauty, we follow it on rushing feet, but no, it is gone before we have even really stamped its picture in our memories. But what a consolation these winging children leave us with their strong, proud adulthood.


March 5. Oh God! The long and short of it is that Alvan has been torn up, almost killed by a bear. My poor, silly Mehitable is the cause of it all and weeps to think her brother might not have been with us tonight except for the grace of God and Alvan's own quick thinking.

The two of them, silly fools, would go a-wandering in the caves. "Please, Ma, let us go down the path a ways. We want to look at the limestone icicles and hear the dripping water the Quaker children talked about at the cabin raising. This cabin smokes worse than the other'n," they said. Finally they wheedled so much I said yes. They left, taking a lantern with them.

Alvan went in first, Mehitable following with the lantern. They got well inside the domed door when they heard a grumbling noise. A mother bear with two small cub was behind them, off to the left just inside the door, and they had not seen her. Quicker than they could even speak to each other, the mother bear lumbered up, lean and hungry and ready to come out of her winter's sleep. She was heading for the entrance, snarling and baring her teeth. Mehitable screamed, dropped the lantern, and fled.

So there was Alvan, alone in the dark with a bear. The cubs huddled in the corner, dim shapes as if seen at midnight. He could smell the mother's foul, strange breath and said the hair on his head rose at the menacing growl in her throat. She lunged and slashed his face, then grabbed him and pinned him under her, breaking his arm. Realizing through his pain and fear that he might have only three minutes to live, Alvan wrenched free from her slashing, knife-sharp claws.

He could barely make out some rocks on the floor of the cave. With his unbroken arm he stooped to pick them up. He tossed them, one, two, at the cubs. They yelped. Momentarily distracted, the mother bear turned from him and he dashed past her into the daylight, blood streaming from the gashes on his face and arms.

Mehitable had run for us; we met him halfway, staggering down the trail. The bear had not pursued.

What kind of brutal homeland is this? Today I think I will heed the pleading of my brothers and sisters in Newbury and return to civilized Massachusetts, pack up and take the wagon out this very afternoon to the Quaker camp and then head back to the East.

But no. Wait a bit. The grape hyacinths I put in in the fall are poking through the ground. Just yesterday I planted strawberries and the other plants where the flood receded. I shall see if they grow and if they do, count it a sign. Through dark times in the stock pen to the light of new growth. We shall see.


April 9 and we are still here. The strawberries are blooming in the large field, where John worked so hard last October to "girdle" trees by chopping a ring around the bark to kill the growth. The strawberry blossoms have the largest yellow cups I have ever seen. I cut back the rose and it has scores of pointy, red shoots around its base.

Tomorrow we all plow and plant the seed corn between the dead forms of these trees we ringed last fall, as John directed us, ever mindful of our care. Best not think of that. I have consciously told myself that my thought must walk on the hills, not skirt the swamps. Our thought is really our home. I am going to choose to have mine swept out, free and cheerful.

Susan says all the neighbors beyond the Quaker settlement are digging ginseng. She meets them at Brooks's horse mill, and they talk of the money they are making.

They have little pronged poles to get the root out. It is disgusting to think that they will dig this root for others' habits of vice, so that men in far-off China may have their manhood restored. No! About some things there can be no compromise. I have had the opportunity to meet some of these far neighbors. They are so superstitious! If a child seems too short to them, they pass it through a hollow tree hole each day. They calm snakes, cows, or even agitated people by playing the fiddle at them. Still, some of the knowledge is sound. They say, "Plant corn when the leaves of the trees are as big as a squirrel's ear," and that is what our new maple leaves will be tomorrow, when we plant.

April 12. An infestation of squirrels, like locusts, has come down from the hills and devoured all the new seed corn in the fields. When Betsy, up early to look for birds, first saw the flashing tails of the animals yesterday dawn, she ran into the cabin to awaken us. We took brooms, branches, whatever we could find. They left, only to return last night and sweep the fields bare. Whatever shall we do?

April 13. Susan can find little game in the woods. The flood has unsettled the animals, destroyed their nests. Now we can not even find the ornery squirrels. And we have had nothing to eat but a little corn meal mush for the last three days. Word has come that the ginseng buyer is at Paoli and that he is buying the roots for 50 cents a pound. It is ironic to me, but all of southern Indiana searches the woods for this lust-enhancing root.

Food! Food! We all think of it constantly. There is none in our cabin, and the wheat harvest is six weeks away for our neighbors who planted winter wheat. Still, there is food about if you have money to buy it. And we do not, more is the pity. My body is large and slow. I drag it about, worrying that I should be eating good food to have the child inside me grow properly.

April 14. Little Johnny cried all day today. He is not getting the food he should. No one can offer us help. Others are starving. I heard a story from Sylvester of a woman down the Buffalo Trace who was alone with a babe while her husband had gone on a fur trading trip. White River flooded there—their food stores were destroyed. Her milk supply failed, and the babe had nothing to eat. She went to the woods determined to drown the babe rather than watch him starve, when suddenly an Indian woman appeared with a horse and sledge carrying corn and salted meat. She had known the need and brought food. God's providence is wonderful, and I know that some way it will supply us too.

April 15. The Quaker cannot help us with food and more seed corn. There have been failed crops, the flood, and now a money shortage here. People are in want everywhere. In desperation my children asked what we should do. There are only four shrivelled turnips and a half a bag of meal in the cabin and no way to plant again.

I went to the woods, near where my dear John is buried. I fell on my knees and prayed Divine Providence to send an answer. I watched my tears fall on the ground onto the odd, heart-shaped leaves of a thick cluster of plants. I rose, weak with this eight-months burden I am carrying but stronger in heart.

"Get the shovels and whittling knives," I called as I returned to the cabin. "We will do what we have to do. This afternoon we dig the ginseng, enough so that we can buy food and enough corn to plant again. Sometimes God uses human weakness for purposes all His own." Out of old men's lechery will come our food. We will survive to bless His name! And so I have learned something. There can be compromise. There has to be sometimes.

May 1. Word has come from the Markles. They insist I come to their house in Madison for the birth of the child, and the children with me. I will go, for the sake of the baby. Snakes have come out everywhere here; there are huge holes of them. The worst are the copperheads—poisonous, coiling about each other in the swampy spots. Now if only my neighbors were here with their fiddle—.

It is, however, a serious matter. The other day Amanda came

upon Betsy down by the creek with her water buckets and tote stick over her shoulder, frozen with fright. Near her, swollen to enormous size, was a rattler. There was a terrible stench all over the clearing; the beasts must exude some liquid like a skunk. Amanda picked up a large, thick stick and stuck it out towards the rattler to change his fixation from Betsy. The young child ran for home, and when she came in, she could not speak and was violently ill all afternoon.

Meanwhile Amanda stood with the stick poked at the rattler trying to decide how to evade him and run. Could she just drop it and flee? Could he travel fast enough to reach her? She did not know. And as she was deciding the snake made a sudden move which almost did the poor girl in; he lunged forward, up her stick and over her shoulder. In a trice she had dropped the stick and run away, without his fangs finding her arm or leg!

We are still digging "sang," as my fiddle neighbors call it. Ugh.


May 5. Now that it is time to go from this cabin for a while, I do not want to leave. Spring has healed the flooded land. Small, white-green strawberries flourish on my vines in the new garden. Each morning I glory in lettuce, new peas, and onions just beginning to bear. I hate to leave a garden just bearing. I want, need to see its changes daily.

The cabin is well-built, the Quakers having added something to its logs and clapboards that most others do not have: a sense of beauty. There are flower boxes under the windows, and someone had a piece of bottle glass for one of the windows. How good they have been to us. They are truly followers of the One who said, "Help the widows and fatherless."

The field is replanted with corn from the "sang" sales Alvan made in town and the shoots have come up this time. Not long ago, many, many troublesome squirrels were bagged in a great hunt by the men from the area and now our crops can grow.

We have food on the table and the children roam the woods as skilled, wary pioneers now, fishing the stream, gathering wildflowers. This is what John dreamed of. I do not want to leave it. It is home. But I hear Judge Markle's wagon.

To: Mehitable Chambers, Newbury, Massachusetts
From: Hannah Chute Poore, Madison, Indiana

May 10, 1819


Dear Mehitable:

I know I have not written to you, my sister, in such a long time, since John's death. I had to content myself with sending word through our brothers. I simply could not find the energy to do much but live through each day.

Now I feel like I am on holiday! I have come to the Markles to have my child, and we are settled into the mainhouse and guest cottage of this lovely home in Madison. Timidly a day or so ago they asked if I felt up to an outing. "I have never believed in a lying-in period," I said, buoyed with the happiness of being away from the wilderness. "Should the young one choose tomorrow to appear, well, it can come there as well as here."

So the Markles took us on a two-day visit to a not so far-away village, Corydon. We went to the Falls of the Ohio, Louisville and then overland by a good hired carriage. It was the first time I had been on a steamboat. My, the sparks and noise and speed! I was not at all tired by the journey.

We stayed all night at the Spencer Inn at Corydon. How odd it is to be away from the cabin. How different a state capital this tiny Indiana town is from Boston!

Almost every one of these log houses is turned into an inn or tavern when the assemblymen are here. It amuses me, and yet I must not be smug about the rough taverns, the legislators they speak of who put their feet up on the desks, the spittoons for constant tobacco spitting. Indiana was a territory only three years ago. And after all, I have been smoking Indian herbs in a pipe! I have not thought fit to tell the Markles that.

The little capital building, the office building and various headquarters are as lovely as anything in the East. So is this house we have returned to in Madison. One of its frequent visitors is the Markle's new son-in-law, the state representative from western Indiana, James McClure.

I am impressed that a legislator is in the house, and I want to tell you about him. He ran away with Auraleigh and the Judge was furious at first. But the indulgent, good-hearted parents soon got over the elopement and welcomed him. This McClure is a Scotch-Irish "laird" from a rich family near Vincennes. There are so many of these Scotch-Irishmen. They came in poor as churchmice ten or twenty years ago and now hold thousands of acres of land and serve as mayors of the towns and governors of the state.

He is ambitious. That is how I might best describe him. He keeps his counsel, generally, but when he speaks, he is as shrewd as a Jew. He has come to understand frontier politics, better even than the Judge himself. They are on opposite sides of the fence, the Judge being for Governor Jonathan Jennings, McClure being a Harrison man.

But Judge Markle and his son-in-law James McClure are cordial not only because of Auraleigh, but because they are hatching a grand scheme for a town west of Paoli in the rawest wilderness there is, on the White River. James McClure and the Judge sit in the parlor and talk of their dreams for this speculation town, and Susan and all the chidren sit and listen to the tales of Taj Mahals and Maharaja palaces that these people are constructing in the air for (odd name) Hindostan Falls. It is already prospering, they say, with immigrants arriving by the scores, even hundreds. Representative McClure and his wife will live there most of the time this summer.

Auraleigh herself has interest in another town—the famous Harmony on the Wabash. She convinced James McClure to take her there for a visit. There she met George Rapp, the leader of the religious community which founded the town. All is held in common as they wait the end of the world. They have fine fields and buildings. Men and women are separate, as with the Shakers, and Quakers, too.

Jim McClure says, "Well, yes but they certainly live well for havin' renounced the world. Sauerbraten and plum puddin' isn't much of a renunciation. And as far as holdin' everything in common—everybody does that and gives the proceeds to Rapp. He gets rich off their poverty."

And then Auraleigh comes and tweaks him on the nose and he kisses her. They are still basking under the honeymoon; three years is about what it takes for the shine of that moon to dim, unless, late in marriage you enter a new honeymoon period. I can almost think of that time with John with gratitude again now. Time, say the folks in Newbury, is the great doctor. It knits up old bones, eases sharp pains to dull aches.

Dull aches is what I have. Henrietta Markle has insisted on calling in a physician, one who has just come to stay a while before going down the river to (of course) Hindostan Falls. I shall meet him tomorrow. There is about a week to go, as I calculate. Tonight was a perfect May evening and lightning bugs by the thousands, no, millions rose from the Ohio lowlands. Where do they sleep all winter?

I shall try to correspond better, dear sister.

Hannah

My Journal again—

May 12. I am having "false labor pains" and am deep in my Bible to still the fears I have about the birth. The last was so difficult, so long, and only the skill of the Indian doctor seemed to bring me through. So many, so many have I known who have "died of the last" child. And taken the babe with them because, bodies worn out and hearts deadened by all they have lived, they gave up or gave out in childbirth. They simply could not do it again.

And I am not at all relieved by this new physician from Pittsburgh, Dr. Malthus Ward. He is a brash young man recently come from Kittanning, Pennsylvania, who seems to think only of making enough money to support himself in style. These doctors! "My practice nets fifty a month," or "I have no rivals in the practice." As if we were chickens and they members of the chicken-pluckers' guild.

No, no, I am not satisfied. But the rest of my family seems blissfully contented with life here. Harriet and Betsy play about constantly with James and George Markle, and Johnny loves having the little year-old girl to be with. They chase pigeons near the coop outside, and they splash and dig in the sand pile under the watchful eye of the nurse, while Henrietta and I eat tarts and watercress sandwiches with Emma Rose and Amanda in the grape arbor. What luxury. Yet, I believe my peas will be in pod today. And the beans in bloom. When I return, we will have our first mess of beans and bacon.


May 15. So much has happened. I began labor in earnest day before yesterday and it progressed ominously, as before, starting, then stopping—wearing me out and frightening me. Dr. Ward was out on calls trying to drum up trade and was sent for as he came in from a nearby village.

I had already dispatched Susan to get an Indian doctor the day before. She went to the Quaker Delaware and it took her most of that day, riding the horse hard. She brought back—the wife of Mark Ebenezer. I lay weak and worn, my labor already twenty-four hours old. Dr. Ward held my hand that midnight hour. My pains seemed to bring no progress, just weaken and rack me; he did not know what to do.

"Exactly what is your medical school preparation, Ward?" Judge Markle said with a hollow, stern voice that echoed through the darkness.

"I attended Dartmouth for a while and spent a few months apprenticing to a physician in upstate New York. I have tried to make my practice at several places and had a good many cases—" He shrugged.

Mark Ebenezer's wife, Ruth Sharp Bill, came in right then, and I found the strength to say, "Thank you Dr. Ward. I think we will try Indian medicine for a while."

And so I remember the next two hours fitfully as she gave me a concoction of urgutrate and other herbs steeped at the fireplace. I recall the contractions starting again and growing stronger and her voice, soft but commanding, and I can dimly call up in memory the rush at the end and the great push that took every fiber of my energy.

A baby girl. She wailed weakly, and Ruth held her up to drain her lungs and smiled at me with just two teeth. It made me laugh, weak as I was.


May 20. Ruth takes care of me and tells me tales of the Delaware in her very nice Quaker English. She watches the maids clean the room and says, "We Lenni Lenape are very careful about cleanness. It is above all else the important thing. We have a cleaning ceremony. It helps us appease the spirits and keeps them from hurting the world."

"Tell me of it," I say, nursing the little girl, glad to see she pulls so strongly.

"We have our big house, built for the cleaning ceremony. Men and women go in, men to tell visions, women to sweep clean after each part of the ceremony. Twelve days and twelve nights it lasts.

"Each man may tell his vision and each may think about its meaning. The vision-speaker shakes a turtle shell filled with pebbles. Men beat animal skin drums. People leap and dance to help the cleansing.

"No one may be defiled. Men may not go to women. All must be clean as new babes and the room clean as brooms can get it."

Her voice is intense and low. I look up.

"My people still do the ceremony. But Mark and I and the others at the Quaker village do not attend."

"No," I say. "You are Christian now, these—how many—years?" I look up, questioningly.

"John Mark Ebenezer is the Christian, eighteen years now. I am the wife of the Christian." Her voice is firm, as if she is preserving something of her own individuality in the way she says each word.

"And—" I hesitate, searching for the right words, "do you sometimes wish you could go to the big house and sweep the floors and listen to the visions?"

"I do not, for we must learn to be content with our choices, and I have chosen to leave my people of the Ohio Delaware to be with my husband. But Mark Ebenezer wishes to go."

"John Mark Ebenezer?" I say, thoroughly surprised.

"And so he does," she says, gazing out the window at trees moving before a storm that is coming off the river. "Just now and again, at time of the Big House rite, he wishes to be clean. Sometimes he feels he has defiled his manhood."

"How?" I ask, astonished.

"By being a man of two faces. Lenni Lenape by birth, Chris-

tian by choice. But he feels this way because—" she looks stead-
fastly at the drops of rain beginning to pelt against the panes.

"Yes—" I prompt.

"Because he is son of a priest but not priest." As if that
answered it all.


June 1. I am recovered and we leave the Markles today. We take
one last glass of lemonade in the gazebo on this bright, glorious
day. The babe sleeps in my arms as the children run about with
their friends. The air is sweet with white clover, the perfume
intoxicating, and the girls make clover chains and bring them to
me. Through the veil of years I see myself and my own sisters
chaining the clover and the daisies, carrying them to our own dear
mother, now gone. I suppose she too, as a child, carried them, to
her mother in the New England of long ago.

Life on this earth is like a daisy chain, with custom and wisdom
passed on from child to child and adult to child. Ring-a-rosie, hide
and seek, the ways of love and strength to build a good home, love
of animals, are passed on to the next generation. These things
never get into books. I shall write no more until we are back—
home.


June 5. I sit before my own cabin now and life is good—good as it
can be for me. The corn has sprouted, the rain is right, the roses
bloom and late strawberries burst with juice. But my cloak of joy
bears a fringe of sadness—my Susan is going from us. "I leave
next week to go to schoolteaching, Ma," she has told me today.
Judge Markle has hired her, and she is the new school marm of—
Hindostan Falls! The Mecca of the West! The hope of all mankind! The realization of Thomas Jefferson's democratic dream—a
real true city to be proud of. Pshaw. They have never seen Boston.
But there they all go, flocking like silly geese to a gathering of
drafty, rough cabins lying in a swampy river bottom. Well, all the
dreamers and fools can make a new start. And I suppose they did
that at Boston, too, once upon a time.

The doctor, Malthus Ward, is setting up practice there too, so rumor goes, with other characters as odd and assorted as the players in a Vanity Fair show. Hindostan Fair.

So all the world goes mad. All but me. I stay here in front of this cabin, shelling peas. World enough and more to me. Until the next crisis comes.

# Chapter Seven

# The McClure Papers

To: Jack McClure, Hindostan Falls, Indiana
From: Daniel McClure, Vincennes, Indiana

March 15, 1819

Dear Son John (Jack still to most I guess),

And so your at Hindostan Falls. You keep tellin me to say it Hindoo-stan but everbody here says it Hindossan.

Some dandified place 'tis, eh? Your last letter tole of how the houses was a sprinkled on the hillside now like pepper on a fried egg. How the head man—Sholts did you say?—was movin everbody and everthing around in the State Assembly so Hindossan would be the county seat.

Some of the she-nanny guns smell a little like a dead catfish washed up on the shores of the Wabash. Sholts is bound and dettermined that he is a goin to be a land baron. Deals for land he thinks he's a goin to own pretty soon when he forces some poor farmers off it. Land transfers with titles that don't ring true. And Jim is taking some of the land Sholts deals out. Jim's a goin to live to regret it.

Jim says he owns it fair and square cause he paid Sholts a few cents a acre for it. And the directors of the Vincennes State Bank seem to think the same thing. They have loaned out a lot of deposit money on this operation. Taint secured by anything but the pie in the sky idee of whats a gonna happen. I say what the Bible does, "Keep your heart, for out of it are the issues of life."

We had plenty of chances in this here fambly to cut the short corners. The onliest thing we ever done was keep slaves—your uncles, that is.

Speakin of that, your cousin Archie, brother Will's boy, won't let go of his slaves even though Indiana is a state now. Says they was willed to him. They have kicked him out of Upper Indiana Church for slaves and too much whisky drinking. And Johnny, that you always said looked like a rabbit, looks even more like one. He was kicked out for the same reasons. Well, not many of Will's younguns amount to much. Acourse Elizabeth married good.

Luke Dugger's got slaves he calls indentured servants. He still whops em too.

Quite a operation there at Duggerville at the mouth of White River on the Wabash for flatboat loading. If that's all that's goin on. I doubt it. I suspect he's a slave tradin up and down the river.

Your children are fine, but your wife Lizzie seems to pine for you. But I know you got your reasons for bein gone. The farm is a goin good, all our farms are.

I got rheumatiz, just like your Grandma Jane did when she was old. Caint sit in the chair for long these days.

Uncle George says hello. Quoted something to me about your being a Brutus to Indiana's Cashyus. Whatever that means.

Your Pa,
Dan'l McClure

To: Daniel McClure, Vincennes, Indiana
From: Jack McClure, Hindostan Falls, Indiana

March 25, 1819

Dear Pa:

Thanks for the news. I will try to get home next week for several days. Tom did write to tell me he's planning to put in tobacco crop over half my acreage. I just never did like farm life, you know that. But that 400 acres is the difference for me between security and poverty, and I thank you from the bottom of my heart for it.

You are right about the political shenanigans. Sholts has bribed, coerced and enticed the legislators into setting up a separate county where he can reign. I use the word consciously because Sholts has built a big frame house on the hill above White River and servants wait on him and bring him juleps as if the place were Louisville or Memphis.

I'm staying out of politics. Jim has me supervising his lands while he is up at the legislature at Corydon. "Construct a mill," he says, "It is sorely needed for all." Only trouble is, it's impossible. The river's too swift. Many have already said so and gone on to other waters.


Hundreds of folk are pouring in each week. A reporter from New York is here interviewing all of us, as if we were creatures from the moon that were in that book Aunt Jean loaned me and Ish so long ago.

Sometimes I think of Ish, that bad sprout from the family tree and wonder about him. What if we had done different with him, Pa? He was always such an obnoxious skunk that we all shunned him, but what if we had cared about him? Would he have done all those things that drove Aunt Jenny crazy? Would he have resorted to murder when he worked for Aaron Burr?

I can't help but remember that it was my kith and kin that was swept down the Mississippi when Ish's raft broke up that day. It all ended so sadly, like so much of life, or my life at least. But as Uncle Will used to say, "Regrets are like windfall apples. If you pick up every one of 'em that you see an chew on it, you'll never get where you're goin'." And he should have known. If every regret he had was an apple, there would have been a bagful.

Your son, Jack

To: Honorable James McClure, Corydon, Indiana
From: Jean McClure, Vincennes, Indiana

April 24, 1819

Dear James:

You may be surprised to receive a letter from your Aunt Jean McClure. I believe it is the first I have written to you, and for that I should probably apologize.

I write from Christian concern for your mother. Janie has— well, I must be frank about these matters—Janie has a man living at your old mansion house now. The man is Retreat Granger, the man all call Witch Master.

The unfortunate situation started when Mr. Granger began coming up last spring when your mother had a spell. Then he moved into one of the outbuildings to dry the herbs she seemed to need. Since your father died and all you children are gone—well, you know. She has not been herself.

I have not been able to talk about this to your sister Mary and your brother-in-law Sam Emison, because they have been travelling in Kentucky for two months visiting their relatives. At any rate—Mr. Granger has moved into the big house and occupies a bedroom upstairs. Past that I cannot comment.

The matter is the talk of the town (which really could have better things to talk about). The ladies from Upper Indiana Church Visiting Committee came to see Janie last week, and she appeared at the door looking wild and wearing a dressing gown. She slammed the door in their faces.

I will be seeing you sometime soon. Reverend Rob McClaren— remember him from when we all fought against the Shakers around here?—Rob is bishop of the Methodist Church now. He has appointed a committee for missionary work at Hindostan Falls and I'm chairman. That series that has been running in the *New York Trumpet* has convinced him "Hindosson," as all the local people are calling it, is in need of salvation. When I come, we'll talk about what, if anything, you wish to do for our Janie.

Your loving aunt,
Jean Jordan McClure

To: Jack McClure, Hindostan Falls, Indiana
From: Daniel McClure, Vincennes, Indiana

April 30, 1819


Dear Son John,

Jest a short note. You say you are managing the Hindostan Land Company's acreage on the river. Get yourself somebody to put you up a mill. And get one of the new ones—the ones that grinds grain fine and saws wood and grinds up linseed oil and even operates a blacksmith's bellows. Jack, get you somebody who will build the mill no matter what and you both will get rich. The Emisons have always been rich and I say a mill is the key to the future. Get you that water power and put it to work and your sons and grandsons will live secure. A mill, Jack. Put one up and don't take imposible for a answer. Do whatever you have to do to get a mill.

From one who never stopped
for nothing (except your ma)
Your Pa Dan'l McClure

*Chapter Eight*

# The Account of Thomas Jefferson Brooks
## (Continued)

Resolutely I, Thomas Jefferson Brooks, hurt but not crushed by the death of my friend Doc Drake in the winter of 1819, pulled down the shades of the windows of the past and opened them on the other side of the mansion house—to the future.

Bright enough did that seem when I met with my two brothers Daniel and Lewis in Cincinnati that April of 1819 to discuss prospects for my new life in Indiana. We sat in a tavern near the river and drank our ale. At first I listened as Lewis described the small trading post he had established near the upper White River in Indiana. He talked of Delaware Indians, marten and buckskin and brain oil and beaver. I watched the sullen curl of his lip, the odd hesitant spark of his eye and thought that Lewis always had been a tentative person. It must have been a disadvantage now, since he worked as a trader and needed a confident demeanor to strike a bargain.

Daniel was his usual blustering, bungling self, gesturing wildly and almost knocking over a bowl of apples as he described the horse mill which was making good profits for him over by the Quaker settlement. "Whatever happened to the fortune in whetstones you wrote about?" I asked.

"There was too much, uh, expenditure of labor required for the return," he offered a little apologetically, remembering his reputation with our sisters at home for being lazy. He spoke also about his corn squeezing still.

"Stay," I told Daniel abruptly. I was unable to tolerate talk about stills, fresh as I was from the turpentine explosion.

I changed the subject. "Tell me more about this area west of Cincinnati. It is the beginning of the road into the wilderness, is it not?" I had just arrived in Cincinnati, having spent close to three months on the Natchez Trace and in Louisville. As I went, I asked many questions about this neck of the woods I was betting my future on.

"Cincinnati is only one of the roads that leads to the wilderness," Lewis explained. "There is also the Louisville Trace." He spread out a rudely drawn map he carried in the pocket of his coat. "The road into southern Indiana and Illinois country from Cincinnati is called Captain Kibbey's Road."

I raised my eyebrows in inquiry. "Captain Kibbey was an adventurer," Lewis said. "He was hired to cut a road through from Cincinnati near the turn of the century. He cut the trees and then lost himself among the virgin oaks and maples. He wandered around for over a month and finally staggered in here naked and thin as a bear in March. He almost died, but the road was through."

"And the other road, coming up from Louisville?"

"The Buffalo Trace. It goes all the way to Vincennes and then across Illinois to St. Louis, if new settlers want to go that far."

All around us in that tavern the very settlers we were discussing were crammed around the tables, forking (and knifing) in their expensive plates of stew. Children wailed, dogs scurried amidst everyone's feet. Outside the streets were jammed with outfitters selling teams and wagons. The whole world was jumping to go west, and Cincinnati and Lousville, if Lewis was right, were jumping-off places for the great, rich timber lands of the Northwest.

"How many are coming across these roads these days?" I asked.

Lewis took a long breath, almost as if he himself could not believe the numbers. "Over twenty-five thousand, so they say, last year came to live in Indiana, and they are still coming at the same rate. And for Illinois country, almost the same. Thousands more are massing in Pittsburgh, Philadelphia, Wheeling, to join them."

I had heard of the exodus, of course. They were calling it the "Great Migration"—the emptying out of the East. But tens of thousands of people in one year into one state. It addled my brains for a few seconds.

"You've come at the right time," Daniel said. "All of these folk buy things, and we are businessmen." I looked at him contemplatively for a moment. It was difficult to think of my impetuous, handsome, ne'r-do-well brother, the one my mother always called Brookie, as a businessman. But I found I could actually accept the idea, especially in this virgin market of customers. In the Great Northwest even Don Juan himself could make money.

"Tell us, then, brother," Dan insisted, "which of us you'll join. Lewis with his fur-trading shack on White River or me in Orange County with the horse mill."

I smiled a little, secretively. "Both. Neither. You will be joining me." They dropped their jaws incredulously. A nineteen-year-old stripling telling his older brothers anything? The presumptuousness of it frightened me also, so I rushed ahead. "What you are doing," I said, "is child's play. You will make no more than a pittance at it. You waste your time."

Dan leapt to his feet in consternation; Lewis turned his eyes away disgustedly. "Give me the maps," I demanded. "Tomorrow I will outline a plan that will make us real riches, that will establish us as rich as any man in Indiana. Meet me here for ham and eggs at eight."

I threw down a silver coin to pay for our suppers and drinks; the bar-maid picked it up suspiciously and flipped it into the air before putting it into her pocket. Both Dan and Lewis sat down, still angry, but chastened and obviously impressed. Specie was scarce and they did not see the flash of much silver. Any man who could throw a silver dollar about as casually as if it were a hazelnut had to be taken seriously.

When they left I mopped the sweat from my brow. Whatever had made me behave that way? In spite of the weeks I had spent in planning, the time spent finding out about this very subject, I had waded in much deeper that I had expected in some sort of impulse to impress my older brothers. Still, a plan of immediate action had flashed into my mind that was as bright as the coin I'd tossed. I would need to burn many candles tonight to perfect its details.


"Look at this map," I said to Lewis and Dan as morning sunlight streamed from high windows, penetrating the smoky haze that still stood in the tavern's great room. "Here, and here, are two roads, both of them marked Buffalo Trace."

"Northern and Southern limbs," Lewis said. "The northern one goes from Louisville to Paoli in the hills and on across the east fork of the White River—"

"Yes, I see. And the southern limb starts at the same place but avoids the worst of the knobhills and goes through the wilderness to the west fork of White River to Vincennes, and of course west to St. Louis. And the road from Cincinnati joins the Buffalo Trace—"

"Right here, near the center of Indiana, at Paoli," Lewis said. He was looking with some interest at the criss-crossing of the roads. Perhaps, like most people, he had never really studied them. But I had always perused them; maps had messages for me. Roads and rivers were like a man's circulation pattern, like the pictures you saw in physician's books, with a man's life, like the web of a spider, spread out fragile and eerie. Well, blood flowed through the waterways and roadways too—the blood of commerce, of people's lives.

I went on. "That joined road goes on to Hindostan. Now look at this area here, near Hindostan Falls, Lewis. About thirty miles from the Wabash the White River bends like an elbow and becomes—"

"I see!" Lewis said with unusual vigor. "A canal—a path between the two arms of the Buffalo Trace."

"Three of the most important roads in the nation right now. Most of the immigrants who don't float the Ohio and come up the Wabash into Illinois and Indiana country go those roads. That's ten thousand people the rest of this year alone, I expect. They get off at Cincinnati or Louisville and take the roads to—"

I looked up to see my brothers' expectant looks. "To us," I said triumphantly. "To Brooks Brothers Trading Enterprises. We go together and control the areas at the joining of the roads. Set up what is needed to supply ten thousand pioneers and take five or ten dollars apiece from them."

"But they outfit in Pittsburgh, or Louisville, or Cincinnati," Lewis protested.

"Of course they do. But they cannot buy nearly enough to supply their needs for the first year of homesteading or fur trading.

You can only carry so many barrels of flour and salt pork in a Conestoga with five children. We are the midpoint oufitters. Supply for hire when their stock runs out. Offer salvation when they have been two months in the woods and the crops have not come in yet. Charging higher, of course, to allow for transportage from our markets—"

"Yes, I see, supply the pioneer's needs," said Daniel "It's what I have been doing anyway with my horse mill near Paoli."

"Horse mill, horse shit," I said definitively. Their eyes opened wide. "Lewis, how many large, efficient mills are there along this road system?"

"None, yet. But you're too late if you're thinking of having one at Hindostan. Frederick Sholts who owns most of the land has the same ideas. And another of the proprietors, Representative McClure, has his agent already looking for someone to put up a large overshot corn grinder. Looking for a master builder."

"And so we will be his master builders." Their eyes became tea saucers. "Brookie is a millman and I have had significant experience in the new mechanics." It was only a small lie, a necessary commercial exaggeration. What I had was a copy of Oliver Evans' book *The Millwright* and more sass than common sense.

I went on. "And as far as grinding corn, that's the piddling part. We'll grind twenty-five things at the new Hindostan Mills." Tea saucers became dinner plates. Then Lewis's naturally suspicious mind rasped into gear and he began to fire turkey shot through the weak points in the plan.

"What makes you think we want to work for you?"

"Did I say you would be? We will be equal businessmen associated to control trade. Each will be his own free market capitalist." I had heard the words in Louisville; they sounded good rolling off my tongue. "Brookie, that is, Daniel," I determined to address the bounder brother as respectfully and earnestly as possible, "if you wished to, you could manage a new mercantile operation on the lower Buffalo Trace across the river and up a piece from Hindostan Falls."

"Lewis," I tried to nod my head deferentially, You will manage our selling enterprise at Paoli, where Kibbey's and the Buffalo Trace meet, incorporating your trading business with the Indians who range north and east of there."

"And you?" Lewis snorted, increasingly irritated with my grandiose behavior.

"I'll manage what we are going to do at Hindostan." I was silent and so were they. Unsaid was the truth we were all beginning to sense. The three of us could control the trade across the central road of the new Ohio Valley. Tens of thousands of people would be our market. There was a brief moment, a mood akin to religious awe. But Lewis's small imagination had run out of steam already.

"I told you about Sholts. He's older and a lot richer than you. He's not going to let some grass-green upstart come in and build an empire in his domain. And what about the others who will want to cash in on this mercantiling thing?"

"We will allow no contenders," I announced with more confidence than I felt. "And should they come, we will reduce them to the status of housewives with cent shops." I cleared my throat. "Well, first of all, we will have squatter's rights. We will be the first real outfitter out here. Then we will get our own"— I paused because I couldn't quite think of the word I wanted—"we'll develop our own inn sign. Something that really tells what we do, makes us stand out. Something nobody else can ape. We'll be our own inn sign. We'll be the Yankee peddlers."

Daniel nodded. He was used to being identified as a Yankee among all these people who had come up from the South.

"We'll dress for the part. Wear suits instead of buckskin, put out printed circulars for our merchandise, sell only the best, different, better lines."

"Out here in the middle of the bramble bushes and possums?" Lewis asked.

"People buy things out here, maybe even more than in Massachusetts. They have to, because they don't have the stuff, don't have much of anything. And out here they hanker for nice things, particularly the women, maybe because of the dirt and roughness."

"Hadn't thought of that," he conceded.

"I have been checking out the mercantiles in Louisville, meeting men who supply goods from Pittsburgh and even as far away as Philadelphia. Crockery and willow china people, fine yard goods men as well as the basic tool and plow people. We will have the finest enterprise in the Ohio River Valley."

Both my brothers shook their heads, but their protest, if it was that, was very weak indeed. The promise of the venture was shining forth, melting the shadows of their hostile disbelief. Finally it was Daniel who looked up to ask in an outraged, articulated whisper, "And capital? Where on God's green earth will we get enough money to set up such an undertaking?"

"We will see if we can take a partner from the beginning."

"Who—"

"Who is the richest man in the territory?"

"Not Sholts," Lewis demanded incredulously. "You do not mean Frederick Sholts. Why would he want to have anything to do with us?"

"Because he will see that we have what he needs to build his town. I have drafted a letter this morning offering to join his engineers and builders as superintendent."

"I don't want to work with Sholts," Lewis sniffed. "He has the head of a gas balloon and he's crooked."

"Then he will precipitate out of the action when he has completed his mission."

"What?" The terminology eluded them.

"Look, brothers. Controlling this new land is nothing but a matter of chemistry. I learned something of that science from a friend"— here a shadow crossed my mind—"in the South. Get the right compounds, elements, put them into the crucible of this new land and—"

"Since you are such a great master of the chemist's art, pray tell us what the correct elements are," Lewis said scornfully.

"Well, unlimited opportunity and a virgin land, that's the base metal to provide the stuff we work on—Sholts' money and political power, that's the acid—and our Yankee shrewdness—didn't some people in Lincoln call it cussedness?—and ability to work—that's the fire under the cauldron. Most of all, the ready market. Thousands of eager pioneer women and men."

And so it was all agreed, all planned as a chemistry experiment. Yet I had the feeling it could be dangerous and, more than I conceded to my brothers, hoped and prayed it would not blow up in our faces at Hindostan Falls on White River.

# Chapter Nine

# The McClure Papers:

## The Note Book of George McClure

Entered by George McClure, Esquire, of Knox County, Indiana on the occasion of his having been commissioned by the *Vincennes Western Sun* to write a series of articles on the phenomenon at Hindostan Falls. Commenced this first day of July, 1820.


I shall attempt to put down in this old farm account book some personal musings on this place, in my typical role (self-assigned) as The Spectator of the bottomlands. These random jottings should also expedite the process of writing the newspaper articles I promised. Well, this old account book will finally see some practical use as a private diary; it certainly wasn't any good for keeping my records straight. Probably because I never used it. Never did have a head for money.


July 3. Jean and I arrived and settled in for our month in the backwoods. The Hindostan Ordinary is a huge log structure just built. Hindostan Land Company, Sholts and his fellow proprietors, operates it, as they do most of the business here. Hostelry is somewhat slovenly, serves cabbage and pumpkin and bear for bill of fare. I thought I had left all that behind. I'm a gentleman now, with two hired hands. But underneath the tail coat and top hat I wear to church beats the heart of a buckskin boy.

What a lot of years have gone by, like the pages of a book you flip, each with a little animal on them, to see the animal move. Stop and look at one page, and you freeze the action. Tonight my mind flips back and freezes—where? In Pennsylvania, where fire-light illuminated logs like the ones of this inn. I see Dada (odd Irish term) kneeling with me on the floor of our small log cabin, making a little broom with a draw knife, pulling long shavings down one way, turning the birch stick over to draw the shavings the opposite way and bind them down to sweep clean. The Delawares about. Odd, as they are now here in Indiana.

I flip further and see Dada's grave, almost sunken, as I watched John kneel there and promise the old man to keep the family together. And further, floating the Ohio in the lead boat, going to Caintuck with the Lytle flotilla five hundred strong. Men were getting off to scout the Indians and eat jerky and drink on shore together, while the women drifted prim and serene in the middle boats and read their Presbyterian catechism.

And on, in Caintuck at McClure Station, where I brought Jean back to be my bride to the biggest she-bang the county ever saw. Fiddles and food enough to feed the starving Hindoos—why did they name this place Hindostan Falls? I think it must be the mania for all things British which still grips America, even though we should know better.

India, Hindoostan, land of jewels and dusky servants fanning their betters with huge peacock feather fans. Poor second sons of English nobles getting rich at the end of the world. Chances taken, fortunes made in trade.

And so to this Hindostan. Jean and I have come indeed to the end of the world. She to save the lost, I to observe them. And write. My friend Badollet keeps writing his letters to Washington city, I keep writing for the papers. Never could do carpentry, make beauty in wood like Dada and Dan'l did. I was only an indifferent farmer, though Brother John tried to teach me. Now my sons do it, and I create in words.

Took my first walk this afternoon and saw the town characters, as in a play. Sholts himself, phlegmatic, huge jowls, with high Spanish boots and a leather crop with which he constantly whacks his riding trousers. He stammers. Took me about on a tour with my nephew Jim—pardon—Representative James McClure. Our keep-it-to-yourself, runt of the litter has become a legislator.

Before we went on the tour, I took Jim aside and told him the odd news Jean and I had brought. His mother Janie McClure has married Retreat Granger and run off with him to Tennessee. And his sister Mary and husband Samuel Emison are beside themselves. There is nothing to be done about it. When I told Jim, his face was stony. I think he cut the ribbons on that bonnet years ago. Or maybe being in the State Assembly freezes your features.

There is a new sureness in this James McClure, son of my older brother, John. Perhaps it is the talented wifey with the pretty, piquant face. Auraleigh Markle McClure is oddly intelligent for a woman and flaunts it. Has a governess to care for her child. Or perhaps her political chit-chat is natural. She speaks of nothing but "social experiments," and New Harmony and Robert Owen and his "ideal working community" in Scotland. She is now corresponding with him.

Why shouldn't women be bright? Jean is.

James and his wife are both the leading lights of southern Indiana society, and soon will be powers in the new capital city out in the swamps. A committee got together and decided where it ought to be. Tom Emison, with several other kingpins, went up to a trapper's shack in Indian country, dropped a pin on the map and made up a name "Indianapolis." India no place. And this city, Hindostan Falls, is India someplace? Well, it's bigger than Indianapolis by a long turkey shot. Sholts pointed that out as we walked through the streets. He said they should have chosen Hindostan Falls. Stammered out that he "t-t-TRIED."

Give Jim credit, he is beginning to distance himself some from Sholts. So is his father-in-law, Judge Markle. They all started out close as young robins in a nest, but that was a year or more ago. Rumors are flying about Sholts. He is over-extended.

Conversation as we walked through streets as raw as Harrodsburg's forty years ago when I first saw it:

Sholts: On the right, there's the c-c-c (pause, red face) county courthouse starting. We're hurryin' it 'long now that we are a county.

George M.: Yes, that was certainly quite a feather in your cap. To get the Indiana legislature to make a new county out of parts of two old ones—

Sholts: 'Twasn't easy. I had to be up at the a-a-a (longer pause, redder face ) Assembly for the best part o' two full sessions. When I had other bus-bus-bus—(after lengthy wait, I aiding in the word) FISH to fry in the business world.

George M.: Must have taken quite a lot of—convincing of legislators.

Sholts: (eyes narrowed) Well, natcherly I had to explain everything—upstandin' nature of the settlers here, the future at this location, what we'd already done with the library, the jail, the academy started, over there (pointing to a foundation and three courses of bricks). We had 'em down here and when they uh, uh, uh (pause so long it made me fear apoplexy was building) UNDERSTOOD, why, some of 'em even invested in land here themselves. Yessir, more'n one did that.

George M.: The new name is Martin County. I'm surprised it isn't going to be Sholts County.

Sholts: Well, that wouldn't be too proper, now would it? Named it after some Kentucky politician in the War of 1812. They can always change it later on should they so desire, acourse.

George M.: It's rather small.

Sholts: At the next session I'm proposin' we take parts of three other counties to add to it. Should work—

George M.: So long as the legislators still own land at Hindostan.

Sholts: Well, that's the way it's done you know.


At least right now it is. In many of these counties in Indiana, Ohio, or Illinois there is one County Czar who owns more land than others or has sufficient political power to control things. Each town speculator has to go to him to ask if he can start a new town. These czars are lords of the land, or rivers, really, where the towns are all built. Very medieval, really in the land of equality.

Sholts proceeded to show me the spot, now high with burdock, where the Vincennes Bank will soon open a branch. "And I, my friend," he stated modestly, "am already on the board of that p-p-PRESTIGIOUS 'stablishment.''

Enough notes for today. Jean is meeting with what she hopes will be the Methodist society of Hindostan. They need it badly enough. Now the sun has set over the river. There is a rare beauty here, as the last rays turn the falls of the river, above the mill, into a brazen furnace.

Now they are lighting torches to illumine the rough streets of the town. As I look out the bottle glass window, I see the faces of its inhabitants—orange in the setting sun, also—many the flotsam and jetsam of the pioneer wave west, no matter what Sholts says. Some go home to families in the cabins up the street. Others, landing here from anonymous failure or indifferent success everywhere from Louisiana to Minnesota Territory, creep out to dissipate themselves. They do not have far to go. There are twelve taverns and eight brothels in this town of 1,200.


July 4. Huge celebration here on the banks, overlooking the falls. Workers for the new mill, almost finished, tradespeople and men of means met to hear speeches and eat sumptuous feast carried in dishes covered with teatowels. Jean was circulating about, telling folk of the Methodist meeting that will be held tomorrow. Judge Andrew Markle gave a long-winded, rambling talk (he stoked up on too much whisky before he started). "In less than one year we are the pride of the West, the miracle of modern industry." Then, under oak trees, we offered the customary toasts to the President, the Congress of the United States, the Veterans of the Revolutionary War, and some new ones to the crossing of the Atlantic by steamboat and the author Washington Irving.


July 6. Cast of town characters continued:

Dr. Malthus Ward has set up his doctoring shop on Highridge Street. A strange bird, this one. He even looks like a bird, with long crane's legs and a head that nods in short pecks constantly. He tried to set up a practice that would make him money in Kittanning, but he says that "envy and bad politics" made the clients go to two other doctors in the town. And so on to Pittsburgh for a while, and now here. Like everyone else, he has heard that "opportunity awaits" in Hindostan Falls.

Jack McClure is fascinated by the doctor. I had a long talk with this naughty-boy nephew of mine last night. I saw him first at the doctor's yesterday, staring into Dr. Ward's instrument case, looking at the lancing knives, the tourniquet canvas, the bleeding cup as if he would make love to them.

"Jack, see me tonight at the Ordinary," I said, and he nodded. He sat across from me there, later, and we each had an ale and talked of old times and new. His same round, earnest face now older, with flaccid lines around the jaw. Whatever is he looking for in life? He has left his wife and children to find it. And yet something new has flared in his soul. I sense it but am just beginning to find out what it is.

Dr. Malthus Ward has apprenticed him informally. Has been letting him go about on calls, apparently for several months.

Jack and Dr. Malthus Ward have gone up White River to the Delaware. Ward has some sort of paid commission from the state to visit them for their illnesses, which are as varied as Job's. Poor savages, after all their journeys, they must make one more. The U. S. Government has decreed they must go west and their chief, William Anderson, is getting them ready, mournfully, to move across the Mississippi.

Here is the gist of Jack's conversation to me about it: "Uncle, I have gone with Dr. Ward for some months. He allows me to come and treat the Indians with what he is teaching me of healing lore, the physician's art. He himself finds the red men distasteful.

"He wants something from them, something I have not as yet discovered. He tries to take the chief aside and the chief reluctantly goes to discuss—what? Something. I am trying to find out what the Delawares have that is so interesting to Malthus Ward. In the meantime I am doing what I love for the first time in my life. I am doctoring."

And somehow, as I look at that face through the light of candles on the table in that cabin-inn, I see again the silly, round-faced boy, harassed by his mother, putting together concoctions to make us all sick at the revival meetings. But I also see the serious boy nobody really knew, away from the others, splinting the leg of a rabbit and nursing it back to health in the woods behind McClure Station. Nobody knew this Jack, I think, but me.

I thought I had lost him along with my own Catherine in the days when we all first came to Vincennes and the heady atmosphere of the place blew like suds into both of their brains.

So now Catherine is reclaimed, a clerk's copy of her mother

with a houseful of children. Yet also like me, with projects and dreams brewing in her always. She has taken up weaving for ladies in the neighborhood, as her grandmother did.

And Jack McClure? We shall see as I get to know this place, and him again.


July 7, 1820. Draft of proposed article to go out today with the post:


To The Editor of the *Vincennes Western Sun*


Dear Sir:

Having been given the opportunity of playing The Spectator in our own new state, I hereby submit for the approbation of you and your readers a vignette of life here in this miracle metropolis along White River.

Since this newspaper boasts readers in Kentucky and Illinois and other far-flung places who cannot possibly have seen Hindostan Falls, I shall attempt to draw its design with my quill and ink. Reader, indulge me, if you will.

Picture a criss-cross of streets not unlike those of Louisville or Cincinnati only five, or perhaps ten years ago. Rough one-room cabins, two-story log homes and even painted board houses are sprinkled along muddy lanes that remind you of the Kentucky of the last generation.

But what is different from the frontier villages of my young manhood, reader, are the shops and mercantile ventures. Every second door is a small service or trader. The high boot of the shoemaker stands next to the solicitor's office, with its scrolled shingle. At least six taverns show their signs, and a tooth-drawer has just come to the village and put out his giant bicuspid.

And what is also different, at least in degree, is the grandness of the pecuniary designs, the grandiose nature of the land speculation, complete with broadside circulars sent to cities in the East and even abroad. *Transylvanian Paradise, to be opened up on the shoals upstream a bit. Access to crop shipping equal to the best. Weekly symposia on important subjects relating to the new scientific farming. Encouragement to all religious persuasions.*

And of course Hindostan isn't the only place like this in the new Northwest. Only the biggest and most grand. I would remind you of New Attica, the Greek community of the mind, which is being laid out over by Big Bear Creek. Only those who can speak koine or are willing to serve the needs of intellectuals should apply.

Bought at a dollar and a quarter an acre, the land is now supposedly double in value. But dear reader, don't demur at the new price. Listen to these incorporators, university professors from New Jersey. They speak of Plato's *Republic*, of the ideal towns they are building. But watch their eyes, my friend, for the glint of greed.

Towering above the shores of Hindostan, this low-built town of high opportunity, are the interests of Frederick Sholts and his partners: the "Hindostan Land Company." This business is the father company and it has spawned many legitimate and bastard enterprises: the Mid-Country Surveying Establishment, the Hindostan Ordinary, which is the inn, and the Agricola Mills and Farming Importing Company.

This last is managed in total by a true Yankee peddler. His name is Thomas Jefferson Brooks and, like his namesake, he has truly wrought building marvels in the wilderness. This Brooks, only twenty years old now, is just finishing the gigantic Agricola Mills.

Several mill-builders passed the site at Hindostan by as being almost an impossibility. The river flows too rapidly here, they said, and its course is too unpredictable. "Nay," said the Brooks prodigy and, having gotten a contract from Sholts, proceeded to dam up White River, divert its course, and since has employed thirty-five men to put up a huge three-story undershot mill with a broad, handsome millrace.

Now reader, you may presuppose this mill is planned to grind only wheat and corn. Forget your preconceptions, although it has just this month begun to grind grain inordinately well with new-type sifters that make fine white flour. This mill uses the latest in mechanics. Many are its "diversions" of the power of the water—a sawmill for wood, a molding plane for rope harness, a huge bellows for the forge, even a cider mill, all turned by ingenious shafts, pulleys, conveyors and trip hammers.

Brooks drew the plans, hired the crews from the best skilled workmen he could find up and down the Ohio, got the incorporators to pay well and soon will be completing the last phases of this looming three-story monster on White River, put up in record time. Now he himself is a stockholder. At the shivaree which marked the first grinding early last month, Thomas Jefferson Brooks was toasted in native cider from his own presses and wine from nearby Switzerland County for his Yankee cleverness. Usually the term Yankee, as we know, is used with opprobrium, but not with the Brooks brothers.

Yes, brothers. Daniel Brooks manages the Portersville River Outfitting Company, a bit upriver, and through his agents gives Indian warnings all along the river. And Lewis Brooks operates Brooks Post near Paoli, which trades with Indians north and east toward Indian territory.

Each day at least three or four new families arrives to domicile here. Land changes hands faster than cards in a game of whist, and the speculators have been active in western Virginia, Ohio and New York State. Land which sold at $1.25 an acre went to $2 and then to $5.

All of this in spite of swamp sickness, which raged last summer and is active again now. Nothing, it seems can stop the headlong, down-the-hill rush of progress. Oh heady days! Oh benefits of Democratic Republicanism and our President James Monroe! Ah, Adam Smith's free market spirit, may you glow and flame forever as you do at Hindostan Falls on this July day in the Year of our Lord 18 and 20. More next week.


July 8. I shall include here in my notebook a copy of Jean's report to the Methodist Bishop.


To Bishop Robert McClaren from the Mission Field


Dear Rob:

Our work here is progressing. We are sowing seeds, and it does not yet appear when the bringing in of the sheaves will occur. But in God's good time.

I can report that the rival Presbyterian attempt at churching the Hindostan community has not prospered. The Scotch-Irish who are here are not church-going; just the opposite. Last Saturday night a man lost his ear in a knifing and there were two murders this month that are being blamed on drunken Indians. In truth the murderers may have been drunk, but they were not Indians.

But I am attempting to win the village to the religion of Love. I held my second meeting last night in the cottage of Widow Small. She is a real backwoods lady who smokes a pipe of tobacco every evening, but she was a Methodist in western Virginia and invited the other Methodists in town and made her small cabin hospitable. She has but a compacted dirt floor, but she had swept clean, and taken a sharp stick and drawn a design all around the floor: a rugged cross with passion flower vines twining about. Very pretty and touching.

Mrs. Sholts was there, a quiet, kind woman with stark, white hair. She has scars on her arms received at the age of eight, when she was captured by Munsees and Indian women stuck hot sticks in her. She and Mr. Sholts made their money in freight traffic in New York and eastern Ohio before they came here to build their town.

With her came a devout young girl of strong character, Susan Brooks, who lives with the Sholts. She is tall as a willow and has a beautiful singing voice. She comes from a staunch, New England Presbyterian family. The mother and eight children are alone in the wilderness trying to survive by farming, so Susan is teaching school to help out. The last summer they even had to gather gin-seng to buy necessaries, but now, with Susan's help and that of some nearby Quakers and an Indian who have aided in clearing the land, they are beginning to realize good crops. I do know one thing—this Hannah Poore has a fine daughter who will make a fervent Methodist should she choose us.

We sang, how we sang! I preached as lay preacher, but I was conscious I could not do justice to the sweetest story there is. But I did try and my heart sang too, at thinking of the love that sent Christ to us all.

And Susan sang loudest of all. But she said little. We shall hold class every night next week and then see who comes to the altar of grace. What a moment that will be!

Yours in Christ

Jean McClure

July 10. A letter from Brother Dan'l back in Vincennes. My Catherine is worried about her little Nancy Jane, who has caught the whooping cough and is in danger. Jack's son Alfred also has it; he and Nancy Jane played during dinner Sunday last. Dan'l will write tomorrow—

July 13. Thank God, my granddaughter Nancy Jane is out of danger. Others of Catherine's children and John's little daughter Jewell have the disease, but only light cases. Jack took his horse and went to Vincennes; Alfred is the light of his life. He came back tonight; Alfred also seems to have weathered the crisis. How uncertain these little ones' lives are. Of our second generation of McClures, eleven have died before they reached seven years of age.

Jean's most recent communiqué, as before, copied into my journal.

To: Bishop Rob McClaren
From: Jean McClure

July 13, 1820

Dear Rob:

God be praised! We have begun in truth the Hindostan Falls Methodist Church with twelve true believers. Mrs. Small and her five old believers, two workmen who helped build the mill and then stayed there and their wives. And, to my gratification, the wife of the great man in the town, Mrs. Frederick Sholts, whom I wrote about to you before.

There was indeed, I think, a dramatic awakening in the village. We had to hold services outside the last night. It was a love feast, and I had asked Reverend Baker to come over from Vincennes. Over a hundred people were there.

Afterwards, at the commitment meeting, inside Mrs. Small's cabin, the twelve came forward and either gave, or re-gave themselves to Christ. And as they did, I scratched each name beside the cross on the dirt floor.

Rob, I had gone to my knees in our room the night before and brought Susan Brooks before our God. Her character, her loving heart, her very strength seemed to me to cry out to be given to Christ. She must have felt it too.

She spoke to me before the service.

"In doing this," said she, "I part with almost two hundred years of the orthodox religion. Calvinism is and always will be the very heart of my mother's life. Yet my heart is moved by the gospel of love you teach."

It was a rough hill to climb for her, and yet she gave herself to God on her knees as the wind blew in a rough storm along the river.

As did Mrs. Sholts. With tears running down her cheeks. She is a good woman and I do not think any of us know the suffering her life has brought her. She lost three children and has none left and Susan has become almost like her own child. Her husband seems to have had many thorny places in his own life and much remains hidden with him, but he too seems to care for Susan with a father's love.

And yet, Rob, our greatest surprise of all was that Frederick Sholts came and sat beside his wife late in the meeting. What may come of it I do not know. I hope and pray he too has opened his heart to the living God. Only He redeems and saves, tending us as flowers that grow in His own dear garden.

I do know that I was deeply touched to see his wife and Susan with him, one on each side holding his hands. There is a good deal of criticism in the town, and even among his own directors, of the way Mr. Sholts has conducted himself since he founded Hindostan.

And if either his wife or Susan was the instrument of that man's salvation, what reward in heaven they have!

We shall continue to hold our classes and, if God wills, out of them will grow the commitment to start a church building.

Yours in Christ, dear old friend,
Jean Jordan McClure

July 15. Today Nephew Jack and I took a hamper full of victuals and sassafras tea and went for a walk back from the river. Two miles north, on a beautiful low ridge, are grassy knolls like Caintuck. He carried some sort of book, and after we ate, showed it to me.

My Dada's old orderly book! From the Indian wars in Pennsylvania. I felt an odd stirring in my heart when I saw those parchment pages, that straight, neat handwriting. I was so young when he went. Others remember a man, I only recall a dream. For Jenny, though, he must have been just a shadow. But then everything is a shadow for my poor sister these days.

The French and Indian War, dwarfed in these new history books by the War of Independence which followed it. Jack stroked the leather cover gently and then opened to entries in 1756, the year before I was born. Dada, John McClure, was on a mission to an old Pennsylvania fort Ma always talked about—Fort Granville. Dada was watching the fort for Colonel John Armstrong. An incompetent officer was in charge, it seemed, and the Indian threat very strong. I glanced at the reports and saw that the civilians in the fort were afraid the Delaware would come from Fort Duquesne and slaughter them, which they did, of course. Dada was taken prisoner and later freed.

There were tears in Jack's eyes as he handled the old leather dispatch folder. He said, "This case sat by my bed in the house for two years. Pa gave it to me as namesake of Grandpa. I first looked into it just before the Battle of Tippecanoe. I used it for my own diary." Jack's eyes were vague. He had led the troops in the final charge at that battle, but he realized I knew of his often cowardly heart. To his credit, the fuss the town had made over him embarrassed him, because he knew he hadn't earned it.

"Lately I've been reading these entries," Jack went on.

"They are intriguing, though they stop 'fore the capture by Indians and torture at Kittanning."

Isn't that the way, I thought, letters you read always stop just before the meaty part or leave out just what you want to know.

Jack showed me a personal note from Dada attached to the military records with cobbler's thread.

"Listen to this," he said.

*"We moved forward through mountains. I stopped at Ft. Tuscarora to see Will Lytle, but he had absented himself to get more supplies to feed horses and men in event of the long seige that is expected.*

*"Forty casualties now, in this dreadful year of Indian uprising. Women, children mostly. All at the fort condemn the bloody savages. They do not, cannot know my secret heart. I do not think I know the depths of its secrets myself.*

"This note," Jack said, "was attached to the page just after his arrival at Ft. Granville. There's more—here's the note attached just before the attack. *Women distraught and afraid the Indians may return and kill in awful ways. For some reason, my own mental torture is greater and more acute than in many months. Perhaps it is that death hovers near. If God does indeed exist, I shall go to His throne in greatest guilt and trembling. There is no hope."*

Jack looked up from the book and into my eyes, wonderingly. I found myself dumbstruck. My father wrote this? The elder of the Big Springs Presbyterian Church? The man they called the Scotch Quaker for his good deeds?

I knew nothing at all about any "secret" of great guilt.

"Has Dan'l ever read these entries from our father?" I asked Jack.

"No. Pa doesn't have much curiosity. You were the inquiring one in the family, Uncle."

"What in the world could Dada have been referring to? Sin?" But Jack only shook his head. He did not know, either.


Later—Thomas Jefferson Brooks has been visiting Jim McClure and Jim's wife Auraleigh almost every night for hours. What are they up to? Politics, likely. The great interest in life along with love. Word about town is that all the Brooks brothers are sweet on Susan Poore, but she will have none of them. Considers them worldly minded, apostates. Especially since she has been taking the Methodist church class from Jean. I hope I haven't been responsible for defeating cupid in this matter. T. Brooks has some decent instincts from what I can tell, only, he is a Yankee peddler through and through, wears a coat and clean linen every day. Suspect he was born tallying accounts. Probably used a pickle barrel for a teething ring. I have found out that he has bought into the Hindostan Land Company within this past year and is now a proprietor.

A load of new arrivals came down the trace and went out to their claims bought from one of Sholts' agents in Virginia. They found they had been sold three times already. The bank is calling in Sholts' loans. This lord is in trouble. Uneasy sleeps the head that wears the crown.


July 20. Jack's wife Lizzie and children, Alfred and Jewell, came from Vincennes for visit. Liz is a prissy woman with a pretty, high bosom. What is it she and Jack talk of as they walk about the streets, followed by the prancing children?


July 22. The Methodist classes are the talk of the town. Interestingly, Jack has begun attending them. Wonder follows wonder in this exotic place. Lizzie has returned to Vincennes. If she knows of his foray into John Wesley's religion, she cannot approve. She is the daughter of a Presbyterian minister.

July 23. Jack came to me late at night at the Hindostan Ordinary, all a-twitter. I rose, put on my dressing gown, and went with him to an empty chamber nearby. "Uncle," he said, "I have been poring over the first John McClure's military journal. I cannot get it out of my mind." I nodded, lighting the paltry lard lamp they provide in this place.

"I got to thinking about these notes attached to the back of the military reports with a loop or two of cobbler's thread. I wondered where they had been written and kept while John McClure was on active duty. There was a very slim, neat pocket on the inside of the back of the leather case. I had seen it, even run my fingers inside its rim to see if there were any more papers, but I had never really paid it much heed.

"Then I took a little opener and probed it, wondering if that was where the letters had been stored. Was I careless? The stitches gave, snapped. They were sixty years old after all. The little pocket opened revealing—a pocket inside hidden all these years from the eye of man. I probed again, headed in with the tip of the pen knife and drew out a folded piece of paper." Jack leaned across the table where we were seated and put a piece of paper into my hand.

In the smoky light of the lamp, I read aloud:

*December 1, 1764*

*I, John McClure, originally of Dunleigh, Ireland, now of Cumberland County, Pennsylvania, do testify to the true circumstances of my life. Believing I do not have long to live after repeated attacks of lung fever, I commit to paper secret facts known only to God and not even communicated to my beloved wife Jane.*

*On the Fourth of June, 1737, when I was eighteen years of age, I did in a fit of anger engage in a fight with an English government clerk after an argument over my father's land. I stabbed at the clerk with a knife, intending to kill him, when a young woman who was with him got in the way, and I killed her instead. I took upon myself then, and still do assume guilt for her life.*

*Cast out, as I thought, by my church and fleeing God's retribution on the unjust, I came with my family to America. But my sin followed me. Behold, your sin will find you out. Though I had some success as a farmer and as a father and friend in the neighborhood, my own conscience bitterly ate at me like a canker.*

*I hated fiercely and defied God on the very day my troops and a contingent of innocent settlers were captured at Ft. Granville and taken to the Delaware Camp.*

*I watched the torture of an old enemy, the commanding officer of Ft. Granville. Under the influence of fever and more exactly, through the influence of Divine Intervention, I finally experienced my salvation. God revealed his very presence to me and took me over all the earth in a vision to see all of mankind and know in truth their brotherhood.*

*I awoke and begged the Indians to put an end to my old enemy's suffering. I myself suffered no more, for I had found love and forgiveness. I cannot speak of the true miracle of grace that transformed me. Transformation can happen. It is God's plan for all of us. I think I write this for one particular set of eyes. Let him who has eyes see.*

I sat back, stunned. I felt as though I had peeked through the years into my father's closet, looked through a cobwebby keyhole into a man's heart. Yet I did not think it was I the letter was intended for.

"Can there be transformation, Uncle?" Jack asked me in a low voice. "I am like him, responsible for a death. I think I am the eyes for whom our grandfather's letter was intended." I did recall a bar-maid he had scandalously carried on with for four years. She had died in odd cirumstances, it was true. But was he responsible?

"I cannot judge your guilt, Jack," I said. "But a good heart is the first requirement for changing. At least somebody told me that once."

"I cannot live in the past, Uncle, I know that. The truth is, perhaps I have found hope for transformation. Perhaps I have begun to find my own life."

I looked at him questioningly.

"I have told Lizzie I am returnin' home. Next month I begin my own medical practice in Vincennes."

I rose, truly pleased, and shook his hand.

"It would be good if I could go to one of the new medical school programs, but most of the best physicians around have learned on the job, as I have, anyway. It is time, of course for me to go home," he said. "Little Alfred needs me. He is a strange, almost eccentric creature."

"You were a little odd yourself as a child," I could not resist saying.

"I finish up here in about two weeks. First I must say goodbye to my Delaware friends."

"You're abandoning them? Leaving them to the tender ministrations of Dr. Malthus Moneybags?"

"I have found out, by the way, what he wants from them. Some sort of sacred artifact—"

"What do you mean?"

He told me Ward had let slip that the tribe up the White had a rare written history of the Delaware. And with his breast puffed up like a pouter pigeon's Ward had mentioned "wealthy antiquarian collector" and a "sum too large to scoff at." I cannot sort it all out.

It is now 2 a.m. I must retire, if I can sleep with all the ruckus in the streets following the town's turkey shoot. Tom cats yowl constantly in this place, and dogs yap. Yap, yap, yap, yap, yap. And so to bed.


July 25. T. Brooks and Jim McClure have been closely conferring in the last few days. Now the last proprietor has arrived, Judge Andrew Markle. What does it all mean?

Jean is closing the first set of Methodist classes. She has twenty new Wesleyans. Not bad hatching. Susan Brooks continues to be a mainstay. Mrs. Sholts still comes, Sholts himself once or twice. The Circuit-riding minister is due in again day after tomorrow, for the Chartering Meeting. New coverts will be accepted here, and the site for the church building chosen. Such doin's, as Dan'l would say.

Glad I remained a Presbyterian and can sit in the back of the church and let the minister and elders do the work. Methodism makes you work, and emote, too much.


July 26. Jack has come back from the Delaware with the most remarkable thing. I have seen it although no one else has, nor should anyone. It is called "Walam Olum" and is on painted, long wooden sticks. It is sign language, but Jack has had an interpretation. It is the miraculous document of a beautiful people, a real farewell song. How old is it? The Indians did not tell him. Dr.

Ward is furious. They gave their treasure to Jack instead of him. Here is how it occurred. Jack helped the Delaware, he set their bones, cleaned their wounds, most of all he gave them quinine for the swamp ague along the White River.

The chief's son drew Jack aside on the last visit and begged him to take the holy sticks. For, he said, Ward plagued them to have the sacred relics which he found out about quite by chance from the Indian agent there who is his friend.

"Ward will sell them," the chief's son said, "and they will get into white man's books and our father's holy tales will be made a mockery. We cannot keep them because Ward will force them from us; he is a friend of the man who takes us west. Soon we must go. But let us take our sacred tales with us in our hearts and minds and let not the greedy white men have them." The last part was the most mournful thing of all for the chief's son said, "Oh, MacLooer with the gift of healing, the white men have taken all else, let them not take the Delawares' sacred memories. Let not dirty hands touch them."

So Jack, touched by their plight, took the *Walam Olum* and swore he would guard it from white men as long as he lived.

And he says he could never tell his cousin Jim, who knows him so well, about the sacred sticks and the promise, because Jim hates Indians with a blistering passion. I ask Jack why he, the hero of the Tippecanoe Indian battle, did not hate Indians also?

"You cannot hate what you pity," he said.

True, and yet I think the Indians will some day want more than pity.


July 27. The whole town buzzes with the Hindostan Land Company Proprietors' meetings going on yesterday and today. How will the proprietors satisfy angry land purchasers? Still the talk of wildcat speculation and move the town forward? Rumor has it that the last meetings have been closed to Sholts, with McClure, Brooks, and Judge Markle closeted together.

Politics may boil, but religion simmers too. Jean and her Methodists got up at the crack of dawn to take chairs, benches and an altar into the woods so the circuit rider can conduct his meeting of consecration for the new church.

Later—Jean has just come in highest spirits from the morning woodside church consecration meeting. As all the would-be Methodists knelt in a glen up the road a bit, Frederick Sholts thundered up on his horse. He sat on a back bench, then came forward during the singing of the hymn. Susan Brooks, with tears streaming down her face, knelt beside him while his wife, who was leading the singing, praised the Lord.

Sholts has promised to give an acre on a back street of Hindostan to the Lord; the Methodists have promised to pray for the town. As far as I can see, it's going to need all the help it can find.

I must put down my pen to go to a meeting on Main Street. I have promised to write a report tonight for the Vincennes editor and post it first thing tomorrow. Will there be anything worth writing about?

9 p.m.
Something worth writing about, indeed! I here append a copy of my dispatch.

To the Editor of the *Vincennes Western Sun:*

Your correspondent has witnessed an interesting series of events today which throw light on the character of our new western "overnight" river towns.

The proprietors of Hindostan Falls met today and dissolved themselves, astounding the town's proponents and inhabitants alike. In a public speech at the site of the new courthouse State Representative James McClure, (whose connection to the present correspondent is known to readers) stood side by side with the town's leading merchant, Thomas Jefferson Brooks.

"In the name of justice," said McClure, one of four proprietors, "we must stand for veracity." He then went on to reveal that Frederick Sholts, the town's founder and first proprietor, oversold the land and speculated illegally and that Sholts used his position as board member of the Vincennes State Bank to finance ventures at the Falls which threaten to cause financial ruin to hundreds of small investors and the bank itself.

Then Brooks told the awe-struck crowd, "The books of the Agricola Farm Company are in disorder." He reviewed several recent transactions in detail and explained problems stretching back two years, when Sholts first began selling lands here. He produced docket sheets showing lawsuits against Sholts for debt and land fraud. Brooks, like a vengeful angel of the Lord, spared not the man from one ignominious revelation.

Judge Markle announced that he, McClure and Brooks, the other proprietors, now have acquired controlling shares in Hindostan Land Company. They have taken over management from Sholts, dissolved the corporation and declared bankruptcy, at which news the assembly was visibly affected. General Washington Johnston, Vincennes attorney, has been named receiver.

"In this reorganization we will first sell the assets of the corporation to whoever makes a responsible offer to pay at least some of the debts, help settlers get extensions of loans, and clear titles," Representative McClure promised. "Judge Markle, Mr. Brooks and I feel responsibility to this town. I believe all of us have been duped and ill used by Mr. Sholts. Now that he is gone from the operation, we can look forward to a new era of prosperity for Hindostan Falls. We will take care of you all!"

The cheers resounded noisily, rivalling the sound of the pouring waters at the falls of White River.

Thus was an astonishing afternoon at the new Mecca of the West terminated.

Frederick Sholts was not present; he had told several of the citizenry that he had been forced to sell out his lands for a pittance, that his character was being impugned, and he would be with the Methodists at their meeting in the woods.


Additional Newspaper story in The *Vincennes Western Sun*, (Page Two)

Mr. Thomas Jefferson Brooks has announced the expansion of his own personal business interests and those of his family. Lewis Brooks will enlarge his trading interests at Paoli and in Indian country by doubling his present mercantile stock and building a new store structure. Lewis Brooks also announces the formation of a new Brooks Stagecoach Line with fleet-footed horses, which he says "will fly from Louisville to St. Louis" by way of Hindostan Falls in a matter of hours. It will be the first stagecoach line across Indiana.

Thomas Jefferson Brooks has announced his intent to buy the assets of Hindostan Land Company and all of Frederick Sholts' enterprises, paying ten cents on the dollar to retire debts. This newly expanded business "will rival similar mills and the outfitting stores in Cincinnati or even Pittsburgh."

The other two partners in the former Sholts Enterprises have tentatively agreed to the new arrangement and will be withdrawing their interests over a period of time. "They have been satisfactorily compensated, indeed they have," Brooks confessed to this reporter.

Agricola will open a new branch in Vincennes featuring the latest in merchandise from all the Eastern markets and New Orleans itself. Mr. Daniel Brooks will operate this new mercantile.

In an expansive mood at the time of this interview, Brooks even indicated that he might be taking up the option to open a bank which could be called the First Bank of Hindostan Falls.

July 28. By express rider to editor of the *Vincennes Western Sun*:

Your correspondent has learned that Representative James McClure has formally announced he will seek re-election from this district. He offers himself to the people of Indiana to introduce "Reform legislation and progressive expansion for the whole state."

In a social note, the well known British industrialist Robert Owen is planning a visit to the White River home here of Mr. and Mrs. McClure. Judge Andrew Markle and his wife Henrietta and their children are presently house guests of the McClures.

Frederick Sholts, former chief proprietor of Hindostan Falls has fled the town and was seen boarding an Ohio River steamboat bound downriver. Mrs. Sholts and the household are in seclusion.

The lord is dead. Long live the new lord. And so, your correspondent leaves all this behind to return to the calmer pastures of Vincennes and pastoral Knox County.

I close my notebook by observing that Brooks has managed to line his own fox's den and those of his brothers quite nicely. And my nephew has managed to pass through this messy operation with his coat-tails clean, like the farmer who insisted on slopping the hogs in his tail coat. To do it, however, he had to walk on tiptoe and learn to ignore the dung on his shoes.

## For Banjo, Guitar, and Fiddle

Sing me a song of a town that lives, A town that's built by men Planned on a hill by the ri-ver-side Sing me a song a-gain

Tune by Ann Price

# 1828

## The Song of the Town Builders

*Sing me a song of a town that lives,*
*A town that's built by men,*
*Planned on a hill by the riverside,*
*Sing me a song again.*

*Cut down the trees, dam up the stream,*
*Make a wheel as fast as you can,*
*Build me a mill 'fore the sun comes up*
*Or you ain't half a man.*

*Call in the trades, lay log streets,*
*Start the academy,*
*Put up a town in a month or two*
*And name it after me!*

*Sing me a song of a town that lived,*
*That one day chanced to die,*
*Where the wind sings a lonely, mournful song*
*Through streets where grass grows high.*

*Show me the death of the people's hope*
*With cabins crumbling away—*
*And I'll show you a town on a whole new shore*
*They've rebuilt for a bright new day.*

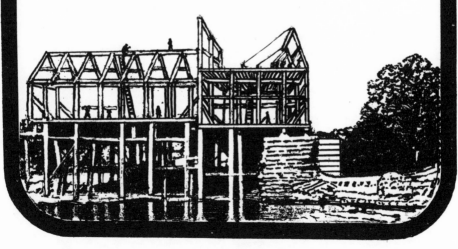

## Chapter Ten

# The Deposition of Kezegat Dauja, of the Potawatomi

You have asked for my testimony in one of these endless land disputes involving my people the Potawatomi and thus I do give it. I shall commit my full and entire story to paper and your lawyers shall use it as they wish.

I was born Dauja, Dawn Yet to Come, in Indiana at the Lake of Boulders, Mocksinkickee. I came in the cold of winter, 1811, as the earthquake shook the land and comets flashed overhead. So my mother, Swiftly Running Feet of Quash Quay's band, has told me.

My father was one of the bravest and best of the Miami warriors. He was called Asondaki Alamelonda, son of Mulberry Blossom, who was herself daughter of the Band Chief Rising Star of the Ohio Miamis.

I never saw my father; he died at Tippecanoe and his body was never found. The brute beast white men must have dumped it in the bloody river as they exulted in their triumph.

I shame myself to tell it; my father was half-white. My name could have a McClure added to it should I desire to do so. I do not desire it.

I did grow up on free and wild lands in northern Indiana, where no white men went, except to trade. Perhaps it was because the marshes covered the lowlands where we dwelt, making them really fit in many places only for the handsome crane birds or musk-rat. Perhaps it was because of the quicksand bogs, slippery to feet not clad in Indian moccasins. At any rate, the white man left our land alone while he gobbled other land in gulps after the Battle of Tippecanoe.

My mother, as a widow, with her own father dead, was taken

into the winter shelter of her uncle, the shaman Kasgo. And so I grew up beside that cooking fire. And what I did learn there! It was not the girl-matter that the women in other lodges doted on, the bark-stripping to make the shelters, the mending of soft-tanned moccasins, and the tanning of the trading furs with deer brain oil.

No, not these, although in truth I could do all those things well enough by the time I was six. No, I learned the stuff of magic, of chanting to ward off sickness which has come to someone, of the amulets of elk teeth or beaver tail or bone of marten.

But most it was the evil eye that I learned of, learned to fear and loathe I should say. From the time I was on my cradle board I heard the grumbling of this uncle, Kasgo, as he did his incantations. I can see him now, on his haunches before the campfire, his eyes dull and hateful, chanting:

*He who walks the rolling winds*
*Whose thunder burns the sky*
*Break your limbs, dim your eye*
*Take you to the death isle*

"And who, my husband, has offended you now?" his slightly-built girl-wife would ask, herself a little frightened.

"Strewn Sticks, in Twin Lakes village. He knows what his offense is." Strewn Sticks was a boy who had hooted at friends as the shaman chanced to pass by. It does not do to hoot near a shaman. They must maintain their reputation as untouchables of great power.

Shamans can drive out evil powers and let the body heal, they can brew herbs, they can use chants. You can, you had better, pay them to do it. But do not cross their paths, at least the bad ones. Animosity towards a Medicine One can be a boy's turning stick: once you throw it out, it will go in a circle and hit the thrower. The unseen Manittos light the fires of his powers, but fear fuels the flame.

That is how my aunt, the child-bride of the shaman, had come to marry this Kasgo. She and her family were afraid not to.

A lovely thing, Gitche Nissiman, Sweet Berries, she was. She lay, only twelve years old in the winter shelter with her parents. As other Indian maidens, she hoped that a man she could love would someday come to her, lie by her side without touching her till dawn and thus tell her parents that he wished to marry her.

But instead came this slinking cat, the shaman, who lay beside her and told her parents, "I shall come for Sweet Berries tomorrow. Be sure she is clean and your presents good ones."

She cried for hours, but what could she do? "You must go to him," her mother said sadly. "I knew a woman once who scorned a shaman. She married another, had a child, and a bear came from a tree and tore her child to pieces before her very eyes."

And so Sweet Berries went to the shaman and had no day of peace ever after, living in the midst of his constant demands, his jealousy, and his odd doings.

Only my mother could ignore the shaman. Her father, his brother, had been band chief and the shaman seemed to have some grudging respect that did not allow him to cross the line and frighten us.

So we did not fear, only watched with disgust what went on in that lodge.

But sometimes I saw things that interested me. Truly I saw the healing, too. I followed, unseen, behind the shaman through the humming summer night or the silent winter snow and peeked through a crack into the lodge of the sick one. I saw him take off his clothes, gesticulate wildly and dance in the firelight, wave the feathers and bones about, suck the skin of the sick one to oust the humors, make the sweat tent, brew the pungent herbs. And I saw the ill one rise from the pallet, healed.

I marvelled, that such good could come of bad. And yet, to tell truth, he was not all bad. He took us to fishing camp in Michigan with the St. Joseph Potawatomi, and we rowed canoes in the silent green lakes while he speared giant pickerel.

We ate delicious fish with corn cakes under stars. He spoke of the groups of stars, the constellations, of big and little bear, of warrior and lost maiden. He knew a bag lot of things, this uncle of my mother's, and at the camp he was free of his evil eye, as if it had been transformed by the purity of the northern waters.

But when we returned to Lake of Boulders, the old malignity returned. I think truly he was afraid of the villagers as much as they feared him. Afraid he could not heal and would lose his living and manhood respect. Afraid the other shamans, from Twin Lakes camps and the high hill camp would best him and get the sickness trade. And so he acted indifferent and turned quickly on his heel at imagined slights, poked his head from out the tent at unexpected moments, looked hither and thither constantly. And yet, to tell truth, more than a few did sicken and even die when he mumbled at them for not paying enough, for talking against him.

"*Mautchi, mautchi*—curse of the shaman" widows and children whispered. They spoke, of course, only to friends, that he might not hear that too and send more evil.

And of course, as do most old men who marry young girls, he lived in torment lest his wife betray him and this poisoned his love. He shouted, he cuffed her, he spoke with scorn. This says nothing of the times in the dark when I heard him use her roughly on the sleeping mats in the corner. As for Sweet Berries, she uttered not a word except for an occasional smothered cry of pain.

"Let us go from this shelter," I said to my mother when I was about eight, when Sweet Berries had been with us for about a year and was living this life of a dog before our eyes.

"We cannot," Swiftly Running Feet said without looking at me. "We have no other shelter relatives. My step-mother, the fat one, hates me because I was the apple of my father's eye, and there is no one else to keep the winds from our backs and venison in our mouths. There is much good food and a fine shelter here. I want a good place, good future for you, my Rosy Dawn." Here she looked at me and rumpled my red hair, heritage of the McClure white people who were my father's parents.

It was true enough that we did eat well. People paid the shaman with the best they could find, and if he healed as he sometimes did, people with bad diseases, their gratitude knew no bounds. We had partridge, bear paw, even once a buffalo hump from the Michigan camps.

I chose to find comfort in the world outside the shelter. Often I went with Sweet Berries, this child wife of my mother's uncle. She took me to the creek to fish for mussels or to wash the clothes. Soon we became fast friends. Since her childhood had been interrupted by early marriage, as rude winter snows sometimes fall on the yellow leaves of Smoky Moon, she seemed to become a child again playing with me. We laughed together and threw sand at each other and slept by the creek. Sometimes we made a little camp ourselves, when the shaman made long visits to heal people near the Miami camps on the Wabash.

One particular summer when I was nearing my coming-of-age time, Sweet Berries and I spent much time out in the nearby woodland camps. My mother slept alone, working on beautiful beadwork she was creating, and she did not care to come. Sweet Berries and I captured rabbits with snares and roasted their meat with the small tomatoes the crazy white man thinks are poison.

We put bits of rabbit and tomatoes on sticks with onions over the campfire and savored them together, and then we ate sugar lumps until our teeth hurt. Sweet Berries was my friend, almost like my sister. I loved her, truly I did.

One night I awoke in the shelter after one of these late campfires to find Sweet Berries gone. I went out of the camp shelter, pushing aside the cattail mat that was its door.

I heard moaning off in the brush. "A warring party of braves has accosted her," I thought with a leaping heart. Roaming parties of vagrant young men were known in these days of plentiful white man's liquor, and had been even invading the menstrual huts where the tribe isolated the "new women" until their time of purification. It was dark as I crept into the brambles and willow shoots. Soon I came to the place where the noise was, but it was not as I had thought. There in the brush was Sweet Berries, and she was with a man. She was willingly doing the act of love I had come to know about so well in the closeness of the wigwam.

But was it the same act? Sweet Berries was making noises I had never heard, moving about as I had never thought she moved with the shaman.

Who was this *alanya* brave? I thought from what I could see that it was the very good-looking young Illinois Potawatomi who had been adopted by the tribe when others of his nation shifted their camp a few years before.

I closed my eyes and returned, numbly, to the camp shelter. The flame of the fire seemed to leap up at me as I passed by, saying, "Trouble, there will be trouble here."

The shaman came back in midsummer month, and I put myself

into the life of summer camp, when bonfires blaze high, dugouts glide over still lake waters and children chase the tiny lantern bugs through grass higher than they are.

I was twelve and intent on using every hour of the summer twilight to play games and be in contests, the occupations our northern children have played forever, I suppose. There were the tag chases and the foot races. There were the wooden stick throwing contests, the "creep up" Chief Quash-quay or the shaman himself led to teach Indian children to be alert. In those games we put a rag over the eyes of a child, and we all tried to steal sticks from him without his knowing who did it.

And there were also the customary "cousin" games which we children who were almost ready for man and womanhood played constantly, the teasing of opposite sex, the wrestling on the ground, the taunting, "And so Little Lynx cares for Green Leaf," songs we sung. I think white children have always done so too at that age, but Indian children do it more.

Of all the young *alanyas* who teased me and whom I teased also in the "cousin" games, Paukooshuck, son of Aubenaubee, was the one most in my life. Paukooshuck was older than I. He was from the Tippecanoe camps but stayed with relatives each summer at Lake Mocksinkickee. Do not think I liked him. No, I told myself, he was a slinking *ginbig*, a snake. A stinking skunk who jumped out from behind oak trees to frighten me, who pulled the pins from my hair and let it tumble in my eyes.

"A jester you are. You are from the tales told by the women, Michiboo the trickster hare born again," I used to yell at him when he had played a particularly trying trick on me.

And yet I knew he liked me. I saw him looking at me, smiling a mocking smile as I worked hoeing corn and pumpkins, making skirts from new trader's cotton, while my mother was cooking beans and new corn over a tripod nearby.

All in our wigwam were trying to stay out of the way of the shaman. Since our return, he was insanely jealous of Sweet Berries, suspecting something, I suppose. His eyes followed her everywhere and he even went to check her in the menstrual hut, a great taboo and a thing never done. It infuriated me to see him and hear his mumblings.

And I could see the fear and loathing in Sweet Berries' eyes.

The Illinois brave was staying apart from her, but sometimes their eyes caressed each other as they passed on the way to the stream or to the dancing circle.

"Who is Kasgo the shaman, anyway, to act so?" I thought with an outrage that surprised me. "If there are Manittos, they do not like the way he acts. He has power to heal legs burned in the fire, wounds that putrefy, and see what he does with that power."

The shaman no longer held my respect, and I decided to do something; I was a reckless child that "cousin-teasing" summer. I started doing little mocking, irritating things to the shaman that he did not know about. I piled up bad-luck snakeskins at the door, so he would see them when he came out as morning sun hit the door flap. I poured water on the fire torches he threw in the air so they would not light. I scratched his shaman's symbol, fire-tiger on a waterfall, on the sets of small leather balls the women threw in their sport games. They laughed as they tossed the balls in the air.

After I put hot-plant in the greens that the women brought as an offering, he cursed and spat them on the ground. Then something made him turn and look at me with questioning eyes. Perhaps it was some sign my mother had made to me; she was very suspicious of my part in the annoyings.

But I was clever of mind. "Oh shaman-uncle," I said with proper reverence, "Someone toys with you. I have seen someone about the shelter lately. . ."

"Who?" he demanded.

"Well," I rolled my eyes, "Paukooshuck, son of Aubenaubee, Band Chief."

"That young man. I will ask the Bat Manitto to see to him." *Mautchi?* Shaman curse? An ugly shadow had passed his face and I felt a pang of regret. Had I gone too far? Paukooshuck was irritating, it is true, but I did not wish him really harmed.

It was too late. Pauk's sister, who was also visiting in our camp, began to develop boils. She could not walk, because of the boils on her upper legs. I felt guilty. I had put the shaman on their path. I went to see her and said I might know a remedy. I really felt I did and put a poultice of hot mustard on the boils. I stayed with her all the night changing the poultice, and by morning the boils had broken. She walked about to get water, much better.

Nothing more happened to Pauk's relatives for a while, but I dreamed of wolves visiting them, of rocks falling on their heads on the trail. Still, I could not control my anger at the shaman and his evil eye. One night, after the shaman had grabbed Sweet Berries' arm and shouted "Who are you seeing? I will curse both him and you with foul part sickness," I determined one more trick. Alone, out in the woods I squatted, making a beaver bone cursebag. I would place it among his most sacred medicine bags, which I had brought with me. Yes, here they were—his pipes, his sacred smoking herbs. I fished through, thinking of where I would put it, when—

"You have done a bad taboo," said a cold voice behind me. It was my mother, Swiftly Running Feet. She grabbed me by the collar of my calico blouse. "How dare you touch the sacred medicine objects, even if they are of the evil shaman?"

My mother looked at me and her eyes were hard. "I have been too long at my bead work. Perhaps I do it to forget. I have not seen what is going on in my own lodge."

I was afraid for the first time in my life. Swiftly Running Feet was a woman of power—quiet it is true, but with strong magic. She was band-chief's daughter and in her own childhood a winner of races still sung about in the tribe chanting. And also, I loved her. "I shall take you to the woods for a woman's time." I looked at her with asking eyes. None of us, Potawatomi, Kickapoo, or Miami had becoming-a-woman times any more. The white men had changed that, along with everything else, since they came in great herds into our lands and brought the killing liquor with them.

"You shall have your own becoming-a-woman rites. With me."

And so we went out to the woods above Twin Lakes. "Here it was your father and I camped to kill the Snow Deer," she said.

"Tell me of my father," I said. She had not spoken often of him, particularly before the shaman. He did not like her Miami marriage, the half-white who was my father.

"Asondaki Caipawa Alamelonda, Shining Morning Sun, was a true man," my mother said, looking over the hills at a time long past. "He came to my camp as a strong young *alanya* looking for a "great hunt" to prove his manhood to Little Turtle, chief of the Miamis.

"I was huntress, too, and told him of the Snow Deer. We came here and found the albino and his mate at sunset. The next night Asondaki Alamelonda tried to kill him and could not, the second night he struck home with spear and the great stag fell at his feet. But before that deer died he spoke—"

"Spoke?" I asked scornfully. Such things were only in the stories of the spirit world.

"Spoke with his eyes. And as he looked into those dying eyes of the great beast, your father changed. He began to seek for the great magic of the universe, the power that ruled."

"Like the shamans?"

"No, not like that at all. Your father tried all things in the white and tribal world. He ran white men's businesses. He made much money. But finally he put it all aside. He gave up his life for his people. So The Catfish his kinsman has told me. My husband—he was a true Son of the West Wind."

"Not really—"

"Who knows?" she smiled. "They say this spirit of great power is reborn in some generations—but your father was as like the West Wind as the face above the stream to its image in the waters."

I was cutting a fish we had speared, making long strips to cook in a fry pan above good maple coals. "But West Wind's son, Manaboozhoo, was a clever trickster." She had told me the story—all Indian children knew it—of how he stole fire from the spirits by deceiving them.

"But that is not why we really love Manaboozhoo above all other spirits, except for his twin Wisky. Is it not for Manaboozhoo's wisdom, his kindness and his sacrifice? His love for us all?"

I looked up from the fire without answering. I had never thought about it. My mother, Swiftly Running Feet went on.

"When Son of the West Wind went to get the fire, he braved the coming winter to go to the land of fire, paddling the raging river with ice in his face, almost destroyed by bad magic. Still he went on, because he knew that our peoples needed fire above all other gifts.

"That is the difference between us and the whites. The white man lives for himself, for his own gold, his own family. An Indian exists for the tribe."

I could not meet her eyes because these ideas troubled me. "And what of you, now that my father is gone? You do not have a new husband," I said. Why is it children, just at growing-up time, find ways to punish their loved parents? She held her head high, turned her profile away. Suddenly, as I saw how she had loved him, I began to look at her as a woman, not just a lump in the corner of the wigwam who provided food and love.

"No, and never shall, though I have had some bid for me."

She was handsome yet, though older than most of the women who were mothers. "I live for my tribe, to make the best bead-work in the north lakelands. I can do that, because I am of the older ones. But you, you are of a generation that must leave the tribe. And for you," she reached out to pat me as I dished up corn and fish, "I wish to see you reared and married to somebody good. Maybe a white man."

"Devils! I do not like them, with their hogs and Bibles and whisky that turns us into fools."

"You are wise woman of the *Neshnabec*, the People. Still, there is not much here for us and soon it will be worse. I promised your father that we would leave all this. Go west, where the tribes can live as the children of the Master of Life."

"What is better there?" I wanted to know.

"Few whites, many tribes live among the Stony Mountains, trapping and growing wealthy. That is what your father would have done, what we could—" her face darkened—"what I can never do now."

"But a white man? What does he have to do with the cycles of sun and moon?"

"If we do not go west, marriage to those who will control and survive is the only way out. Whites are the people of power. We are as ants. The new treaties take more and more, and soon we will have nothing left. You are part-white and are beautiful, too. So marry a white man and go to the city. May my eyes live to see it!"

"Your eyes may fall out before they see that," I mumbled, irritable with the smoke in my eyes and all these ideas. Still, we ate our good camp food, watched a beaver build a dam and lay down painted in pennyroyal and wrapped in deerskin robes against the insects, and fell asleep before the fire.

I awoke at dawn, with the wind stirring the ash leaves above us. For a moment, just a moment, I stirred with it, feeling a longing I could not even put a name to.

"Tell me more about my father," I said to Mother after we had eaten. She did, talking most of the morning of him, of his father the Kentuckian who now lived rich with a thousand acres near Vincennes, of the beautiful Miami mother, dead of smallpox. Of my father's days of trading furs, and of the white men, the Lasselles, he worked for who used him and then cast him out, owing him a goodly sum of money. Of his strong, handsome face and loving spirit, above all those she had ever known. And how he had cherished her in the last days, when he stayed with Chief Tecumseh and put his hand on me while I was yet in the womb, loving the child he would never see, because he finally chose to fight with his brothers at the great battle.

And as we walked the long track home, I felt a pain that was at my heart and would not leave, even when I swallowed hard and ran.

I recalled Manaboozhoo, son of the West Wind, so they say, did not know where his father was when he was a child. And he went to this shelter and that wigwam, on hill and over valley, looking for him. He would follow a curling trail of smoke into a door and look in, peering in an Old One's face to say "Are you my father?" And the Old One would shake his head slowly, sadly.

Finally a Manitto in disguise told him to go to climb the highest tree in the northlands and take a white ash basket with him. When his father blew through the trees, he could trap him and clap the lid on. So Manaboozhoo did as he was told, and when he had climbed a giant oak and felt its branches sway, he caught his father the wind. But when he took the lid off—

"Alas, he is gone," Manaboozhoo said sadly. "He has slipped through the cracks."

Now the search of Manaboozhoo was mine too, and I yearned to know my father, even though I could not, because he was dead. And in this mood I returned to the home village. My becoming-a-woman trip was over. But instead of finding the guiding spirit of a bear or deer as the old women had on their times in the wild, I had discovered the spirit of my father, and it haunted me on the trail home and for many days to come.


There was ill news waiting when we returned to the village. Pauk and his sister had to leave their relatives and go back to the Tippecanoe camps. They felt evil eye on them night and day, it was said. It had made Pauk feel sad, and he would not be comforted.

And, Sweet Berries, unable to live without her lover, had gone to him in the night. The shaman, warned in a dream, he said, had risen and followed and found them in each other's arms. He had denounced them and the two had fled to Twin Lakes, where they had reluctantly been admitted. Who knows what evil would follow them there. "You cannot evade a shaman's powers," the village people said. "*Mautchi*, the evil curse, follows everywhere."

Late fall came, the month of Smoky Moon, and with it news that Sweet Berries had borne a child too early, and that it was marked and dead.

After that the shaman, ugly man, strutted about with leering pride. The Manittos had avenged him, so it seemed.

He relaxed enough to decide to go duck hunting and asked my mother to let me come as canoe paddler. She raised her eyebrows, knowing my distaste for the man. But to refuse would be to offer offense; all young girls or female relatives were expected to paddle canoes at duck hunting time.

We went to the lakes north of St. Joseph portage and made camp on the hills above the duck marshes. My heart was not heavy, because I would be under the stars, the place I loved most, and because I hoped the shaman's evil eye would leave him in the wilderness, as it had before.

That night I cooked quail and wild rice into a savory stew and I built a leanto covered with canvas. We gathered pine branches to put our wool blankets on and before going to sleep, I sat in the crisp, clear air before the campfire. The shaman jested with me, almost like a "cousin" game. Then he went into the leanto and to bed.

I slept out by the fire. I dozed, then awakened. It seemed I saw the brush part and yet I heard no noise. My heart was in my mouth; out of the wood stepped the Snow Deer, just as my mother had described him when he came to Asondaki Alamelonda my father.

He stood almost six feet tall, with huge racks of antlers; somehow I could not seem to count them, although I wished to. His eyes were red; White Ones' eyes are always so, and in them was a terrible sadness. I yearned, I recall, to know the cause of that awful sadness.

He spoke and his voice sounded in my mind, not my ears. "Daughter of the West Wind, I salute you. You are a 'Gifted One' the spirits watch with care. I am your vision animal, finally come to you in these latter days. Guard my gifts with care. I give you three herbs. The first is prickly ash, for good-seeing eyes. You will be *Manitto Wabo*, seer of the spirits and able to understand the will of the Great Spirit. The second is mandrake for the kind of womanhood the Master of Life has decreed for you. The last is black willow bark, a balm for the feet that will travel far on many roads."

I raised my hand out to him, yearning to touch his beauty, and he began to glow, as if the light of all the stars above us had come into him, and then he faded away.

And within an hour, when I had gone back to sleep on my pallet in that northern campground, I was awakened by arms around me, turning me about. The cat shaman was awake at dawn time and planned to use me for his lust.

"*Agachiti win,*" I shouted, "Shame on you." But I was afraid of him and did not defy him. And thus was I robbed of my virginity on the very night I saw my vision. Strange watch it was indeed that the Manittos were keeping on me. I laughed a bitter laugh.

When we went back and I told my mother what had happened on the pallet, her face hardened. She left me, and when I asked where she had gone, someone said she had taken a horse and gone to see the Indian agent in the Twin Lakes village.

That night she said, "I am sending you to the new Mission School. You will go as soon as they open it north of the St. Joseph's camps. There you will be taught the white man's ways and kept out of harm's way too." And so I prepared to leave my childhood village, with all its charms and dangers.

When the ground froze that winter of 1823, I went. One lone tear came down my cheek slowly. I would not see my mother or cousins or friends like Paukooshuck for nearly a year, perhaps more. The Mission School was in Michigan and students must stay there, not seeing relatives.

I put up six stakes in a row beside the wigwam, pointing northeast to St. Joseph's River. When my mother saw them, she would think of the absent one. And the Manittos, if they existed, would know where to find the "gifted one" to bestow all the favors they were supposed to be giving me.

Chief Quash Quay took me to the mission and, old man that he was, dawdled on the trail so that it took three days. When we arrived, he helped me off the horse and said, "Here is Dawn Yet To Come, a bright star of the Potawatomi. She has white blood, too. Indian agent has sent her here and will pay."

A tall woman as slim and lovely as a willow wand bent down to shake my hand, which startled me. Tribal people do not shake hands. "I am Mrs. McCoy, Dawn," she said with a voice as rich as French satin. Chief Quash Quay stayed that night to translate for me.

That night she took the lonely Indian child into her own log house. How strange, yet beautiful it was to me. Here the fire did not go out a hole in the top of the room but burned cleanly in a stone place at the end of the room. Here were no bumpy pallets on poles, but real bird-feather mattresses. Soft! Tomorrow I must start my instruction, but tonight after Mrs. McCoy put her own three children into cot beds, she talked to me and Chief Quash Quay before the fire.

"My husband and I have come from Kentucky to minister to the Indians in the name of Christ." She tried to say some of the things in Potawatomi, which she wanted desperately to master. Perhaps I could help her, I thought.

"We have been at Ft. Wayne but have moved the mission here."

"Your home is full of plenty and ease."

"Not at all. Perhaps to you—" she was an instinctively kind

woman and did not wish to wound me. "Ah well, it is comfortable," she finished. I nodded.

"But my way has been hard. I shall tell you about it; perhaps you may be interested to hear of it." Anything she said I would have been interested in. She had on a simple lawn dress, but at the sleeves was delicate, looped material that looked like a spider's web. She was so very beautiful! And, truth to tell, although my mother said I was beautiful, I was plump as a young bear.

"We do not live off the hunt as you do. Our corn and meal had to be hauled one hundred miles to Ft. Wayne in wagons, and most of the way through a wilderness.

"Corn was a dollar and a half a bushel. That might not mean anything to you, but my dear it meant that we ran out of food in the middle of the winter. And I had no one to help with the children. We had come to bear Christ's cross to the pagan peoples, but our own crosses became too heavy.

"I had thirty Indian children in my family, in my own home and a cabin next door. They were suffering from cold and illness and I must cook all their food, see to their sickness. Soon we had nothing to eat, no help, and no money to get necessities of life."

I looked at Chief Quash Quay warily. I feared he might be getting tired saying all these things. Although it did take a while, I did not want him to stop translating. I had never heard anything half so interesting.

"I broke down before my load. My husband, Reverend McCoy, had to leave us in that wilderness to go to Ohio to beg of strangers what we needed. I was almost too worn to pray as he went, but somehow I found the strength to ask the Lord who aids the weary for help. And He did aid us. In Ohio Reverend McCoy found those willing to support the poor Baptists in the woods and we were saved."

I did not ask her what kind of Manitto this Lord Who Aids was. I thought I would find out tomorrow, when I started my lessons in religion. Potawatomi boys went to the Meda house when they were eleven and stayed several months. Now I was going to the white man's Meda house to stay and we would see what it brought.

Quash Quay bade goodbye to me, saying he would be on the

trail at dawn and would not see me again for a year. I nodded without showing in my face the emotion my heart felt.

And so, after rising at six, getting my skin scrubbed with lye soap till I bit my lip, after eating porridge (so they said the thin mush was), I started learning to be a Christian.

Odd we Potawatomi did not yet know the story of the Nazarene, but it is the truth that we did not. We were poor weak villages far from the posts and missionaries. Some children who came to the mission knew much, some had the story mixed with Manaboozhoo's and Michaboo's, some like me had never heard a bit. And so Mrs. McCoy always started fire from tinder, as we say, or from the beginning.

There was, Mrs. McCoy told us, a man named Jesus who lived in a place where there was no snow. It was across the sea lake. People did not live by hunting bear, deer or mink fur but tended wool-bearing animals. These woolly sheep sang, or so I thought she said, when He was born.

His mother did not know a man, and the Manittos wrought a wonder with her. This Jesus, so I got it through Mrs. McCoy's bad Potawatomi, was a wise one, *Manitto Wabo* as I was supposed to be, but much better at interpreting the spirits.

When this Jesus was a child, he sat in the war council and told stories that even the Wise Ones could not understand. He went on a long moon-in-the wild—forty days, forty nights. A bad Manitto called Devel came and tried to throw him down the hill, but they wrestled and I guess Jesus won.

People came from all about to hear him talk, and he gave all food to eat from one small cooking pot; his magic was great and of the Master of Life.

He was a great shaman and healed all without sucking, torch-throwing, or incantations. But wonder of all, his power came through love. He did not need to scare people. No one was afraid of him, except the chiefs and fellow shamans who did not wish to share power.

Finally the other chiefs ambushed him. A friend, trying to scalp them from what I got, cut off one member of the war party's ear and this Jesus put it back on. Magic of magic, he did it all!

But most of all, according to Mrs. McCoy, after he was killed he came to earth again and said we all could live too. She described the white hunting grounds Jesus would lead people into and they did sound good. But I did not like the part about rising from the tomb. Doing that, I thought, this Jesus sounded like a ghost and I was afraid of him.

"Take Him into your life," Mrs. McCoy said, and showed me a picture of Him, with blood dropping from brambles on his forehead and a strange spirit light all around him. "He will be with you always."

"No more, show me no more," I said, astonishing everybody. But I did not want a ghost with a bloody forehead following me around in my life.

I refused to listen any more to such talk, having had enough of it with the shaman. But I did say I would sweep the house and do the dishes and all the work Mrs. McCoy did, if only they wouldn't make me take religious classes.

I heard the minister and his wife conferring before the fireplace of the main home, with other Potawatomi all about. At last Mrs. McCoy came to me.

"I regret you cannot take Christ into your heart, Dawn, but you are a good girl and—I need the help." So I was to stay, but remain as "pagan" as ever. And I did stay, through all the embroidery lessons, the basket-and-biscuit-making sessions and the learning of the alphabet. And through it all I developed a very good knowledge of English and a true love for Mrs. McCoy and the children.

I stayed two years, going to my home village only twice, and I learned the English language well enough to become interpreter when Reverend McCoy went to the villages and they all spoke rapidly. He never did get to speak the Potawatomi tongue well.

As for Mrs. McCoy, she got so she clasped me to her heart and could not have me from her. It was not just the work; I was a friend, as I had been to my poor Sweet Berries. I say poor because I think of my lost sister as I last saw her on a trip with Reverend McCoy to the Twin Lakes villages. Hollow, emaciated, her beauty gone, she had been cast out by her husband. Soon she died, of the shaman's curse or her own fear of it. I do not know which and it does not matter; her life was wasted either way.

Mrs. McCoy was to have another child late in the summer the first year I was there. She had been told not to bear again, but what is that to the white women? Their husbands follow them about, make mooning faces, pine around until there is guilt. Or the women themselves are bad as bitches in heat although they know they must abstain from loving in bed. Tribal women and men are not so; they have the strength to stay apart if they must.

And white women do not know the power of herbs. So, sad to say, they must bear and die and many, many do out here.

All at the mission said Mrs. McCoy must be taken care of in a good home with no cares, flat on her back. For this she must go to Vincennes, to a sister who had moved there and lived in a fine new home. Nothing would do but that I, her little Dawn, must go too. Why not? I thought. It would keep my hands out of the dishwater and my knees off the rough puncheon boards I scrubbed.

"How shall I go?" Mrs. McCoy asked her husband as they stooped over a map of this state of Indiana.

"It is hard to know," Reverend McCoy said. "The roads do not go from here to there. You could go on horseback to Indianapolis and from there—." He stopped. A woman going over rough roads in her sixth month of pregnancy was in danger.

"No. Not by horseback. What if I should go by river? Down the Wabash," she said.

"Ah, no, my love," he said, taking her hands. (It made me sick. As if he had not gotten her into this web of trouble himself!) "It is over three hundred miles, through a wilderness, with only Indians—"

"I shall have Dawn along," she said, smiling a little.

"Let it be so," I thought. It would be good I was there. Unless of course, we ran into Kickapoo, who would as soon drown us as not.

And so with the three younger McCoy children, Mrs. McCoy and I entered an open canoe. Even the Indian people about us were in tears and Reverend McCoy was on his knees, beseeching God to protect us. Or perhaps it was to help him find someone to cook and clean for the forty-seven youths he had to take care of while his wife was away.

Since it was his lust that got us into the trouble of this trip, I wish he had been there to know the torment of the mosquitoes that first and second night. The season of hot weather had set in by the river and Mrs. McCoy and I had to be up all night seeing to the fire and driving away the wicked bugs. All the pennyroyal in the world cannot keep mosquitoes away in the midsummer month after Wabash rains. They are as a cloud before thunder comes. Nine days we were on the river, and nine days it rained. Our clothing rotted and mildewed, our corn meal was spoiled, the children grew ill.

And yet we did arrive and find Mrs. McCoy's sister. Staying in the fine house, Mrs. McCoy grew strong again, and we all dried out. In good time the babe came, with a physician standing by, and all was well. And I, who had the gift of languages, learned some French.

We returned by land on horseback. After that trying trip was over, we came into the settlement and presented Reverend McCoy with his new little daughter.

After that, I stayed with them some months, teaching the youngest Indian children to read and write as I had learned. And I was happy enough, I guess, there, until one day I opened the door and there stood Paukooshuck.

I went outside to talk to him. We walked and talked a long while.

"I have known you were here this long time and have not come to see you. Until now," he said. I looked at him walking beside me, wearing Potawatomi leggings and a trader's cotton shirt, with a knife around his neck on a leather thong. He was a strong man now.

"Why do you wish to talk to me?" I asked him. "Do not your wives have voices that they can laugh at your tricks, praise your hunting lies?"

"What do you know of my wives?" he demanded.

"That you have two, in spite of what this visiting minister McCoy and now the priest who sometimes visits among the Potawatomi tells you."

"Pah," he spat tobacco juice. I wondered if he had picked up other bad habits from the white man, like everybody else. "The priest from Vincennes wishes to send his black frocks among us to turn us from the 'savage, heathen ways.' "

He wished to change the subject away from the co-wife situation. I did not say anything and let him go on.

"The priest at St. Joseph's told some of the tribe when Quash

Quay died, we should bury him lying down, and they did that. But his children came back in the night and sat him up and put the offerings and the wolf fence about him.''

"I have heard." My mother had been over to see me in the Bear Moon.

"I am surprised you have heard, since your ears have the white man's ear bobs in them." Paukooshuck's voice was grating and bitter, and it stung me, as nettle plants do when their leaves brush against the skin.

"They try to get the young men to throw away the medicine bags," he said.

"Who is this 'they'?"

"The priests at St. Joseph's."

"I see."

"I am surprised you do see, since your eyes do not seem to know what is going on in your own home camp. And in that of my relatives, on the same lake."

"Let your eyes be mine and tell me what that is."

"Sad *alanyas* sitting about drinking whisky and playing moccasin and waiting for annuities. And when the government money comes they drink until they pull knives and stab them, deep, sometimes into their own wives. And in their stupor they wander about in the dark in the bushes and do abominations. Uncles lie with nieces, sons with mothers—"

"Stop! You have said enough." I knew it all. My mother had told me of the pitiful, sad times now in the camps. Except for Menominee's camp, where such things were not allowed. He sometimes went to talk to the priests, and listened to them, too.

Paukooshuck was silent for a long time. We had climbed a hill which some said was a burial place for the Old Ones who walked long ago in these parts. Now we sat down in soft grass at its top. When Pauk spoke again, it was the old, teasing Paukooshuck. He took my hair and made the braids of childhood for me, then pulled them out. I laughed and tried to pull from his grasp, and he wrestled me down and it was the same as when I was ten. Except it was not the same.

And when we came down the hill, my face glowed with heat like the oak coals in a late fire, when summer moon hangs low. I was filled with joy, greater than anything I had ever known.

"It was I who set the shaman on you that summer in camp," I teased, and started to run from him. He chased me all the rest of the way home, pinching my legs when he caught me.

Pauk came that night and lay by my side in the little cabin where I had been staying by myself of late. And Reverend McCoy came in early the next morning and said, "If you will act so with this very young girl, you must be married in the church. You are committing sin," and called Paukooshuck bigamist and ravisher of young womanhood.

And I laughed and laughed to think that Pauk, with his honest heart and joyous, teasing ways could be thought to sin, while this man, who had got his wife big with child again, was not.

Paukooshuck left, promising to come for me, and Mrs. McCoy stewed and fretted about me and that afternoon her time came upon her. In my mind I believed she would deliver and then she would die, her blood gushing about her in a pool they could not stanch and her face a white, pinched stone. I did not wish to see that, so I gathered my few things and slipped away before I could hear bad things.

I wept and mourned for friendship gone again. And I tell you that I left that place and went to follow the tracks of my lover, but before I found him, I went back to my home camp, where the sticks I set had long since scattered.

"I love Paukooshuck, son of Aubenaubee," I said to my mother, Swiftly Running Feet.

"You are only fourteen. You wish to join yourself to a japester who has two wives?" she said to me, looking scornful. "Why?"

"Because he has joy in his heart, and I yearn for it like a child for honey. The Manittos were supposed to bring me gifts, and all they have brought is sadness. As for being only fourteen, I have lived as much a lifetime of sad and odd events as many women of thrity. I am sick of it, and I will marry Paukooshuck and maybe his joy will rub on me as mushroom dust does when one walks the forest path."

So I became his wife and learned to live as one of three and I will tell you that story when I have rested more.

# Chapter Eleven

## The Account of Thomas Jefferson Brooks
### (Continued)

Hindostan Falls continued to grow, as did other Northwestern boom towns. Cincinnati, the "Queen City of the Northwest," as it called itself, had gone from eleven families in 1789 to 11,000 by the end of the 1820's. Hindostan Falls could not equal that, of course. With a population of about 1500 it had not yet grown to the size of the large Ohio River towns, but we had hopes. After all, Indianapolis had only a hundred people in the early 1820's. For a few short years Hindostan Falls was the largest city in Indiana. Certainly large enough to build the Brooks fortunes.

The Agricola Mill and Farm Importing Company that I bought when the Sholts enterprise went bankrupt prospered. Agricola Mills almost immediately replaced all the old handgrinders, horse mills, and tub grinders that had sat in the stump-filled pioneer outlots. The mill's water-powered services drew customers for everything from power sawing of lumber to blacksmithing from all across south central Indiana.

Lewis's Brooks Buffalo Trace Stagecoach Line grew like a bumptious baby and jolted people all the way from the Ohio River to Vincennes, shortening to two days a journey that thirty years ago took two months for a family.

Successful business operation often means consolidation. In plain terms, close down whatever isn't profitable. We had shut down the Vincennes operation when Daniel's management ability proved inadequate to the task of running it. Lewis and I, with stronger family pride than good sense, I think, transferred him over to the Paoli outfitting store and old Indian trading post to see what he could do there.

There were still many settlers coming across the Trace in the 1820's, and, as we had envisioned in the beginning, we "fed'ed 'em, bed'ed 'em and sledded 'em"—if snow was on the Trace and that was the only way to get through. And of course we took their money.

Or, to be more accurate, Lewis and I did. Daniel finally asked us to help close down the Paoli operation too in 1827, as it was "unimaginative and dreary work" for him. He came over to Hindostan (evidently a less dreary spot) to help me run the Hindostan Ordinary we had just remodelled. Say that I am soft, and you will be right. Blood is thicker than water, you know, and also, I have to admit, more thick-headed. I asked Brookie to be more practical, and he was trying, but his head was usually crammed full of the dreams that Hindostan was good at generating. Worse than that, he had money from selling his original whetstone interests in Orange county. Money and fuddle-headedness are not a good combination. Still, I had to let him go on as he wished.

It was a sign of the times that by the mid-twenties our Indian early warning system was gone. The only Indians left were the few poor old Quaker Delaware over by Susan Poore's family's house.

Susan Poore. There she was, teaching school up Hindostan's back street, drilling on the Roosevelt spelling method and on the round, easy hand script of the times, pounding in to unwilling young skulls the continents of the world and the states of the Union. Wearing out her youth stopping big boys at recess from cutting the grapevine swings almost in half so fat girls would fall on them when they swung. This she did so she could send home three dollars a week to her mother and the children. And she had been doing it faithfully for almost ten years.

Why do I tell you about her? Because I loved her, old maid that she now was at twenty-six. She had never, I suppose been beautiful; her hair was thin and mouse-colored and her nose a trifle large, although she had lovely, wide green eyes.

No, what captivated me, at least, about Susan Poore was the mystery which surrounded her. What drove her so, to stay about that small school cabin, polishing desks and washing slates, each night visiting families of poor rivermen and prosperous farmers alike, going to see the mayor and justices of the town to be sure poor relief was done right.

If anyone asked her why she stayed and worked so for the town, she simply said, "This is my home. I want to make it something." I suppose the zealous enthusiasms and steep declines of life in a boom town, the bursting bubbles of energy that sometimes popped in your face but were beautiful to behold for a while, the restlessness of the town itself, suited her temperament. In that she may have been like me.

But how did she, a woman, stand all the ups and downs of that brutal, bursting frontier town? I wondered, but I didn't know. There seemed to be within the woman some sort of banked fire, some source of energy I could not quite grasp. She was like a steam engine whose power we can see in its effects and motion, but whose source of strength lies smoldering out of sight.

Oddly, she bore me some sort of ill will. I would have said she hated me, if hate was in her. I did see her frequently at the store. One day in the late winter of 1828 she came into the store as I sat amidst the pickle barrels, at my cherry desk. I was "at the accounts." My suit, as usual, was neatly brushed, my shoes carefully cleaned of the muck of the White River bottom (I always hoped she would notice).

But she looked at me as if I were a piece of frozen mud. "It has come to my ears, sir," Susan Poore began, "that you have been calling in accounts."

I looked up at her. Her skin was clear and fair, those beautiful, serenely sharp eyes fixed on me.

"I have been doing so," I admitted, wondering why I felt guilty. I had told myself, long ago in Massachusetts as a stock boy, that I would not allow debt to mount up. "I have been asking that ledger debt be justly paid."

"You have badgered the family of Thomas Slaymaker. He is one of our Methodist congregation." Something in her look made me think I was one of the third level students caught whistling gently while teacher's back was turned. That made me angry.

"These frontier farmers overextend themselves. They do not provide for hard times. Like Aesop's grasshopper they sit before their squalid fireplaces (which catch fire three times a day because they are ill-built) and do not worry if the grocer must pay their accounts from his own money."

"Thomas Slaymaker is a good man, sir. He is starting over here, after some misfortunes in Virginia. That is the purpose of our town, to let people build afresh."

"At whose expense? Not mine, I tell you. Oh, I well know Tom Slaymaker's type. I am surprised, Miss, that you of refined New England stock do not blanch at being in his company."

"How can I do so, sir, when he is honest and tries to provide for his family? It's—well, it's ill fortune that has doomed most of them to a sad lot. He cannot help it that the land he bought here is poor and the market glutted with farm produce. Since the state bank at Vincennes failed and so many with it—"

Yes, it had failed, and many poor souls with it. But I had gotten out and managed to make money in the process. McClure, too. But with McClure, I was loaning myself, holding notes with a decent rate of interest. These were part of what I was calling in. "I trust Thomas Slaymaker can help it that he spits incessantly on his own floor. And that he grabs at his victuals like an orangutan," I insisted.

"Half of the Northwest eats like that, sir, and you know it. We are not now in Boston. One's table habits, or what one *wears* do not define the quality of gentleman."

I flinched, but said nothing. For the next moment a silence hung between Susan Poore and me. Perhaps the words "New England" suggested the great gulf that stood between us here in Indiana and the folk of Boston. Here men cleaned their teeth with pocket knives and ate muskrats. Perhaps we were quiet because the notion of regional kinship, which should have bound Susan and me among all these frontiersmen in the wilderness, seemed instead to encourage repugnance. We should have been friends; we were somehow enemies.

"These lazy settlers earn the agues and squalor they have. Let them learn enterprise like the rest of us," I stoutly maintained. "Let Thomas Slaymaker begin to pay his bill."

"You and I have a differing view of Hindostan Falls. I see it as a chance for new life, you as a boundless marketplace to make you money. It does not seem you have much human feeling for man or woman," Susan Poore said coldly. Her words seemed to hang in the air.

I answered her gaze steadily. "Do I not regard any woman?"

Refusing to even acknowledge my glance, she turned away, and, picking up her packages, strode from the store. I was left with the loneliness I often felt lately. It was getting at me. In a way, Susan was right. I did not feel much human feeling *from* man or woman. Perhaps it explained the odd indulgence I granted Daniel, in spite of my better business sense. He was the Brookie of my youth, one of the few handles with which I could reach into my childhood, and he cared for me in his own way. Lately lots of things had been causing an odd aching in me for the New England I stoutly maintained I still hated.

Mother and Father had not quite forgiven me and my brothers for going west. We did not write often; I did not intend to go back for a visit. I told myself New England meant the memories of stilted religion and Emily, whom I now knew I would never see again. Emily had been declared dead after a search by an investigator I had hired from Pittsburgh located no trace whatsoever of her.

Well, I could not, I told myself, as I returned to my cherry desk, waste time thinking about these namby-pamby concerns, either in my past, or now, this Susan Poore.

Other things claimed my attention. First were my schemes to try to stimulate the local economy, which had become as sluggish as the White River in September. It was obvious that land speculation had slowed. The Brooks Brothers, of course had already feathered their bird nests. Daniel and I now lived in Sholts' solid frame house two stories tall back from the main street in Hindostan. Our informal banking business was prospering. McClure and I loaned—did we loan! We were talking of getting a charter, issuing our own notes, complete with a picture of an eagle standing on a ball of gold, the Masonic eye and the Flag of Freedom.

Actually, I had not often seen McClure lately. He was busy with anti-Jackson politics in Indianapolis. McClure was in the process of distinguishing himself far beyond southern Indiana. He was the general secretary to the governor of the State, James Brown Ray.

McClure's wife and family seldom visited their cabin in the

village, either. Auraleigh was often with her own people, the Markles, who now lived in the great experiment in communal living (and home of misfits, milksops and mealymouths), New Harmony, Indiana.

Judge Markle, as I said earlier, had sold his interest in Hindostan to me. Pursuing his interest in liberal politics and indulging his wife and daughter's interests, he moved to the "great ideal" town Robert Owen now operated over on the Wabash. There he put out his attorney-at-law shingle.

I suppose he had been egged on by Mr. Robert Owen himself. This cloud cuckoo-land philosopher was Auraleigh's idol. He visited the McClures when he was thinking of buying New Harmony from the Rappites for a "social experiment in communal living."

When Father Rapp and his religious following left the Wabash valley to await the Second Coming elsewhere, Owen bought his lands and moved to America. Judge Markle, Henrietta, and whichever of their hare-brained lot of children weren't married, joined him in New Harmony, for ownership of land in common, lectures on philosophy, and afternoon hay-pitching sessions. Pig bath, I said and still do say.

But it wasn't only his wife's parents James McClure had to see to—there were the numerous McClures back in Knox County. Prodigious as rabbits and yappy and demanding as a pack of hounds, they seemed to depend on him to solve their squabbles and quandries. So we saw little of him.

Still, as in the old days, McClure and I cooperated in the banking and numerous enterprises. One of them, an ingenious brokering scheme, was coming to fruition in the spring of 1828. Of that I shall say more later.

I have little room to be talking of McClure and his yapping, irritating relatives.

Brookie wasn't the only one of my own relatives who was causing me chagrin. Lewis had married an heiress in the new town of New Albany, where he had his stagecoach line. About this time, restless as a sandflea, he grew tired of the wagoning of human souls and handed over the management of the stage line to his wife Agnes's brother, opining that there was no real money in stagecoaching.

Lewis's eye was on gold, nothing more nor less, though he

would take credit or promissory notes. "Bent on making half a million," he said "and know just how to do it."

He took up an old connection to ease his way to fortune. John Tipton was an Indian trading, trapping connection of Lewis's from his first days out here. And Tipton had his paw in the honey jar in northern Indiana in the late 1820's. Some men make their money in merchandising, some in banking or law; in those days in the Northwest, there was a wild breed of buck that made money, big money, out of Indians.

At every step of the poor tribesman's day Tipton and the Indian traders stood to make money. An Indian, under the new treaties, received an annuity; Tipton helped distribute it for the government and took a juicy fee for his part. A brave now had money; very well, Tipton had friends with stores, where the Indian could buy trinkets and necessities, as much as he wanted, paid with credit or against future annuities. Was the store bill too large and the Indian distressed? Do not worry, my friend, Tipton will help you sell any furs you can locate from the diminishing supply. You need a letter written to the government? Property bought, sold or pawned? Your supply of goods re-sold? Tipton enterprises can serve you.

And by 1826, though he still officially resided at New Albany, Lewis had become Tipton's agent in the biggest "make money off the Indians" scheme of all. During this period the government, and all its people in the great state of Indiana had decided that the savages (Miami, Delaware, Kickapoo, Potawatomi) were all an abomination in the sight of God and man. They particularly were an abomination to Progress—in the form of the scheme for a great Indiana canal to link, in effect, the Mississippi River with the Great Lakes.

They would have to give up the rest of their lands and leave Indiana. There needed to be treaties, many of them, and fast, so we could build our canals and roads.

Lewis was right when he saw there was money here. Was not Governor DeWitt Clinton getting rich beyond the dreams of Midas himself with the Erie Canal? And it was all Tipton's, and his cohorts', for the taking. If the Indians, through whose land the Michigan road and new canals had to go, could somehow be induced, seduced, traduced into giving the land up, there were thousands of acres to gobble up and sell again if you could get there first.

But that wasn't all. The treaty process itself could drop thousands of dollars in the coffers of Tipton and Company. The government paid for land in cash to be traded for pots and pans and the like, and Tipton could contract for the pots and pans, broker them, and sell them finally to the Indians for exorbitant rates, with the help of his trader friends. It was a true chain of money-making opportunities. The only trouble was, on the other end of the chain, hanging by the neck like a dog being dragged along, was the Indian of the woodlands.

Well, what if we did get what we wished for, the Indians out of the way once they gave up their land for the canals and roads that progress demanded? Lewis and Tipton had ideas about that, too.

We could, well, we could—transport them! That's it! Send them west, in great herds. As cattlemen drive thousands of steers, as the English transported criminals by the thousands, so the American government could remove Indians, for their own good of course, to the lands nobody cared for in the far West. Fair and square, neat as a pin, quick as a wink, the redskins would be paid off in total and herded west.

Who would do the herding? Well, John Tipton and my brother were bursting to try this, too, if it came to that. There were Federal "removal" contracts (hateful word, suggesting the disposing of rubbish). Final settlements would someday have to be negotiated. Why shouldn't Tipton and the other traders help negotiate the greatest payoffs possible to the poor, beleaguered savages as they took them to the West? The Indians owed the traders giant, inflated bills and the government payoff money would just about settle the chits. If we were careful and made sure it did.

All of this was only in the talking stages; the Indians still had the land, but the inevitable was the inevitable. So the talk ran as Lewis took off to be Tipton's agent and right-hand accomplice.

And, to give the Devil his due, the Indians had few other white men even willing to deal with them. They took whatever they could get in those days.

The long and short of it was that there were several Indian treaties 1826-28. Lewis was often up with Tipton in Potawatomi and Miami country trying to stir the commercial and political pots, and I could not count on him for help in managing the mercantile and milling operations. I had my hands full those days, running around getting grinding buhrs sharpened, helping choose delicate foods and wines for the inn, ordering shoe leather and spices.

I certainly wasn't able to count on Daniel for any help. I have said my older brother Daniel was present in Hindostan Falls supposedly managing the Hindostan Ordinary, but there was something on his mind beyond that. Daniel, our Brookie, perhaps to prove that after all he could do something decent, decided to take the profits he had made in our ventures and his own and invest the money in a grandiose scheme for the "Louisville of Indiana"—an entertainment pavilion.

Perhaps it was the influence of the Prince Regent's pavilion at Brighton, complete with Arabian minarets and Hindoo doors, perhaps it was a theatre he saw in Cincinnati, whatever it was, Brookie was building it in Hindostan Falls—three stories tall, made of virgin timber and painted pink, with Venetian windows and turrets and a drawbridge right in the middle of Walnut Street near the river.

It was about to be completed and Brookie was pouring over newspaper ads for entertainment late in that winter of 1828. "Picture it, Thomas. I have hired a French artist who lives in Cincinnati. He is painting a scene of Mars, recumbant on a couch, being fed grapes and bread by Venus. Above, floating on a coral cloud, will be the muses playing their instruments."

"This will go all over the walls?" I asked, trying to be sincerely interested.

"The ceiling will be plastered and show great dramatic scenes, Lady Macbeth washing her hands, Brutus stabbing Caesar—"

"All of that is so gory, the ladies and gentlemen will be repulsed."

"Perfect for this frontier. But I'll have patriotic scenes too, Valley Forge, Lexington and Concord—"

"Lexington, you say?"

"Of a certainty. With Father, as a twelve-year-old watching in the crowd. I'll have to borrow your silhouettes so we can get the face right. All must be authentic."

"Well, of course. When are you opening?"

"March 15."

"Good enough." That was the date I had set for my great free market feat, one destined to establish Hindostan's name above all the rest in the Midwest. Louisville, your name is mud, as well as your streets, I told myself. Lexington, your reputation is in danger. Cincinnati—well, maybe not Cincinnati.

What was I doing? Simply this. Every winter there was a long period when the great market of New Orleans was crying, begging to buy food products, and there was neither brokered grain nor meat in the Northwest to ship nor water enough in the rivers to float it.

In winter those farmers in Ohio, Indiana and Illinois, sometimes loaded with produce, sold nothing and could not buy; people in New Orleans starved and waited.

Desire was especially high in the spring, and the first flatboats in with corn, ham, and wheat flour were greeted like the Second Coming—with much higher prices than later loads would bring.

I was going to purvey great desires for merchandise in the South into fame and fortune for Hindostan Falls. I had been watching the river, as they used to watch the Nile in ancient Egypt, and calculating the snowfall and other factors, I thought I could predict that it would rise about the 15th of March this year, a couple of weeks earlier than most years. We would be ready with a huge fleet of flatboats loaded with foodstuffs, and we would be the first into New Orleans.

How to get enough goods to make a killing? Secretly I had begun to assemble cargos. I bought and stored great supplies of ham and grain and put them in stone cellars which had been cut into the hillside at the time of the building of the mill. It was cool there. As the winter went on and times grew harder, I began to take settlement of the bills in haunches of venison, tubs of salt, sacks of meal. The larders were bulging with tons of stuff.

But of course you are saying to yourself that we would need boats to float the victuals and men to man 'em. I had that figured out too and was constantly calculating with my pencil. But I was not quite ready to reveal my plan; there were other speculators about Hindostan and its environs, to say nothing of Dugger Enterprises at the mouth of White River. Couldn't let the kitten out of the flour sack yet. Might have my idea stolen clean away.

It did have to do with calling in the store's debts. That I can say, and I should tell you that they were large by this time; I had over one hundred families in deep debt to Agricola Mills and Brooks Mercantile, which was now the largest store in Indiana. There were also the lending notes from my unchartered banking operations. And these debts would not, as a matter of my ideals, go uncollected. After all, I was a man of principle. Business principle.

Susan Poore burst in the door one day in 1828, when my predicted February snows were just beginning to thaw. "Sir, I hear you have demanded that Tom Slaymaker become your personal slave." I did not look up at her; I was arranging bolts of red and blue wool in the shelves.

She stormed on, "You have told him and fifty other poor debtors in the village and neighboring area, that they are to give you all their daylight hours for the next three weeks to build a huge fleet of flatboats. And beyond that to leave their wives and families at the very time of planting to go with you as crew for some sort of speculative folderol of an idea—"

"It is for the good of the town," I said, straightening the ends of the cloth on the bolts.

"Good of the town? How could you know what that is? I keep telling you this is an experiment in new life out here. Why do you think I've put so much of my heart into it? So many of us are trying to make it a decent place where people, even poor ones can start anew, raise Christian families, find meaning in their lives, and make an honest living, and then you attach their souls to your account books so they can never get ahead—"

The fire in her eyes was beautiful, irresistible. I turned from the shelves, walked to her quickly, and grasped her hands in mine firmly. Surprised, she struggled to free herself. "Why do you despise me so?" I asked. I was standing not a foot from her; no one else was in the store.

A moment passed; she emitted a long, almost inaudible breath. "Because you destroyed a man I cared about for your own gain and profit."

"Sholts," I said, finally understanding.

"Frederick Sholts, my second father. He had just come to Christ and you ruined him. The very day of his conversion. He fled and died in disgrace in Memphis and his wife, who was dearer to me than my own family, gave up to the ague the next spring.'' She did not try to conceal the anguish in her voice.

''And what of the innocent people Sholts ruined? The land he sold fraudulently? The promises he made and did not fulfil? The legislature bought? He was a sham, I tell you.''

''But he had repented whatever he did that was wrong. He had come to Christ.'' Her face was flushed, her green eyes flashing like the northern lights. I wanted to pull her to me, hold her in my arms. But instead I said what I had to.

''And if he was shamming that too? If he repented to avoid the revenge of the town and the law? So lawsuits might be withdrawn? No, Miss Poore. I think he went into your woodland prayer glen, came forward, fell on his knees and lied.''

Her hand went to her mouth in disbelief. She had never thought of the possibility. ''You—'' she said and could not finish it.

''Yes, I. Well I may be an apostate but I have never lied to God. If, indeed there is one, which the doings of Frederick Sholts have made me doubt.''

She raised her hand and delivered a stinging slap to my face. I pulled her to me and, as she struggled, put my lips on hers, feeling the warmth of her face. Not letting her go for a moment, I reached one of my hands in back of her, moved it over her hair and loosened the clasp on it. I had been wanting to do this for such a long time. As I continued kissing her deeply, just for an instant she stopped struggling. Then she broke free. Flushed and outraged, without meeting my eye, she left the store. I sank heavily into a chair, dismayed at the scene with the woman I now knew I loved beyond all hope.


February days passed quickly that winter of 1828. My brother Brookie's pavilion, now grandly called the Western Emporium of Culture, was taking shape. He had forsaken his usual lethargy to rush it to completion in time for the opening, already announced in papers all over southern Indiana. Just recently I had been coming to see him in the lobby of the theatre to check progress.

''We still have over four more weeks until March 15,'' he

would shout over the noise of clapboards being nailed in final place up on the roof. "The plasterers should be here next week and then the Cincinnati artists will follow them. They won't wait until the plaster is dry to put up the scenes of Terpsichore and Calliope."

"Who?"

"The muses, of course." He curled his lip at me a bit contemptuously. I had been taught well enough at the Lincoln school for all that matter, but it had always been Brookie who was the student. He had devoured novels and even Father's dog-eared library of the classics in the parsonage when he was in his Lord Byron phase.

"Why do they work in wet plaster?" I asked, suddenly struck with the oddity of what my brother had said.

"I am having them do Florentine fresco. Like Leonardo da Vinci or Fra Angelico."

"Who?" I asked, really watching the flatboats being built by my "slave laborers" down by the river. They were just starting the frames; it had taken over a week to whipsaw the wood, even with the new steam saw at the mill.

"Never mind. I just hope the plasterers arrive in time."

By the last week in February the flatboats were done, but I scanned the heavens anxiously. By now the rains should have started, if they were going to speed that heavy snow melt in northern Indiana and feed the river, as I had figured. Brookie scanned the Trace—nary a sign of the Cincinnati plasterers. Finally he got on his horse and rode to get them, returning with less than two weeks to go.

"I had to prod them, beg them, bribe them to finish up the new Masonic Hall and come with me. But while I was there I checked out my attractions for the opening festivities."

"Which are?" I wondered.

"A fiddle orchestra, a man with a two-headed pig, and a Shakespearean emoter who can play all the parts in the big scene from *The Tempest*."

Suddenly my old friend Doc Drake flashed into my mind, but I put aside the pang the recollection brought.

"That's Friday night. Everybody in two counties is coming in for the opening. It's better, they say than a Shaker meeting or a

Baptist revival. The Hindostan Ordinary is booked up, and every private house is taking people in, you know."

I did know that, of course. The Ordinary was my own personal favorite of all the interests I owned. I often slipped away from the mill, leaving it to competent managers and millhands, and sat in a Windsor chair in the inn's fancy new parlor and drank tea. Sometimes, when Brookie left the desk near the door, I checked through his books. "What will you do as a follow-up act Saturday?" I asked.

He was watching the plasterers put up their scaffolding. "Umm, we're staging 'The Landing of Lafayette at Cincinnati.' Auraleigh Markle McClure is in town and has agreed to play 'Freedom.' I'll be playing 'Industry' myself."

"How appropriate," I murmured, and left. I had enough to worry about if the rains didn't come up north, the river didn't rise and I was left with 4,000 rotting hams.

On March 10th the rains began. They did not drift down gently and melt northern snows; they came in sluices and after a day showed no signs of abating. I needed to be quick. "Prepare to leave within five days," I said to my debtors. "We will load the boats Friday, leave Saturday." It would take that long for White River to get to crest.

Brookie picked his way along the muddy streets the next day, cursing. "The plasterers have just finished. They say the plaster isn't drying as well as it should have," he muttered to me as I headed towards his culture palace. "And this rain may hold up the visitors coming in on the Trace."

Inside the palace a Frenchman with a goatee and a painting pallet was climbing the scaffolding. "Zees is impossible," he said. "For fresco zee plaster must be just right. It needs to dessicate at least two days and zees fools have dallied and just finished it. Ah, well, I shall try."

Brookie's prophecy that the wet weather might hold back the crowds was not well-founded. The sun came out as the river rose almost to crest and a wind came up. By Thursday night the roads had dried and people began to pour in to Hindostan Falls.

I could not, of course, appreciate their presence much. I was busy completing the loading of hams and thousands of bags of flour.

Late Friday, a crowd assembled to see us load the boats. The men, resigned to being made honest debt-payers, were kissing their relatives and shaking hands with their neighbors. They would be leaving at dawn.

Susan Poore came out of the crowd with one last volley for me. "I hear that you have implied the threat of court action to these men should they leave you before this lot is delivered."

I acted as if I were ignoring her. Her self-righteousness was as irritating as wool against bare flesh. "Listen, men," I said. "I am giving you a fair way to retire your just debts. No man wants to be the community's responsibility. When you come back over the Trace from New Orleans, you can look your neighbor in the eye with a clean ledger before you."

Susan looked steadily at me. Why did she so unnerve me when I really believed I was right? "And I want to announce that I am giving you a share in the venture too. The money we realize from the sale of these flatboats. It's yours, men!" I wondered what had made me say that, and when I looked in Susan Poore's direction and saw a slight, surprised smile play across her lips, I knew.

My flatboat crews went home to sleep one more night, the night of the opening. I put on a long-tailed coat I had bought in Cincinnati and a top hat of the latest fashion. The entire town would be there tonight, and the store had sold a lot of feathers and furs to dress up the usual sunbonnets and homespun. I had even heard that McClure's wife was wearing jewels. Who said Hindostan Falls was the end of the world?

We sat in the auditorium. The new frescoes gleamed with classic beauty in the light of the candle chandelier and the stage lights. I could hardly believe my eyes at the assemblage, chattering happily as they picked mud off their shoes. The town's day had come. Outside waited the loaded flatboats, inside was an "elegant entertainment worthy of the theatrical extravaganzas of Paree or London." Or at least the broadsides put up on trees had said.

The fiddle band sawed away on "The Last Rose of Summer." The lights flickered. The curtain on a wire was pulled back by a very pretty young woman with pointy black shoes and a wide smile. Behind that curtain the two-headed pig stood, wearing a big blue bow on one neck and a big yellow bow on the other.

The applause was thundering. Brookie came out, prepared to

make a little speech of welcome. Then, all at once there was an ominous rumble. People quit clapping and were just looking up apprehensively at the ceiling when it happened. Several tons of improperly-aged, sloppy, wet plaster came down from the frescoed ceiling.

People screamed and hid under benches. When it was all over, I saw that only one person was badly hurt and that was the bootmaker, who had a broken leg.

Daniel was beside himself, but all he could think of to do was yell, "All monies will be refunded, all monies will be refunded" as the cream of Southern Indiana society filed out of the ruined theatre, dazed looks on their faces, plaster bits in their hair and teeth.


The next morning my flotilla took off for New Orleans. We floated the crests of White, Wabash, and Mississippi to fame and fortune. We were listed in papers all across the South as being the first flatboat fleet to come into New Orleans in the spring of 1828 and received a bag of gold, so to speak for our trouble. More to the point, I was able to negotiate a brokering agreement with three major New Orleans firms. Under my agreement Hindostan interests could broker grain and meat shipments from southern Indiana for the coming summer on an exclusive basis in exchange for distribution rights for the goods I had brought.

Hindostan Falls! Your next phase of growth is assured!

Thomas Jefferson Brooks! Your lucre is enhanced fourfold! Fortune, you have often trampled me beneath your feet, but now you have put me on your very shoulders!

All these things I told myself as I wandered about the odd little death houses New Orleans people are buried in, in the customary cemetery trip I took in every town I visited. I spat in the eye of the lurking spirits of my Puritan ancestors, or whoever it was that followed me about chortling on these trips. Go away, follow me no more, I am fortune's darling.

So I thought. And as we returned along the Natchez Trace, our group was set upon by a band of brigands, highwaymen who beat us and took most of the men's money and left us by the road.

One man they killed—blew his brains out with a pistol. And as

I limped along that despicable trace I knew I faced the most awful trial of my life. I must meet the eyes of Susan Poore when I had to tell her that her Methodist charge, Tom Slaymaker, had been killed in my mission. And that while the men had lost everything, my money was all safe in the First Bank of New Orleans, covered in full with the letters of credit that the robbers never even recognized in my pack.

# Chapter Twelve

# Deposition of Kezegat Dauja of the Potawatomi
### (Continued)

Being one of three wives is like getting a very fine and perfect sweet cake and then having two good friends insist you divide and eat it with them.

Paukooshuck's father Aubenaubee had had four wives. Aubee was a powerful band chief; one of the strongest in the Northlands here. He commanded who would take what furs along the St. Joseph and Tippecanoe rivers and the lake country around us. There were other chiefs, but he was one of the main ones who signed treaties with the white men. So he could command and "gift" all those wives.

Aubee spent three months with Ripple Woman (Pauk's mother) at the Tippecanoe village. Then he de-camped to the north side of Lake Mocksinkickee to his favorite wife, the sister of Chief Neswaugee. Then he went across the lake to the east side wife. Finally, then, he went to spend some weeks with the wife at the St. Joseph river. Hunting and wife-visiting, Aubee ranged as far as the Michigan border.

I suppose for Pauk, it was son walking in moccasins of father. I knew about Black Wing in the camps at Tippecanoe and Ears Ringing in the Twin Lake camps near to us, when I took Paukooshuck to husband. But I wanted him badly enough to live as one of three. And, of course, we three wives did not live in one lodge.

Had we done so, I knew, as youngest wife I would wait on the older ones, who could accept or reject me as they wished.

Although there was nobody who was a co-wife in my village,

there were others in Twin Lakes camp who had more than one wife. Even the priests who visited the St. Joseph River Potawatomi camps, and whom some of our band consulted, couldn't stop co-marriage among the Potawatomi.

So I was willing to try being a co-wife, even though my mother Swiftly Running Feet railed at me without mercy about it. "You have not married a white man, as I said you should. Foolish Rosy Dawn! These are the people of the future. Destiny has chosen them. But to marry one who sleeps in three tents! Have they taught you nothing at the Christian mission? Ah, but then you are very young."

It was true. No more than fourteen summers. But it was also true that I loved Pauk desperately, with a wildness that made me feel like a caged animal loosed. Perhaps it was because I had been so restrained in my years at the Baptist Mission, rising at 5 o'clock to the trumpet playing, "Oh sun that shines by day/Arise and praise the Lord," sewing each day at 10, and eating jowl and beans (I detest the dish to this day) at 12 noon. I was half a woman.

Pauk as a youth was a man of cocky confidence, humor, and good, strong sport in the bedroll. At least that was a part of him. I found after I really got to know my husband that he was as complicated as a web of weaving.

Darkness came over the sunny woods of his disposition, shutting out the laughter. The gossiping women of our tribe had spoken of it in hushed tones when the shaman (now dead) was in power. I had known it briefly earlier, at the mission, when Pauk had spoken coldly to me for not seeing the changes in my own village. Now he showed me this other side of his face.

When the mood hit him, Pauk sank into this blackness for a week, perhaps two at a time. Usually it had to do with the white man and his slimy, deceitful tricks, but it was sometimes over the slipping of the Potawatomi themselves into the mud of slack ways. They had departed from the purity of Indian law and religion, was Pauk's chant.

He had spent much time just before he came to me at the mission at Twin Lakes visiting the camp of Chief Menominee. This good Potawatomi band chief made his men and women stay free from white man's liquor and say prayers, together on their knees, each day to the Master of Life. Pauk liked that, even though he was confused because Menominee had Jesus and Mary some-where in there too. But what my husband really mourned was that the spirit of our times had moved beyond his control; it hurt his heart.

I recall the first time I saw the Black Mood come after our marriage. We had decided to go with the tribe to the payments of the government's annuity money at Ft. Wayne Indian Agency. The payment was set for Saturday; on Friday band chiefs with followers began to drift into the camp outside the fort and village. We went into the Hot Toddy log tavern near the St. Mary River there at Ft. Wayne. Close to a hundred tribal people from all over the river region crammed into it.

"We have whisky, all you want," said the owner, a mixed-blood French and Indian *métis*, to Aubee and his followers.

"My belly is cold from the road. It cries out for the warmth of the whisky jug," said Aubee, the father of my husband. He patted the belly that was every bit as tough and round as a log drum, and you could almost hear it reverberate.

"He will be drunk again," Pauk whispered, turning to me. He had been jesting with the men in the corner, where some prime otter and mink furs were being shown around, but I noticed the anxiety in his voice.

Aubee drank irregularly, but when he once picked up the jug, he drank for days at a time. It had been so in the Tippecanoe camps where Pauk was born and grew up. When Aubee felt the binge coming on, Pauk told me, he would take himself to the woods, to the next camp. Perhaps he thought he could head off the drinking demon, but it rarely worked.

At the new camp, he would give in to the drinking fit. It took a certain pattern, Pauk told me as we watched his father there in the Hot Toddy tavern. "The first day, he provokes all those around him, like a new brave wishing to fight for his manhood feathers," Pauk said. "The second day he fights. The third day," he said, his voice lowered, "he has killing in his blood. He stabs. If there is a gun, he shoots."

"And he is not the only one." So said Paukooshuck. Ah, so sad, I thought. It is as if the Bat Manitto spirit had decided to eliminate our people, punishing them for unforgivable sins. Instead of destroying them in the flood, as the grandfathers' stories say, he would kill them off by poisoning their insides and brains. Little by little this evil Manitto would torture them, robbing them of respect, honor, even manhood as they drank the Bat poison. Finally they die, lying in filth in the mud, strangling in their own vomit or lanced through the kidneys with a poinard of their own kinsman. As I was sitting in the corner of the Hot Toddy thinking this, all around us Potawatomi and Miami were getting drunk.

"And yet we have not sinned so much as Noah's people in the Christian Bible." I told Pauk the story.

"Have we not sinned, too?" he asked when I had finished. "All is changing." He was muttering, drinking sweet cider. Pauk did not drink strong spirits, ever. "Potawatomi do not live according to the ancient law of the people." I raised my eyebrows. Most Indian people did not talk of ancient law or the Old Ones anymore.

"The white men wish us to have band chiefs who will do their bidding. Our 'chiefs' are weak yes-sayers. In other times the chief man of the *Neshnabec* was the wisest man, the Speaker-chief, who was able to stand against all, if it came to that. This is the type of chief I would have wished to be, should I have been chosen. But I have no way to prove myself.

"In other times," Pauk went on, "I could have had medicine bag and hawk feathers on the war trail. Not now. It is hard, but in these troubled times we must keep our hearts true. A people can only grow and prosper if they are strong in spirit and pure of heart." I looked in even greater wonder. True man was here. I had, really, only thought of him as a clever joker and lover.

He went on, growing more bitter. "In these times a Potawatomi brave, drunk or sober, may have his own aunt, or mother-in-law. In times of our greatness one could not even speak to his mother-in-law!"

I knew it was true. Even the cousin-teasing games, which had as their real purpose the building of reverence for family and strong ties among kin in a clan, were passing away.

Pain grew in Pauk's face and after a while he rose and stalked from the room.

I tell you that what I recall the next day at that annuity time in Ft. Wayne was worse. John Tipton, the government's Indian agent, and his lackey Lewis Brooks, set up tables outside to give out the money. But they also had account books before them on the table, the books of their trader friends. Beside the names of people like Penamo, Nambo, Shawbenum, were columns of numbers and sums for furs brought in, $1—buck, $4—beaver and more.

But on the far right was the column that killed our people—charges at the store: $3—2 yards of calico, $4—five bushels white corn meal; $2—stew pot. Here is how the talk went at that table:

"Nambo, you have charged against the forthcoming annuity," says Mr. Lewis Brooks, his small eyes-of-the-weasel looking off at the grazing horses.

Nambo looks at the list questioningly; Tipton repeats in his rough Potawatomi, "You owe. We need to collect."

Nambo's face contracts in bewilderment and pain. His family is hungry and without blankets; beavers and even buckskins are getting harder to come by, and it has been many moons since the last annuity.

"If you put the X here we will present these accounts against the annuity. We will take what you owe from the funds. Then we will be free to give you what is left."

Nambo looks at Tipton, Tipton smiles a tight smile and points at the X, Nambo takes up the quill and puts an X on the page. Mr. Ewing, the store-keeper and friend of Tipton, has been standing behind the table.

"You have some dollars left in gold, Nambo, I see," says Mr. Ewing. "But should you take the amount in credit at my store, I can give you six quarts of whisky as a special gift. You want to keep your credit good with us, now, don't you?"

Tipton translates, and Nambo throws down the quill in anger with an oath in Potawatomi. The goods in Ewing's store are overpriced, and Nambo wishes to spend his coin in his own way. But Nambo is as the beaver whom the trap has caught, but not killed; his yelps will do him little good. The only other stores around here are owned by other trading friends of Tipton's. Ft. Wayne is in the wilderness; there is no other place to go. Nambo's family needs to eat, soon. There is no choice but to take credit on the stocks the provisioners have brought in for much money, which Ewing and the other trader friends of Tipton have placed on the shelves for much more money. Nambo is of Aubenaubee's St. Joseph village. But Aubee cannot speak to the vulture traders for Nambo, cannot say that all of this year's payment will be used up in a few short weeks with the credit system and the high prices, and Nambo will have to start charging against next year's annuity. No, Chief Aubenaubee has already broken into the case of whisky bottles gifted as the "tribute" Lewis Brooks has for him.

By this time Aubee is walking around slapping people on the shoulder too hard. By dawn he will be sitting on the ground arguing with the ghost of Tecumseh.

Clouds darker than I have ever seen shroud Pauk's face and he goes off by himself for hours. When he returns, he gets our horses and we go off at a run, leaving our band chief to collect for us.

At that first annuity payment after our marriage, Pauk did not speak to me, or anyone for almost two days. But perhaps his reaction to it was better than the others in the tribe.

That night, while bonfires blazed, a man killed his sister right before the eyes of others; and lewd, indescribable things happened in the woods beyond the camps.

When the Black Mood finally departed from Paukooshuck that annuity season, he left to go to the Twin Lakes wife, Ears Ringing, and he stayed for a month, returning to me just about the time I grew desperate with dreams of what was occurring over in that other camp. Did he show his dark side there, too, or did only I bring it out? Did he talk about me, laugh and share our little jokes? At night on the bedrolls, ah, what did he there? But I did not ask about it when he was with me. Somehow I did not ask. Perhaps it was because my mother had told me I would be jealous. I could not help but throw jealousy in his face like dishwater, Swiftly Running Feet said.

I did ask Pauk meekly enough what the others were like, and he said of the Tippecanoe wife that she was too busy and of the Twin Lakes wife, Ears Ringing, that she was not busy enough. Then he laughed to himself, quietly.

He stayed two months, then went on to the Tippecanoe wife, and thus it went till the middle of the summer. By this time he had a girl child with Black Wing at Tippecanoe and a little boy at Twin Lakes. I had not quickened, though we were constantly at bed-roll sport when we were together.

My mother, Swiftly Running Feet, said she had great difficulty in getting with child; I was her only quickening. "Asondaki Alamelonda was often gone, months or years at a time. For us who quicken only with difficulty, it is necessary to have one's husband about all of the time." This pained me more than all she could have said.

And then, one day in that summertime of 1826, I could stand it no longer. I do not know what stick knocked down the tinder pile, I only know that I knew I could not live alone a married woman any longer.

"Goodbye, Mother," I said to Swiftly Running Feet in her small hut on the hill above Lake Mocksinkickee. I told her I was walking to Twin Lakes, where Pauk had just gone. She turned from the journey cake she was frying in a big iron frypan and her eyes had nothing but love in them. She did not say, "I told you to marry a white man," or "We live with our mistakes." She just went to a chest in the back of the lodge and opened it. Soon she put two objects in my hand. One was a crucifix made of silver. I pulled back.

"This is the ghost god," I said.

But she closed my hand around it. "It belonged to your grandmother, M'Takwapiminji, Mulberry Blossom. Her trials were great, but she was a woman of wisdom, band chief's daughter as I am. Having something of hers may bring some of her strength to you. And here is something else."

It was an odd, porous rock that looked more like a deer's brain than anything else. "What on Turtle's Back Island is this?" I demanded.

"A madstone. It was sent by someone to the shaman, but he was afraid of it. I think it will be worth much to you."

I touched her arm and picked up the odd presents. As I went through the door of the shelter, she called after me, "Each of us takes his own trip to the stars. I shall have to watch yours from afar, now."

I arrived at Twin Lakes camp in late afternoon of that summer day. Pauk was coming in from the hunt with a group of friends and two large deer tied to carrying poles. He saw me and came at once, fearing, I suppose some mishap at the other camp.

"No," I said. "I have come to be co-wife. I shall do whatever it takes,'' He looked long and hard at me with the beginnings of a frown tempting the edges of his mouth. Then he broke into laughter. He laughed like a silly loon for fully two minutes. But when he took me by the hand to the lodge, I could read the pleasure in his eyes. He was glad I had come.

He put my things on slab shelves near the rear of the rather large lodge which had been his wife's parents. ''A madstone,'' he said incredulously, pulling it out of the pack.

''Yes. It was the shaman's, though he did not claim it. I do not know what it is.''

''Great magic, it is,'' he replied, fingering the dry surface, that was almost like that of a toadstool. ''They come from the stomachs of deer or bears, the large ones. No one knows why they form in there. Some who live by the ocean say the mussels there form stones in their shells like this, but beautiful. The madstones are ugly, but the Manittos send them as a great help to man.''

''How so?'' I asked.

''You know that if a man is bit by a mad animal, the froth-at-mouth sickness comes?''

I nodded. Two children had died horrible deaths in our camp last winter after being bit by a squirrel.

''When a mad, frothing animal bites, you put the madstone on the wound and the stone will stick. It sucks out the poison until it is gone.''

''It does that?''

''So they say. Even white men value madstones greatly. They are rare. There are only three in this territory. One of them, so the Meda priest told me in my sacred studies, is owned by the brother of your Reverend McCoy. But that is on the Beautiful River, Ohio, many miles away.'' My life with the McCoys came into my mind for a moment. There were former students of the mission at Quash Quay's camp, as there were here at Twin Lakes. One of them at the former place had told me that Mrs. McCoy did survive her child-bearing when I left. It gladdened my heart.

He put the stone down. ''Good magic will come to our lodge because this is here. And because you come with it.''

Ears Ringing, the Twin Lakes wife, did not think so. She was a tall, handsome, young woman with Shawnee blood in her and the oily hair of the Shawnee, plaited in the modern style. But she was sullen, always imagining some slight when none was intended.

When she saw me, and Pauk told her what the new arrangement was, she closed her eyes a moment and then opened them wide. She gestured towards the lodge door. "We need wood. Bring it from the woodlot," she said. I went out the door; she was elder wife.

Being with Pauk again that late summer and fall, I was like a bear cub rolling in a wildflower patch. In this new place we reawakened the old playfulness of our childhood, and when we were out of sight of men and women of the village, we splashed in stream water, chased each other along roads and lay lovingly in each other's arms by the fire in our fishing camp leantos.

Still, the old folks' saying tells truth. "Two wives in the same lodge are as two bear mothers in the same winter den." Pauk had said Ears Ringing was "not as busy as she should be." Lazy is the word I would use. She let the year-old child run about with its deerskin napkins unchanged, and she threw food scraps into the corner. The dogs smelled; the clothes were not washed. No wonder the white man had thought Potawatomi filthy; the smell from the lodge was awful.

But I was not of this mind. I came from the band of old Brown Squirrel, which was known throughout the Northlands as the most fastidious of all tribes. So I tried. I swept the dogs and their doings out the door; I washed the clothes with lye soap in the spring as the white women do. And I loved the little brave, Waterdog, although he caused me a pang of longing to have my own child.

But I was not very happy, especially after fall rains drove Pauk and me inside the lodge at night, where all heard each other's sounds. True, my bedroll was at the back of that roomy shelter, and Ears Ringing was near the door, as far away from me as she could get, but when Pauk sank down beside her of a night instead of me, my heart fell.

Sometimes, outside, I threw things, as I had used to do occasionally at the Baptist mission. "Ooh, Manittos of the underworld, you have stomped on my life. You promised I should be *Manitto Wabo*, a wisewoman of the spirits," I shouted as I threw rocks at trees down by the stream.

"Why, what is the matter with you, Rosy Dawn?" Pauk said, truly surprised to find me this way.

"Oh, I do this now and then. You have just never seen me so," I told him. "My mother says it is my McClure blood from the hot tempered, red-haired white people."

He nodded gravely, then pinched my hind end. But I was not in the mood to be pinched.

One day, when we travelled north near Lake Michigan with Aubee to see about some furs, I visited a white man's church. Inside, folding snow-white satin clothing besewn with gold, was a priest. He turned to look at me and smiled.

"What is the clothing?" I asked him in French. "I do not recall ball gowns in other white man's churches."

"It is so in our church," he answered in French and then switched to English. We carried on a conversation about the Catholic Mass and sacraments for some time. "And so how do you, a Potawatomi, know languages?" he finally wondered.

"I have the gift of tongues. My father was so, too. And I was with the McCoys at the Baptist Mission."

"Ahh," he breathed, looking at me with some small degree of wonder.

"I might come to the Masses if you came out to Twin Lakes," I said. "It would be something to do, I suppose." Truly, there were things about the Mass that I liked that day as I stayed, sitting on a back bench while Indians from this band took wafers and drank from a cup. I studied the altar cloth with the scarlet embroidery, the gold plate and cup, the spicy smoke from the chafer he swung about. And I listened to the odd language, like the French but less liquid, more regular. Awe, and something like sharp, sweet sadness mingled in my feelings while I heard it, and I felt as I had felt when I had watched the dances done in the camps as a small child under the moon of harvest time.

"I will ask my bishop to send someone to Twin Lakes," the priest said as I left the Mass. "It is hard, for you are far in the woods and he is in Vincennes."

Before I left, he asked if I would like to think about being catechized and baptized. I looked up at the dead god two feet high on the rude tamarack logs of the church. "We all need faith," the priest said.

"I have faith. Faith in my husband. Faith in my people. If I find a little faith in myself, I shall have all I need."

"No," he said coolly. "Not all you need at all."

Who was this man, this man who stayed north in Detroit and travelled around to set up crosses and holy drinking cups on stumps in the woods, I asked myself as we returned over dry woodland trails. Something was in him I had not known. I suspect it was with the McCoys, too, though I was too young and shut inside myself to know it.

This priest was turning his back on his own white race; his only ties with whites were letters sent over the five hundred miles between him and his Bishop Bruté in Vincennes. I had seen some powerful medicine here—it made me uncomfortable. What did it mean?

When we returned to Twin Lakes, I took myself to the woods immediately, although that fall evening it was cool and drizzling.

I spent an hour or two building a leanto and then stayed in there all that night thinking, sitting before a sputtering fire. Sometime around midnight I began considering what my mother had told me about my father. It was here, at Twin Lakes, where he had seen Snow Deer, the great animal I had seen in a vision, with the pained eyes that spoke for all my people.

I remembered what the Great One had told me when he appeared that awful night I spent with the shaman near here. That I would be *Manitto Wabo*, seer of Indian peoples. Suddenly I could see the Snow Deer's eyes in the darkness. Was it only in my mind? It does not matter. I saw them again, wounded, desperately pleading. To whom? I was the only one there.

What was it those eyes were asking me to do? What did I have to give? Well, of course there was something I knew how to do . . . certainly doing something, anything, would be better than the emptiness I was finding fetching, carrying, and learning to hate my co-wife.

The next morning I took my madstone from the corner of the lodge. I asked Paukooshuck to help me move to the woods. Ah, wonderful man that he was, he listened to my scheme, chuckled a bit, and helped me pack my things and go.

Together we made the large leanto watertight. Pauk made two windows with crude shutters and hung blankets over the door. We put in simple furniture: bedsteads, blankets, a table. And that night, I began to put the word around this camp and the other two on Twin Lakes that I would take the sick in.

So, gradually, because there was no good healer there, parents began to bring children with infected limbs in, and I tended them. Women with female troubles came to the bright fire outside my leanto. Men with fevers sought me out. What magic did I, the *Manitto Wabo* use? Certainly not all the torch-throwing and screeching and leaping my uncle used to do.

Through all I had seen, I had formed ideas about how to heal, and now I could put them into practice. Bring the sick into a light, fresh-smelling room with a clear fire. Put them on a clean pallet with warm blankets. Fix them good broths to eat, speak kindly. Administer herbs grown outside the door. Cut and clean wounds with a knife stuck first in the fire. Do not promise anything, do not frighten, do not threaten. Speak words of encouragement, think thoughts of love. This is how healing should, must be done.

And, truly it was like that in my little healing lodge. When spring came round again, I planted a garden with every herb I could find that the old women in the other camps had told me of. The beds in my little shed were often full, but not for long. People came in sick, went away well.

I soon had the chance to see the madstone in action. A frantic woman who had come all the way from the St. Joseph River on a horse with a three-year-old child said a raccoon had bit the boy's leg. She was so afraid she could hardly speak. Froth-at-mouth sickness is terrible indeed.

I clamped the madstone on the child's wound, which was as big as a walnut. Ah! that ugly rock stuck on the wound. We bound it about the leg and took the child to the pallet. Twelve hours later the madstone came off and I bound the wound with a cloth. Later on in that year the woman sent a messenger to tell me the child lived and was thriving.

Was this Manitto magic? Did the stone have a little sucking mouth of its own, a spirit of the rock? I do not think so. Perhaps this very dry stone does what the Iroquois and Miami do to cure snake bite. They suck out poison from the wound and spit it on the ground. Or, perhaps the raccoon was not mad.

More likely, as I came to believe, the sick ones were healed by faith, the faith in the stone, the faith in me. All I knew was that they were healed, and that I had a whole new purpose for why I existed. I did not leave Pauk; he came to be with me at my lodge. But there was peace and harmony in both lodges now.

The priest I had met came on horseback to visit the Twin Lakes camps. I welcomed him, showed him my healing lodge. "You do the work of the Master, whether you know it or not," he said with a smile.

"I do the good my own heart tells me to," I said.

"Perhaps it is the same thing," he said. But he did not promise if anyone would ever come to make a church at Twin Lakes.

One day in that fall of the white man's year 1826, Paukooshuck told me, "There are treaty proceedings to be held next month at the Mississinewa. I must go; many odd things are afoot. I wish you to come as interpreter for the Potawatomi."

I had heard of the treaty; all the men in the village were grumbling about what had happened. Tipton's evil totem Brooks had run before him into the village promising there would be many fine presents, new annuity payments, even reservations for some if the treaty lands were signed over.

"They wish to build a road over our lands. A wide, new road from Kentucky to the great Lake Michigan. Many white men will use it and whoever owns the land along it will be rich, very rich. That is why Tipton sends to get us to sign. We are in the way."

"And yet his words are smooth enough. He says he is a friend."

"Tipton hides his war paint beneath a linen shirt. He sends Brooks to carry the totem and then comes in after the battles are all won. He must appear to be impartial, above trouble. He wishes to run for white man's office in government."

"But is he? Free from trouble?" I asked my husband.

"No. It is Tipton," Pauk went on, "who will buy the land as soon as the treaty he forces through is signed. He will set up a fine town on the new road to Michigan, become a lord, as the English say. Lord of the Eel River." He laughed, but his laugh was heavy with sadness and scorn.

"Houses will be put up where our people have camped," he murmured. "There will be seminaries. Barns where people have shows and dress up and pretend to be other people. Piles of horse manure crawling with bottle flies, on the hill where the sun has always risen over waters as clear as bead-glass. And we, dirty Indians, will be shoved back, our noses pushed into dung, like the white men punish puppies for doing what is natural, being who they are.''

"Your father Aubenaubee will be there—"

"Yes. And the other chiefs. If they refuse to sign and stay together—perhaps we can hold decent space for ourselves. Let them build the road elsewhere. The Old Grandfathers fished these lakelands for ten thousand years and we were given them to be chiefs. And even the whites have promised in their treaties that these lands would not be touched." He was silent for a moment.

Then his light-hearted mood returned. "Rosy Dawn, do you know the story of when men did not have the gifts of fire and water? In the beginning time, when men lived in a desert place and ate meat uncooked. Manaboozhoo, Son of the West Wind, decided to steal the useful fire from Sisninikoo, the magician who had hidden the embers in the caves of the West."

"I think so," I said. It was like the other story of the West Wind my mother had told me. Once, twice, Manaboozhoo, Son of the West Wind, had to steal fire because people were careless and lost the fire when it went out. This was the first time he brought it back.

"Manaboozhoo went into the cave," Pauk went on, "and braved the three trials and won and brought back fire to men. As a special gift, because Manaboozhoo loved the *Neshnabec*, our Potawatomi people, at the same time he also gave to them the waterlands of the north, where we came.

"Chiefs of the waterlands he made us, and keepers of the fire. The Son of the West Wind himself so named the *Neshnabec*," Paukooshuck said. "And so we have been. Now we will see who these men are who wish to take the waterlands from us."

And so our bands of Potawatomi went to the Mississinewa River in October of 1826. The treaty-signing scenes from 1826 come before my eyes like shapes from an awful, nightmare ghost dance. I can see the commissioners, one of them the famous white chieftain of Michigan, Cass, hard of spirit as a piece of filing stone but fair withal.

With him were the *métis*, half breeds whose fangs glinted savagely as they prepared to profit from either side and who slavered over the traders' boots and whispered in the Indians' ears to "sign, sign." The Ft. Wayne traders were there, with faces like limestone, taking time pieces out of little pockets on their vests. With them were Tipton and Brooks, dressed in fringed leather and wearing red and white blankets to show that they were "of the savages themselves."

Finally there was the governor of the state himself, determined to get his road lands at any cost, strutting about with his squaw man, one McClure. I wondered if he were related to me and kept imagining I saw some sort of family resemblance.

My husband's eyes watched, watched Aubenaubee and the lake band chiefs as they tried to hold the line. "They have locked up the liquor in a shed with a key," Pauk said to me. "If it stays locked—"

I was busy enough myself, interpreting. Tipton and the rest had accepted me without question when Pauk presented me. My English was almost perfect, and the commissioners had me move among the groups of Potawatomi and half-breeds telling their ideas as "Official presenter." There was another, one William Conner, but I was to be the native Potawatomi speaker. The officials said they wanted our people to fairly know what the governor and other officials were proposing for the "fine new treaty." Really, as far as I was concerned, what I was doing was listening to see if all was done fairly and our people's thoughts said truly.

"We will raise payments $2,000 a year. We will give you a blacksmith and a mill on the Tippecanoe, and one-hundred-sixty bushels of salt." So said the white man.

"No. We will not sell. We have sold often enough. Learn we can say no, too." So said the Indian.

"Your great chiefs are gone. Topnebee is dead and Metea, here, ill. Listen to your own mixed-bloods. They want you to sign." So said the white man.

"They serve the god of gold. We listen to ourselves."

One week, two passed. Governor Ray, ever more obsessed by his Michigan Road, began to grow ugly and demanded the Potawatomi settle the treaty terms.

At one council, Aubenaubee spoke to Governor Ray in this way:

"Father, we have heard all you have to say. We have considered the proposition, we do not wish to hear any more."

Governor Ray said, sharply, "We do not have any new propositions. We want you to think about what has been said. If you will just *listen*—"

And my father Aubenabee answered, just as sharply, "When we came our ears were opened wide to hear, our eyes wide open to see. We heard, we said no. Is there some reason you cannot understand that word?"

Ray swore at the chiefs and he ordered me to tell them this: "You are poor and starving and we will distribute goods to get you through the winter if you sign. We can make you sign, you know," he said. "Get ready to go west. You have no other choice, finally," he said. He showed scorn for every one of our people by selling Aubenaubee a broken down horse which must have been twenty-five years old for $200.

And Aubee, awed in spite of all he had said at the prospect of having the White Father's own horse, paid the money.

Finally Brooks came to the tent where Pauk and I slept. "I want the squaw to take a message," he said.

"I am not a squaw. That means an immoral woman," I said.

"Tell them we offer $30,000 worth of presents, blankets, corn, wheat, flour, cloth, wagons and houses for the chiefs, everything they want. They can name the gifting terms."

"The lands of lake and cattail cannot be bought with bribes."

"Tell them, I say," he spat out, and left the tent.

"Can Aubee stand fast?" Pauk wondered. His eyes were hollow. I saw him go over to his father's tents, tell him what had been said, put his arm about the stocky old man's shoulders.

When he came back in, he told me, "My father is sweating. It is as if his body is being held above a fire and roasted."

But Aubee did stand. He and the others would not bend; there would be no sale of our land at this time. Some of the commissioners and followers were packing up to leave when, at dusk, I saw Brooks and Governor Ray at the door of the liquor shed. My eyes widened; even their own officials in Washington had expressly forbidden treaties with liquor—

"Does Tipton agree to this dispersal?" I overheard Ray ask. "Not that it matters much—"

"I have not found it necessary to officially inform him," Brooks said and snapped the lock off.

By the time I had run back to find Pauk and we had returned to the shed, Aubee and two of the other Potawatomi chiefs were advancing towards the door of the shed.

"So you say it is open," Aubee said to the white men, the sweat of his drive for the alcohol pouring off his face.

"Father, do not pass," Pauk said, putting himself across the door.

But, snarling like an animal, Aubenaubee used all his bear-bulk to throw aside his son and enter the shed.

And this is my true deposition as you asked to have it: that the Mississinewa Treaty of 1826 was brought about by connivance, bribery, and degradation of my people so that the Michigan Road could go through.

It is public record that John Tipton had his agents buy the reservation lands at the mouth of Eel river, which were to be awarded by that treaty, from Potawatomi traitors, even before the treaty was signed.

For himself, and his town. When the others of Aubee's bands put their drunk chief on a litter to take him home, they spoke long and seriously to Pauk. They asked his advice, put him in a place of honor among the council. "You will speak to Tipton and the rest now," said the elder men to my husband. "You know how to deal with him and the others so the old ways and our interests will not be lost."

"These white men are chiefs of these northern lands now," Pauk said to me as we broke camp. "There is no negotiating now. They simply tell us what they want, and we have to agree. They buy, conquer and take Indian lands so they can become lords of these rivers. Lords of places like Connersville, the place of Conner's brother, Evansville, Hindostan. Now what will it be next? Tiptonburg? Small domains they seem to me." —His voice was heavy with sad scorn.

"They seemed as gods when we were among them," I murmured, wonderingly.

"They are but men as we. But they have power." After a long

moment he added. "It seems to me the Master of Life gave the red man wisdom, but the white man power. Why is that, my Rosy Dawn?" He chuckled grimly as we found the horses. For some reason, I suspected there would be no evil mood this night.

Wisdom! Paukooshuck of the Potawatomi had it! What a great chief he would make some day, I thought. If there were any of us to be chief over. I looked at my husband on the trail, tall and strong and thought that perhaps his wisdom, strong in the ways of our people, was what I had been looking for all along. Finding my husband and his strength, had I not ended the quest for my long-lost father?

And yet he did not feel strong and wise to himself. "The very lakelands we love are gone. What will they do next?" Pauk mumbled to himself, shaking his head.

I remembered the snoring, besotted figure of his father, Aubenaubee of the Potawatomi camps and asked myself, "What indeed?" And my thoughts were as troubled as if the shaman were among us again.

# Chapter Thirteen

# The McClure Papers

To: James R. McClure, New Harmony, Indiana
From: Governor J.B. Ray, Indianapolis, Indiana

January 10, 1827

My Dear McClure:

I write to you in haste. It is imperative that you return from the delights of your idyllic paradise on the banks of the Wabash to the real, grim, and dirty world known as Indiana politics.

Since you left a week ago, affairs have been hastening towards the precipice and I doubt not that if you and I do not use our wits, we shall both fall off into the pit—of being retired to furrowing, ditching, and other disgusting parts of the occupation known as FARMING.

Damn them all. The snide calamity-mongers in the Indiana Legislature are hypocrites. First they instruct us to undertake a road from the Ohio all the way to Michigan by getting the government to grant lands.

Then, when I set up a commission and acquired the lands from the Potawatomi and Miami at minimal cost to the United States, but at great personal cost and the loss of my health and family harmony, I am accused of improper conduct at the treaty.

James, our political enemies are serious. I am threatened with public censure in my own legislature. Prepare to leave at once to come help me defend myself.

Yours,
Governor Ray

To: Jim McClure, Esquire, Indianapolis, Indiana
From: Jack McClure, Vincennes, Indiana

January 12, 1827


Jim Dandy:

What in hell is going on there in the capital? The *Vincennes Western Sun* says you and the governor are up to your brass buttons, stewing in intrigue over the new Michigan Road.

The legislature is going to impeach the governor of the state? Over the Potawatomi Treaty last fall that you helped negotiate? I told you when we all got burned by Aaron Burr that politics is like the first year of an unhappy marriage: a short hot summer of delight followed by a cold winter of regret and blame.

I have sent a courier. Please, let him not wait long for your answer. Send complete details for my eyes alone; I shall give some made-up answer to your brothers and sisters and cousins; all here are anxious.

The tangle over your mother Jane's estate continues; Samuel Emison as executor is trying to sort out all the considerations. Since she was not, as we found out, ever married to Retreat Granger but living in common law, Granger has no claims. Still, it appears that debts will take half your father's magnificent acres, including the stone horse-barn. I am sorry—and sorry you did not believe you had the time to handle the matter yourself. Still, I cannot blame. As my Pa once said, "I've had my times too."

Jackie D.

To: Doctor John McClure, Vincennes, Indiana
From: The Honorable James McClure, Esquire, New Harmony, Indiana

January 30, 1827

Jackie Dee—

I am about beside myself at what the ass of a governor has done, and now asks me to help repair. I shall tell you a few truths, since you have always known my inmost heart.

Truth One: At my urging the governor took up the project of most import to the state, the building of a Michigan Road. Was this road as necessary as I have said? You have eyes and know that from around the very capital where the governor abides, farmers must cart wheat and corn to Cincinnati through mud holes and rock piles to sell it cheap for seventy-five cents a bushel. There is no road through Indiana! In the War of 1812, the miserable paths of the Northwest, particularly of Indiana, where soldiers had to travel, were a grave threat that almost cost us the war.

Truth Two: To get the lands secured, the Governor appointed HIMSELF a commissioner, along with General Tipton and Governor Cass, to force a Potawatomi treaty the way he wanted it last fall.

Truth Three: At the treaty grounds up near the Mississinewa, the Potawatomi didn't wish to sign. Governor Ray instructed me to use certain kinds of "persuasion" on them. (Do not lecture to me, my dear cousin. We have known each other too thoroughly for that. Besides, we are not the first officials to threaten them or use liquor to still the war-paint feelings of the savages. Or to use traders like Tipton and the Ewing brothers to our advantage. Or to withhold the shabby trade goods and the very food they needed to survive until we got our wishes.)

Truth Four: After the Potawatomi finally capitulated and gave up a great section of the northern part of the state and received their miserable pittance of annuities and salt, and we had the lands for the road and new settlement, our opponents in the Judas-legislature now demand that Ray answer to accusations of criminal intent.

Impeach him? Ruin me? Not at all. I have not pushed "internal improvements," countless officials, and even the governor of this state uphill for these years to allow the whole kit of us to tumble down the hill like Jack and Jill.

I have my strategies.

As far as the family business goes, Jack, you will have to handle it. You are the settled and successful dispenser of pills and now surgeon. I cannot handle my own family in New Harmony; Auraleigh is oddly distant and the children hardly know me.

I suppose all of this will be worth it. What I am doing is important. I think we are mortaring in the stones for the foundation of a state's prosperity.

Still, I still can't help but wishing that at this moment we were fishing in one of the good old "cricks" of southern Indiana.

> Your devoted Cousin
> And former plotter 'gainst
> B'ars and Injeeans in Caintuck
> an' all them furreign provinces
> Jim

To: Mr. Lewis Brooks, Care of John Tipton, Eel River Settlement

From: James McClure, Indianapolis, Indiana

February 2, 1827

Brooks: Please pay careful attention. I made certain financial and political arrangements with you to be sure the Potawatomi signed the treaty giving the State of Indiana land for public improvements.

Governor Ray and I put aside scruples to join your trading interests: you got the debts owed you by the savages paid, the State got the land.

Now enemies of the governor and the new road system are

claiming he acted irresponsibly at the treaty, grabbed land, and even paid himself unfairly as a commissioner.

I call upon you to draft a letter to the legislature and the Indianapolis newspapers providing affidavit that the governor handled his commission correctly and that the treaty signing was according to lawful procedure.

I assure you, Brooks, that we are all blackbirds popped into the same pie. I stood by as you entered the tents of Chief Aubenaubee and provided demijohns of whisky and rum, as your trading friends wheedled and cajoled and promised and, I think threatened. The things that went on at the treaty grounds are too dark to put on paper.

You and your mixed-blood trading friends now have collected $16,000 in debt money the government provided as a result of the treaty. You and Tipton are negotiating with individual Indians for countless acres of their personal reservation lands. Already Tipton's pockets are lined with land sales money from Indian grants he doesn't even own yet.

Tell Ewing, Tipton, Coquillard and the rest of the trading interests involved in this that I want a joint statement from them exonerating the governor. Otherwise, their part in it will come out. My courier will accompany you to see it is done, then return to Indianapolis with it.

Do not delay in this matter.

James McClure


To: James McClure, Aide, Governor Ray, Indianapolis, Indiana
From: Lewis Brooks, Agent for Tipton Trading Enterprises,
Eel River

February 3, 1827


My Dear Sir:

Surely you did not intend the peremptory and insulting tone of your letter. This is not the manner of men who knew each other cordially before, as we did in Hindostan Falls. I am afraid I do not understand the rough ways of most of you "Hoosiers." In the East we know how to value the subtleties of transactions among gentlemen.

Your employer, the governor, is to blame for his own problems. We did not officially initiate treaty proceedings; Governor Ray did. He has himself urged that the savages be "broken" from their dependence on the hunting lands. He it was who told us all that once most of the lands were gone and the savages were restricted to small farming plots, they would lose their affections for Indiana. He wants the Indians gone! Now that some people believe the methods were a bit rough, he is backing off and acting outraged.

You imply we traders are vultures, pressing for Indian treaties so we can have the government settle the debts the tribes owe us. We collect only just debts. Indian traders have lost revenues and goods dealing from supplies that have rotted on us, spring floods and official delays. Working with these hopeless "children of the woods" is not easy profit. Shipping costs are high, the government pays late, the Indians in drunken rages kill even the agents who feed them. Whatever we get we have earned, I tell you.

Still, we will agree to do as you wish—Tipton has signed the affidavit absolving the governor and I am sending it on to John and William Ewing, the two other main traders in this.

Past that, the legislature will have to do as it pleases. We will try to save Governor Ray from charges of corruption and mismanagement in the treaty, but no one can save him from being the fool that he is!

Please direct correspondence to New Albany, as I am going there to handle some family business.

Your servant, etc.
Lewis Brooks

To: Dr. John McClure, Vincennes, Indiana
From: Honorable James McClure, Indianapolis, Indiana

February 10, 1827

Dear Doctor Jack:

You will have read by now that the governor of the State of
Indiana has been censured in the State Assembly for ill handling
of the Treaty of 1826. The affidavit of the traders that I secured,
privately circulated and supporting Ray to some extent, probably
kept the vote as close as it was and forestalled sterner measures. It
was I who had to unravel the snarls in this colossal mess. What did
I say to this oaf, Governor Ray, who brought about all these
troubles by screaming at the Indians and cursing them like span-
iels? Who sold to the chief of the Potawatomi, Aubenaubee, a
spayed twenty-year old mare that couldn't even walk right? And
beyond that—I cannot tell the worst in a letter.

Last night I went to the home of Governor Ray and asked to see
him in private. Door shut behind me I said, "Here is what you
will do, SIR. You will write a blustering letter to the legislature
which I will help you write, informing them they have exceeded
their jurisdiction, misrepresented the treaty situation, and endan-
gered the state's functioning.

"You will sit as my parents and I used to sit in McClure fort in
Kentucky, in the days when Indian renegades came by the fort
hoping to steal horses or perhaps do worse. 'Wait it out,' John
McClure, my father said. We will try waiting until the opposition
politicians on the warpath at the Indiana legislature have tired of
the game and gone home. Let time pass; let them sit in the cold
and get hungry." So I told him, and so we are doing.

The legislature will finally remember more important matters
and leave the governor alone. What is the difference, so long as
the road is built? And built it is going to be, within five years,
opening up the South to the northern Great Lakes.

I hope the war party takes its paint off soon and lets us run the
government of Indiana. The road is an issue that is past. We have
something new to do now. We have to build a canal to hook up the
Wabash River with Lake Erie.

Your cousin,
Jim D. McClure

To: Honorable James McClure, Indianapolis, Indiana
From: Dr. Jack McClure, Vincennes, Indiana

June 10, 1827

Dear Jimbo:

Well, from your last letter, which has waited for an answer these weeks, it seems you've pulled it off. The Indian Treaty and the Michigan Road. All I can say is, "Shore is good tidings. An hyars a slap on the back from the Wabash valley."

And so the Wabash and Erie Canal is the next step in your dream? We may make Indiana the richest state in the Union in our time. Now wouldn't that be a pretty little kettle of perch? We'll show "them folks way down East a thing or three!"

Come to think of it, you've had this dream ever since we were tender sprouts in the Young Patriots of the Wilderness Club. You went to join Aaron Burr (when I was too scared to go) so's you could build the New West, far from the selfish, worn-out, effeminate East.

And so you see us all as the heart of the nation, with produce flowing to market down scores of waterways. Industry filling up the cup that will run over. Progress.

Or, my dear Young Patriot of the Wilderness, are you in further than you know? I call to mind that stream out yonder in back of the stockade at McClure Station in Kentucky. You and I could wade out through harmless shallows and eddies and of a sudden we'd be smack dab in the middle and up to our shoulders before we even knew it.

It was too late to go back; it was dangerous to go on—is that you now? Am I beginning to sound like Pa? No. Only Dan'l McClure can sound like himself, after all.

"Fambly news." Archie McClure has left Vincennes and gone to Luke and Jay Byrd Dugger's White River camp, Duggerville. Motliest lot of slave traders, reprobates and escaped small-time criminals I ever saw, down at the river. And above it the old Luke and Delva Dugger's huge plantation house. What I never could figure out is, if the Duggers want to be Southerners, why don't they move to Alabama?

Archie's going to be their overseer. He's taken some of your ma's old slaves with him to help him run the camp. Charlotte is one of them. Remember her? Your ma sold her to Archie. Charlotte married one of Uncle Will's slaves—Moses. Archie's drawn up papers to bind them in 99 year service to him. The rest of the old McClure slaves are held by his brothers and sisters.

Johnny's drinkin' himself into spongehood like his Pa, Uncle Will, usta, before he got religion or whatever it was. Elizabeth worries about her brother—Johnny don't act like the eldest in that family. As ever, he's a rabbit.

Cat and John Hogue—all of us are going to their house, some sixty people, for July 4. Some of the little ones are getting to be striplings. I can't get it through my head that Alfred is fifteen and so is Nancy Jane, Cat's eldest.

They're all going to the academy in town now, not at all like our off-and-on log cabin, slate school with Aunt Jenny.

Still as a stone Aunt Jenny is. And even when John Robert comes into the room, she knows no knowin'. Mahalia, John Robert's good wife, keeps trying to get Aunt Jenny to come back to living, says she knows there is a spark in there that is Aunt Jenny Scott.

Mahalia and John Robert have a son, James. They waited long for this 'un and hope for a passel more.

I meant to tell you before. Uncle George had word that a man answering our mean, late lamented cousin Ish's description has been found dead in Texas. He'd been employed as a spy by the Mexican government to find out what the new American settlers were up to, and somebody ambushed him.

So Ish wasn't drowned after all. I knew it all along. He was too mean to go that easy, but not too mean to die, I guess at the hands of the Mexicans.

Well, keep in touch and tell me the strange, mysterious ways of the capital city. If I don't hear your pithy puns and the puny politics of the particular parties there, I wither and die like a violet in the summer sun.

Your cousin Jack

# The Poore Papers
## The Journal of Hannah Poore
### (Continued)

May 10, 1828. I, Hannah Chute Poore, take up my pen again to record my thoughts. I have not written for too long a time, and if for no other reason I should express my gratitude to the Giver of All Good. Truly, the harvest has become plenteous in Indiana for all my family.

I look around me, out the window of this new, two-story log house built by Alvan my son, and I see fields of wheat, yellow-brown and ready to cut, rippling flat in the wind. We lived through the ginseng time, when there was nothing, through the corn time when we first cleared and planted, when there was enough, and now we enjoy the wheat time when all is plenteous.

Alvan says the best of our farm is the rich bottom land where wheat grows well. My dear John's concerns that this would not be productive land were not well founded; we have grown enough fine grain to even pay the debt we took on when we came to this county. At first we had to grow some years of corn to take the silt from the soil; the first wheat we planted shot up and fell over from overabundance. Now we have fine-ground wheat flour and a bee-hive oven to cook it into bread. I have a cooking shed at the back of the house, a spring house and pens of hogs to feed my family.

Except, of course, that they are not all here to eat what I fix. How odd it seems to me that when you finally have plenty of fried chicken and good hams and white bread to feed many children, the children are gone. Mehitable has found her Will Merrell and gone to Cincinnati, Amanda her Moses Pearson.

And Alvan married Julia, too, and has been running the place, the frugal farmer his father never was, poor man. So I have Betsy,

Hannah, Harriet, young John and Amelia here, surely plenty enough to content me.

I do not count my Wendell back east or Susan, of course. She is lost to us, in a manner of speaking. Oh, I do not refer to her becoming a Wesleyan, although I do not particularly warm to Methodists. It is an undignified, overly effusive way to worship our God.

Ever since I saw the Methodists barking like dogs and falling on the floor in religious ecstasy at revivals when I was a child, I thought they might better call their churches menagerie zoos.

But Susan is free and over twenty-one. A good deal older. She, blessed girl, is what they call a spinster, and yet she stays there in that place, Hindostan Falls, for whatever reasons I cannot imagine. We no longer need her money, although it does allow me to buy special things.

She has her reasons. I pray I can always welcome her when she does come to us, freely, with an open heart, instead of wanting to shout, "You are only half a day's ride on the stage from us, why do you stay away?"

She has her reasons, I suppose.

"Hindostan Falls is my home, now, Mother," she says, and when I say that a woman does not live alone in a wild town, she simply smiles that odd little smile of hers and says, "I do."

She does try to explain; I do try to understand in the way mothers and grown daughters have had since the time of the Pharoahs, I suppose. "Mother, I must have my pioneering time, when I stand alone and build something, as you did. You had Orange County, I have Hindostan. I wish you could be there and see the important families moving in, the children in the school. Why, in a few years—" The gist of it is that it is hers, not dependent on me. I do understand, a little anyway.


May 15. We are preparing now, in the spring for the fall apple gathering and drying. Mark Ebenezer has been coming over and he and Alvan have built a drying oven, in which we will keep a Franklin stove forever running. Long drawers will hold sixteen bushels of apples at once! Modern inventions will make us all slothful, I think.

Sylvester still comes to help us although I do not quite know why. I have little to give him—except my gratitude. He seems to be satisfied with nothing more than friendship, although he is as fine a friend as I have ever had. Still, a friend is not a husband, although I could have had that too. I can never forget the day, just a year after John died, when Sylvester came to me and took one of my hands in his, and looked at me.

"Be my wife," he said, taking his eyeglasses off to look at me searchingly. "I do love thee, Hannah."

But I had to shake my head, sadly, and try to say the correct thing not to wound this great, good man who was savior to our family.

"And I love thee, Sylvester, but in the spirit. Let us leave it there and always love each other that way."

I do recall that that was about the time the Indian, Mark Ebenezer, had his great time of sadness. His Delaware people were moving away from Indiana. They had agreed to go when the government wished them gone.

"Why did they go so peacefully?" I asked him one day as he helped me and the younger children shuck corn.

"Because they have the wisdom of the land in them. They knew it would be senseless to resist. Why should they not know? Resisting did not serve them well in Pennsylvania or Ohio. I have seen the sea. One may stand and scream at the ocean, but one will not hold its waves from breaking on shore."

Lately he has been around much. Harriet has been looking at him with concern, as only a twelve-year-old can do. She has adored him since she was a toddler and he let her follow him about as he put in garden for me. I must admit (though I could never tell it to Sister and the others at Newbury) that he and Ruth took Harriet back to their home at the Quaker village for visits. Poor souls! They were not blessed with offspring. They adored her so much; I only know I trusted them. Mark Ebenezer and Ruth gave her a little corncob doll with a skirt made of ribbon. And of course Sylvester was there.

I must go now to bake bread. The beehive oven does us well. Alvan rakes out coals from the oven through the hole to leave the bricks piping hot for seven loaves, six pies and two batches of cookies, if you hurry to finish before it loses its heat.

May 20. Corn all planted as of yesterday. Fruit trees have made it through blossoming time without frost and are setting on good apples, peaches, pears. I whitewashed the bottoms of the fruit trees last fall to disappoint the weevils.

Exhausted last night with putting in fifteen new rose bushes, I had fallen into my bed when a sharp knock awoke me.

Apprehensively I arose and lit a taper. Alvan and his brood were up the stairs in their comfortable beds. I grabbed up John's old rifle, though I could not have shot it, I think, if my life depended on it. But perhaps, I thought, if there were brigands of some sort, robbers a bit off the Trace—

I raised the latch. There, outside, shivering in the misty, cool night, were three colored persons! A huge man and two women with shawls pulled fast about them. And behind them, in the shadows, Sylvester.

"Quick. I have no time to explain," he whispered. "Take them in and put them in the potato hole. You have a rug above it. As you are a Christian, hide these fellow Christians from deep trouble."

He disappeared into the shadows and without a word, I brought the Negroes in, shut and latched the door, and hurried them to the potato hole.

No one came all through last night, nothing but the blowing of the wind, scattering clouds and bringing in a change in the weather. But this morning I sent Alvan to Paoli to find out the news there. He has returned to say an old man named Luke Dugger was stomping about from bar to bar looking for his "lost nigras," who must have been the ones in our potato hole.

Sylvester has just come to tell me that he is helping these illegally held Negroes to escape bondage from the Dugger man and his kin. There is another group of colored men and women, fled at the same time as our "guests" with him in the Quaker village.

What an outrage! That in the free state of Indiana, men in Knox County still hold colored folk as if they are slaves. Oh, they will tell you that they are merely indentured servants, but these poor souls are held as surely as if they lived in Mississippi. They are "under contract" for paupers' wages and they are in debt, ignorant of their rights—they stay on because they do not know what to do.

Lot, Pambra, and Billie are the names of the ones brought to us. I am determined they will remain with us come what may until this dreadful Dugger man returns to his rivershanty town, or plantation house, or whatever it is, on White River.

Thank God he did not find them. For revenge he would have shipped them instantly to be sold as slaves in Mississippi.


May 21. Pruning apple trees in the orchard. We should have done it earlier, but did not get around to it. We shall have quite a crop of Rome Beauties and Spies next fall! Alvan thinks to trade cider from a new press we will make for several things our neighbors have: good honey, lard. Our new guests, as I call the colored folk, have constructed a very decent shanty and now occupy it. Today they helped with the plowing. Crows were everywhere, following as Alvan and Lot dropped corn into the furrows. Amelia and John had to follow, beating them off with brooms until the corn was covered. Dugger has gone home; the entire Quaker community conspired to keep news of his human chattels from him and by a subterfuge gave him to understand they had fled to Michigan.

Lord forgive our dishonesty! I shall keep them here and pay them wages. They are, indeed, a great help.


Mark Ebenezer is often about these days and broods a great deal. I hope that Harriet can help to lift his spirits. Poor man! He has tried so hard to make a life without his wife Ruth. 'Twas a blow when she left that day six years ago on a pony, with bells jingling strangely out of tune.

Sad lot those poor Delaware, starting from near here and travelling to Terre Haute and across the Wabash, a mournful, silent crowd carrying old ones and sick on litters, leaving these woodlands to go west! All of us went to Terre Haute to see the journey pass through there. I held Harriet by the hand and she waved to Ruth, sadly.

"Why did she leave, Mark Ebenezer?" this small child of mine said that day as the ponies disappeared down the dusty trail.

"It is Delaware custom. Women are family heads and go with families," he said to no one, his eyes on the western clouds.

"And you stay?" I put in.

"I stay with my Christ. The Delaware Long House has done without me now these thirty years; it will stand in the new land without me too." So he said. But his voice was gloomy, his stance defeated.

Still, he has found much to do in the years that have intervened. He has travelled with the Quakers among the other tribes. They have opened small schools, teaching Miami and Potawatomi to farm, where they could. Lately, though, he has not travelled much and his spirits seem a little gloomy again. Ah, we will revive them with work. We are making a cider press, the neighbors, Mark Ebenzer, Harriet and I, building a cabin to hold the press and barrels in which good cider will last long into winter. Harriet is beside herself with joy at getting to put up a little house. She says she will use it for her corncob doll and the wooden animals Mark Ebenezer has carved for her. Our next neighbors, the Bothfelds, are over to help and will stay the night. I am fixing pork and dressing with gravy and dandelion greens for them. There will be fiddle music and exchanging of stories about the folk round-abouts. How soon this wilderness is become a neighborhood!

Today Pambra helps me with the wash; Mark Ebenezer and Alvan are building a bridge to cross the creek. It will help us take the horses to the barn without bringing them all the way to the house when the creek is in flood.


May 25. Word has it that Dugger has threatened to go to the law to get the return of his "servants." What kind of a case has he? Anyway, I now have learned that the other group at the Quaker village is almost all indentured to one family—the McClures of Vincennes.

Odd our paths should cross again. James McClure I have not seen since the birth of Amelia at the Markles, but I hear of him often, in the papers, of course. Who can escape knowing that he is the assistant of that nefarious Governor Ray in Indianapolis?

But I also hear from Henrietta Markle that her daughter, Auraleigh McClure, now stays long months with her parents in New Harmony. How they twitter about the social experiment over there on the western Wabash! Free piano lessons for all, community fields to till, lectures on English trade guilds in the evening. They have imported scientists and fine educators to teach children in a new way. The Markles' twins are going to the new school with adults who want to learn, too. I may write to her when I get a moment to tell her of our doings and the escape of the "slaves." None of the McClures may see fit to tell her, knowing her own hatred of the institution of slavery.

Henrietta mentions that the members of the New Harmony community argue constantly with Robert Owen about how it should all be run. Really, I wonder how James McClure's children fare with staying away from their father. The McClures seem to thrive on marriages of separation. I hear that Jack McClure lived in Hindostan for more than a year before he returned to his wife and children and became a doctor. Respected enough he is now, I know.

Hindostan. Susan is here now with us, visiting.

"Who are your friends? Who your companions?" I ask as we quilt pieces together in the light of an oil lamp. Johnny and Amelia are squirming about, trying to get their lesson on the other side of the table. When their sister Susan visits for a month, they are whittled into shape.

"Johnny is growing up a savage, Mother," Susan says, screwing her mouth up into a tight knot.

Alas, she is quite right. My younger children know more of Indian lore and fishing for bass than they do of participles and Latin verse.

But we do meet with our little Presbyterian Church up the road. And I have taught John and Amelia to read the catechism and the Bible some. "The fear of the Lord is the beginning of wisdom."

"You ask who my friends are," Susan says, pulling back hair from her forehead. "My brothers and sisters in Christ." Methodists always talk so. Some way it embarrasses me to hear such open effusion about a private subject like religion.

"One of your friends, I think, was more charlatan than Methodist—"

She turns away, abruptly. "Do not speak of Mr. Sholts. He was much misunderstood. You sound like Brooks."

"Brooks? Dan Brooks?" Into my mind flashed the handsome, rather bumbling operator of the horse mill and whisky still when we had first arrived. But of course he was now a business giant, in Hindostan.

"Not Dan Brooks—Thomas Jefferson. Never mind." She stood up, dropping pieces of quilting on the floorboards. "He is not worth considering. At any rate, he is betrothed to someone in Hindostan he has just recently met. A daughter of a business associate of his. I hope he may have better sense when he is married."

Mark Ebenezer is preparing to return to the Quaker settlement. He and Sylvester, he says, must plan a trip to the Potawatomi camps up north. The government is pressing the Indians up there to leave and the Quakers here are interested in their cause.


June 1. Alvan and Lot are repairing fences. First roses in, large as saucers and so fragrant I think I will faint. There is serious business this day, though. I, Hannah Chute Poore, am a litigant of a law case. Sylvester and the Quakers have decided that Lot and Pambra and Billy must sue for their freedom to test the courts, and I have said I will sue in their behalf. To think that in this free state, Negroes must go to law to get what the Constitution of 1816 gives them. It is outrageous! I am attempting to talk to Susan more about her life but she is testy, unhappy. To have a grown child unfulfilled and miserable is like feeling an icicle at the heart.


June 3. I was awakened in the night by the sound of thundering hoofbeats. I put on my linen wrapper and before Alvan could rouse himself from bed, get his coat, and reach the door with his Kentucky rifle, I had John's old musket loaded and was out the door. Not a moment too soon did I cover the door of the "guest shack" with my body. Luke Dugger and his clan had come to claim their own.

"Git out 'the way, Miz Poore," he snarled at me. "Them's my Nigras and I'm a gonna take 'em home."

I was silent, but my gun was pointed at his heart. I was ready to strike a spark.

"Now, Miz Poore, you jest don't unnerstand. These here's like children, never had any schoolin', always had somebody to put sweet potatoes and hog on their tables. Why, they cain't even think for theirselves. I got to take care of 'em.''

"They are making a living for themselves right here. I am paying them.''

There was a low, surly mumbling. A younger version of the old man spoke up. "M' names Jay Byrd Dugger and I tell you, Ma'm, to move aside. I got Johnny and Archie McClure here, too. When we're done getting our Nigras here we're a-gonna go to them Quakers an' take the McClure servants. All of 'em escaped from Dugger's camp together. This here ain't women's business.''

Another man mumbled and I could see him, like a shadow in the corner of my eye, moving forward.

With my hand trembling on the gunstock, I said, ''And I tell you all that it is precisely that. This business is mine, as it would be any Christian's. My name is on a court case, filed this very week in the county courthouse in Paoli, to help these people claim their freedom. And I order you off this land as trespassers.

''Be gone!'' I walked menacingly towards them. I could feel eyes glittering in the cold moonlight. Heavy dew wet the grass by my foot. The door of the house opened and Alvan rushed out, a lantern in his hand. The others were behind him. I waved them back.

The Duggers and Archie and Johnny McClure took a step towards me. ''I tell you I will fire this gun and you will have to drag me aside to cross this threshold,'' I said. ''My children will stand as witnesses that you manhandled a grandmother and a Presbyterian deaconess. I shall press further charges.''

They hesitated a moment and in that moment Alvan advanced with his gun and threatened them from the other side of the house clearing, Susan behind him. Finally, with menacing looks, the four swung into their saddles and rode up the road.

I felt the blood go from my head and had to swing it down between my knees in a most unceremonious manner. Not women's work indeed! Well, I had made it my job, and I certainly wasn't going to be one of those fainting women in vogue now. After all, they live in Massachusetts. I am an Indiana pioneer woman now, and Hoosier women don't faint.

June 5. Oh, Lord, when you send children why do you not send the wisdom to deal with them? Susan has left after a bitter agument with me. I spoke the truth—I think I did—and told her she was allowing herself to shrivel up like a sugar plum. That her bitterness—toward whatever her situation was in that deplorable town down the road—was leeching out her soul like lye. Could I have said it a better way? Probably I was too direct. Remorse fills me.

June 7. Sunday. As usual went to meetings. Strange doings this week are trying me, grant patience, Oh Lord. I have decided to go to the Quaker settlement. I can, I think, leave my "guests" in the shack. I need to confirm what I suspect—that the Luke Dugger gang did not kidnap the McClure coloreds from the Quaker town.

June 8. I am here at the Quaker settlement near Paoli. It is as I suspected. They rode right through town and on their way to Vincennes. Too many men were here and the twelve McClure Negroes scattered in various homes. I shall stay and confer about our legal matters.

June 15. I am staying with Sylvester's sister Virginia. She is a kind woman, a "non-observing" Quaker, who loves fashion styles and wears the new straw bonnets even indoors.

I have just been to a Quaker meeting, which I have attended occasionally before. I like these testimonial and prayer times. Silence. Peace. The separation of men and women I do not approve of. Adam and Eve sinned together, were thrown out of paradise together, and it is together we men and women must work out the world.

There is much worry about Mark Ebenezer, the Indian, here. He and Sylvester had ridden north to the Potawatomi. As they discussed the white man's plan to send these tribes west, Mark Ebenezer abruptly left the discussion and rode away. He told Sylvester he was going to his own camps—to the White River camps his people left behind these eight years now. What can he hope to find poking about in the fire ashes of the past?

June 20. I remain at the Quaker settlement. Mark Ebenezer has returned and is acting very strangely. He walks about mumbling.

Eight p.m. by candlelight. Our Indian friend startled the men at testimony meeting tonight, so Sylvester tells me. There in the gloom of that meeting house, with candlelight flickering off his strong, lined face, he spoke, haltingly of his visit to the deserted camps of the Delaware.

"A haunted camp my people have left," he said, "and behind it, on the hill, the past seems to sit on its haunches like a giant spirit. Grass grows between the last logs of the fallen-in Long House. Rain falls on the stones of the steam house. Under a rusty pot is a cup and ball that belonged, I think, to my niece, and beside it a rag of a shirt embroidered by some Delaware woman and now rotting into soil."

He went on to say there was a string of camps like this from the coast to the Big Lakes, ulcers on the skin of the countryside. The ghost villages of the long-gone Delaware. "The leaves fall on the them, the rain weeps for them, until snow freezes the heart of earth and no more tears can fall."

The men's congregation of the Quaker Church was shocked at this odd outburst. An old man in the row in front of Sylvester pulled his coat and told him to "get on with the Christian point of it all." I wondered, when I heard all this story later, outside the women's meeting, if perhaps that was the Christian point.

That was not all Mark Ebenezer had said. With a voice full of emotion he had asked "Can Christ heal the hurt of my people?" he asked and then went on to insist He could not, not while the government cries peace, peace, where there is no peace, while the white man continues to take the land from his other red brothers and threatens to send them away, too. A half a dozen men began to murmur, reacting in alarm to the pain in his voice. But ignoring them, he went on, growing more agitated. "They crucify Him, again and again, my brothers"—his voice was almost a wail— "and see His tortured pain in the faces of the Indian peoples."

He put his head in his hands and wept. That is what Sylvester told me.

June 25. Today I was alone in the house of Sylvester's sister, watching the sunset—gunpowder gray streaked with ochre. Through the bubbled glass panes I saw a man ride into the village and head for the door.

'Twas an old man, short, stocky of stature, but with a face so open it seemed to mirror the sunset's last fire.

I opened the door to him.

"Hello, M'am," he said, removing his trail hat. "M'name's Dan'l McClure. I've come from Vincennes about our property—pardon—about our dependents. About Moses and Charlotte and the rest." His round, lined face was full of pain. I invited him in and stirred up the fire.

I looked at him twirling the big hat in his hands and tried to recall what I knew of him from the Markles. William Henry Harrison's judge—head of the Territorial Defense Committee when Tecumseh threatened, a man with a mansion on as fine a thousand acres of land as any the Republic boasted.

"I am ashamed of my kin, shamed o' my own race," Dan'l McClure said in a low voice. "I tole 'em I was a-gonna handle this, ride over here m'self." I had wondered at how the younger ones in his family could allow this seventy-year-old man to ride through two counties alone, but now that I saw the strength in his eyes I could understand it.

"My Dada left Ireland to find freedom. Then his sons had the bad sense to take freedom away from other men. I have been fightin' with my own kin over this since we were in Caintuck. 'Tis the one thing we don't agree on."

I was silent, watching the coals. I asked him if he would eat some beans and cornbread with me and he nodded, his eyes grateful. When he had finished it and gingerbread too, he went on.

"Well, we have paid," he finally said, almost as if he were speaking to himself. "The very day m' brother John brought home the fambly's first slaves was the day disaster come to us. He came home from his slave-buying jaunt to find his wife had sinned with our other brother.

"The fambly's still paying the price for all the sinnin' that this ownin' of other men brings. Two o' my brother Will's sons are disgraced from the drink that almost got their Pa. Their Ma a-rottin' o' grief in her big house. Brother John's wife dead in Tennessee in a mountain hovel, their son workin' for a crazy charlatan that calls himself gov'nor—" Ah, so that was how James McClure's family viewed his rise to success like a comet in the sky.

"Never mind. I had no business spillin' our cider all over the path o' your house. The long 'n short o' it is I'm here to give our people their freedom. It has taken a while to get the legal papers ready, but here they are."

He fished in his pocket. "I've bought up all the indentures, and here—" he dumped them out on the table. "When your Quaker folks return tell 'em the McClures are all free from human servitude now—whites and coloreds alike.

"I'm a gonna say goodbye to Moses and Charlotte and the rest. I'll be givin' them somethin' to start out with on their own. I knew the Decker darkies too. Wisht I could free 'em as easy as I have m' own fambly's. Would ya tell Lot, Pambra and Billie I'm sorry and—if they's ever anythin' I can do for 'em, jest ask. I hope your case in court for 'em hurries 'long." He stalked out, plumping his big hat squarely on his head.

Interestingly, Alvan has sent me more news of the McClures— a letter from Auraleigh Markle McClure, answering mine. I shall include it here.

From: Auraleigh Markle McClure, New Harmony, Indiana
To: Mrs. Hannah Poore, Paoli, Indiana

June 1, 1828

Dear Mrs. Poore:

How kind it was of you to write and tell me about your family and include news of my own! This thing with the poor bond-people—deplorable! I must admit my husband James does not agree with my liberal sentiments in the matter. I have had an outraged letter from him demanding that someone exert control on his Uncle Dan'l. As if anyone could do that, even if the matter were not a clear moral and legal one. But then James and I find ourselves in disagreement about these issues often these days. Ah well, so the world runs.

You were gracious enough to ask how we fare here in New Harmony. I know there is a good deal of curiosity about this "model town." New York and even Boston reporters have visited us and world travellers manage to put us on their itineraries. I cannot decide if we are famous or notorious. Things do lurch along here. I have decided that "ideal communities" have a lot of trouble surviving. Here Mr. Owen has set up a series of villages which will bring out the best in mankind, educating them from the ground up to live with their fellow beings in industry, fellowship and commonality of purpose. We are attempting to rid ourselves of the exploitation and corruption of the "old way" in Europe and America. The problem is that human nature works to threaten us, as perhaps it always will, when we try to make people live up to a certain social standard. Jealousy, greed, mischief—all of these are directed at Mr. Owen and the things that are not working here, and he keeps trying to "reorganize" the community to make it work better. Sometimes New Harmony reminds me of a watch shop, where all the wheels and springs are lying about on tables, and one wonders if the watchmaker will ever get them re-assembled into clocks, chiming and telling time again.

Still, the educational part of New Harmony is the most interesting of all, and I work with that. I teach at the Education Society, where we have put our children. We are attempting to lead the children into a practical and happy pattern of life using the Pestolozzian system. A Mr. William Maclure, no relation of ours, I think, has set up a school which has done away with all Latin, Greek and higher math and even most grammar. We teach the children to sew and learn trades and do useful skills. Our own daughter Estella is learning to cook and preserve food and Samuel is laying bricks and preparing to learn to set type. Natural history is a great love of Maclure's, and he is preparing to set up a book publishing system here which will bring out useful books on science.

Mr. Owen has a large general store on which the community depends for all its supplies. He has the ordering done to conform to what he thinks a good social order needs. But people in the community also have their say. For your eyes, Mrs. Poore, I will confess that although we are told to eliminate classes and "fancy dressing," by wearing the plain dresses Mr. Owen encourages, I much prefer the frilly gowns a few of the community leaders have insisted he get in lately. My sister Emma Rose now has five of them! Poor frivolous creature, many people talk against her for it, but secretly they too buy the "civilized, upper class" trinkets and clothing too. Alas, poor Mr. Owen does not have a practical head. He has spent much of his own money on this community and a good deal loaned to him, too. Not wishing to have high prices at his store, Mr. Owen orders in huge stocks and then sells them at least a third below their value. All the folks from around the county come to New Harmony Store to shop because its goods are so cheap. How we will ever make payments on the property to the Rappites is anyone's surmise.

You ask if I have been disillusioned by the scheme to improve mankind by setting up ideal living communities. With the scheme yes, although I think it might work at some other place, in some other way. But Mr. Owen himself is too flitty, with too much air in his brain, to make this work and pay for itself. All these people want their own ways and refuse to do the drudgery.

With the people in the town, though, I am not disillusioned. Far from it. Mr. Maclure is an intelligent, practical visionary and Robert Dale Owen is a scientist of the first repute. There are philosophers, scientists, musicians and others of high reputation and intelligence, and I love to be among them. I think our family is settled here. Emma Rose has married the dancing master and they give us all waltz lessons, and Evangeline and Effie have married prosperous farmers.

My husband James does not share my enthusiasm for New Harmony and seems to spend as little time as possible here, at least it honestly seems so to me. But I must not repine; he says he is doing an important work with Governor Ray in getting the roads and canals of Indiana built. I wish James had a man of sounder character to work with, but then politics makes strange bedfellows.

I will say that in the Michigan Road trouble recently, I think my husband rolled over in the political bed and found he had a bear sleeping next to him. So be it.

My parents send their regards. I am glad to hear Susan is continuing to do her bit to build her town in Hindostan; I try to do my bit here.

Your fond friend, Auraleigh McClure

A good but troubling letter, I think. How humankind does run on. It is time to return home.

June 26. I have decided to take Mark Ebenezer back with me. His troubled heart needs healing, and we all who love him can try to make amends for the losses he is feeling.

No word from Susan.

The court case at Paoli courthouse proceeds. Luke Dugger is writing outrageous letters, full of veiled threats. I am not afraid. The Quakers tell me there is no doubt but the law will free these people.

July 5. And so we are back, and I have not written for a while. Alvan has announced that he and Julia are again anticipating an addition to our family. Mark Ebenezer says little, but seems glad to see the children and find work for his strong hands.

July 14. Mark Ebenezer ate at our table this night as he has not done since returning. I am glad to note this; he has been eating off to himself at a fire he builds. I cannot tell if we are helping his gloomy spirits, but I pray so.

July 28. Tonight Mark Ebenezer was jollier than he has been since returning, and told stories about the Great Hare, a very naughty rabbit indeed. Somehow the stories have too many "country" implications for me, but I know that is how the Indians tell them.

As the evening wore on, I sewed a shirt and Alvan repaired the tines on the fireplace toaster, as the fire flickered and popped. Harriet, John and little Amelia sat with Mark Ebenezer as they sorted out green, transparent apples they had all gathered today. The culls will make good sauce, and of the best ones we shall have an ample supply for putting in the apple dryer for winter pies. Green apples pies were ever the best, especially when cooked with maple sugar. Sometimes merry Amelia tossed a small apple at John Mark Ebenezer and he caught it and laughed. He is beginning to heal, I am sure of it. The love of this family, and Christ, is enough to knit any broken spirit. Tomorrow Mark Ebenezer, Harriet and Amelia will hang the door on the cider shed and put up shutters. Alvan will do the final assembly of the cider press when he is finished with haying chores and all will be complete for fall. Harriet is happily gathering up the corncob doll, its family of Noah's animals and the little toy chair and table Mark Ebenezer has made, to take with her to see their new home in the playhouse-shed.

July 29. My God, my God, why hast thou forsaken me? The most awful happening has shaken us to the core. I shall try to summon my wits and spirit late this night to tell the story in order. The three went as I described to the cider shed, about a half a mile back in the woods. The day was dark, with the wind sending black thunder clouds scudding across the sky. About an hour or so after they had gone Amelia burst in, tears streaming down her face, her voice terrified.

"Ma, Ma, Mark Ebenezer is acting so odd. We started to put up the last shutter and he was silent a long moment. 'Twas as if he was listening to the voice of the wind. He put down the shutter and began to talk frightening talk, sometimes crying out, sometimes singing. He went to the cold fire and began picking, tearing through the ashes. Now he's sitting on the floor talking to the Great Hare and the West Wind. Come Ma, fast. I couldn't get Harriet to leave; she stayed there trying to calm him down."

We ran through the woods, tripping over swamp roots and tearing our skirts in our haste. How long did that woodland run take? Five, ten, minutes? But as we approached, I did not hear wailing or the Indian chanting Amelia had described. The shed was completely silent.

Oh, my God, how can I describe the sight that met my eyes? Hanging by the neck from a branch on the sturdy oak outside the shed was Mark Ebenezer, a cider barrel on its side beneath him. His eyes were protruding almost in surprise, his face was marked with crescent moons of charcoal black, the Delaware war and death marks. His legs twisted in the gusty wind in an odd, mocking dance of death.

And Harriet? My lovely, calm-as-still-waters girl? She sat in the corner of the shed, tears streaming down her face, holding onto the corncob baby with the ribbon dress, her own dress torn and disheveled from the struggle to keep him from taking his life.

We took her home and now she will not go out of the house again. She cries and wails, and I do not know when she will be willing to leave the security of this home again.

To worsen my despair, I have not been able to get a message to Susan. I am yearning for her to comfort and help us. Surely she will come at once. I sent Johnny to Paoli with a message to be put aboard the stagecoach, but he has returned saying the coach has been delayed because of some problem at Hindostan Falls. How I hate the place! Oh, Lord forgive me for my anger and grant me patience in this time of trial.

## The McClure Papers

To: James McClure, Indianapolis, Indiana
From: Dr. Jack McClure, Vincennes, Indiana

August 4, 1828

Dear Jimmo:

And so the Assembly has moved forward with the canals and

soon we will be criss-crossed, like Holland! Isn't that the import of your last letter? And you have been thinking of leaving Governor Ray's service? Hurrah, I say! Let me know how you fare in— serving the canal interests, did you say? And what is this about railroads in Indiana? With all these canals crossing all these roads, crossing all these rail lines, I don't see where a cow is going to find a decent place to stand, do you?

Archie McClure can't get over the fact that Pa paid off all his bond servants and then the court found for Mrs. Poore and freed Luke Dugger's too. All our Knox County "slaves" are going to live by a small freedman's community near the Ohio River. Jim, I know you objected to what Pa did, riding that way over to Orange County, but there was no stopping him. You know that as well as I do. When Dan'l McClure gets his dander up, there's no smoothing it down.

Pa's unhappy these past few days, mopes about and Ma can't console him, though she even picked some gooseberries and stemmed them to make his favorite pie. Hurt her fingers for two days. Sam'l Thompson, Pa's best friend, died. Sam'l married so late, he left some minor children, and Pa, and then I after him, am to stand as friends and helpers to the widow.

Alfred sends his love to his Godfather. 'Twas thoughty of you to send him that copy of *Sacred Thoughts for a Presbyterian Boy*. He seems restless in his religion, lately.

And I?

A lawsuit has been filed against me, cousin. If you were around more, you could be my lawyer, but I have had to engage one of the Vincennes fee-seekers. One Dr. Malthus Ward—remember him?—is suing me. He lived in Hindostan for a while and I apprenticed to him—claims I took what is rightfully his.

It is the sacred writings or history of the Delaware, given to me by the chiefs when I was on White River. He wants the scrolls, for such they are, on sticks, to offer to an antiquarian. Ward once told me the collectors would pay handsomely, perhaps a thousand dollars, for a real treasure of early man.

I fear it will end up in some huckster's museum. Ward would sell it to anyone, if he could not find a collector of old things. I know that to be true. I can see it now; people snickering and pointing at the quaint "savage things." The one thing these poor people begged for when they were pushed out of this state was dignity, and the sacredness of tribal memory.

Oh, you will say I am an "Injeean lover"—how we used to say that with scorn. Perhaps I am one, at least in this case. I promised them I would not let the sacred writings be profaned.

I tell you they are fine works. I have them here before me and can recall at least some of what they mean, these pictures of turtles and water waves and suns rising over curved horizons. They are like Egyptian hieroglyphics. I commited a few lines to memory, when the son of the band chief spoke them for me.

*In the beginning, there was water over all the land*
*And the Great Spirit was there. . .*
*He made much land and sky. . . sun, moon and stars,*
*Creatures that die, souls and all*
*Then he made man, Grandfather man.*
*All men lived as friends, all were pleased,*
*All were at ease, all were happy.*
*But then, secretly to earth came the Snake God*
*Came wickedness, crime, unhappiness, bad weather,*
*        destruction, death.*
*This all happened very long ago, beyond the Great Sea*
*In the first land.*

Jim, my spirit moves when I see these scrolls and think of the millennia behind them. They are so like the holy writings of the Christian faith. Can we all be one people on the face of this earth?

Something as important as this must be for all, not for an entertainment museum. Someday there will be a place for them, similar to what Bonaparte has set up at Louvre Palace in Paris.

I promised those Delaware—enough of this.

Sometime when you come home, I want you to look through our Grandfather John McClure's book from the Indian war days in Pennsylvania. I keep reading and re-reading it. Whites and Indians were massacring each other every day in Pennsylvania during the year he died, yet Indians came to his funeral, so Pa says. They wailed in mourning for him and tossed sacred medicine objects on his coffin to speed his journey to the spirit world. From what I hear about our grandfather, he did not need any speeding. I have spoken often to Uncle George about our grandfather. Uncle has given me a miniature painted from memory by our grandmother after his death. I want you to see it. I don't know why, but I think both you and I have something to learn from this man we never knew. I have taken the book to Emison's, to your sister Mary's, for you.

Uncle George has gone to Hindostan Falls to write what he calls "one last article—The Mecca of the Northwest Ten Years Later." I will seal and send this letter after we finish supper. I hear Lizzie calling us all. Alfred is in his room reading *History of the Slave Trade* given him by John Robert Scott. This son of mine is a rip-snortin', plug-tearin' idealist. He seems a throwback to what they said Grandfather John was like. Lizzie is angered by it, but then Lizzie is angered by many things. Still, she has a good side. We must not forget that.

Time is short—I am attempting surgery on a neck tumor tonight on one of the Ewing family. Oh, for some way to put her to sleep! Laudanum and whisky are not nearly enough. Most doctors I know do not want to put patients deep asleep for fear they could not be wakened, but I believe somewhere there must be relief for their thrashing about and pain—

10 p.m. In haste—Patient survives, thank God, but in agony. I cauterized to stop hemorrhaging.

What's this? Post has just brought the word that some strange and awful sickness has hit Hindostan Falls. Five men have died in four days, one the doctor. I feel I must go and shall leave at first light. Old friends we both care for are there.

Your devoted cousin
Jack McClure

# Chapter Fourteen

## The McClure Papers
### The Notebook of George McClure
### (Continued)

August 5, 1828.

Here I sit in the Brooks Inn, waiting for the stagecoach due in tomorrow. God speed its journey! Five deaths, four sick and of what? "Cold sickness" they call it.

I shall review these notes for the article I began to write before the sudden onslaught of this sickness. I shall still print my article when I return to Vincennes, with some mention of the sickness.

Hindostan Falls lives and thrives after these ten years. It grows more slowly now than ten years ago, and other burgs in Indiana vie with it for "boom capital." Still, the spirit of free trade stalks its streets, and if that spirit is not a lusty stripling still, it is at least a healthy youth.

The original Sholts partnership is dead and long buried, the Vincennes and Paoli branches of the Brooks enterprise are now closed, the bottom has fallen out of pork and corn, and still Hindostan lives, one of the largest and most prosperous towns in Indiana.

I have been observing now for over seventy years. Before my vision have passed the French and Indian conflicts, the Revolution, the first settlement of Kentucky and this new state of Indiana. What have I seen?

I have seen cycles. Repeated patterns. There is a wilderness. People come to it. They bring the best of impulses: religious fervor, love of freedom, chance for opportunity and a new life. The northern Ireland of my father's father, for example, when

James I sent the Scotch to settle it. Carlisle, Pennsylvania in 1750 when the first McClures came to it. Harrodsburg in Caintuck when I first met George Rogers Clark.

"Come quickly to the new lands. Plant your opportunities in new fields; reach out for your neighbors' help and give yours. This is the American character," all of them say.

Then a monster follows hard on their heels to gobble up the good impulses of those first settlers. Fangs dripping, with huge jowls and belly, its name is Greed. Speculation. Land grabs. Town planning. "Get what you can while the getting is good. This is the American character," everyone says now.

"Ah, this Monster Greed isn't really us. This greed was a phenomenon of the colonies," I thought before the War of Independence, if I gave it much consideration at all. This cheating, going across the mountains, founding questionable land syndicates which cheat people, is just happening because the King's unjust.

Then, after the Revolution I told myself, "Speculators are eating up Kentucky because Virginia has bad laws. The pent-up energies of war are being flushed out here."

So I said.

But I was wrong. This monster isn't an anomaly, a foreigner in our midst. This jowly, voracious creature is red, white, and blue, Yankee-Doodle-boy American Greed. I should know; I bet the family fortunes on a cotton-ginning scheme and lost.

No, the monster is still here in Hindostan Falls. The streets still teem with action. Landlords are making rent-slaves out of tenants, raising rents quarterly. Two banks have failed and the cash system died, panics have come and gone, but still greed persists. Speculators buy up failed farmers plots to re-sell to Rhode Islanders who still want to "go west." Slave traders range all along the river looking for free blacks to capture and sell south. Pork barons buy boatloads of bacon, whetstone marquises take out wildcat loans to "expand into Eastern markets." And everybody makes money off the Indians.

The apothecary, the livery man must have their "carriages." All turns on gold—or when we cannot get that—credit.

Speaking of credit—what of the Brookses, who used credit to build fortunes for themselves? Daniel Brooks, trying a new career for the sixth time, is forming an itinerant show to tour America. Lewis Brooks is helping his master John Tipton set up the new town at the confluence of the Eel and Wabash rivers, with lands they got after the treaties that they arranged, setting up academies, pushing for a Federal armory there.

And Thomas Jefferson Brooks, the king of Hindostan Falls? Named for the great Democrat? Who knows of him. He owns it all now, with my nephew James still a part of some of his projects. The Squire of southern Indiana Brooks is, and he is preparing to marry his New Orleans partner's daughter after a whirlwind courtship. This town is really Thomas Jefferson Brooks'. Some bad, much good is in the man, as in many who live here. And everywhere, I suppose. (I can just hear my practical brother John saying, "Be fair, George. You alwuz did have your durn head in the cuckoo's clouds. Free trade ain't alwuz a bad thing. All money-making ain't greed.") True. Maybe I should say it this way. Money-making is the most persistent thing in America's history and character. Above religion, above family love, it endures and shapes us. Is that all right, John?

Yes, Hindostan Falls lives. As long as there is an America, there will be Hindostan Fallses—springing up overnight, then expanding like gas balloons on the strong hot air of decent aspirations and the foul gas of greedy speculation.

I left off there. The sickness changes the picture. Will it spread or claim only a few poor souls here and leave as it often does? What are the philosophical implications? Of course you must have those. Here they are, George. When yellow fever hit Philadelphia in the 1790's, some blamed the materialism of the town.

Can such a thing be true? A judgment of God on the sins of Mammon? I do not know if I believe that or not. But I do know what I saw in Harrodsburg, when men killed each other in the streets for a warrant to a particularly fine piece of bottomland. *Radix malorum cupiditas est*—the root of evil is greed.

There now, I have quoted Latin, when I promised my Jean I never would again. Jean, Jean, my sweet lovely dear one, you are gone now these three years. Gone, gone so many of the ones I have loved, and no one sympathetic to me anymore but Catherine.

I had best close the window. Odd chill that is blowing through, miasma from this river. Hindostan is so near the sullen water—like Jamestown in Virginia. Never build on the swamp. This cold dampness makes me shake. Or could it be—?

I have been a mover for most of my life; that last trip will soon come one way or another. The worst part of old age is that all joy is tempered with the thought that it cannot last. Each day is one fewer, a piece cut off the loaf of life, until finally there is no more left to cut. I shall think of what Brother Will said, after our last river trip.

As malarial ague wore him down a little at a time, like a file on metal, he told me, "Waal, mebbe there's a after life and mebbe there ain't. If there is one, I'll be pleasantly surprised and if there ain't, I won't know it anyways."

If I go, I go with my head high. What I did, I did with decency, pretty straight honesty and some humor. And after all, I did know George Rogers Clark and George Washington. Well, I didn't exactly KNOW Washington. Saw him at Princeton on his horse. So much for full honesty, McClure.

Pray that stagecoach comes soon.


To: Squire Daniel McClure, Knox County, Indiana
From: Doctor Jack McClure, Hindostan Falls, Indiana
August 8, 1828


Dear Pa:

I must take time to sort out my thoughts, and the best way I can do it is to write to you. I am in a state of extreme nervous debilitation. I will, must sleep for a few hours. At present I am too nervous to do that.

Pa, Uncle George is very ill with the virulent fever. As soon as you get this letter tell Cat, Polly, Margit, Willy, Bob and the rest. But they must not come! Under no conditions! If we can keep this awful thing from spreading its death to Vincennes—

I have Uncle here in the Hindostan Ordinary, the inn of Thomas

Jefferson Brooks, Jim McClure's old partner. Brooks was kind enough to turn the Inn rooms into hospital wards, sending up food and replacing soiled linen. He is himself nursing some of his own employees. I did not think Thomas Jefferson Brooks was that sort of person, but then I guess I did not really know him.

Uncle George took ill as he waited for the stagecoach. The vile vehicle never came. By that time word had reached New Albany and the other river towns that we were laboring with virulent contagion, and they passed resolutions banning any contact with us.

Uncle George chilled for half a day, then grew feverish, delirious, really, and had terrible pains in his limbs and stomach. He has puked for two days now and is very weak; his skin is a terrible yellow. These are the typical symptoms of the disorder. But I do have hope. He can turn the corner and recover now or grow worse. If he vomits black material that looks like coffee grounds, all is over.

I have been with him as much as I could and still make rounds all over the town as others sicken. We were unable to contain it to River Street; no lane or byway is immune now from the plague. I have just today hired a male nurse, the only person I could find to be with Uncle. Some say this nurse is a felon, but he seems to be giving good care.

I shall keep you and the family informed as long as the post runs.

At present, seventeen have died, eighty-five are ill. I have found and helped old friends, Widow Small of the Methodist congregation, Susan Poore, the schoolteacher I so admire in the Methodist congregation. Thankfully, hers was a very light case and she is up nursing others.

We are not yet at the crest of the disease, I fear. Panic and despair are beginning to take their tolls; whole families are preparing to flee.

I am the only physician in town. Doctor Latham died, one of the first victims. As if we did not have enough to face, word has come that the town's old physician, Dr. Malthus Ward, is coming to "relieve suffering among his old acquaintances." Pshaw, I do not believe that he has enough humanity or sensibility to help a humble bee. He is coming at my time of confusion to try to find his own advantage with the property he claims from me—

Enough of that. As Hamlet's mother says, "Troubles come not singly" at times like this "but in battalions."

As for treatment, I think I have found it, after some frustration. The first few cases I treated I tried salts and gentle purges, but two in one family died. I would not bleed, though some begged for it. You know I detest bleeding.

When Mr. Timoleus, the boot maker, sickened, it occurred to me that a light dose of calomel and jalap might do the trick.

It seems to work as at least half my patients are better today. That calomel is so efficacious! Life's ironies! The purge I used so many years ago as a jest at the revival was calomel.

I make rounds constantly among the streets where grimness and strong fear live. I am physically spent and mentally strained, and yet, Pa, I want you to know that I have never felt more alive in all my days.

I am aware of Ma's concern for me, and yours. Lizzie writes constantly begging me to return, but I cannot. Finally I have a chance to pay a token or two for some of the things I have done in this life that I regret. I feel that after too long a period of growing up I may finally be a man.

Eyes closing above this candle and quill—

Your son, John McClure

## The Account of Thomas Jefferson Brooks
### (Continued)

When it became obvious that Hindostan was in the midst of some sort of dreadful and malignant spreading fever in that August of 1828, there was only, finally, one real question, and that was, who would take care of the sick?

Normally a family answers that question themselves when there is sickness, but you must understand the nature of this virulent epidemic to see why that became all that mattered.

The impulse in a plague is to flee, to take horse, cart, shanks' mare and leave to healthier areas away from the miasma causing the fever.

The streets of Hindostan, the Buffalo Trace, the ferry docks were clogged with hundreds of people bent on getting out, many in a state of near panic as bells tolled behind them and hearse carts made their way to the cemetery. Rumor was the ugly, deformed queen of the day. "Can't go to Cincinnati; many cases are reported there and it is universally fatal." "Put a small packet of tar around your neck; 'twill keep off the vapors." "No, vinegar at the nose is best." "Should we ship and go to St. Louis? They've had rain there and rain stops it, they say."

But rumor is an ill informer. Cincinnati had but few cases; rain, at least in small amounts, did not seem to stop it. And it was only fatal in about half the cases; those cared for decently had a chance of recovery.

So, since many could not leave because there was already sickness in almost every home, "Who will nurse" became a question of living and dying. Some who were leaving should not have gone; I am ashamed to confess that common decency and even family ties were forgotten in the fear which gripped the town. My chief miller lay in want of even basic care in the last stages of the disease, while his wife of twenty years left to go to Salem to her relatives. Servants left masters. Grown children left their parents without even a drink of water.

I saw things in Hindostan Falls those two weeks that are the worst mankind has to offer. I saw carters charging exorbitant fees to take people to Louisville, and carpenters making fortunes on wood coffins. I observed landlords who charged rents for people dying and bereft and one who set furniture out in the streets on two poor orphans. I saw children wandering, crying, with both parents dead at home, pulling on the coats of people who could hardly respond.

I know that two of our boats from Hindostan Falls were refused dockage at Duggerville ferry, and that the younger Dugger himself stove in a freight boat from Hindostan that was supposed to pick up grain to feed our survivors.

But I also saw things that are the best our race can give.

I saw Branstable, the sextant at the church, go on burying even though all knew that to touch the corpse placed one in greatest, mortal danger. Day and night he moved from house to house collecting the dead until finally we had buried one hundred and two from Hindostan Falls with three times that many ill.

Why did I stay to help? Murmur not with admiration that I was some kind of saintly hero. Perhaps ever in my mind was the picture of the virulent fever I myself had had and the loyal friend Doc Drake, who had seen me through it, mopping my brow, cleaning my bed, whispering to me to live when I had given myself up to death.

Or perhaps it was that I felt Hindostan was my town. I busied myself with Agricola Mill people, getting them out if they wished to go, arranging for care if they sickened.

There were a handful of people at the inn; many took sick quickly. One, George McClure, uncle of my old partner the assemblyman, I saw through to his death. Sad to go, far away from family and even friends, in a strange city. I ended up bringing him water after the keelboat man that had been hired for him ended up taking the poor old man's purse and fleeing in one of the last canoes on the shore.

His nephew came in at the last and cried, unashamedly, to see his uncle so.

And then this nephew, Jack McClure, whom I knew well from former days in Hindostan, a fine doctor with a promising practice behind him in Vincennes, got the chills himself and sank into the fever. As the symptoms came upon him, he cursed and pounded against the floorboards saying that there was nobody to care for his patients should he succumb to fever.

I took the linen off the very bed his uncle had vacated and burned it, then put the poor man in the bed; there was no other place to lie in the inn. So he sank lower and lower, and as he grew delirious, he yelled out, saying, "Ma, 'tis your fault. You never told me what it was really about and now that I have just found out it is being snatched from me."

Within only a day Jack McClure was raving out of his head. I tied him into bed as he cried, imagining he led the Parke Dragoons at the Battle of Tippecanoe and speaking, finally, piteously, to "Adahbelle" and "Alfred."

Just before he died, he looked me straight in the eye. "Take care of them all," he said. "Don't let them drink the river water. That wretched stuff is to blame." Ravings of a poor dying man. What else was there to drink? I had given it to him plenteously in his last hours.

Certainly I did what I could for him and his uncle. Tried to get the other doctor, Malthus Ward, to prescribe for them, but he came and went as fast as a will-o'-the-wisp. I think he did look in on McClure once. I had been down seeing to food and I passed Ward in the upstairs hall. He brushed past me without speaking.

McClure seemed disturbed and when I went in his room, he yelled, "Keep the dirty hands away!" Over and over. Strange, but then there were many strange things then. I ordered strong cherrywood coffins made for this uncle and his nephew, shrouded them in camphor and wool, and marked their graves with wooden crosses. Perhaps someone, someday would wish to rebury them when soil and time had cleansed the graves, when hell stopped and the world took up again.

"Take care of them—" I saw Drake in that dying doctor's eyes.

And so I stayed. Just say I was there, and someone had to see to it all. The mayor had died; so I became the mayor and ordered that they stop tolling that dismal church bell, that the streets be sloshed with salt water twice a day, that lime be thrown into all the privies.

We became a town of shadows. No one, not a Christian soul from the outside world, would have anything to do with us; we were quarantined, made abhorrent by town resolutions from Kentucky all the way to Pittsburgh. The few helpers who were well enough to do the necessaries slipped away or themselves took sick. Finally Mr. Branstable, the sextant, took to his bed and there was no one to bury the dead.

The time finally came in those spectral streets when there were only two people left who were not ill or recovering and too weak to be of aid: myself and Susan Poore.

Odd irony. I should say that during the last few months I had wrenched my heart away from Susan Poore and was by now engaged to marry Blanchette La Rue, the daughter of a rich New Orleans merchant who was my trading partner and had come to town for the season, poor unfortunate gentleman. She had been abed for a week with a light case of the fever but was now up and, though very weak, was trying to nurse her father and mother, who were serious cases.

I had not seen Blanchette for a day or two; the awful affairs of the moment had kept me from their house on River Street. Now, as I headed towards River Street I came upon Susan Poore, walking more slowly ahead of me.

"You are still among us?" I asked, catching up and walking beside her. I had seen so much pain that nothing made me wonder anymore.

Her eyes were weary, but her gown was clean and her mouth firmly set. "How could I go? So many of my children at the school are ill—or worse—how could I leave them?" She turned her head so I would not see the pain in her eyes.

"We are the only ones left, it seems," she commented. "Where do you go now?"

"To Blanchette's." Words that two weeks ago would have been fraught with emotion for both of us now fell like clods of earth between us. We had seen so much suffering in the town that personal feelings, even the history of the recent past, seemed to have withered and dried, like the shreds of flowers blasted by December cold.

"I will come with you to see if I can offer some relief to her in her nursing duties," Susan said and I nodded wordlessly.

But when we came into the small frame house, we found, to our dismay, a scene of awful sadness. My dear little curly-headed girl was sunk upon her daybed, relapsed. Behind her, in the back room, her mother and father lay dead, several hours now.

"My God," I said to myself. "I thought I had seen all there is to see, but this is wretched. She has seen them both die and now is fighting desperately for her own life." Her breath came in harsh gasps; her yellow skin was dry as birch bark.

"Mr. Brooks," Susan said, seeing my agitation, "You must go. I shall see to her needs."

"Blanchette—my dear," I said, my voice breaking.

"She does not know you," Susan said to me, steadily, but with compassion. "Go. We must—do something about those—" She gestured toward the back room. "Get a litter and Mr. Branstable's horse and cart."

And so I did what I was told. Having to do the practical matters kept me from frantic worrying. Surely Susan Poore must have planned it that way. And when I returned I knew what she had done—she had spared me of that most awful of tasks—watching a loved one who does not know you die.

"How quickly, quickly, she went," I said numbly, looking at those small hands, which Susan had folded. Scenes of our recent courtship flashed through my mind, our first meeting in New Orleans when I sought solace from the rejection Susan had dealt me, picnics in the fields above the falls, the carriage rides through the steep hills behind the town. I had told her I would allow our children to become Catholic. What difference did it make to me? Now there would be no children.

"Lately the deaths occur almost overnight," Susan said softly. "I am truly sorry." She looked at me with wide eyes, and I believed her with all my heart. The two angry beings who had argued in the store did not exist any more. Nothing existed except the bare, stark contraries of human existence: death and life, courage and cowardice, decency and ignominy.

"I will grieve later," I said. "The only honor or succor we can bring these poor folk is to do well with their corpses—the best we can."

And so that tall, strong woman and I between us both got the two rigid bodies someway onto a litter one at a time and to the burying wagon. And then, as my heart nearly burst with pain, I helped Susan lay the sad, limp remains of a beautiful young girl beside them. And, I do not to this day know how, we entered eight more houses and brought out the eight who had died in the last two days. Two of them were little girls from Susan's school.

Do not believe what you have heard of Hindostan, that we buried our dead in one common pit as they did in London in the plague. No! Compassion and decency did not completely die, though they were sore beset in those unspeakable days.

Old Man Branstable and his last two helpers had already dug so many graves that the burying ground looked like a plowed field. Susan and I put our town dead into simple plank coffins that I had ordered and threw dirt over them. Over an idea that was dying. Over a third of our lives.

And after that, carrying a pine chip lantern we went about the town and into every home. We scared the rats out of deserted cabins, sloshed them with vinegar water and shut their door latches. In houses where the sick were, we brought broth from an iron pot and the rest of the loaves of bread in town, and we aired the rooms and gave them the last of the clean linen from the inn.

That day lasted through two centuries. But the worst came last, when we found Old Man Branstable at the edge of town, in back of the livery where the church's horse was kept. In his delirium he must have meant to feed the horse. He had lain there, I guess, a couple of days in the sun and heat. His body was putrefied and maggoty. Never man on this earth should be called upon to do what we had to do to get that good old man to his final resting place.

In the midst of it, I looked up at the woman who was helping me. "That ever a woman should have to do this"—my voice broke.

"It was women who helped bring Jesus from the cross and who tended his body," she said.

"Seeing you here, I can almost believe in God," I whispered, my words swallowed up by the growing darkness.

"Seeing you here, I can almost believe in man," she said.

She leaned on the spade above this, the last of the graves. "Were we really so bad here? We had so many dreams: the academy, the hospital. We were to be the second Louisville. Now the courthouse will never even be finished. Nobody will rebuild—"

"Nor should they. This is an unhealthy place. Sholts should never have set the town here."

"I was wrong about Sholts," she said quickly. "He would never have stayed, I know that. Not everyone who signs the church roll book is a Christian. And some who never sign are."

"Pshaw. I was probably wrong about poor Sholts too. He died a tortured man—who knows what his private regrets were?"

"We were the town builders." Now the tears finally began to fall and spilled over her hands onto the new grave. "You and I—all of us—put so much into the dreams and now they are broken like a milk pitcher."

"Not broken, just dented badly. This pitcher's pewter, not fine china. Maybe we'll take the dreams and reshape them a bit. Maybe they could have stood some reshaping."

And so we stumbled on through the night hours, catching only a few brief snatches of sleep as we sat by beds of pain until the sun rose. As we made morning rounds, we found only two more had died; perhaps the crest had passed. At noon we sat under a huge elm on the rise above the river.

"It's no use. We cannot do it, Thomas," Susan said to me. "Many are recovering. With food, clean sheets and care they might live. But we are spent, totally. The worst is, none will help. They have forgotten Hindostan. My brother wrote until the last posts. He is holding my frantic mother back from coming only through threats of contagion to the other children. He keeps begging me to come home. Yet he did not come himself."

"Men are a poor, beastly race at best."

"You have always said so, and yet you have given more than anyone could ask here. Your actions belie your words."

I put my arm about her shoulders and we slept there, as peacefully as children, by the road into Hindostan Falls.

We awoke to the light of the setting sun and the sound of horses snorting. A tall, beautiful woman with a blonde halo of hair with one gray streak in it stood above us. A giant of a man in fringed deerskin stood by her side.

"I am Catherine McClure Hogue. This is m' husband, John." She turned to gesture towards the group of about a dozen men and women behind her. The horses they rode and led were laden with saddlebags.

"These are elders of the Upper Indiana Church." I gazed in wonder. "We have come to claim our kin. T' mark their graves so sometime we can come again and bury 'em in the church yard on our road, where they belong, with the rest." Tears welled in her eyes. "And to help you, as long as you need us."

"You can't stay here. It's death to be at Hindostan," I said sharply.

"None o' that tomfoolery. You cared for my father in his dying hours. Now we shall stay and do for you. We have brought food."

And so this angel, for so she seemed to me, directed the rest as they made camp on high ground and cooked soups, brought out dosages of clean herbs and powders and went into houses and scoured and nursed and prayed.

As they returned to camp that night, Catherine Hogue took my arm. "Tell me m' father's—George McClure's—last words," she said. I had thought about them more than once, because I did not know what they meant.

"He said, 'I found her in a fever, once, now perhaps I go again to her the same way.' "

"Oh, Pa," the beautiful woman said plaintively. "He had stumbled to my mother's house, wounded by an Indian and feverish and she took him in and loved him. Once, so long ago in Kentucky. Only Uncle Dan'l is left, and he soon will go—I shall be the oldest one of my generation."

I looked at her with surprise. She could not yet be fifty.

"Ma, Pa, both gone now. Oh, how short we make our little stay, sir. How soon we leave." She left me and took her grief up the hill, alone.

I thought of Catherine Hogue's words as Susan and I stood, in November on that hill above the deserted town of Hindostan Falls. The wind rattled doors half off their hinges and the caw of crows sounded stridently above the silent streets.

'Twas true, completely true, I thought. How short we do make our little stay, how soon we all do leave.


Note in the *Vincennes Western Sun*, January 5, 1829.


Mrs. Hannah Chute Poore of Orange County announces the marriage of her daughter Susan to Thomas Jefferson Brooks, owner of Agricola Mills and Trading Company.

Theirs is the first marriage performed in the newly built village of Mt. Pleasant, two miles back of White River and the late lamented town of Hindostan Falls. Brooks will continue to operate the mills at Hindostan, but his main enterprise will be a new, three story mercantile store in Mt. Pleasant for the many families who have recently re-settled there.

Come you Mick from Cork or Ul-ster and get your pick me pal We'll whack a ditch thro this mur-ky swamp and call it a can- al Wa-bash and E -ne Wa-bash and E-rie Dir-ty, dread-ful stream I've sold me soul for com-pan-y gold And the A-mer-i-can dream

Tune by Ann Price

# 1838

Digging the Canal

An 1830's work song

*Come, you mick from Cork or Ulster and get your pick,*
*    me pal,*
*We'll whack a ditch through this murky swamp, and call*
*    it a canal.*

*Refrain*
*Wabash and Erie, Wabash and Erie, you dreadful, dirty*
*    stream,*
*I've sold my soul for government gold and the American*
*    dream.*

*Flies and heat and sweat so bad that I can hardly see,*
*Pass the whisky, this canal won't get the best of me.*
*(Refrain)*

*Move the clay 'till your arms fall off, and your hands be*
*    black as pitch.*
*I've dug my way halfway to hell for this great big son of*
*    a ditch.*
*(Refrain)*

# Chapter Fifteen
## The McClure Papers

To: Mrs. Auraleigh McClure, New Harmony, Indiana
From: James McClure, Indiana Canal Commission, Indianapolis, Indiana

March 5, 1838

My Dear Wife:

I take my pen in hand tonight with a good deal of sadness, after your last letter. The news that you are considering making our separation permanent falls like drops of molten lead on my heart.

I know that I have not been much of a father to Samuel and Estella. I came to you in New Harmony as often as I could—well, let us not dwell on that subject. I am glad Samuel has gone to Hanover College and that he will read the law. I was afraid the sporadic and inadequate education he received in New Harmony would have handicapped him.

Estella will make a good mother someday, should the man who can tolerate her "spirited temper" win her.

I have been sorely tried as I have attempted to be a loving parent and a loyal public servant at both the same time.

What I have been doing is—well, I think time will show the importance of this grand Hoosier scheme. I always promised you I would not be at it forever, that I would return to southern Indiana someday, although I do not see myself, or you, living on the family acres (reduced as they are now).

No, instead I shall probably hang out my shingle in one of the small towns. I had always thought you would be with me. I cannot believe you think in another way.

You cannot doubt my fidelity, although I have had my chances. Indianapolis is small, but it is the world at times. I do not doubt your loyalty to me, although I will admit the early ardor we shared has not been manifested in physical ways much any more. The fires so often common to McClures have in my case been much dampened by the demands of public service, and I suspect this has often been less than pleasing to you.

You make other charges—let them rest. The one thing you say which I feel I will, MUST answer is this: "This THING has altered you. You have picked up the corruptive nature of the whole canal building enterprise."

By "This THING" I take it you mean the whole Improvement Program, the Wabash and Erie Canal—the grand scheme I have given my life to, which is now about to come to fruition.

Can you not wait and see the momentous events that are about to occur? Can you not put aside these petty, personal concerns and give yourself to this grand vision of the future for the State?

I had thought when we married that you shared my concern for society—let it alone.

Now as to my being corrupted. I feel I must go back with you to the time I first became a commissioner for the Wabash and Erie Canal. You remember the soul searching I did then, after poor unfortunate Jack's death at Hindostan—a noble death that put my poor life as the governor's whipping boy to shame.

Now, Auraleigh, I admit that as Governor Ray's assistant I did consent to some of the man's chicanery; more, I instigated some of it. But after Jack died, and Governor Ray's fortunes fell, I determined to use my talent and experience to seek employment which would serve the cause of internal improvements in a square manner.

I had friends in the assembly, it is true. They asked me to be on the commission to build the canal to link Lake Erie with the Ohio River—the great dream for two hundred years of every French voyageur, every Indian having to portage, and each settler with corn to sell.

And so we commenced the important task of connecting Ft. Wayne and the Maumee with the Wabash River. Ohio, after all, was doing its part on the other end to build this waterway to Lake Erie.

"High-flying, wasteful spending," you say.

Let us examine that. First, let me concede with you that there were problems from the beginning in paying for this great dream. Indiana's legislature voted to approve this canal while Governor Ray was yet in power, in 1829; yet they sent no money bags along to buy their dream, only some lands to sell. Where were the rest of the funds supposed to come from—the golden rain trees on New Harmony's streets?

Passel of buzzard-brains in their soft chairs in the House of Representatives. I should know, being one of their own. But I was as addled as the rest.

"Money to come from future revenues," the legislature, the newspapers, the farmer ready to ship his grain, said. All of us, without exception and from all parties, looked at the Erie Canal in New York. It was raising a million dollars a year. Why should anyone not think our canal would do the same? The goods of all the heartland West would be passing through this canal to magic markets that stretched on and on, beyond the horizon.

I put full faith in the canal. I took the last of my money out of Brooks' Agricola ventures and bought the best land I could along the canal route from John Tipton, cheap. He had reasons to keep me happy, and I do admit I capitalized on them, if you will pardon the pun, my dear. I sold the Tipton land at a fine profit, and we are rich today because of it. Surely you cannot curse the very canal that buys you bonnets and furs.


I did object to the borrowing that was done without security. Two million dollars in 1832—but I was overruled. But how much sweating and swearing there was to be done in those early days to get that canal started! I was proud to be made labor commissioner. Let the others on the commission take other duties, raise the money, let contracts—I'll recruit the men to dig the canal, I said. After all, I had come from poor folk. My father and grandfather labored with their hands, and I thought I could speak to the Irishmen we needed to dig our "ditch."

You did not strongly protest when I went to Ireland, to my

father's home country. Well, I admit you did not know the number of months I would be gone—going from pub to pub in County Cork and about Dublin and even Ulster, the home of the McClures! But "press game tactics, false promises used to recruit the Irishmen for the canal." You are quite wrong, my dear; instead it was the opposite, as I think you know.

Did I lie to get these hundreds of Irishmen to Ft. Wayne? Did I show circulars, as commissioners from other states did, that showed tidy European-looking little villages when they knew all the time the men would be heading for rude log shacks in the swamps of the Maumee and St. Mary's rivers?

No. I knew what Ft. Wayne looked like—wolves ten miles out of the village stealing sheep, muddy, ridged mule paths for roads, drunks, both white and Indian running horse races in the streets—I knew and I did not water the whisky in the thing.

I told them about the high prices—flour, $10 a barrel, corn, $1.50 a bushel—I can still feel their eyes, staring coldly there, in those villages in Cork; yet, after six months I had my crews, 60 the first sailing, 114 the second, finally a shipload.

Why did they come with me? Because I told them my father John McClure's story, about the enormous stone barn, the brick-yard with servants cooking hams, the fox hunts in the final days. I needed no press gang to recruit this army; the truth was pressing enough, pardon the phrase.

They looked through me, past the poverty of their lives and to the shores of America, and they saw 2,000 acres and a mansion if they worked as hard as my father did. So they came for $78 a month.

Work they did. I sat down at the tables in the pubs in Ireland and pulled out drawings of the canals we would be building in Indiana, between Ft. Wayne and Logansport.

When they came, did they find I lied? No! Grubbing and chopping and shovelling, they pulled out tons of soil and mud that it had taken nature and 10,000 years of river floods to deposit, just as I had told them they would.

I helped to set up that very four-car system your southern Indiana newspaper scavengers are so fond of describing and praising, now that the canal is "good news."

But then, Auraleigh, you were visiting—your only visit—and

saw the four-car system work: fill a one-horse cart, and as soon as that cart is full it leaves, then push another one in its place, fill and it leaves, and so on, so no time is lost.

"No humanity," you say. It was I, your husband, who told the commissioners that my Irishmen had to have relief sometimes, that we must bring in axemen to cut the thirty-foot high walnuts and poplars. The Irishmen were not good at axe work, as it turned out. There aren't a lot of trees left in Ireland, it seems.

I saw to it they got their wages, even when I had to carry them by night from the head of the commission's house. Doctor Coe—now you talk, Auraleigh, about the "seamy underhandedness of the commission"—surely you couldn't find a better Christian man than Doctor Coe. All Indianapolis sings his praises for coming to help us in the fever epidemic, and starting our Sunday schools. He, surely, is an honorable business man, if ever there was one.

Doctor Coe has made our state's name famous and convinced the money-lending people in the big cities, Philadelphia and New York City, to loan Indiana over three million dollars. Three million dollars, Auraleigh, in one swoop. And your husband is at the center of all these proceedings. You should be proud, not carping like a fish wife—let it go.

Now I am going to tell you something, my dear wife. To show you what faith I have in the integrity of this canal and Doctor Coe and my fellow commissioners, I have this year taken all the money left to me by my father and $25,000 I made in those land sales with Tipton and Ray. I have put it into stocks in the Morris Company, Coe's big-city Eastern contact. He has major stock holdings in the company; that is enough for me.

Well, I can see you are mad as a cat in the crick about the credit part of it all. I know you are not the only Hoosier to be that way—over the fact that the legislature has just now blown the whistle for us to start building a whole new, big system of railroads and canals in the state without being nearly done with the Wabash and Erie.

To think that you would rank yourself among the conservatives, and I would seem a liberal in this! Let us have more faith in our state, my dear. Soon this canal will function, Ohio will finish its part to the lake, the Whitewater Canal will span the southeast part of the state, and the Central Canal will hook up to both of them.

I hear you say that we have spent ten years and eight million and have only ninety-nine miles of the Wabash and Erie and thirty miles of these dream canals finished.

My dear, how little faith you have! I know I could have restored it if I had had you with me for the opening of the Wabash and Erie for the little stretch in Wabash, Indiana last year.

If you could have seen the water coming in, merchants from the town kissing the ground, ladies rushing up the banks to meet it. On July 4th three ships came in. Well, the first was not worthy of your note, being a converted maple sugar trough manned by another commissioner and Yours Truly.

But then the *Prairie Hen* and the *Indiana* sailed by before our very eyes on what used to be farmland! Actually sailed all the way from Ft. Wayne on artificial waters I had a share in bringing forth. Being allowed to be on that first boat, to actually see those brave ships and crowds and feel the surging waters of a new age flood beneath me—I felt as my father must have felt as a young man when he reached the docks of Philadelphia and felt a new world beneath his feet.

Auraleigh, their local Indian Chief Allolah whooped and hollered and a band played "Hail Columbia." I never saw anything like it, I tell you since the foxhunt with William Henry Harrison when I was a youth in Knox County, which was a foxy occasion, pardon the pun.

You, my dear, have been involved in air castle schemes which are far less sure than this. Your New Harmony "ideal community" has died a dreary death. Talk about indebtedness—your Robert Owen had his lawsuits before he left, abandoning his dream. But our canal system! The depression can't deflate it; small-minded, low-faced, nay-sayers who talk about the overwhelming debt can't slow it down.

What a silly bunch of schemers your Owenites were. It isn't with philosophers and political undertakings (as I found out) where the future lies, but in commerce. The land, I say, with its crops and raw materials taken to market! Credit and confidence!

Our Indiana legislature, spitting in the very eyes of the debt and fired with the spirit of the future, has authorized full completion of one hundred twenty miles of canal. All projects are to go forward simultaneously.

The money will be found, somehow. Doctor Coe has gone to

raise more money from the Morris Company. The corner is about to be turned.

Tut, tut, don't tell me Coe will be prospering as he does it. That, my dear, is our American system! And the beauty of it is, as he prospers so will we. I cannot think that is bad and I ask, beg you to reconsider and put your faith back in me and our state's projects.

Your husband James

To: Catherine McClure Hogue, Vincennes, Indiana
From: James McClure, Indianapolis, Indiana
May 30, 1838

Dear Cat:

At the very time I am having so much trouble with the canal and matters at my own home, I hear more bad news from Knox County. What's this Lizzie McClure writes me about your young 'un Nancy Jane and my godson Alfred taking up with the Quakers? Listening to Cousin John Robert Scott talk and going to meetings with him? Lizzie is beside herself. She always did call the McClures a bunch of "crazy Scotch Irish hotheads stuffed into fancy suits."

Says they are nothing but poor white-trash Movers, who always got restless sitting around watching the corn grow and the hogs root, so they'd pick up and move. With every wind that blew, the McClures moved on to another house and took up another strange idea. Not too far from wrong, though she makes me mad acting like her people, the Elliotts, are the cream at the top of the bucket all the time.

As if I don't have enough to do as head of this family, trying to see these canals through with the personal trials I face—my godson going over into the next county to Quaker meetings. Do you know how odd those people are and what shame comes to their families when war comes and the Quakers refuse to go? During the last war there were tar and featherings in Indiana, and I don't know what all.

Now it's the abolitionists they bed down with. All I need as a public servant, Whig sort, is having it rumored my kin are trucking with abolitionists and Negroes and whatnot. Some of the Quakers over by Richmond have Negroes in their HOMES and it makes people rabid around here. Course it isn't that I am indignant about, 'tis that I always loved Jack best of all people (except Auraleigh, of course, can't forget that) and I promised Jack if anything ever happened to him, I'd look after Alfred.

Quakers. Don't you recall how John Hogue and I and the others had to ride after you when you and Mary McClure joined the Shakers? Didn't you learn even a thimbleful of sense, Cat, in all that? Haven't we got enough common sense churches that people can attend?

Uncle Dan'l, rest his soul, and our pa's, John and George McClure, held no truck with these peace-mongering, tall-hatted fools that call themselves the Friends. In Pennsylvania they set the Indians on the settlers; our own pa's saw it.

Now Cat, I can't be there and I expect you to handle this. I'll write to John Robert Scott, too, although I don't expect much from that neck of the woods. Always was an odd boy, whole family odd, if you ask me.

Jim

P.S. Now don't any of you tell me our grandfather was called The Scotch Quaker—only a way of speaking, it was.

You settle those young'uns squirrel hash and write me that you have done it quick.


To: James McClure, Esquire, Indianapolis, Indiana
From: Catherine McClure Hogue, Vincennes, Indiana
June 10, 1838


Dear Jim:

I can't understand your snit over the young'uns going to Quaker meetings. You may be out on the shed roof in a cold wind on this one.

"Quaker" isn't "Shaker," although the Friends are odd enough anyways. Let me tell you, I'm not so sure they aren't right in wanting us all to stay away from wars. But then I'm not going to expect a veteran of the Battle of Tippecanoe to agree with me on that. You old members of Harrison's brave militia are ready to rout enemies out of every blackberry bush you pass.

Nancy Jane HAS been a trial to me, I must admit. Sweet and beautiful as ever my mother was; indeed, she favors her. She has a will stronger than my own. You will know what I mean when I say that, cousin.

And I'll tell you about Jack's Alfred, since he's the one you're really concerned about, being your godson and all. I don't think Hanover College helped him to be anything else but a dreamer. Since his father is gone, and since Aunt Martha and Uncle Daniel were taken in the cholera, every filosofical wind that blows up he sniffs at. First he and sofmoric friends read about Mezmer and he tries to mezemerize his brothers and sisters and made em bump into trees.

Then the frenola, that is, phranologist (dang these big words) came to Vincennes and Alfred started feeling the bumps on everybody's head. Not mine I can tell you.

Smart as a bullwhip ever since he was eighteen months old but as flighty as a barnswallow. Nancy Jane calls it the "dreamy smarts," and she worries about it in her cousin. Still, she worships the very dirt he walks on.

I know you have tried to write him some settlin letters, had him up to Indianapolis to visit you, but Alfred is who he is. And I am going to tell you something, some of what he does and says—even some of the abolitionist talk—makes sense! There, I've said it. Bout time some of us in southern Indiana started thinking about the brotherhood of man and peace. The Scriptures do teach it, you know. But all that sort of talk makes Lizzie run around like a rabid terrier. Lizzie never could understand a word Alfred said, but then all she ever understood was the receept for watermelon pickles and the Book of Job.

Man is short of days and full of sorrows.

Only Jack could have handled Alfred, but he gave himself up to Hindostan. Can't think of that without thinking of Pa, so sad.

Wisht I had my mother's faith, a gift, and the ones who have it greatly are gifted indeed, as the Indians say.

What I want to tell you, cousin, is this. Should've got to it earlier in this letter, but I wanted to work up to it. Nancy Jane, Alfred and cousin John Robert have gone off with a Quaker missionary group from Orange County. They and an old man named Sylvester Brown and one other Quaker have taken a steamboat down the Mississippi. They have gone on a mercy mission that they say we McClures ought to be proud they've taken on. Pshaw. I won't go that far.

Here 'tis—Jay Byrd Dugger and his sons, you know they've been running that slapdash camp at the mouth of White River— they've kidnapped Charlotte, your Pa's old slave, and her husband Moses and their son Little Abe, from the colored settlement down by the Ohio. They are selling them as slaves in Natchez, so 'tis said, even though they are free people.

This Quaker posse intends to track and free the colored folk. I thought you would want to know about this. Cousin, tisn't anything to be done. Both Nancy Jane and Alfred are free, white, and twenty-one and anyways, they've already left. My heart hurts to think what they may meet on this trip.

I'm sorry if you don't like it. I don't either, although I'm on the new Non-slavery Committee at Upper Indiana Church. Common sense should tell us 'tis dangerous to run afoul of men selling human property.

Your cousin
Cat

## The Poore Papers
### Hannah Poore's Journal
### (Continued)

July 1, Mt. Pleasant, Indiana,

Cares of the distaff, women's chores, have occupied my time, which I have not had to devote to this journal. 'Tis regretful to me that I am not at my home in Orange County, while Thomas Jefferson and Susan take a long-postponed trip back to the East.

They say I am needed to take care of young Lewis, Emily, and Little Susan. But I know the real reason I have been asked here is that Susan and Thomas Jefferson have really fretted about me living alone out in that still remote Orange County home of mine. It seems odd that with such a big family I am alone at last, but Alvan and Julia moved to Cincinnati and the rest married, even my babies Johnny and Amelia, and all are in their own homes.

Except for Harriet, and that will change next month.

July 3. A letter has arrived from Sylvester, which I shall copy exactly into this journal:

Friend Hannah:

We are baying like Quaker bloodhounds on the trail. My outrage keeps me hot and fuming. I can still hardly believe that these despicable—I cannot call them men—beasts have kidnapped a family freed from indenture for over ten years. They snatched our friends from their own home near the Ohio river and spirited them off to a flatboat, where their confederates waited. But they will not succeed.

We have been two days on the steamboat and are at Memphis. Friend John Robert Scott is a true Lion of Judah. What a convert he is: zealous and strong in his witness. The two young people are as eager as their cousin to witness to Christ's love to the world in the way of His appointing. I shall describe them to thee.

Nancy Jane is a willowy girl with a complexion as light as a milkmaid's. Her cousin Alfred McClure, compared to her is like the evening to the morning, dark skinned, with a black hank of hair and soft gentle eyes. He is intensely sensitive. Thee and I met the grandfather, Dan'l McClure, and it seems to me Alfred looks like him; Scott tells me he favors in remarkable fashion his great-grandfather the Irish McClure, at least from a family miniature.

On this steamboat trip, Nancy Jane is the practical one in our group, seeing us into the dining salon, as they call this small cabin with a gummy table, watching our satchels and bags.

We are going to camp now. The Quakers in Memphis have sent an inquiry down the line—thee will know what I mean.

We go onto the trail; these people-snatching Duggers have not gone to Natchez; we know that, but into Tennessee. We shall pursue the slavers discreetly. This is dangerous work. The Duggers carry their "slaves" at gun-point. I almost wish we had not brought the young folk with us. I do not mind facing guns and hatred myself, but do I have the right to place others' lives in danger? Let us hope God directs.

I shall write as soon as there is an outcome.

Thy Friend
Sylvester


Back to Mt. Pleasant doings:

July 8. Harriet is going to make a charming bride. We have had the local dressmaker fashion a satin gown and veil. John Poore's parents, his father's side particularly, would have been impressed to see the guest list, everyone in three counties. Pity John could not see how his family has come up in the world. A carriage, a mansion house (well at least Thomas and Susan have one) and Harriet betrothed to John Houghton, nephew of one of the wealthiest man in southern Indiana.

Aaron Houghton, John's uncle, has a prosperous mill and the ferry on a bend of White River near here. There are two mills in this area now, Thomas's and Mr. Houghton's, and grain enough and more for them to grind. How we do grow!


July 14. Four more days until the nuptials. Today I planted Massachusetts grape hyacinths and strawberry slips in the garden of the cabin where the newlyweds will live. I did the same eight years ago at Thomas and Susan's large house up the road and around the corner. It should make me happy that these sisters will be near each other, but today I am in low spirits.

Nobody says it, but of course there is a sad shadow on this wedding, try as we will to make nothing of it: the bride is so shy, if that is the word, that she speaks only in whispers, and she does not go out of the house. Some sort of anxiety binds my beautiful daughter to her home.

It is a severe trial to Harriet that she must move to a new place when she marries. I have seen her wringing her hands and heard her pacing in her bedroom at night. What a disorder she has had since that awful day when Mark Ebenezer took himself from us! She can only rest when she is under the home roof. Cold sweat breaks out upon her brow when she must go only across the road to chase her kitten.

Coming here for this long visit with Susan was almost impossible for my poor Harriet to accomplish. She so wanted it, but when the moment came to put valises into the wagon, put the dust covers over our laps, and have Johnny drive us—she wept and shook and I had to lay her head in my lap the whole way.

So she has not been to church or to visit any of the young people here. She has not been able to enjoy any of the spelling bees and picnics that she has been invited to. Finally the young people have stopped inviting her and accept this indisposition of character she suffers.

Miraculously, John Houghton found and loved her here, in her sequestered nest. God grant that the married state may unbind her heart and give her freedom. Her sweetness and giving heart touch all who meet her, but to her mother it is a sad pain to see the throttling of her spirit since that day ten years ago.

I anxiously await news of the progress of Susan and Thomas's visit in the East. Some Mt. Pleasant folk talk behind our backs of Susan's not being here to be bridal matron for her sister. I think the illness of Thomas's mother sufficient warrant for their going to Massachusetts. Beyond that—Thomas has never been back home. He left Lincoln so many years ago in haste with rancor in his heart, with more pain than he will admit, tearing his roots from the soil.

As we all did. How many of us here in this Northwest have left half of ourselves in New England, or Virginia? I have never looked back, no Lot's wife I, but some part of me still lives in Newbury, among the daisies in the garden of Father Chute's old house.

They all wish me to move here to Mt. Pleasant, but I cannot;

there is no one to take care of the house and see to my roses and peonies. More than that, I must continue the important work Sylvester and I have begun—too secret and dangerous to speak of even in these pages—yet.

I await his word, and the wedding of my dear daughter!


July 18. Thanks be to Christ who has blessed this wedding of my dear girl as he blessed the nuptials at Cana. Thomas and Susan's children were angels, Emily as fine a six-year-old flower girl as could be wished for, strewing petals of roses, Lewis at three a fine, serious bearer of the bridal bouquet.

I shall always remember the beautiful bower of flowers on the bank of the river, and John Houghton's sister playing the pianoforte, Moore's "Believe Me If All Those Endearing Young Charms,"

> *No, the heart that has truly loved, never forgets*
> *But as truly loves on to the close*
> *As the sunflower turns on her god when he sets*
> *The same look that she gave when he rose.*

John, John, I miss you yet, and especially today.


Harriet clasped her handkerchief into a million wrinkles, yet said out clearly the words "I do." But when she stood in line in that bright sunlight, taking the hands of well-wishers, she could only nod and smile and look at the garden gate, realizing soon she would be going through that portal to the world she so fears.


July 21. Letter from Thomas and Susan. They had a safe trip and are having a good visit in Massachusetts. Thank God they are safe. The stagecoach stuck fast in the mud near Boston. They were over two hours freeing it. Two gentlemen refused to help free the wheels, as all the other men were doing, and there was an argument and fist-fight, Thomas says. At least it was not the dead of winter and the infernal coach on sled runners having to be pushed up the hill. Progress! Susan and Thomas and baby Tommy will start back next week. Susan reports the corn in New England is stunted and dwarfish, nothing like our mile-high grain in Indiana.

July 28. A letter from Sylvester, herewith copied into my journal:

Dear Friend Hannah:

Moses and Charlotte and Little Abe are safe. Let me tell you how the Lord has worked in this matter. We went together, I and our brother Frederick Lindley from Orangeville meeting, Nancy Jane and Alfred and John Robert Scott, in a hired wagon into the countryside in Tennessee.

We journeyed out the road not far from the river, where our contacts said the poor, kidnapped, colored friends were. They had been sold as slaves to a dirt-farmer who has a few fields of cotton and hemp and many, many pigs.

We decided to go as the sun began to sink in late afternoon, allowing only time to take care of our mission and return to the river camp. We bravely came to the slovenly farm, kicking chickens from our path. When a sour-faced man came to the opening of the house (I cannot call it a door, 'twas a blanket) I bowed low, sweeping off my hat. "Neighbor, we've come to strike a deal with you."

John Robert Scott told him we had come to buy his slaves (almost choking on the words), that they were family retainers from our old southern Indiana family.

The man looked at me suspiciously. Out of the corner of my eye I could see our colored friends come out of a run-down cabin down a rubble-filled path.

I asked this Tennessee farmer if he could part with his property if he got sufficient money for them.

"Cain't do it," he said in a guarded voice, obviously wondering why such a group of us wanted to buy his new slaves. "I got 'em fair and square with some money I made on the corn still." He smiled a toothless smile. Give him credit, he was honest. "Bought 'em so's I can be a gentry. Step up to a big house with them thar pillars on a hill." He had met Luke Dugger down at the river and they had struck a deal. "What's it to you?" he asked, his voice suddenly harsh.

'Twas then that Alfred came in. "Sir, please," he said, hat in hand. "I'm thinking of moving to Caintuck and taking these folk with me. Start a stand of my own and I want to take nigras with me. Pay 'em a dollar or two, take care of 'em." It was only a small lie. We were going to take care of them.

A worn woman with a sunbonnet on had come up behind the man, and the smell of potatoes cooking with onions floated out the door. Alfred went on, seemingly inspired. "Sir, these nigras have been in our family for forty years. Why, my great uncle bought Abraham's ma and pa at a sale near Frankfort. If it wasn't for the damn northern laws in Indiana—well, you understand. That's why I'm heading for states rights territory."

Nancy Jane stood behind her cousin, smiling so sweetly at this gnarled, suspicious man. She did not once look at the rifle he held firmly at his side.

The man seemed convinced on "moral grounds" of what Alfred and John Robert had said. He looked to me to see how much would be offered, and Frederick Lindley, our well-off friend from the Orangeville meeting, said, "We are ready to pay you twice what you gave Dugger."

The woman behind the new slave owner tugged at his sleeve. I could see Charlotte, Moses, and Little Abe watching with their eyes wide open. The man cleared his throat.

" 'Twill be hard to get new niggers. Still—"

Martin pulled out a bankroll. "We need to be on our way within the hour. We have boat space."

And before we knew it, we had a deal. The wagon pulled away from the house, loaded with all of us. As soon as we rounded the bend on our way to camp, our colored friends began laughing and crying and slapping us on the backs, and it was worth all the trouble. And I thanked God that we were away without the dirt farmers having any second thoughts. It wouldn't do to be classified as "interfering abolitionists." Others who had risked these dangerous rescues had been shot at, and two Quakers had already been killed defending runaway colored folk, at Copper Creek in Virginia.

We were determined that the Duggers would not remain unpunished. We would pay court costs for Moses to sue that kidnapper in the courts of his home county. And, if the Duggers chose to be ugly about it all—well, "those that wait upon the Lord" do dwell under His shadow and protection.

The young cousins have been bricks of courage and witness. As I write this in our camp tonight, Nancy Jane is ill. Her cousin Alfred tends her in her canvas tent at the edge of the clearing. As I listen, I can hear their low voices in the dusky darkness. What friends they are, although sometimes lately they seem irritable with each other. Probably the strain of this holy escapade. Their uncle and our colored friends, quite exhausted, are long since asleep. I shall seal this and post it at Memphis; I long to be in the arms of Morpheus and sleep after all the excitement.


Next morning—

My dear friend Hannah, a strange and unsettling thing has occurred. The two young cousins have gone off with each other, to the consternation of their older relative, John Robert Scott, and my complete amazement. I cannot account for it. I shall inform thee as soon as I can determine what has caused this untoward event. We must hasten to catch the steamboat.

Thy friend,
Sylvester


## The McClure Papers


To: Catherine McClure Hogue, Vincennes, Indiana
From: Nancy Jane Hogue McClure, Memphis, Tennessee
August 2, 1838


Ma—

How can I put pen to paper here in Memphis knowing what you and Pa will feel. Still I must.

Come to it, pen. Alfred and I are married. We were made man and wife by a small country parson along the Trace in Tennessee. We will catch the steamboat today and join Cousin John Robert and our Quaker friends in Louisville, hoping for their forgiveness for what we have done.

And so the truth. We have married in our own family, and we've deceived you about it. Ma, it was partly your fault. You and Pa and Cousin Jack when he was still here and John Robert and the rest have thrown us all together, all of us, the McClure family—for as long as I can remember. I can't recall a young people's meeting at Upper Indiana Church or a Christmas Eve when Alfred and I were children when we weren't together, and when I didn't love him.

Ma, we have tried. Somehow it seems odd or wrong to fall in love with close kin. Even though we are second cousins, not first, it has a strange ring to it. Maybe it was just that the family would disapprove, especially Aunt Lizzie. She never did like me, or any of us McClures, really. All those things she says about McClures, that there's two kinds, the wild, drinking, fighting ones and the prissy, smarter-than-thou ones. And both are bad. Says Alfred's pa was a combination of both. Don't know why she said that—he didn't drink much.

Then, after Alfred's pa Jack died, Lizzie kept Alfred away from us all. 'Twas as if all the bitterness she felt in her unhappy marriage poured out on us McClures, and I felt it, always. She didn't understand why we all always wanted to be together. "Too much McCluring" was how she put it and didn't even come to Christmas.

Ever since Alfred and I first knew how we felt, we have hid it from ourselves and denied our love, tore ourselves from each other, paining to be together and paining more when we had to be apart. When John Robert Scott started taking us to Quaker meetings, he couldn't know. Then, we thought we had got over each other in the new faith we'd found. I wanted to come with John Robert, and Alfred did, too. We hadn't planned anything, I swear it. In fact, Alfred said he thought friends in Christ could be together for the good of the cause. God knows we tried.

But, Ma, 'twasn't to be. Coming here on this mission I have seen him day and night. I shouldn't have come, I guess, but I thought I was strong. God gave me the strong faith of my Grandma Jean and I thought this would be the test.

We failed. That night by the campfire, when I was so tired and he came to take care of me—well, we knew we must be married. Ma, we can't live apart. He needs me, needs me take care of him. I need him to make me see the world outside my piece of country. He talks so of what he reads, and he reads all the time. Some day he will be a famous lawyer, I know it. He is the smartest, knowingest man I have ever seen.

Maybe our being McClure is a large part of what happened. You always say all the McClures are so much alike, and it lasts through the generations. I think that is so true. He is as different from me as a dog from a doughnut, but he sees things the way I do. When I hear him laugh, it seems as if it is my own voice I hear—Grandma Jean always said 'twas old Jane McClure from Ireland laughing in whoops in all of us. When he cries, I cry twict.

We love our relatives more because they understand us, accept us. So my love for Alfred is one plus one.

Alfred is most afraid of his sister Jewell's tongue on this. He knows she will not speak to him. "Uppity," Jewell called him, "Blue blood." She railed at Alfred when she saw us together and guessed at our love. Poor little farm gal, happy married to Archie Simpson, with his common ways. She can't start to understand, can she? Alfred was born for bigger things than Knox County backwater.

I cannot say more. The post is ready to ride.

Tell Pa I love him, always have loved him.

Your daughter
Nancy Jane McClure

P.S. You say I most favor my Grandma Jean of any of your brood. Did she not run off, so to speak, with Grandpa George?

## The Poore Papers

To: Hannah Chute Poore, Brooks House, Mt. Pleasant, Indiana
From: John Robert Scott, Louisville, Kentucky

August 10, 1838

My dear Madam:

I need to write particularly to you about matters of both public good and private need.

Our Quaker mission shall return with our colored protegés within the week; we are arranging for their safe settlement in Indiana, at Richmond at the Quaker community there.

I know you will keep this letter in the bond of secrecy of our sacred cause—shall I write the words? Simon's Net.

I have had some occasion to check out our Southern contacts down here. After the murder in Virginia that all the papers were full of, I have had to be circumspect. I did see the Tennessee Tanner and the Society outside Nashville on the Alabama and Mississippi undergrounds.

All they can do, they say, is give very secret information and advice at this time.

Any help these poor colored souls get to flee to freedom will have to occur north of the Ohio River—Southerners are very much up in arms about runaway slaves and treat anyone who would be sympathetic to helping slaves flee with law and violence. These new laws enforce that slaves must be returned if they run. Property rights—pah, how can these folk count themselves Christians? But for the slavers, there are financial rewards in chasing down their fellow beings and returning them to the life of imprisonment that is slavery.

Indiana stations are ready, as they have been ever for the last five years. How many folk have we helped? Fifty? Seventy-five? God bless you for your part, Mrs. Poore. I know you did not wish to leave your farm there in Orange County even for your daughter's wedding and to care for your grandchildren. It does you credit that you fretted because new runaways might come to your station while you were gone.

Only a real Christian would have exposed herself to the dangers you have without a man there in the woods. Fugitive slavers deprived of their prey and reward by the underground railroad can be violent. It is hard to believe that the Dugger clan are not the worst of the lot, but it is true.

It is all too vicious in a free society. These new laws expose us all—you a lone woman who wishes to help her fellow humans, I as commander of Simon's Net in Indiana, our Quaker friends who are a part of it, and idealistic young folk like my cousins Alfred and Nancy Jane. All of us have banded to create a net of help for poor runaway slaves who wish only to live free. All of us live with guns at our heads.

My dear friend, it is now too dangerous for you to occupy that key station in Orange County. I need to be frank; the situation calls for those who can be physically agile. Younger folk, for the good of The Net.

I know that only by ordering you away from this place that is now fraught with risk can I get you to leave your post, so I now do it. I ask that you remove yourself for a while from the firing line there outside Paoli and the direct road north to freedom.

You have told me your daughter Susan and Thomas Jefferson wish you to live with them. I urge an extended stay. You may consider it a new assignment if you wish. We need a small message station at Mount Pleasant, and so you can be of service to the cause there.

Now for the favor I have to ask of you—I should be saying "thee," but I am too old to begin that. Should you grant this favor, it would serve both our cause and my own family.

You recall my young cousins, Alfred and Nancy Jane. They have become Quakers recently and joined the mission from conscience. They both say they wish to redeem our McClure family's slaving history; for, Alfred McClure said recently, " 'Twas my relative who owned the ancestor of Charlotte and Little Abe, so we all have blame to expiate."

They are fine young people with sincere vision.

But they have run off now from our mission and married; I believe Sylvester wrote to you of it. It is a matter of strong consternation in my family and some of them are not speaking. In Kentucky folks shoot each other from behind mountain tops over family fights; in southern Indiana they shun each other, wounding with words that spread throughout the farm neighborhoods like poisoned arrows.

We have never spoken much of my family. You have often inquired of them, so now I shall take a minute to answer your kind questions. I know you knew my Uncle Daniel and through your daughter, my nephews Dr. Jack and Representative James McClure, who is now in Indianapolis with the canals. I am an only child; well, I did have a brother, Ishmael, whom I barely knew. Ish brought disgrace to the family years ago and we are told died in Texas in 1827, under dark cirumstances.

My father, James Scott, died at 82 last year. My dear mother Jenny stays at home with my family at Scott Farm, which is across from Harrison's ruined Fort Knox.

Mother does not know me and has not for several years, but oddly enough she does seem to respond to my baby twin children. We have an older son, James, and my wife Mahalia bore twins last year. My mother seems to brighten perceptibly when Jacob Joe, a sweet, easy child is in the room; strangely; when his difficult brother Zach is with him she seems agitated. We do not know how to explain it.

Now, on to my personal request. The sister Jewell and mother Lizzie of Alfred McClure are adamantly opposed to his marriage with his cousin. I do not think it so awful myself; the two young people are strong in the bonds of Simon's Net and strong in Christ. But Lizzie and her daughter say they have had enough of McClures, that it was the McClure wild strain that caused all the trouble in their lives.

It would be very painful for Nancy Jane and Alfred to return to Knox County right now. My cousin Catherine Hogue, Nancy Jane's mother, joins me in this request: could the newly married couple occupy your house and farm your land for you, with proper arrangements of course, while you stay at Mt. Pleasant? They are eager to be active station managers for Simon's Net, and I think it highly advisable they do so.

We shall await your post at Louisville. Should you allow it, the young folk can go to housekeeping and farming immediately.

Alfred wishes to read law but has said he will have to defer it for many reasons for the present. They would relish the opportunity to join Sylvester and the active Quaker community there.

Yours, in the bonds of affection and of Simon's Net.

John Robert Scott

*Chapter Sixteen*

# The Deposition of Kezegat Dauga
# of the Potawatomi
### (Continued)

From the time of the Indian treaties in the white man's year 1826, both Potawatomi and Miami in western Indiana and states nearby were pressed as if by an enemy in war camp.

Like drums in the night came the voices to us in the years 1830, 31, 32, each year with ever stronger reverberations. In harsh and insulting tones, one group of people was speaking to another:

"Listen, savages. You have sold most of your land. Sell the remnant! Take more of the annuity money and tinsel toys we offer and give up the last forests and riverlands. You are the people who killed our fathers. You scare our cattle and steal pigs. Our children do not like to look at you. Prepare to gather up your things and move out of here."

We determined not to listen and, hard as it was, to hold on to the small parcels allocated to various tribes in the treaties and to lead our lives on them. After all, they had been granted to us by the Congress of the U.S. government.

I decided to move my medicine tent to the large camp of Menominee, a mile from our camp at Twin Lakes. Pauk spent most of his time with me. He did not part from Twin Lakes wife, Ears Ringing, and although he parted with the Tippecanoe wife, he continued to visit Ears Ringing sometimes. He loved his son Waterdog. If truth be told, so did I, and there was more than a little yearning in me when I saw him. I wanted my own child.

I did not complain about Ears Ringing, but the priest at Menominee's camp, Father Deseille, and the chief himself, mentioned the English word "bigamy" to Pauk.

"The Old Ones allowed more than one wife, and you know I always honor the ways of the Old Ones," Pauk answered Chief Menominee. The chief said nothing more. This wise one did not wish to confront the son of Chief Aubenaubee.

Pauk talked much about the ways of our people these days. "We no longer honor the ways of the *Neshnabec*, the People. It was not enough that we gave up war totems and manhood quests in the wild. We allow the women to touch us even at times when we must be brave and strong. Some of this Menominee tribe who are Christians do many new things. They do not bury their dead in log pens facing the rising sun but in Christian graves."

He went on. "First Menominee said that he was a prophet. He told his own tales of Virgin Mary and Christ and connected them with our Indian stories. But now that this Father Deseille has come and built a regular church, Menominee is a Roman Catholic. But he will not get a convert in me!"

"Nor I," I affirmed. I wanted to reassure Pauk, because I sometimes went to the Masses at the new log church. I enjoyed the smells of the incense and the chanting in the odd, choppy language, much as I had enjoyed watching the shaman do his rites so long before.

But Pauk was not thinking about me. He was continuing to rage about the changing times. "These weddings are the worst of all. Soon I will see braves of my band stuff themselves into long-tailed coats like the whites, wear top hats and carry nosegays to their brides. Soon we will all eat yellow wedding cake." I knew he mourned for the great giftings, the exchange of fine ponies and clothing and silver such as had happened at the marryings of my mother and father, Asondaki Alamelonda and Swiftly Running Feet.

I had brought Swiftly Running Feet to the Twin Lakes camp from her home at Lake of the Boulders, Mocksinkickee. Her relatives there had died, and I wanted her with me.

She did not share the views of Paukooshuck my husband. "We should not hang on past our time," she said, "like an old woman who is of no use but clings to life. We should think of moving where there is more land to hunt and where those who want to keep our ways can be free to do so. Some of our chiefs have gone to scout across the Mississippi, so they say, and some say it is good land, with deer and bear and many trees along clean streams and even fur-bearing animals we can sell."

But few listened to my mother, Swiftly Running Feet. Menominee and Paukooshuck were fighting to hold on to these last riverlands—the "Potawatomi Reservations" left after the treaties of the last ten years. My mother said that was of no use.

"The white man worships gold and knows how to make it work to do things—to run time clocks and look at the stars and operate railroad trains. We cannot do any of that and should give up this old life and learn the white man's ways. That is the future, and it cannot be stopped any more than the flood in spring can be held back. I knew Tecumseh and lived in his camp. If that great one could not beat the whites, you will not either. Besides, we must learn to trust the white man. If we show trust and friendship and do as they wish, they will treat us fairly. It is that we have always fought them."

She was saying this in the summer lodge. Pauk, who did not believe a man should speak to his mother-in-law, grew exasperated and said, anyway, "We will honor our own ways and keep ourselves pure of their corruption. And we will learn what we have to, the good things to make life better for our families. But we will not trust them. They cheat even at moccasin game, which as any fool knows is stupid. We will use the brains the Maker of the Universe gave us and use the white man's laws to hold our land."

But my mother would only shake her head.

"Let the white man have his way. Do not fight him; it will call forth the Bat Manitto—trouble and chaos."

But it was too late. My husband and Menominee were already fighting hard to keep the land. They spoke often with Father Deseille, the priest who came to Twin Lakes and who had built a Christian log church there. He pored over treaty law with them to be sure they understood it.

All this was as a wind blowing over a lodge at night to me while I was warm and safe inside, because my healing practice was my life. I was developing the skill of bone-setting. Because of the fighting and drinking and falling off horses and cliffs there were more bones to be set than ever.

I practiced snapping bones cleanly back in place, binding skillfully and strongly, and giving strong tea of bone-set plant for pain and healing. The wrists I bound did not twist like a bird's claw and form bone lumps, and I was glad.

I took my madstone almost as far as the Illinois border and never did I let it out of my sight. No! I often put it right on a gaping, bleeding bite wound of squirrel or raccoon, dog or cat, and it stuck fast and absorbed the poison. It worked; I knew not how.

But none of us could live in peace, try as we would, for the white man kept calling us back to council. I, as a skillful interpreter of the tongue to English, was often called on. And because they gave valuable presents and because it helped me be wise about these men's ways—I went.

So did Pauk. Often did we all break camp, often talk together, often wonder sadly, anxiously at these fallen times. Something was broken from the times we played together, without care at cousin-teasing games. Broken, like the bones I set. I knew what it was. It was the life and will of my people.

In the spring of 1832 Aubenaubee, chief of our Potawataomi bands, began to have messages that we of Indiana, Illinois, and Michigan must come together with the speakers for Secretary of War Lewis Cass.

"They will push our faces in the dung because of the Black Hawk War in Illinois. It was not our war, was Sauk and Fox, but we must eat dirt for it. They will use this war to take more of the pittance that we have," said Pauk.

And so, in October we went to Tippecanoe River, Pauk and his father Aubee, along with Menominee to talk of treaties, I to interpret. Three "great men" of the whites were to talk to us, but two were fools.

At first council meeting, my father Aubenaubee stood and said to one particular fool, Davis, "Does our Great Father intend to insult us by sending such men to treat with us? Why did he not send General Cass or Tipton? You, Davis, are a big man but a damn stupid fellow."

"Good, my father," whispered Pauk, after I had translated the statement to the commissioners, who grunted with displeasure. "Perhaps now that the dogs have snarled, the white men will not kick them in the ribs quite so hard," Pauk whispered to me.

But he did not know how wily these men were. My mother was right. They plied all of our men with wines, fine wines, and brandy and whisky. Through my sadness as I watched them drink and roar about, I looked gratefully at Pauk, glad that he had pledged never to touch this white man's poison. Who knew what he would have been like if the Black Moods had been fired by liquor?

Oh, the white officials were clever. John Tipton and his herd of trader friends had stampeded to the treaty grounds voracious for land and determined. The government had decided to offer over $150,000 worth of trade goods should the Potawatomi give up the rest of their land, and the traders were ready with pots and pans as abundant as acorns in Smoky Moon. They were licking their chops like wolves.

The commissioners divided off the prairie Potawatomi from the Illinois and finally got some minor chiefs of each to sign. They separated off the St. Joseph Potawatomi and some of them, drunk, gave up all claims to lands in south Michigan, northern Illinois and Indiana.

And then they went after Aubee. "Out of the lands we take, you will have a reservation of twenty-six sections if you sign," they said.

"No, Father, no," Pauk pleaded. "Do not listen to this bribe. They tease you with bait and make you a decoy," Pauk begged Aubee in camp that night.

"I shall not send them the white belt of peace," Aubee said to his son. "Do not worry, Pauk."

But he was already half-drunk when he said it, and by evening these clever men had thought of something else.

The next day, as I stood as interpreter for my husband's father in the matter of our homeland, the white men added more minnows to the baitline. "Ten more sections for you at beautiful Lake Maxincuckee."

Aubee's eyes were at first evasive, then narrow. "*Sawcon,*" he ordered in Potawatomi, pointing at me. "Go."


Aubenaubee of the Potawatomi caved in to white greed and signed at the Treaty of 1832 for the reservation lands they offered him and some other considerations.

And my husband Paukooshuck beat the dirt at the treaty ground with his fists and painted his face with black charcoal.

And this I do certify, that the traders who camped about John Tipton's nearby town of Logansport, who swore, and gambled and drank and ate like pigs waiting for the results, when they heard the news of the signing, rushed to the grounds with $68,000 of goods to be immediately distributed as token of the rest.

And I do say that they sold $3 blankets for $10 apiece, $10 horses for $50, and watered whisky at three times its fair price. Ewing and the rest of the traders banded together and fixed the prices of everything ridiculously high, so they would not have to compete with each other.

These traders, some of whom were related to our own Potawatomi, arranged for chiefs like Thunder Comes Late and Crows Fighting to sign that they had received three times the goods they got. The traders gave the band chiefs baskets of trinkets for doing it. Then the traders went to the government to collect for inflated sums.

This I saw myself. The next thing I did not see, but it is said by those who know. The commissioners raised prices one more time on invoices to the government and kept what was over.

The Black Mood was hard upon Paukooshuck when he came home, and others mumbled too. "Aubee should not be chief," some braves murmured. "You are the strong man," they said to Pauk. It is odd to me, when I think about it now, that some were friends of the white traders.

"I say honor the old ways of our people," Pauk told these murmuring men. "A chief cannot be removed because you say so."

And all the camp was anguished because of what had happened, and Menominee said he had not signed, and there was fighting and more drinking and the women said, "What will happen next? We cannot bear and raise little ones when it is like this." And children hid in the lodges as the men hit each other and stabbed their relatives.

Broken bones, broken people, Lords of the Rivers, Keepers of the Fire.


The Black Mood settled also on Aubenaubee, Chief of our band, and he drank watered-down whisky day and night in his camp near the Tippecanoe. He would sign no more treaties ever, he said. He would stay in his camp and not come out for any white man. And as for going west, they would have to kill him to take him there. He told it to all, for two years he kept saying it, and all knew this time, in his humiliation, he meant it.

But the Bat Manitto haunted his dreams. And none in his villages really respected him any more, no matter what he said. His main wife, the mother of Paukooshuck, threw Aubenaubee's venison at him and did not fix fresh beans and corn any more. And one night she laughed when he came to her mat. She said, in scorn, "A true man may lie by me, but this Indian's manhood was left at the white man's Tippecanoe River camp."

So it is said. I did not see it with my own eyes. Perhaps she did not say that, perhaps the Indians who knew the traders only said so. Perhaps they had their reasons for saying so. They said Aubee took his wife and carried her outside to the giant cooking rock and beat her against it with all his might and knocked her brains out and crushed her skull, and she died. So it is said.

The council of our band met to rule upon the killing, coming from all the places Aubee was chief: St. Joseph, Mocksinkickee, Tippecanoe, Twin Lakes camp. Pauk must appear before them, they said, and Aubee. After much talk they called Aubee in and said, "The law of the tribe from oldest times says if Paukooshuck comes upon Aubenaubee, then Paukooshuck, the son of a bad father must kill Aubenaubee." And so Aubee left and went away to the far St. Joseph's camp.

And then the elders called in Pauk and said, "For one year, if you see your father, you must kill him for the murder of his wife. You must bring the justice of the *Neshnabec* to him. Times may have changed, but our law remains sure."

And Pauk nodded. He knew of the law of the tribe and had told all to honor it.

But he did say to me, "I shall stay away from my father for a year. That way I can honor the law of the tribe and will not have to kill my own father, poor as he is and possessed of the Bat Manitto. But I fear the worst, because I know when wrongs start running down the trail, they go in whole tribes."

Still, almost a year passed and my heart rose. The whites had left us alone after the treaty; little had happened to implement it.

Even though they pressed us to consider going to Nebraska Territory and sent their exploration parties west, so they would return and tempt us, we would not have it.

Reverend McCoy, my old missionary teacher, took some of his former pupils at the mission and went to scout, and they all returned giving whoops of affirmation for the new spot. "If I know the Potawatomi," said McCoy, "I can promise they will like Nebraska Territory." But when did he ever know the Potawatomi? Not when I knew him, not now.

Still, we knew the government wanted even the reservations Aubenaubee and Menonimee had left, pitiful pittance of the Old Ones' hunting grounds. Like buzzards preening themselves they patiently waited beside a dying animal.

And so a year almost passed, and Aubee and his son had not seen each other, keeping themselves away from family gatherings. But I was nervous in April of that year of 1836, because a wedding was to occur. It was one of those mixed white-Indian weddings that Pauk so despised. Pauk's half-sister, Trisby Rose, whom he particularly loved, and who was born to Aubee and Chief Neswaugee's sister on the shores of Lake Mocksinkickee, was to be married.

At sixteen Trisby Rose was marrying a British soldier. Pauk came into the shelter speaking of the wedding and complaining the day one of his half-brothers brought the invitation to the gifting. My mother and I sat at the cooking fire fixing fish soup.

"My sister is Catholic," Pauk said. "The feast will last for several days, as is the tribal custom, but they will have the nosegay and the wedding cake, and kneeling before the cross of the sad white God."

"Do not look at me with accusing eyes," I said to him. He resented my visits with Father Deseille. "I only talk to the priest because he knows much and I learn French. I do not honor the ghost god, you know."

"Well, we will think on going. There will be feasting and spear-fishing at night with the torches."

I looked up at him. "Will your father—"

"My father will not come," he said quickly. "He knows what we must do, and what not do. But pray to the Manittos that he does not come."

"I do not know if I believe in the Manittos any more. Good bone-set and the madstone are my sacred objects. I trust them and myself. That is all we have and that must be enough."

"And that is what the guiding spirits have told the *Manitto Wabo*," my mother said from over by the cooking fire. There was more than a little scorn in her voice, though I pretended not to notice. She and I were at odds sometimes lately.

"Do not go," my mother begged Pauk. "You are opening the door of the lodge and inviting trouble in." But he brushed her off.

"Some council members say I am afraid and that I must go. They say I speak always of the old ways, but I do not have the courage to honor them," he said.

Ah? I wondered to myself. And some council members are trailmates of the whites who want us to go west. They do not know Pauk, but Aubee they know well. Can it be that these remember how hard Aubee fought the treaty and what he now says? What if he should not drink and sign? What if he should be the one to say, "We will not go west, no matter what." Ah, would not they have good reason for wanting Pauk to go to the wedding, for having him kill Aubee there and remove him from the treaty process? I wondered at it all.

Together we loaded the horse to make camp at Lake of the Boulders.

And thus we went to the wedding and all was as my husband said, except that Aubenaubee, "Chief leader of the Potawatomis," as the whites called him, was there. He stood at the edge of the clearing above the lake, quietly talking to his child, Trisby Rose.

The Catholic priest Father Deseille stood by the altar, unfolding gold and white vestments and preparing wine for the ceremony. He saw me and Pauk and spoke a word of caution to me. "Dawn, the great God condemns vengeance killing. He says, 'Thou shalt not kill.' The law of the State punishes those who do."

"We are on Indian lands. Our laws apply."

"It is not clear because of the treaty. Aubee has been to the sheriff and has an order that Pauk may not approach him."

"The laws of the Ancient Ones apply here."

This priest's eyes were like gunmetal. "And who is the most ancient of all?"

That I could not answer.

And so, on that fourteenth day of April, 1836, Trisby married Melford Leonard, in a Mass above the shores of Lake Mocksinkickee. As the Mass closed and the two knelt, I saw the Black Mood fall around my husband like a misty rain at dusk time. I watched cautiously after the ceremony, my emotion suspended, until I saw something that made fear rise in my heart. Paukooshuck, who never drank strong spirits, went to the feast table and took up a jug loaded with whisky. He tipped it up and, in a few minutes, pausing only long enough to let it settle and to let himself breathe, he emptied the small jug. Then he began another.

He, who spurned whisky as white man's poison sent to shatter our people, drank. He drank until he was soundly, but not falling-down drunk. And some Indians on the council drank with him. As the dancing commenced on that night, with the cool wind blowing the women's skirts, and a huge moon lighting all the scene, Aubee left, morose and drunk, taking himself on the back of a horse up the trail towards the Tippecanoe.

Pauk watched him go. "And so I have to go up the trail too. My destiny follows me like a dog I flee from, who will not be lost," he said.

"I go too," I said to my husband. "I shall prepare the horses at once." Others were drifting away; we said hasty good-byes.

We rode south, through the black dirt of the boglands, where skunk cabbages opened their green, cup-like leaves beside us and muskrats scrambled about.

Finally lights twinkled ahead of us—lights of the settlement whites were calling Richland Center. We were coming to Blodgett's Tavern. We hitched the horse to the post and entered. Inside, standing between us and the light of the fire at the end of the room, was Aubenaubee, "Chief leader of the Potawatomis."

He was tapping a huge whisky hogshead. No one else was in the room. The cold wind blew the door open behind us. I grabbed Pauk's arm. "My husband, think what you do," I said.

"I do think," he said. He took out his long knife and, hesitating only briefly, raised his arm high to throw it. A long minute passed and I wondered that the old man had not turned and seen us. But then Pauk put his arm down with a tiny sigh. He could not kill his father. At that moment a knife flew past us, thrown right to the mark from behind in the open door, and Aubenaubee dropped, dead of a knife in the back. Then the door slammed, and the sound of horses hoofs pounded into the darkness.

"The men of the council have exacted the Old Ones' justice when I could not. I was a coward in the face of the law of the *Neshnabec*," Pauk said, refusing to even pursue. We told the men in the other room of the tavern the story of the knife thrown at Aubee, but they looked at us with disbelief. Still, they did nothing but send for Aubee's relatives from nearby Tippecanoe camps.

As we left, Pauk said again that the men of the council had done their duty. Ah? I thought. Some men of the council are half-breeds and they are in the pockets of the government agents and traders. And with the old chief gone and the new chief paralyzed with his own guilt? Ah. It would be easy to dispose of the final treaties taking the last of our lands, sending us all away.

"I shall know joy no more," said my husband, as we made bleak camp by the Tippecanoe. As I thought of the past, of the cousin-teasing games, and the jests and the happiness this man had known, I anguished over who was to blame for all this. I thought with scorn that it could be the bad Bat Manitto who might, just might still be out there controlling things. Perhaps I was being punished for not believing in him, or any of the old spirits. It was clear that something had turned things upside down. Broken people, broken lives.

What more could this Bat Manitto have to throw at us from his ordure cave? I did not know, but I thought we should probably expect it very soon.

# Chapter Seventeen

# The Account of Thomas Jefferson Brooks
### (Continued)

Well, in the summer of 1838 I went back to Massachusetts at last, to the stagnant fens of New England, to the stifling religion that had engulfed my childhood and to the parents who had unwittingly been the tools of my unhappiness. Strange, when I returned after so long I found not the objects of irritation I had left, but two old people I could love.

I found Bathsheba Dakin Brooks, ill and stooped with age but wrapped round with a quality I had never recognized in her when we were at home: dignity. I found Daniel Brooks, who had the courage that surviving sorrow gracefully gives, and the honest peace that living almost seventy years as a thoroughly good man bestows.

The sisters turned out to be not the flibbertijibbet, waspish rivals for the parents' affection that I remembered. They were, it seemed now, middle-aged women with decent children and, in the case of Becky and Lucy, even some humor in their dispositions. We laughed together and had things to say to each other that made us feel like long-lost friends. Improbably, I invited Becky to come be a schoolmarm at Mt. Pleasant. Improbably, she accepted. I wished I had not stayed away so long.

Even my Emily had been forgiven. "The Dakin streak of madness took her off," Tryphena was always telling anyone who still cared. She had told Emily's two children that. I met them, a young man who looked like the sweet-potato Puritan, and a girl who looked like nobody in the family. Well, at least my dear childhood companion could rest in peace now. I would never know where she was buried, and that bothered me. But then, I told myself, things don't usually turn out in real life as neatly as they do in novels.

Daniel had recently written a letter to Mother and Father saying he was now the proprietor of a travelling menagerie and show which went about Kentucky and Ohio. They gave me the letter to read. Mother smiled mysteriously as I read it; Father looked bewildered. Tryphena sniffed. They had never forgiven Brookie, really, for being himself, and kicking the traces of the faith he had been brought up in.

I knew my father wondered about my own "Christian commitment." Susan and I went to church with him. Afterwards we took a trip to find the pilgrim burial cairns he had shown me in my youth. He had not been there for three years, he said.

When we went to Concord and walked the road a little out of town, we could not find the cairns. A house sat where they had been, and when Father went up to inquire at the door, he came back saying, "Brookses. Some of the Brookses still live on the land. But they know nothing of the burial pits."

"Think you that this means that all traces of the pilgrims' existence are now gone, Tom Jefferson?" Father asked, after we had returned home.

"I do not know what I do believe. I know I believe in the several hundred thousand dollars I have in the banks. I know I now believe in man. I go to church sometimes with my family, but my mind strays." I felt strange talking about this. "I know I believe in this young man," I said, bouncing year-old Tommy on my knee. We had brought this young sprout of ours with us. My mother and father adored him, making over him constantly, as if through him they could come to know our other three children, back home with Grandmother Poore. My parents would never even catch sight of these grandchildren, back in far-away Indiana, at the end of the world.

When the time came for Susan and me and little Tommy to leave, we parted with the family with sincere regret. I never saw Mother or Father again.


I left Susan and Tommy at Cincinnati. They were going by stage on to Mt. Pleasant. Susan was eager to see her sister Harriet and John Houghton, the new bride and groom, and hear about the wedding she had missed. She was also needed to help Grandmother Poore settle in permanently with us, at Brooks House in Mt. Pleasant. I had decided to go north to find my brother Daniel.

I said before that Daniel, after his experience at Hindostan with the falling-down Museum Hall, had decided to go into the itinerant business, as it was then called, circus, as we would say today. 'Twas in his blood, he said, and besides there was money in it. He had mentioned in his letter to my mother and father that he would be in Cleveland about the time I was returning, and I had decided to come in and surprise him.

The Brooks Wonder Show and Travelling Menagerie had been at Cleveland for some time now, and I took the stage there on what I hoped would be my last ride on that diabolical vehicle for a while. My back, never good in recent years, was beginning to feel as if some housewife had decided to rest her hot flatiron on it, and riding on a stagecoach did not improve the situation. Just outside Cleveland we had to go get fenceposts from the side of the road to pry the coach out of the mud. I would not beg off, I admit it, for fear of being thought less than a man, so I strained my back further.

Finally we came to the City on the Lake, and I limped out.

Broadside posters were on posts and trees everywhere. "Tightrope performers. Freaks of nature and FINAL MYSTERY ACT," they said. I found my way down the street.

Outside a hall which was lit up like a sunrise was a juggler with two plates on sticks, and there was Daniel in a top hat with a tight, checkered vest, speaking to a small crowd. "Inside tonight ladies and gentlemen, you can experience an extravaganza never seen before in our Northwest. Mr. Daring-do Drissel is only one of a spate of specialties designed to terrify, awe, and possibly titillate (excuse me, ladies) you. Mr. Drissel has been in the great cities of America—Philadelphia, Pennsylvania; Salem, Massachusetts, and Charlotte, North Carolina. Oh yes, he has challenged all comers in the art of balance and won. He can keep more torches afloat, balance more plates while jumping between sawhorses than any other man alive! But also inside is Gargantua Taylor, the giant who stands seven feet, ten inches tall and his beautiful bride, whom we have just added to this entertainment and who is seven feet herself.

"We have trick dogs and our own trick fleas, who do not perform together for obvious reasons" (he waited here for the gratifying laughter to cease).

"And then you will want to see our own stuffed and life-like exhibits brought from the far corner of the world, placed in diorama cases.

"See the Battle of Fallen Timbers tableux and our new, all new addition, not here last week, should you have visited our establishment before this—THE DELAWARE INDIAN WEDDING DANCE AND SECRETS OF CHIEF PESHAWBE EXHIBIT.

"Come on in. Ladies, you are welcome. A woman attendant will be on hand for the evening performance."

Sweat was popping off his forehead like popcorn on a hot griddle. He had not seen me, so I decided to play the wag with him for a while. I recalled the stuff of his letter—

"Ah, sir," said my voice from the shadows. "And may we see your automaton? Your Gypsy maiden?"

"Well—ah—sir, my Gypsy Fortune Teller is presently not being exhibited."

"But sir," I went on, "I have travelled from Toledo to see it. I have heard it has marvelous mechanisms inside it which make it like a human being. That it can think and tell fortunes which are astonishing."

"That is true sir, but it is out of commission." He put a finger inside his collar nervously.

The man next to me said to his neighbor, "Mebbe the ol' music box flung a spring."

A woman said to him, " 'Tis really a marvel, I tell you. I had my fortune done in Columbus, and it pointed at cards about my finding true love, just like a real gypsy would. They came true." She smiled a toothy smile and grasped the arm of a bandy-legged farmer with worn boots.

I could not stop baiting my poor brother. "Let us see it—Brookie," I shouted in my own voice, using that old family baby name.

He looked into the shadows in disbelief and then smiled a broad smile. He told the crowd, "My friends, let my small partner with me here take your coins, and you hasten into the show, which begins in only five minutes."

The crowd headed towards the table where one of the smallest dwarfs I'd ever seen was selling tickets to the show.

Brookie soon found me. "Tom Jefferson, you shameless deceiver. How could I know it was you bantering me from the crowd? What brings you here?"

I told him I'd come on the spur of the moment to see him and the itinerant show.

"Let's go in," he said. "We'll talk later. In the meantime, enjoy the show." He left me.

Church benches had been set up in front of a slightly raised platform, which was surrounded by hurricane lamps. A beautiful young lady with sausage curls and dainty pointed slippers pulled back the curtain. It reminded me of Hindostan, and I hoped the roof would not fall on us here, too. I looked up, and it seemed to me it was quite secure.

Soon Daring-do the juggler came out. Daniel and the dwarf, whose name was Hugo, backed up the act and seemed to be everywhere on the stage, lighting the torches the juggler threw in the air, setting up the plates and oranges he threw about, hup ho-ing him with their hands onto the sawhorses.

After the juggler, we saw the dog, a chow-chow who barked several times to answer questions and the two giants, whose laughs rocked the small hall. We clapped for the living tableaux of the Battle of Fallen Timbers, where men wearing uniforms of George Washington's buff and blue dramatically shot muskets at three Indians, who lay with arms out over long logs.

"Those are real Indians," I said to the new bride with the teeth who sat on the bench beside me.

"Savage Delawares," she said. "Imported 'em from Missourah or wherever 'tis they stay now."

"That so? Why'd they want to come," how could I say it, "when the show demeans them? Their ancestors fought at that battle didn't they?"

"How should I know? They ain't hardly any Injeeans any more in Ohio. An' I hear tell they're shipping the last ones outa Indianney.

"So they say." Lewis had written me about it and it was in all the papers. Not the last Indians in Indiana, exactly, but almost. The Miami were not going yet, though they soon would. But all the Potawatomi were being shipped away in groups to Nebraska Territory. In recent treaties most of them had agreed to go.

"Bout time they got rid a all them savages so's civilized folk can sleep a nights. Anyways these yere Delawares do a dance, bout ta start now."

And so it did. Seven of them came sort of mincing out. They had a family resemblance, to my way of thinking, and sat down before a stage set, a painted tepee typical of the Sioux in the West. Another man came from behind a tree, his arms full of gifts. A blushing maid arose and came to stand beside him; red blankets were exchanged and a dance began.

All of this tableux was accompanied by chanting, and as the Indians circled and stomped, they grew more animated. The audience began to chant and stomp also.

A small boy in back of me said in an earnest voice, "I wisht I could 'a been here when they was all over the woods, Grandpa."

"No sir, you don't, Bertie," said a gruff voice in answer.

After the show I went with Daniel to his quarters at the Hotel English, one of the new European-type hostelries Cleveland was sporting.

"I'm taking in the money in this engagement. Had a house of four hundred last Saturday night."

"How can you make any money?" These acts, I knew, were for sale, and they weren't cheap. Sometimes they sold midgets and fat people as if they were slaves.

"Well, I'm promoting the business. You have to promote. I write articles for the *Herald* myself. In point of fact I spend a lot." We were eating chicken and biscuits and fruit, sent up from the dining salon. The lodgings were costing a pretty penny. "I had a giant contest for the whole state of Ohio and advertised it in the newspapers in all the major cities. I challenged all comers on behalf of my Gargantua Taylor. Two Saturdays in a row I did it and they came from Zanesville and Springfield and even as far as Gallipolis. I offered a $100 prize."

I let a surprised sigh escape my lips.

"Well, I wasn't worried. I knew my giant was the best around.

We brought all the comers out, paraded them while a lady played the pianoforte. I had a professor of higher mathematics from Western Reserve University measuring with a measure stick—and surprise!'' He looked at me with that sort of gushing boyishness that in spite of everything, endeared him to me.

"Your man won."

"Yes, and a few weeks after that we had his marriage. My, my you should have seen it! One of the contestants in my contest was Miss Ida Jean Slabotny, the Polish giant, from Tiffin. I paid her parents handsomely to let her join the travelling show and now she is one of my regulars. My giant fell head over heels in love with her. The night of the wedding I had two shows without an empty seat in the house. I took in $400. Fifty cents a ticket.''

I nodded in admiration, then was silent as we both ate.

I could tell from the way he looked up that he was going to change the subject. "How are Mother and Father?" he asked wistfully. I told him about the visit to the East, and I knew it cost him pain to hear it. Brookie was the scapegrace, the one who "didn't amount to much." Running a circus was not in the catalogue of Holy New England Occupations. But he seemed to be making a success of this! Finally. "Stay about at least till Saturday," he said confidentially. "See my *coup de grace*, my Mystery Ceremony of the Delawares.''

"Do they do their ceremonies—in public?" I asked, still chagrined by the savages paid to sprawl in disgraceful death at the Battle of Fallen Timbers.

"These do. What they don't know they make up. They're all from one family, and they're half-breeds. Their father runs a trading post and farms a little and their mother's a Delaware. Most of the time they wear jean-cloth overalls and grow sorghum and hogs, but for me they put on breechclouts and leggings. They do some of the old dances and play like old-time Indians. This was big Indian country, you know, but now only the old folks remember it.''

"What is the special mystery ceremony?" I asked.

"Wait until Saturday night and you'll see it yourself," he said. "Oh, and stay with me. The bed is comfortable.''

I decided to take his advice, and the next morning, after sleeping on a board in his good bed, my back did feel better.

I took some time to see a bit of Cleveland while I was there. I travelled the streets looking at the sights of this rapidly-growing city, which was now as big as Columbus and Dayton, but not Cincinnati, its arch-rival. The hotel sat on the beautiful square in the middle of town. A graceful courthouse with a huge cupola dominated this public commons. I watched bustling water traffic on the river and the new canal.

Meanwhile, Brookie ran about taking advertisements with startling Gothic type to the editor of the newspaper and making sure the Wonder Show performers were well provided for in the cheap accommodations he had hired for them down by the livery stables. His dwarf, Hugo, who was a clever, silent little man, handled a good many of the details of the business, packing and unpacking stage properties, providing for care of the hyena and armadillo and alligator that were the "menagerie" Brookie advertised.

Friday afternoon, as Brookie rehearsed the "Delawares" behind curtains, I walked about to see some of the exhibits he carried in the basement of the hall.

There was a stuffed dodo bird and a pink flamingo, a hornet's nest the size of a barrel, a diorama of Louis the 16th and Marie Antoinette at tea. The oddest thing was an arm, severed at the elbow and stuffed. The hand on the end of it carried a sword. The sign beside it said, "Arm of a Napoleonic soldier, cut off at the Battle of Austerlitz as it raised a sword to defend the great hero."

"Oh, if only I had an elephant," my brother sighed, later that night in the hotel. "I could show it for weeks at a time in a town like this, or Cincinnati, or Louisville. If I had an elephant, I could settle in one town, only go out for part of the year. I'm ready to do that. I could be rich. Or better yet, a giraffe. There's only one in the whole United States of America."

"How much would a giraffe cost?"

"A thousand dollars, maybe. There are hardly any of 'em available, but I know a sea captain back home that could get one."

I brought up what I had avoided for two days, now. "What about the gypsy fortune teller? The automaton."

His eyes grew vague and wary, just as they used to do when Father asked what he and Miss Hepzibah, or whoever the fair maid was, were doing for so long on the walk home from church.

"Well, just as you say. It works automatically, with machinery inside. I bought it from a Hungarian who was a genius at wheel and lever machinery, although the folks at the show don't know that. It points at cards which have tarot symbols and interpretations on them. Uncanny luck. It's just machinery, but people flocked by the hundreds to see it in Cincinnati a couple of months ago.''

"The editor of the paper threatened something—"

"Oh, they all claim humbug about travelling shows. Want to expose whatever we do as chicanery. I never made any real claims about the gypsy. I told 'em my fortune-teller was machinery. He's raising the hue and cry just because some women came to think she could really act, think some way.''

"I read the article in the *Cincinnati Gazette*. It said your automaton seems to answer questions by knocking out 'yes' and 'no.' The editor said he was investigating because he sensed fraud.''

"Nothing for you to worry about." He began talking about the canals that Ohio was trying to finish and the worry about the state debt, two topics which were on every tongue these days.

"The State of Ohio has asked the government to pay off the canal obligations, which amount to millions of dollars. But the U.S. Congress declined,'' he told me.

"The Honorable McClure, my old partner, is knee-deep in the Wabash and Erie,'' I told him, and we both laughed at the pun McClure himself would have liked. "The legislators keep running a race with the debt to get a goodly section of the thing finished. I think the debt is going to win. The news in Indiana isn't good.''

The next day, Saturday, Brooks' Wonder Show had an afternoon "Family Outing" performance. It was at this that the "Delaware Mystery Ceremony" was to be performed. I got up early and took a walk to the river. I rubbed my hands together as I strolled through the streets on this beautiful morning in Cleveland. It should be a good day for Brookie.

But when I returned to take morning coffee with my brother, his expression was anything but happy. He was reading the newspaper at a table, shifting his weight discontentedly on the chair in irritation. "Listen to this obnoxious article,'' he said. "The editor of the *Cincinnati Gazette* has a front page notice. 'To the citizens of Cleveland and other cities where the popular Brooks Wonder Show performs. We in your sister city have a civic duty to inform you that the company is perpetuating a deceptive humbug of the first magnitude. Investigations which leave not a shred of a doubt cast a shadow on the miraculous performance of the Gypsy Lady during the past two years in cities across the state of Pennsylvania and in the Northwest.' '' He looked up with vexation.

I didn't know what to say, so I shrugged my shoulders, with a puzzled smile on my face. He went on reading: '' 'We in the Queen City on the river challenge Mr. Daniel Brooks to produce his famed device, which has astonished so many people and is on the way to gaining him a fortune, for public inspection. If the automaton can really tell fortunes from cards, let all inspect her again with complete forthrightness in light of this paper's new information. Mr. Brooks, we extend you the gauntlet. Come forth up there in Cleveland and show us your miracle. The editor of this paper will be at the performance next Saturday. Bring forth your marvel, we dare you.''

"Well, what are you going to do?" I asked, helping myself to coffee and raised biscuits and jam.

"What can I do? Well, I guess I could display my gypsy again for all to see. I certainly have nothing to hide. I do not know what he could possibly be talking about."

"You have not seen fit to confide in me, your own brother. How does this automaton work?"

"She is like others of the sort, conceived of in Europe. She has intricate machinery in her back, like a clock or music box."

"And how does she tells folks accurately about themselves?"

'' 'Tis the secret designing of the Hungarian from whom I bought her. These folk know many wonderful things.'' His eyes seemed far away, and I suspected he was thinking more of some Hungarian woman who had stolen his heart than of the man who had sold him the device. Daniel had never married, but he had loved more women and under more circumstances, I suspect, than all the husbands of Mt. Pleasant put together over their lifetimes.

"Well, then bring out your woman after the show tonight. Welcome the Cincinnati editor. Call up someone from the audience, let your lady whir her wheels for all to see."

He nodded his head, thoughtfully, and I went on. "Come what may, at least you are sure to have a friendly first-night audience, that is, if your Delaware Mystery Ceremony goes as well as you think it will.''

''Yes, yes,'' he said eagerly. ''That is how I shall do the thing. I shall submit it to my audience! Why, I shall even call upon the editor of the *Cleveland Herald*. I have made his acquaintance through my advertisements, and it is his niece who is my honorary curtain maid. I choose one in each city from among the prominent maidens.''

Oh. I had wondered who she was.

By seven o'clock people began to line up outside the hall. By 7:30 there was not a seat in the place, and folk were jostling shoulders in the back behind the benches.

The curtain was pushed aside by the pretty girl, whose name was Miss Effie, at exactly eight, and the usual acts began with the giant and his wife posing to music from a pianoforte, standing on boxes, kneeling and so forth, menagerie animals on leashes led out by Miss Effie, with bows both on the animals and herself.

Then, so those who had seen the show would have new amusement, slightly changed versions of the old acts: the juggler doing his stunts but on a wheeled box this time, then the tableux of Indians, now called, ''Attack on a Kentucky Station.'' The ''British Troops'' had on the same shabby George Washington pants, but this time wore what appeared to be ragged red musicians' uniforms with white banding sewn on. They stood before a painting of a stockade, leading ''hostile savages,'' the Delaware family who now assumed confident, defiant poses. It seemed as if they could as easily be settlers as Indians; on the other side of the stage, some of the faces under the sunbonnets were from this same Delaware family. Brookie must have been short of actors.

Then the curtain closed for about ten minutes. Heads were turning, and I followed them. A dandily dressed gentleman with an old-fashioned sword cane had come in and stood in the aisle. He was impressively taking off fine kid gloves for the benefit of those around him, who buzzed and oohed in deference. The editor of the Cincinnati paper, I presumed.

When the curtain opened again, however, we all forgot everything except the scene before us. The stage was as silent and dark as the inside of Mammoth Cave. Then Otto the dwarf sneaked about covertly placing lanterns on the side and at the back of the stage, illuminating a scene of craggy rocks. It was almost as if the sun was rising, and the effect was eerie.

The mixed-breed Indian family were found bent in reverence before the rocky cliff, and on the cliff was the tallest of the clan in only a breechclout, with his hair shaved off except for the scalp lock. A terrified shudder went through the audience.

Then my brother's voice came out from behind a canvas screen. "Honorable ladies and gentlemen, you citizens of Cleveland, Ohio are witnessing for the first time the sacred Delaware Indian Manitto Rites to welcome the rising sun at Harvest Festival. (The sorghum half-breeds began to rise slowly from their positions.) They are turning to the four cardinal points of the compass (they did) to show the power of the Great Spirit over all the earth. They are crying aloud to the Manittos of the hills and sky to banish the bad spirits. (They cried, although it was more like hungry dogs howling.)

"Now they dance, singing loudly. They depict the bad dreams they have had during the year."

As the Indians circled, issuing blood-curdling yells that made the hair rise on the necks of most of the audience, I thought how silly that was. Drake had told me of the customs of the Delaware; he knew them well and they did not sing to the sun. And their harvest festival dances were done indoors by individuals telling dreams—this was all wrong. My thought strayed for a moment. How my friend had loved the Delaware!

The "Indians" sank in a circle on the floor and the "Chief" resumed his position at the top of the rock. "For the first time on the American continent, and anywhere for that matter," Brookie announced solemnly, "Brooks Wonder Show and Travelling Menagerie will present for you an authentic Indian marvel. The Sacred *Walam Olum*, the Bible, so to speak, of the Delaware Indians, purchased recently at great expense from a scholar and man of science who received it directly from the great Delaware Indian Tribe of Indiana before their emigration west."

He described how this mystical work was composed of tales told for countless generations, passed on from chief to chief, written down on sacred sticks recently and given to the "man of science" who reluctantly parted with them so that Brooks Wonder Show could bring them to the American public. Something clicked in my mind, but I could not place it; years ago in Hindostan it seemed to me the folks had talked of this. I did not recall in what connection, quite.

The pianoforte rolled dramatically into arpeggios. "That the past might not be lost!" Brookie shouted. Only one light was left on the stage, flickering across the "chief's" face, as he stood alone by the artificial cliff. He began to speak:

*In the beginning, there was water over all the land*
*And the Great Spirit was there. . .*
*He made much land and sky. . . sun, moon and stars*
*Creatures that die, souls and all.*
*Then he made man, Grandfather man.*

The sorghum chief's voice went on, reading Lenni Lenape (as their language is called), then English, reciting the Delaware Indian creation myth and history of ancient times.

As I sat there, in that smelly, hot room with those enrapt spectators listening to that half-way Indian recite the syllables and heard their meaning reverberate through the darkness in that ancient tongue, something happened to me.

I came alive to what the lines meant, what they were. This was the tradition of a thousand years, the dignity of religion, the collective memory of a race, now bruised and beaten to earth. Was anything more beautiful and sacred than the creation myth of a people? Could anything say more about their dreams and view of themselves?

"That the past might not be lost—" But was this preserving it? Letting some mercenary pretenders gutturally mutilate and mouth what must be truly beautiful poetry? Letting the white race which had caused the dismal downfall of the mythic race it described ogle the work as a sideshow attraction? And what would happen to it in five years, if my brother tired of it? Would it end up as cage paper for the lion Brookie would probably have then?

Lost in my own disturbed thoughts, I was suprised to hear

thunderous applause. The performance was over. The chandelier was re-lit and raised. There was Brookie's voice. "And now, ladies and gentlemen, you may remain a few moments afterwards to see the sacred objects themselves, handle them if you wish. But return in fifteen minutes for the final presentation." The men, lighting cigars or spitting tobacco, the women, gathering their skirts, hopped off the benches and pushed towards a table Otto was setting up.

I edged forward to see what they were handling: small, flat sticks painted with hieroglyphics. "Don't make no sense t' me atall," said one very thin man with very dirty fingernails.

"They cain't even spell their name, haveta draw in little pitchers," his tall scarecrow of a wife opined. "I sure am glad they're outa here. 'Twould give me a fright a day to have 'em out in the woods. I don't know how Ma and Pa ever put up with it. I'll feel better when ever last one of 'em is-gone from Indianney."

"Let me see, Ma—" An unkempt boy pushed up and grabbed. He had a piece of taffy sticking to the palm of his hand.

For some odd reason, no doubt because Hindostan had been on my mind, my thoughts flashed back to poor Doctor Jack McClure and I saw him raving, out of his head, yet strangely lucid, saying "No dirty hands, no dirty hands." Of course it had nothing to do with this, and yet it fit. I turned away, dispirited, and returned to my bench.

The table was put away. My brother lowered the stage lights and stood in the center of the stage saying, "My friends, you all know about the challenge issued by the *Cincinnati Gazette*. They have sent the editor Tilden Shewsbury here to denouce us, to reveal some sort of chicanery and humbug, so they say."

There was a roar from the crowd, half friendly to the Wonder Show that had just given them the Delaware Mysteries, so I thought, and the other half ready to see the Wonder Show or anybody, denounced and humiliated, so long as it would be amusing.

"I have asked Mr. Tilden Shewsbury to come up here on this stage and I have agreed, without fear, to answer his accusations and give him and all of you time to view the renowned automaton, The Gypsy Woman! Mr. Shewsbury, are you out there?" He peered into the dusky gloom. "No? Well, it may be he has stepped out a minute—never mind. Perhaps he is afraid." He chuckled and the audience chuckled, too. "We shall go forward with our presentation." The curtain opened to show a table with a long tablecloth spread with cards. Beside it stood a huge, seven-foot tall gypsy woman, arms outstretched.

The audience gasped; most had never seen the wonder, of course. "Now I will ask for a lady from the audience to come up here with the fortune teller." Several stood; Brookie pointed at a respectable, gray-haired woman in black mourning, who was sitting on the front row.

"Ma'm, will you honor us by participating in this exercise for the name of the Brooks Wonder Show? In the name of plain dealing and honesty?" At first the woman demurred, then, urged on by her relatives, cautiously made her way to the stage.

"Now friends and neighbors in the audience, I will ask you to observe. Here are the cards, each with an age-old Tarot symbol on it, beneath which is a fotune-telling interpretation. Do you see those?"

A voice came from the back of the hall and the Cincinnati editor came forward. "Yes, do you see them? Just like the ones he put out in Cincinnati when he committed his frauds—"

Brookie interrupted him. "Welcome sir, come right up here." He turned to the audience with an enormous smile, waving his arm expansively at the editor in introduction. "Mr. Tilden Shewsbury." He conspicuously ushered his diffident guest up to the stage."Do you do understand that this kind woman here, Mrs."— he leaned over to the woman, who was seated in the chair,— "McDougall—will be able to ask the Gypsy Lady as many questions as she wishes. At any time the gypsy may point to a tarot card which may or may not give correct information to the kind lady about her present or future circumstances."

"Yes, cards, which you—" the editor attempted to say, but Brookie would not have it.

"Now, now, you will have ample opportunity to say what you will sir, in the town I have decided to adopt for my own. Yes, from now on, Cleveland will be the home of the Brooks Wonder Show and Menagerie."

There was a brief ripple of surprised applause. I was caught unaware. Well, this small but raucous town was as good a place as anywhere else. Raw, rough Hindostan Falls, after all, had suited him much better than placid Mount Pleasant. And the young girl who drew the curtains back seemed to adore him. Perhaps there was something there. Well, at any rate.

The Gypsy, painted garish colors with a bright red scarf about her yellow painted locks began to whir. Her arms moved up and down, her head nodded. Mrs. McDougall began to look a little alarmed; my brother reassured her with a pat on the shoulder. "Just a mechanism," he said smiling at the audience. "Ask her a question, my dear madam."

"What has happened to me lately?" she said in a small voice, and Brookie repeated the question.

There was a moment's hesitation, then the whirring began again, and the long, ring-laden finger of the gypsy pointed at a card. Belladonna, woman in black. Beneath it, in large black letters was the saying, "There has been a death."

"It pointed to the death card. My dear husband"—here her voice faltered—"died four months ago. How did she—it—know?"

The audience, which had been snickering and coughing, now quieted down for the second question.

Mrs. McDougall looked questioningly up at Brookie. "Ask something you want to know," he told her. "It has amazed others with predictions."

"Who—will take care of me?"

Amidst the odd noise, like an army of cicadas, the finger pointed to the young man card.

"My nephew!" she gasped.

"Command it. Tell it to point to other cards," Brookie said. She nodded and, loudly enough to be heard in the back, began inquiring.

Each time she asked a question, the automaton pointed. Hanged man, young maiden, each fittingly answered her inquiries.

The audience nudged, nodded and whispered. Finally one man said, "Get it to tap the table."

"It can tap, once for yes, two taps, no. Or it can count for you. More I do not promise it will tell you, never have," my brother said, smiling confidently.

"Tap two times," the widow woman commanded, and the hand came down, once, twice.

"Eight times," a young man in the audience called out. Hesitating a moment, the arm began tapping slowly. One-two-three— on up to eight.

The audience, directed by Brookie, kept testing the Gypsy for about two minutes. "Now put the gypsy to the ultimate test. Ask her about what you are wearing, where we are, anything that can be answered by yes or no, " he suggested.

"Am I wearing gloves?"

(Tap.)

"Is Mr. Brooks over forty?"

(Tap.)

"Are we in Cincinnati?"

(Tap tap.)

"New York?"

(Tap tap.)

"Cleveland?"

(Tap.)

The audience roared its approval, and as it did so, the portly man who had been standing fairly silently on the stage spoke up loudly. "May I address the audience now, sir?" he asked.

Brookie hesitated only a moment, bowed deeply and then graciously stepped aside.

"Ahh, ladies and gentleman of our sister city of Cleveland. You have heard my name; you know I have a respected position in Cincinnati. I have come a ways to tell you of something—something we in Cincinnati think you ought to know." Mr. Tilden Shewsbury looked over at Brookie, the Gypsy, and the widow woman, who seemed almost irritated at being interrupted.

"When the Brooks Wonder Show was in our city last winter, I saw the mechanical device you see before you perform in the civic hall. It was only shown twice, as if overexposure would dim its novelty." He smirked ironically.

"Something about the performance, similar to the one you have seen tonight, bothered me. Now we have sometimes heard of marvelous automatons who can raise machinery, tell time, water plants. But a fortune telling gypsy automaton?"

"And I showed you the inside mechanism," Brookie said loudly, not willing to completely relinquish the advantage to this man.

"Sir—" the editor said, turning to look Brookie full in the face, "I ask that you do that tonight for this group."

The audience began to nudge and whisper again. " 'Tain't fittin' to ask the magic show men to show their secrets."

" 'Tain't done. Still, if thar's humbug—"

"I shall be happy to show everyone the way my mechanism works. (Grunts and murmurs of approbation for my brother's generosity.) I am in the business of creating things for you that amuse, and I have nothing to hide when it comes to amusing you."

He went to the automaton, revolved her with some difficulty because she was heavy, and turned a switch on her painted back. A large door swung open and the audience cooed and clapped a little to see the machinery inside the woman. Her whole inside was full of pulleys, levers, weights and turning wheels; only a small box at the bottom was unmechanized.

Brookie went to her and pushed a lever. The arm raised. He pushed another; the eyes blinked. "Ah, but on what impulse does she move?" said Mr. Shewsbury. "That is what I asked myself. Could Mr. Brooks be pulling her with a rope?"

The audience craned its necks to see if there could be any hidden ropes on the stage but could not find any. "Was there a trapdoor beneath? No. I searched for answers that would reveal humbugging here. After all, the fine citizens of Cincinnati were paying thirty-five cents a performance, and they did not deserve to be lied to and cheated!"

Just the fringe of an angry hum edged the comments of the crowd, as if a line of hornets was approaching a happy family picnic.

"I was in Europe on business and I made it a point to make the long and somewhat trying trip to the nation of Hungary," Mr. Shewsbury continued. "Hints I had been given told me I might find something rewarding there. I hate humbug!"

The noise of the hornets intensified a bit, spurred on by curiosity and the strident, mocking tone of the man's voice. The audience was just beginning to wonder, to ask itself if the popular

Brooks Wonder Show could, after all, have in it anything of—say it—fraud.

"I found a man, an old man wonderfully skilled in the art of machines, in a shop in a small village which had huge music boxes, grandfather clocks, calculating machines. The shop clicked and ticked as if it were alive."

The audience which had grown silent as he spoke, chuckled a little. I rose apprehensively. This group was turning, coming around to the editor's side. He went on. "I spoke for a whole evening to this man, this wizard of machinery. He conceded he had made two live-looking automatons which took him five years. One was a turk, the Terrible Turk, which is in England, one was"—he turned with a savage sneer—"the Gypsy Fortune Teller."

The hornets really tuned up now, and an unhappy buzz filled the room. Hungarian clockmaker? Brookie had some way let it be believed that the creation of the gypsy was his. "My gypsy," he had called her.

I looked at Brookie. He looked apprehensive, but not nearly as frightened as I thought he should. Why not? Was it that he didn't care that this man was turning a whole town against him?

"But that isn't all. The worst part of this sham is that in some way this man lets everyone believe this machine thinks. He makes you believe that in some way, partaking of the mysteries of magic or spiritualism, it can sense thoughts and relay them. Well, I am here to tell you that it is a fraud, complete and total." Shewsbury walked to the gypsy. Brookie took a step forward.

"Inside the machine"—he walked rapidly to it and reached around to its back, as if embracing the odd dummy,—"is a spring which the clock-maker told me about—here."

In a twink he had reached in and yanked out by the hair Otto the dwarf, who had been hiding in the tiny box at the bottom of the gypsy's machinery.

The audience roared and soon began throwing things. Eggs, soft peaches and even a blob of butter flew at the stage. Carefully avoiding the barrage, I edged towards the gypsy. Brookie would be hit, I told myself, but no! Where was he? Nowhere in sight.

The dwarf stood nervously stretching his limbs and hunching up his neck like a cat, the gypsy smiled her enigmatic, half-stupid smile, the editor of the *Cincinnati Gazette* glared triumphantly at the audience, but where was the owner of the Brooks Wonder Show?

The audience pointed to the stage. Was Brookie coming out? I turned my head. No, there was a man I did not know but whom the audience seemed to recognize, coming out of a rear door of the hall. My voice murmuring "Who is that?" must have been sounded through through all the din, because a man next to me said, "He's the editor of the *Cleveland Herald.*"

The editor, if that's who he was, raised his hand. Almost instantly the audience came to attention, surprised at his appearance, ready for the next event in this odd evening.

"I am Lyle Caruthers and I run the paper here in Cleveland. My friends and my honored colleague in the profession," he began, eyeing Tilden Shewsbury rather coldly. "We have certainly behaved shockingly tonight, haven't we?" A slight smile twisted his lips. "We have humiliated a lady, invaded her chamber, so to speak, by exposing her undressed to the mob. Seriously, though, my fellow citizens, let us not be too quick to listen to cries of fraud and deception. Let us remember that Mr. Brooks is not guilty of anything, really, but entertaining us. Did he ever say that this machine thinks? He said it told fortunes. Did he ever say there wasn't a dwarf in it? Never, to my knowledge.

"What is deception, my friends? I think it is often willing self-deception. Aren't we really deceived by our own desires in life? Don't we really love to be deceived, accept it willingly? The fact is, we enjoy it. What young maid doesn't deceive her suitor, telling him how he is the most wonderful, most handsome of all men? He doesn't believe that any more than she does, but he lets himself believe.

"Can you tell me you really bought a ticket to this show believing that a wooden doll can tell you how your life should be run or that magic is better than prayer or good old Buckeye common sense?

"You didn't believe that this gypsy doll had thoughts any more than the people in New York believed that the woman Mr. Barnum was just showing around was 160 years old. We know she couldn't possibly have been George Washington's nurse, as the show sign said, but we went to see anyway.

"We have been entertained, and it has cost thirty-five cents. We have had our money's worth. Besides"—Here he put a glaring look on his face—"the source is suspect. Why has a Cincinnatian come all the way up here to tell us this, to *interfere*?" Here he raised his voice to a crescendo. "Is it because he wishes truth to be served, or rather is it to see us, his city's rival in reputation, look like we have been made fools of? Well, we won't buy it, Mr. Editor. An attack on our new permanent show, with all of the things it will bring to this city, is an attack on Cleveland itself.

"No, I have enjoyed the Brooks Wonder show. I have enjoyed it last week, and tonight, and I want to enjoy it a month and a year from tonight. I'll gladly put down thirty-five cents for what you call humbug so long as the show's good. I'll come here and I'll let myself be deceived, just for a moment. I'll forget my cares, as I did when I was a child, and pretend. That's what a travelling show is all about."

The audience was still for a moment, then a man at the back took off his farmer's hat and waved it and shouted, "Hip, hip, hooray!" Others stood up and clapped, and soon the Cincinnati editor was retreating like a cur with his tail between his legs.

"Now, come out here, Mr. Brooks," said the local journalist. (Brookie did.) "I want to present you to the people of your new home." With a sort of bashful smile on his face and his arm around the Gypsy, Brookie smiled and waved and promised half-price tickets for the show tomorrow.


"What a Yankee peddler you are," I said to Brookie as I packed my things at the hotel later that night. Miss Effie Lewellen, the honorary curtain puller, and her uncle, the *Herald* editor, had just left after taking coffee with us.

"Well, it will all work out well," said Brookie. "I have just agreed with Mr. Caruthers that Effie and I will announce our engagement after church tomorrow.

"We will be married in two weeks. There is a need for haste, of course in the situation, so he says. I think she does have a strong inclination towards me and she is a sweet young thing. Her temperament, and connections"—he looked sheepish—"will be good signs for me in my new home city." I looked a little doubtful.

"Well, I have always wanted a child. And if it isn't mine but some cad's who loved and left her, what of it? As solid citizens of Cleveland, Ohio, we will probably have several of our own."

"You are going to have to produce new wonders for the show. You have already told me that."

"I will be travelling with the show much of the time, but when I am in Cleveland—well, you're right. If I only had an elephant—"

"How about a giraffe?"

"How am I going to get a *giraffe*?"

"One Yankee peddler to another, what if I offer you a deal?"

"What could I possibly have that you want, Tom Jefferson?"

"The Delaware Indian Mysteries."

And so I offered him prime farm land around Mt. Pleasant which was in my possession for the Delaware sacred book. In answer to his baffled expression, I simply said, "Just say I want the writings to honor the memory of a friend who loved the Delaware. As fine a friend as e'er my heart has coped with." I had it in my mind to send the *Walam Olum*, or whatever the Indians called it, to a Kentucky university in my friend Doc Drake's name, which I did do. I do not know what has become of it today.

"There are some strings attached," I went on, closing my valise. "I consider this an investment. That farm land is worth a lot more than an Indian memento, no matter how sacred. I want a fourth share in the giraffe. Your show and acumen in this transaction have convinced me you're a worthy investment property, Brookie. I'm going to tell the family so, too."

We shook hands. "Oh, and don't call me Brookie any more," he said. "If I'm a worthy investment property, redeemed in the beloved family's eyes, I don't need that infantile name anymore."

## Chapter Eighteen

# The Account of Thomas Jefferson Brooks
### (Continued)

After I said goodbye to Daniel in that August of 1838, I decided to go to Ft. Wayne by a good, comfortable stage and then by canal boat to Logansport to see my other brother Lewis. That decision sat on my conscience, because I did not like being away from my children so long, particularly my youngest. It was an odd thing, but I was sincerely attached to the point of distraction, almost like a woman, to the baby, Tommy.

I, Thomas Jefferson Brooks, Yankee trader, hardened business-man, able to foreclose a mortgage, collect a debt, truly doted on a year-old child in a ridiculous manner.

I had three other children, and I loved them too, but Tom was my special pet. He had come suddenly in the night a month before his time, when no midwife or physician could be summoned, and I had to do the services. For a long moment this tiny blue boy did not breathe, and I took him and pumped air into his little lungs and, miracle—he gasped, cried a small, gargling cry and took a breath.

Susan was ill for fully a month, and Grandmother Poore was busy with the other children. I was the child's mother, changing napkins, rocking, even bathing him.

We formed a bond I cannot describe. I could not be without him. When Susan and I went east, it would have been possible to wean him to a cup and porringer at a year and leave him with his grandmother. I insisted he go, pleading that his mother and he could not be separated, but it was really I who could not be away from Tom. I do confess this weakness, if such it was. Love awoke in my life the minute that tiny infant breathed, pure love with no hint of adulteration, and it never left.

Still, I wished to go to Logansport and find Lewis. It'd been better than a year since I last saw my brother. I had never been on a canal boat, and it was quite a different experience from the trips I had made as a keelboatman twenty years before, down the broad, cliff-lined waters of the Ohio. And I did want to see this miracle of progress, the Wabash and Erie, which my old partner James McClure had helped to build at a cost of insolvency, almost, in the state.

The one strip of the Wabash and Erie which was now open passed like a narrow strip of glass through virgin forest that made it seem to be almost an Indian path. Behind and before us packet boats sailed, loaded with green apples, venison hams, and sacks of corn meal. Led by our horse, who walked along the tow path, we glided beneath vast tulip trees and hickories, passing from shadow to sunlight. Now and then a clearing would appear around a bend and we would see a pier and a cluster of cabins with a name like Miamisport or Lagro.

The weather was the oddest that summer that I can ever remember. It was extremely hot, baking the land for days on end. Then drenching thundershowers would fall and roll right off the hard earth into the rivers. For one full day on that canal driving rain fell, and all of us, all twenty people, crammed together below, sitting as far away from the drafty hatch as possible. Water came in from the closed window holes and wet our clothing, and all was damp and steamy. "Not too different from a keelboat," I thought, remembering rainy days on the river with Doc. The company, of course, was entirely different.

Two Baptist ladies were aboard, and they pulled out a tract and looked over their spectacles at the assemblage sitting on the imitation plush seats—at the dandies with silk scarves at their throats, who tippled from small amber glass bottles, at the prosperous farmers who belched and smoked cigars and talked about Van Buren, and at a few clods who "helled" and "damned" and hadn't washed for three weeks.

The skies finally cleared, and we stayed overnight at the Tipton Inn midway, and I was ushered up to the best room in the house because my brother was the owner, John Tipton's, secretary. Lewis must have received the message that I was coming.

All went well the next day out on the canal. It was another "baking" day, and people drank lemonade out of bottles and ate spicy sausages and cake out of hampers the inn had fixed, until we got near Logansport. The unusually hard rains had caused temporary high waters in the Eel and Wabash Rivers nearby, and the banks of the canal were washing onto the towpath, taking bites out of the soft sides as we passed through. We tied up five miles above Logansport to repair the rudder's stern mooring, which was in danger of breaking off. I was smoking a cigar and watching the bank, propping my back against the back of the cabin to ease the twinges of pain I still felt now and again.

I saw, near the bow, a small freshet which was coming out of the bank. Alarmed, I sat up straight to see that small crack open into a jagged breach. All of a sudden it increased in size and, as I watched amazed, water opened a canal into the woods. The swirling waters sucked us along into the breach, breaking our mooring. As we rushed over white and brown water into the woodlands, women screamed and men cursed as they flew off the seats below. I held onto a mooring cleat for dear life.

The bow swung about violently and struck a tree. Terrified women and men crawled or were flung through the doorway. The boat swung hard around and hit another giant tree trunk and lurched onto its side. The Baptist women were thrown into the water, and with their stiff stays and wool crepe gowns dragging them down, they were sinking, screaming. I jumped in, cigar and all and dragged them, someway, to the crumbling shore.

"Hang onto a root," I ordered. Others in the water were crawling onto shore as the boat finally righted itself. Then, canal men from other boats and towmen on shore pulled the Baptist women and other passengers up out of the water.

My valise floated over and I pulled it out. The contents were not wet, so I changed my trousers behind a blackberry bush and walked on over the towpath to Logansport. The odd thing was that my back no longer hurt. I could not account for it.

I was heading for the Indian agency, where Lewis worked for John Tipton. As I walked I looked about for Indians; a few Miami were on the streets, dressed in summer buckskin pants and calico shirts, with turbans wrapped about their heads. I was disappointed not to see the camps about the town, with rowdy traders and wild Indians gambling and doing all the things I read about in the state's papers.

There was no treaty in progress of course, but the truth is that although I would be glad enough to see Lewis, what I had really come to see were the Indians—the Potawatomi—while I could still see them. The government was arranging for them to go west, to leave Indiana, and I wanted to see some of the last Indians in Indiana before they were no more.

Lewis was in the parlor of John Tipton's spacious house. My brother stood up and came to shake my hand, in good health it seemed, and his usual sardonic self. After introductions, the three of us sat around taking sherry and finally eating supper around a beautiful, new Philadelphia walnut table.

An Indian woman served roast mutton and fine wines. I must admit I was impressed. John Tipton was not all frontier general; this man had been a U.S. Senator in Washington city.

Lewis irritated me by telling Tipton of my "odd, redskin-loving ways. 'Tis his only quirk; otherwise he's as staunch a Whig as ever you'd want to meet. But he doesn't like folk tampering with Indian braves or calling them 'dog shit' or other appropriate names." I reddened.

Perhaps Tipton was slightly nervous about appearing to criticize "Indian lovers" as Lewis was doing. I knew John Tipton liked to maintain the fiction that he was a true friend of the Indian, and indeed he was the friend of many individual Indians. Perhaps he wished to justify himself to me. It is true I was one of the wealthiest men in Indiana. At any rate, he began to speak with dignified reserve, explaining the present position of the Indians in a way that was almost pleading with me to understand the government's stance.

"Mr. Brooks, we are at the end of the canyon. No recourse is left to us but to save the last of these Indian peoples by takin' them west."

I raised my eyebrows, but not because of his words. I was tasting the sweet that was being served. Where had he got the figs that were in this delicious pudding? I prided myself on the food Susan and the hired girls set on our table, but this was superb.

"All of this could have been avoided," Tipton went on, "if their tribal leaders had been more reasonable about agreein' to go west. Let me tell you what happened at the treaty of 1836, right after their chief Aubenaubee was killed. The new leader Paukooshuck was difficult in the utmost, and he wasn't the only one. Menominee, his fellow chieftain, even refused to come to talk about removal.

"We told them that there was terrible pressure for these lands—that they could live as they wished in the West, that they would be well paid, that to stay was nothing but trouble for all of us. Paukooshuck spit on the treaty but finally signed, saying something about us having broken his spirit and his people—that his wife's mother was right—there was no way to resist us. Anyway he signed, as I knew he would. Aubenaubee would not have signed, no matter what, this time. The old chief had told us that, but then he was gone, wasn't he? At any rate, Paukooshuck signed, to our great relief.

"Other small chiefs around Menominee were convinced to sign for him in absentia, and they did. The treaty gave up the last rights of the Potawatomi in Indiana and provided for removal to Nebraska Territory as soon as possible."

Tipton waved away the Indian woman who was offering more of the fig pudding. Then there was one of those silences which hang over a group when a conversation is suspended because an unwelcome listener is there. When the Indian woman left the room, he went on.

"Menominee says he never signed and absolutely refuses to go. Other chieftains, includin' Paukooshuck, are livin' in Menominee's camps and they also refuse to remove. They are tryin' to use legal means, encouraged by the priest who serves them and the Catholic Church. Menominee has asked the courts to rule on whether someone else can sign away his lands. We're expeditin' that process, and I can assure you"—here Tipton's lip curled with sardonic determination—"that there will be no reversal."

I asked about the controversies I'd been reading about, where squatters were raising log cabins on the land owned by Potawatomi.

"The settlers haven't waited for the courts' decisions. Squatters have gone onto the last of the reservation lands," he continued. "They are plowin' at the very edge of the villages." He turned and reached towards a pile of papers on the sideboard.

After sipping a drink of cordial, he read from the letter.

*To John Tipton at Logansport.*

*We have got a problem here in these northern counties in Indiana and Illinois too. I have bought my land fair and square from the goverment. But there are many good people who want to buy redskin land. President Jackson has ordered them to go west. They have agreed to go west. Some went west with the Indian Agent last year. Why do these stubborn Indians around here yet remain?*

*Let them that can, till and tend the land and use it, not those that God intended as inferior waste it.*

*The state should not have granted these reservations anyways when the earlier treaties was signed, especially to a species of men who murder their own kin, like Pawkooshuck did, and know no god but whiskey.*

*Countless cows is getting stole and scruffles with knives is still going on ever Saturday night.*

*This old chief Menominee, egged on by some of a suspect and oftentimes traiterus religion, is standing in the way of the whole U.S. goverment. Who knows when he and his followers may break forth into a massacree in this county, killing, as his ancestor did. The Black Hawk war is not far behind us.*

*He is a outrage to us and to the U.S. goverment who he defies. There are those of us who own rifles and know what to do with them.*

*A Friend near the Twin Lakes*

John Tipton set the letter down and stared into the candlelight.

"Does he mean your Father Deseille when he says those of a traitorous religion?" I asked.

"Yes. Deseille has told them of the legal means they may use to test this last treaty, the one that takes the personal reservation land. Time is runnin' out, I think, even for legal means. You knew many of them went last summer to Nebraska Territory?"

I knew. It had been a disgrace. A high-handed hireling named Sands, along with Indian agents and strong-arms, had assembled tribes from Michigan, Indiana, Wisconsin and Illinois who had agreed to go. When the tribesmen showed reluctance, with winter in their faces and no supplies for the women and children, Sands told them there would be no annuity payments until they went west.

They marched through torrential rain, camping in exposed places, while Sands and his guards stayed in inns, ate quail and drank themselves woozy.

The strong-arms stole supplies by the wagonload and forced Indian women to their will, night after night, before they would issue supplies.

I knew about it, all right.

"Deseille died and was replaced by Father Petit. He too is urging Menominee to resist removal."

To his credit, I thought.

"It can go on no longer," Tipton said, and then, when I was silent, insisted, "These are my Indians. I fought to get them food and shelter. I got decent terms for 'em at the treaties. I know what will be good for 'em."

Lewis began to chuckle a little as he drained his sherry glass. It was an odd sound in that sumptuously appointed dining room. "Do you know what Menominee said?" he asked. "It hasn't been in the papers. 'T would be misunderstood. He saw President Van Buren and he claims the president told him that no one would be able to remove the Potawatomi if they did not really sell their lands. There is some sympathy building in the United States Senate about the plight of the Potawatomi here. There's a letter here from Menominee in the pile—" Lewis looked up at me and shrugged.

"May I hear it?" I asked.

He reached to the sideboard and pulled out a handwritten sheet. He put on eyeglasses and in the dim candlelight, read:

*The President does not know the truth. He, like me, has been imposed upon. He does not know that you made my young chiefs drunk and got their consent and pretended to get mine . . . He would not drive me from my home and the graves of my tribe, and my children, who have gone to the Great Spirit, nor allow you to tell me that your braves will take me, tied like a dog. When the President knows the truth, he will leave me to my own. I have not sold my lands, I will not sell them. I have not signed any treaty, and will not sign any. I am not going to leave my lands.*

John Tipton seemed to have sunk completely into his chair. Tallow was dripping on the table. "Ah, but he will," he said.

That evening, after we had left the table and the bell on Tipton's grandfather clock had chimed eleven, I heard him and Lewis speaking in low voices in the parlor office. Finally Lewis emerged and in answer to the question in my eyes, answered: "It is happening, finally. Governor Wallace's courier has arrived. We are to raise the militia and eject the last of them. One of the agents, Abel Pepper will get Menominee away from camp and we will move in. The guns will make the final statement of what the people of Indiana think of the Potawtomi. Tipton has told me to take care of the militia draft. He wants to have as little as possible to do with the direct action." He chuckled in that odd, rueful way again. "I am a poison taster, like the ones the Italian princes used to have," he said.

And then he added, "You've been wanting to see some of the last Indians in Indiana. Give me three days to round up the militia and then ride north with me."

I nodded and he left.

I spent the time looking about Logansport, the town John Tipton had built, the two sides of the river, both of them growing with businesses and operations connected with the canal. Warehouses, shipping docks, taverns, new homes—clearly the canal was bringing this town prosperity, even if it was ruining Indiana financially.

Finally we rode north along the new Michigan Road leading 100 volunteers, collecting others. They were all well armed with deer rifles and hatred that stretched back to the time of their fathers and the Battle of Tippecanoe.

I need to make the story short. I came to see, and this is what I saw.

I saw five detachments of the military circle the Twin Lakes Indian camp and capture Menominee and four other chiefs. I saw them kick down the proud Paukooshuck and his pregnant wife and her mother, and then bind the hands of everyone in the tribe to keep them from escaping, as mothers and children cried in fear.

And I saw the militiamen ride through those northern woods, chasing Indians who attempted to get away, rounding them up like heifers, forcing them in with guns to their backs.

For three days I saw other Indians come into the camp with militiamen behind them, and Abel Pepper and my brother drag reluctant signers to the tables to be enrolled for immediate removal.

And at last they had provisions loaded and were ready to depart, and I saw these militiamen kick and push resisting Menominee, who was crying, "My home, my children's graves" and throw him and the other chiefs into a cage with slats across the top and drive off through the dust. My mind still, to this day, echoes with the sounds of the crying, sick babies and the old men singing the death chant.

And the next day, when the dust was laid, the dour volunteers began exultantly torching the cabins to destroy every thing that had ever belonged to a living soul. "Stop," John Tipton ordered. "There are buildings here that the white man can use." Reluctantly, the militiamen pulled back.

My eyes were sick of seeing. I was ashamed that I had wanted to come to see these last Indians, and ashamed of being a part of an America which could order such things done to human beings as I had seen these last days.

Even Lewis, saying he was tired of being the "poison taster," had enough and went back to Mount Pleasant. Before I left I walked through the quiet woods. The damp heat of that awful, baking summer breathed from every leaf. On one of those odd impulses that sometimes hits when one is alone, I cried out, "Goodbye."

But nothing answered; there was only the rippling of dry leaves on the shaking aspen and the cry of a mourning dove, raincrow as the Indians call her, on the branch of a tree far away across Twin Lakes.

*Chapter Nineteen*

## The McClure Papers

To: Mr. John Robert Scott, Old Ft. Knox, Vincennes, Indiana
From: Cousin Alfred McClure, Poore Farm, Orange County, Indiana

February 10, 1839

Dear Cousin John Robert,

I am having this letter delivered by special, trusted courier so that it will not fall into evil hands. Nancy Jane and I are established here on Mrs. Poore's farm and believe it will be profitable wheat country. We are preparing for spring planting. Mrs. Poore and her family have insisted we hire a man and woman to help tend the farm. Nancy Jane will appreciate the assistance, as she is in the family way.

In these six months we have been able to help several people on their way north to freedom and have been able to learn quite a deal about those who seek this way out of servitude. I think I am doing my job for Simon's Net, but even in this short amount of time, I am wiser than I was when we went to help rescue Charlotte and Moses and Little Abe.

Had I known then what I know now I might not have taken such a foolhardy risk. I should certainly not take it now, with a family on the way. In the South, rescuing colored folk with a woman! Even some of the Quakers in this settlement criticize our bravado.

I suppose we answered our Father's call in the press of the moment, and He supplied the protection we needed.

One thing that I have discovered is that not all members of this Quaker sect that you and Nancy Jane and I have joined have the same views. We Friends are a scattered bunch with some splits in our ranks on the matter of doctrine, aren't we?

And even amongst those in one area, some honor the old ways and speak only in "thee and thous," while some new meetings allow folk to be more worldly. I, for one, cannot change to "thees" when I have "you'd" all these years.

I went to the Yearly Meeting at Richmond and I found some Quakers there were abolitionists, some strongly opposed to helping Negroes because they are inferior in God's chain of being, some unwilling to break laws like the Fugitive Slave acts.

But in some way we manage to put together Simon's Net. Odd bedmates—Friends, political followers of the new abolitionist movement, some Wesleyan Methodists and good Presbyterians like Mrs. Poore. 'Tis a network of help, and Nancy Jane and I are as committed to it as before. Now, though, we have the wisdom to pour a little cool water on our heated opinions.

Let me tell you what I have learned as a practicing operator of a road station for Simon's Net. It has been interesting to observe these poor colored souls as they fly north, abandoning family and security, being unsure of the future and grateful for a morsel and a safe place to stay!

Largely safe, that is. With Jay Byrd Dugger and his sons and friends on the loose all over southern Indiana, no one can be sure of safety. I have hid the men and women I've helped in the caves right on our property, in corn shocks, and in the potato hole Mrs. Poore used so many years ago herself.

Some of these dastardly slavers live on islands in the middle of the Ohio River so as to be near the colored "prey" when they cross over. They train dogs who can "smell out a nigger for six days efn they git jest one sniff of his clothing," as I heard one local farmboy brag.

So, when I am helping a group escape, if we walk about on the property, we cross the stream several times, and I give them different shoes. I sometimes dress the men as Friends in dark gray suits and black hats, and put the women in dark cotton dresses, with simple bonnets.

I have even had some willing young people in the neighborhood from our own meeting dress as decoys and go on the road to Indianapolis, putting the real fugitives in a night coach with one of our men bound for Ohio.

For a long period, the Quaker stations out here have been left alone. Recently, though, Mrs. Poore and Sylvester's stations are suspected of being "harborers." None of us are in immediate danger; there are few fugitives and not much real interest most of the time.

This is because the officials wax hot and cold on enforcing the laws which say we must help return stolen "property" to the Southern states. Just last month, after the Governor of Kentucky had complained again, the constable came out and pounded on the door demanding to search our house, as he was every house in the neighborhood. He had a rough-looking group of bounty-seekers with him; no doubt he was putting on a show for them.

We graciously let him in, assuring him that he had been misinformed if he thought any fugitives were on our property. At Sylvester's place he stalked about the grounds and, coming to the smokehouse, which our friend keeps locked, demanded to be let in to inspect it. Sylvester's temper got the best of him, I guess, and he told the old man he would have to get a search warrant.

The constable hastened to Paoli, but it was the next day before he could get a warrant. When he came out with the rat pack of fugitive-slavers riding behind him, Sylvester was ready with the key.

"I thank thee for operating according to the laws of the land," Sylvester said. Then he opened his smokehouse to reveal a bunch of joints of smoked hams and brined pigs' feet—nothing else.

Actually, the slaves this pack of jackals were pursuing had crossed into Indiana from Ohio and taken the Newport Connection to Ft. Wayne. There are four main "lines" in this railroad, and that is the eastern one. As you know, I expect, they all attempt to get the fleeing slaves to Canada, where Negroes can live free. Some, of course, do stop in other places and settle in, generally living in fear for the rest of their days.

The folk here about do not suspect Nancy Jane and me. We are too young and innocent-looking to be harboring fugitives from justice. How inadequate a phrase that sounds when talking about those flying from being owned.

Interestingly enough, some of them are criminal fugitives, cousin. Yes, not all these brave souls are really brave souls. A certain percentage, even one man who came to me for help, are fleeing from prosecution for serious crimes, for assault, stealing, even rape and I suppose murder. I was caught in a quandary of conscience with this man, who was from Virginia.

"What have you done?" I asked.

"Massa, I stolded two bolts calico from the massa next ours so my wife could make herself some dresses. They got a paper out fo' me, but I ain't goin' go back and I am goin' to find a way to git her up here too. I didn't know so many was fleein'. I didn't know, none of ussins does, that you white folks will help git a person to freedom."

It isn't only black felons that flee, of course. There are also those who want to "divorce" by leaving a mean husband or shrewish wife, those who have heard there's gold for the picking up in the streets of Detroit, those who are unstable and will run all their lives. And there are also free Negroes masquerading as slaves to trap and sell their fellow creatures for $25 or $50, whatever the reward.

But there is a remainder, about half, who are good people who are leaving because they know God made them as free souls and they are willing to risk their lives to live free. It is these that reward us for risking danger in Simon's Net.

I am saying "we." I must not forget Nancy Jane. She is the practical one in our partnership, the one who makes arrangements, who stocks in supplies, who sends post messages in cryptic form, who manages the farm so we have something to offer hungry people and to eat ourselves. I fear I am not too practical at these matters myself.

All this exodus that's just beginning to hit us isn't an organized uprising; it's just random people deciding to leave bondage. How many go? Only a small percentage, and I think it will ever be thus. Most slaves, they tell me, are satisfied or too overburdened with surviving or too docile to think of leaving. 'Tis only the smartest ones, the ones who are unusually gifted, who have been house servants or possibly have had a goodly taste of freedom, who decide to bolt.

Enough of this; you asked for "particulars of our trade." I have supplied them. If I may be personal, Cousin John Robert, I delight to hear family news. You told me of the charming antics of the twins, Jacob Joe and Zach, and the light in their grandmother's eyes, so long dim, and I share in your parental joy and bewilderment. Different as day and night, you say the twins are. I am sure Zach will be less of a worry to you as he grows; many two and three-year-olds are little devils!

I look forward to all that. If our child is a girl, she will be Mary Jane, if a boy, John. Perhaps this new little one will be a peacemaker, bringing our still-warring parties in the family together. I do not have good hope of it. Mother and Sister have not answered our letters. They feel we deceived them and say to those who ask (so I hear) that they do not approve the marriage. Aunt Catherine remains a good mother to Nancy Jane and has been to see us. She and Nancy Jane have had long talks about Simon's Net, and Aunt Catherine seems to be turning into something of an abolitionist herself. She says Grandfather George McClure would have been one had he been alive today. There is now a rift between her and my mother Lizzie and sister Jewell over our marriage.

Animosities die hard in southern Indiana, and once a posture is taken, it is difficult to back away from it. Or, as Grandfather Dan'l used to say, "Once you get a mule to go through a gate, you ain't goin' to get him to change his mind and back up."

Never mind. We have cast our all for the Pearl of Great Price. Should I never see Mother and Sister again, never read the law and set up as an attorney, as I had dreamed, I could bear it. Just so that my children grow up without that ignorance, racial bigotry, and hatred that mark so many others that I see, even in my own family.

Please send word of Uncle Jim. The news from the State Capital is alarming—the State unable to meet obligations, overwhelmingly in debt, creditors abroad and at home threatening the very solvency of the treasury. Can such a thing come to pass? I await your letter.

> In Christ and the Bonds of Simon's Net
> Your cousin, Alfred McClure

To: Catherine McClure Hogue, Vincennes, Indiana
From: Jim McClure, Indianapolis, Indiana

August 15, 1839

Cat—

Sorry about this brief note but my thoughts are disjointed now. The news is impossible to believe, yet dreaded all along. The State of Indiana is bankrupt. Four million in outstanding canal debts. The Morris Company bond house has gone under. Crashed, through mismanagement and fraud. Rothschilds and Lloyds of London are calling in debts, and we are totally unable to pay for all the contracting of canals and now railroads. Work has been suspended; my Irish workers have left their wheelbarrows by the sides of the ditches. I do not know if they will ever take them up again.

The Legislature has put us all into limbo from which there is no return. I guess it's their fault. There's probably enough blame to go around, and I should pick up a pot of it myself.

Cat, I have lost all. My investment in the bond house is gone. Coe, whom we all so trusted, gypped us all and made himself a fortune by re-selling bonds with no backing. I have lost my wife and my children's faith and over two hundred thousand dollars myself in this. I am virtually a pauper.

Sick too—fever, some of it feared to be cholera, has hit the town again; I have been weak all day.

Cat, Jack left me Grandfather John McClure's old French and Indian War diary. My head swims like the lights of these candles—I seem to see my Pa and yours as boys and Grandfather John fighting Indians to the death, defying them in the very headquarters of the Delaware tribe. Agonizing bravery and courage. It pains me to see how we pioneers of this day waste our manhood in offices, taking shares and plotting deals.

One entry here—December 22, 1764, he was desperately ill. He says, "If I should die today I could face my God in spite of what I did because finally, my heart became single. I took the wax and made it into one bright light, I did not pour it out into many sad and fizzling tapers."

Died the next day, didn't he? Cat, what did he mean? I don't think I know.

Weak. Think I need air. Sky heavy and yellow as curdled cream. Shall take a walk and post this. Haven't the heart for much else. Gone, all gone. I wanted so much.

For some reason I am thinking of Caintuck tonight, of you and Jack and I dancing by a bonfire at Bardstown and Uncle George playing, "When the world was young." Do you remember that?

Your Cousin Jim

Article from *Indianapolis Sentinel*, August 17, 1839

Our friends in southern Indiana and many active in the Capital City's politics will be sad to hear a piece of news received today.

James McClure, a representative in Indiana's first legislative assemblies at Corydon and an assistant to Governor James Brown Ray, today was found dead near the downtown Canal Bridge.

Mr. McClure, who was most recently Canal Labor Commissioner, was apparently stricken with an attack of the cholera at some time day before yesterday and due to the inclement weather, the storm and hail, climbed under the bridge for temporary shelter.

It is not known why, after the storm abated, he stayed beneath the bridge. "Surely the exposure to the elements contributed to hastening his death. Galloping cholera—we see it sometimes, but it is rather mysterious here. Why he did not at least crawl out or cry out for help we do not know." So spoke Dr. Malcolm Baldridge, a physician who examined Mr. McClure.

The Central Canal was one of his own projects, and it is also possible he wished to inspect it. The canal was begun six years ago, but since water was first let into it, no boat has used it and only six miles were completed before the recent and notorious failure of the State funding system. The future of the "White River White Elephant" is not known.

## Deposition of Kezegat Dauja, of the Potawatomi
## (Continued)

I was seven months with child in August of 1838, when the evil-minded farmer troops hurried all our people away from the hunting lands where we had always lived, from the lake where my father Asondaki had had his great vision quest of the Snow Deer. For, just as my mother, I had quickened with child only after several years, after Pauk and I had long since given up hope of a child. Now my time would come inconveniently, as it often does. It would be on the sad trail west.

Menominee and the two other chiefs were in cages with boards across the top of them. Paukooshuck, with his arms bound tightly was on a horse behind them, guarded. Mother and I were in the canvas-topped wagon following Pauk.

"Ah, Mother," I cried, almost beside myself with agony of body (since they had beaten me) and spirit. "We have not put out the signal sticks, to tell those who wish to follow us what direction we go."

"My Dawn, there are none left to see them. The soldiers have gone through Michigan and Illinois and Indiana and no one escaped."

"Do not be too sure of THAAAT" I said, a pressure pain shooting down my leg.

"Stretch out, Rosy Dawn, as much as you can," she said. And I thought, uncomfortable as I was as we jolted along, of how my poor Pauk and the other chiefs fared.

Caged and bound. As foxes or bears in traps or as the awful things the white men show about in their circuses. I could not bear to think of it.

These officials had hated Menominee for fighting the treaty all the way to the President of the United States. They despised Paukooshuck for the defiance he showed them at the treaty grounds in 1836, two years before. They had thought he would be more agreeable about signing than his father Aubenaubee, but, alas, they did not know him. Paukooshuck would not sign until they threatened to keep back supplies they had brought for our people, to starve them out, really.

So they had taken him, shouting and resisting, from the Twin Lakes camp. Three men it had taken to get the ropes around his arms.

But by evening Pauk, at least, was out of the ropes on his word that he would not try to escape. They thought he would not leave me, I suppose, and they were right.

I wandered restless at the first campsite where we stopped, there at the Tippecanoe River. The insects buzzed in the heavy, hot night. There by the river, Ears Ringing bathed the limbs of her child Waterdog, now a boy of ten. Her forehead was drawn with worry.

"How does he ail?" I asked. Healing was never far from my mind, although I had not done it for two months as I purified myself for the birth of the child. One must not be about fevers when a child is due; spotted fevers may mark it; that I knew from the Old Ones.

"Throat fever," she said, and my heart sank. One of the worst things for children.

"Is it the gray throat fever?"

"No, the red one. His throat is almost closed."

A small consolation, that. Gray throat fever, the diphtheria as white men call it, closed the breath off and few survived. Red throat, or scarlet fever was bad enough. It caused death in the youngest, or those who were weak. Or who had bad food, or travelled in oppressive heat. Oh, Bat Manitto, you have truly come among us in this year of trouble. Have you not thrown enough at us from your caves of dung?

"Come to my wagon now, and I will give you herbs," I told her, heartsick I could not help further because of the nearness of my birthing time. After she left the wagon, I wandered along the river. Militiamen with Kentucky rifles were thickly posted, tall and strong as corn in July, I thought. I looked into one man's face above his shirt and powder horn. "He is just a boy," I told myself.

"Where do you come from?" I asked and watched him start, surprised at my English.

"I—well, from Delphi. I have come with my brothers. We were called by General Tipton's messenger." There was an edge of apology in his voice.

"A good city. I was there and saw the canal," I told him. He asked me how I learned English and I told him of the mission and something of our lives. We spoke a long time there, as a gentle breeze blew away the worst of the insects and the noises of cooking-pot cleanup sounded behind us.

"You have been beaten," he said, finally. I had seen him eyeing the blood-red bruises on my face and arms.

"Yes. I cried out to the soldiers from Logansport that they were hurting me as they bound me. I spoke in English, and that seemed to enrage them someway. They did not like it that I spoke their tongue. Perhaps it was easier for them when they thought of me as an animal. They kicked my mother when she fell." Each word seemed to drop through the darkness like a stone.

He turned his face away. "I'm Methodist," he said softly into the shadows of night. "Found grace at a tent meeting near m' home. Love o' God shed wide in m'heart, an' I don't cotton to all this—" His arm swept a wide circle and included the camp and its guard.

I murmured something, but he went on, earnestly, "I never saw a Injeean that I could talk to. Most I see—well, we're scared o' 'em, o' your people."

"Afraid of a few hundred pitiful human beings too broken and shattered to even be able to take care of their own?"

"M' grandpa was killed by the Creeks; Ma were jest a tyke but she remembers it. They lived in Florida. She screams in the night sometimes. The old folks in the cabin up the crick from where we live now was in a station in Caintuck. They talk about the horrors of the Injeeans there. Can't forget, I guess. Still, I hate this. Ain't cut out for it. No Christian is."

We listened to the call for curfew, the cursing of some of the soldiers as they swept the woods and found Potawatomi who were seeking solitude or privacy there.

"May God bless and lead you, Ma'm," said the troubled boy. And before I could call after him that I didn't believe in his God, that I needed only myself, he was gone. The next morning the surly soldiers said three of the militiamen, brothers from Delphi, had left without notice. "Desertion," they called it, pursing their lips, but I thought there should be another word to describe their going—honor.

The hot sun glared on us as we walked further up the trail and camped. Menominee was allowed to walk around out of his wagon under guard but then he was returned to captivity; he said little. Paukooshuck walked by me, then helped me into the wagon when I could walk no more. I wanted exercise; it would be good for the coming of the child.

"Waterdog has gone to the Death Isle," Pauk said stonily as he brought food to me.

"Do not tell me," I said, mourning. "Waterdog."

"Ears Ringing has the red throat fever too," he said. "Others, many others are ill."

"I cannot go to help them," I said, anguished. "It would endanger the child."

When I went into the wagon, I saw a bad sight. Swiftly Running Feet, my mother, was ill. Her face was flushed, her throat raw as a winter wind.

"We cannot take her on this awful road," I said to Pauk, and he nodded. So many were sick, young and old alike. They could not drag themselves over that parched road.

That night Pauk and I and my mother, and forty-nine others of the Potawatomi were left behind, guarded, in camp while the others went on. Children cried hoarsely through their pain and fear. Old men sat exposed in the cool river damps, their eyes listless. There were not enough wagons for the sick. "Where are our priests?" the old women who were Catholics cried. But Father Deseille was dead and the good new priest, Petit, who had come to us did not have permission to go west with the march. Would nothing go right?

I tended my mother through the night and she worsened. Her dry lips cracked as I tried to force water down her tightened throat.

"I think we should all be dead," I said to Pauk. I was desperate with exhaustion and fear. "I do believe we all should have sunk beneath the dark waters of Lake Manitto. At least we should not have to choke in dust and die far from home."

I broke off my caretaking and went outside the wagon. Exhausted, I sat beneath a tree and in that midnight darkness I think I dreamed. Again I saw the Snow Deer, my father's vision animal, in splendor before me.

I was angry with him, yes, angry with an animal sent by the Spirit World. "What do you want with me?" I demanded. "You came and made many promises, telling me I would be *Manitto Wabo*, see great truths from the Spirit World. I see nothing from the home of the West Wind, the spirits. All I see is trouble. You lied, I think."

His sad eyes did not look at me. "Prepare for your time of Power. You will heal now as never before."

"I cannot heal. My babe—"

"The child within you will be safe. Great good is prophesied for his life; he is beloved of the Master of Life. Now you go and live obedience. Someone you can trust is coming to help you and the people. Prepare herbs. The Master of Life himself will speak to you. You will be seer. Prepare."

When I awoke my babe was jumping within me for joy; I knew that the vision was a true one, and I was not afraid any longer. When I went inside the wagon, I was not surprised to find my mother Swiftly Running Feet better.


When we came the next day, wearily, to Logansport, many were ill there too. The government had provided a doctor and he travelled about the wagons, looking into them. "Scarlet fever," I heard him say. "And possibly typhus. I don't have much medicine."

"Can we not have better food for our people?" Paukooshuck and the other chiefs asked of the man who was second in command, Judge Polke. The beef had thick, smelly slime on it; the bread was hard and stale. He shrugged his shoulders and said he would ask General Tipton. But no better food came.

The illness seemed to spread rapidly; the babes were taken by it first. Their hold on life seemed as thin as a piece of finger-twisted twine and they slipped away, at least ten of them in that first week. They were buried in tiny graves, over which we threw herbs and sang the chants, by the side of the low, brown, sluggish rivers of Indiana.

I visited each wagon I could, unafraid now since my vision had strengthened me, and I brought what I could—a tea made of marjoram, blue skull plant, and cuckold. They did not work well, so I went to the woods. "Whoever you are who has called me to heal, tell me what to use." Almost immediately it came into my mind to take the strongest infusion of ginseng I could find and paint it on their throats at the first sign of a sore throat. Since this was so different from what I usually did I hesitated; still it was as good as anything. I continued the infusion tea, but I added strong, pungent ginseng. They choked when I painted their throats, but that day my patients did not die, but the white doctor's patients did. One of them, sad to say, was Ears Ringing. I said nothing to Pauk; I did not know what I should say. I was too numb to feel sadness when the news came, even if my heart would have honestly let me. After a string of many deaths, the heart does not feel.

At Logansport happened a wonderful thing; the priest Petit, whom all loved, came into camp. He had been given permission by his Bishop Bruté in Vincennes to accompany us. The spirits of the people lifted, as if clearing of the skies had come after a storm. I went to Father Petit's wagon.

"We start, tomorrow, Priest. Ah, so you are putting up the sacred things of the sad white god." We had become good friends in the short time he had been with us. He knew I would not be converted, and it had become almost a subject of banter between us.

"Yes, I am putting up the crucifix and making an altar. The people yearn for the support of their faith. We can pray for strength and healing." Petit smiled at me. The other priest was serious; this one was a man of smiles.

I told him what I was doing. "The Master of Life works through us all, when we sacrifice for the good of all," I told him.

"So Jesus said," he said, looking at me as if he knew what my next comment would be.

"So said Son of the West Wind," I answered, stoutly.

"I wish to talk to you about something," he said a moment later. He told me that my mother had asked Bishop Bruté to pursue the matter of the back wages owed my father by Hyacinthe Lasselle, a trader from Vincennes. I had come to know this sly trader from the treaty proceedings, and had spoken to him of the debt when we were near Eel River, but he had answered with a light remark and brushed by. It seemed, though, that he could not brush by Father Petit and Bishop Bruté.

"The bishop asked to see Mr. Lasselle and told him the judgment of the church was on him. He must pay the wages earned so faithfully by your father over so many years working for the Lasselles." Father Petit turned to the side chest that ran along one side of the wagon. "I have brought you the sum, several hundred dollars. The bishop insisted on payment in gold."

I thanked him and took the bag with indifference. Money from our own people, collected by Lasselle at the time of the treaty. Anyway, gold was insignificant out here, where we were not free. Ah, well, perhaps I could buy some comfort for my mother and new child, if ever we reached a place where life meant something again.


So the *Neshnabec*, the Potawatomi Indians, left Logansport and passed through Indiana. They followed the rivers they used to rule, a long train of human despair and misery, a muted mourning march to the gravesight of a race.

And our march was accompanied each day by the same tokens: the stares of white people, many cold, many curious, and a few, like my militiaman at the Tippecanoe, anguished, the buzzing of hordes of flies which bit our people mercilessly, and the dust and heat that choked our throats and made us cry for water, water.

And I tell you that the soldiers who marched with us did prod us with bayonets; do not believe the reports which said this was not true. I certify they had their sharp knives at our backs. Our sick were loaded in the luggage vans and had to ride between the canvas tents and wooden hogsheads, and a hogshead rolled over on one poor old man from Michigan and killed him.

And as my time came, I nursed the sick day and night until my potions ran out, and still they cried for relief. The white doctor had no more calomel or jessop because we were far into Illinois, and anyway he was drunk, always drunk.

Now, since you want to know the details of this march, and you are looking into it, I shall tell you how we marched. First came the United States flag carried by a dragoon officer in charge, then baggage carts and a carriage for Menominee, now only guarded, not bound. Then came Paukooshuck and the other village chiefs and a long line of us men, women, and children on horseback or walking.

When camp was made at night, there was a little relief. Then the white doctors, and I, the Indian healer, tended the sick. Always, ever, there were at least two who died and who were left by the road.

On September 25, after I had passed with what comfort I could offer, among over 100 weakened Potawatomi, I stopped by my mother's wagon and I heard a call. I went inside and found Swiftly Running Feet, daughter of the Band Chief Brown Squirrel, lying on the pallet.

"My heart," she said, and fear gripped me. Had the fever gone into her heart? If so—"I will get my foxglove," I said.

"No," she said, waving me off. "It is my time. I feel the life ebbing out of me as heat from the cooking rocks in my father's old camps long ago, by the beautiful lake." She sighed, long, painfully. "Come here, my Dawn. I had wanted to see the son or daughter you will bear. The child shall know neither your mother or father. Ah, *he*, Asondaki Alamelonda would have liked to have known you, fine strong daughter of both of us. I shall tell him of you when I get to the isle away in the clouds." Her voice trailed off. The pain must have been severe.

"It shall be a young brave, I think." She pulled me to her. "We can give him his mother's name. Make his name McClure." Her thin hand was like a bird's talon. "It will be best."

She did not die then, but in the night. I was beside her, and I thought as the wind sighed outside the wagon, that it was also sighing in the ash trees at Mocksinkickee, where her father and mother both lay buried in peace on the hill above the dancing waters. It is sad to die far from home.

"Pah," said Paukooshuck when he heard of what she had said of the child's name. "See what pinning hope on the good faith of the whites has given all of us? See what it got your mother?"

We saw to the burial rites and put her to rest under a cottonwood tree. She was lying down, in the style of the whites, as the soldiers insisted. Now I was a child alone. She who had looked for her father so long now had no mother either.

The heat left the land only a little as we advanced across Illinois. We went through Danville, on over to Sidney and to Long Point. We traced each jolt in the road with our bruised bodies. We defined each difficult hill with the torture in our minds. September left and the flies with it; but then clouds of gnats and bees, late autumn's messengers, came about us and tormented even as the flies had before.

As we went one or two white doctors, when they were not in their cups, continued to tend the sick ones, over sixty, and I tended others who wanted ancient medicine, over forty of them there were. My patients did not die; the white doctors' did. The vision I had was right; I now had the healing power.

"Spirit of the White Deer, or whoever you are that now helps me, I thank you," I said. "Somehow I know the medicines which help. Sometimes I hold a hand and healing comes. You help me stand with confidence in myself."

I had to be alone; Paukooshuck now led the hunting parties which swept the prairies, bringing in venison, seeking the precious water. Off on a horse in the trees, he did not fret; he did not even think. But though because of this my canteen was never empty, and he brought me the choice pieces of meat, Pauk could not really help me. He could not even help himself, though he tried. Bravely he tried. And let no soldier lay a hand on him or me again! One or two tried, and he gave defiance to them in the face of the guns. Still he, I, all of us were numb most of the time. I dragged my laden body from wagon to wagon at nights, living only for the healing.

We continued, as in a bad dream at night, where one cannot escape and must drag heavy foot after heavy foot, through the central part of Illinois. The horses reared, the children cried. But still we pressed on. Month of Burning Prairie came on; Tipton left; Polke now led the train. Pride in being *Neshnabec* filtered back into our hearts, in spite of what we were enduring. We marched through Springfield, Illinois, wearing fine regalia so the folk there would know we were the Potawatomi, Keepers of the Fire, Lords of the Rivers. Our heads were high.

That night there was laughing again in the camp. I should have had some rejoicing; my labor was near. But instead, that night my sadness began. I do not know what caused it; I had never been subject to Black Mood before, but it set in. Perhaps it was the constant tending of the sick, perhaps the death of the beautiful and courageous runner woman of the Potawatomi, Swiftly Running Feet. Or the knowledge that I must see my husband through this, be the strength that had left him after Aubenaubee died.

Perhaps it was those pains of early labor which could have made me happy but instead reminded me I was bringing a captive soul into a weeping world—a burden on itself and on us. Most of all, though, I think it was the burden that I already bore—the awful, dull, remorseless hatred of the whites that had done this all to us. Potawatomi people, noble and free. Crushed like peaches under cartwheels.

So many graves, lonely under alien trees, so much agony, so many tears, dropping on the dusty earth, tears an uncaring universe did not seem to recognize. I hated the whiteskins with a loathing that was as sharp as pain, as pure and uncompromising as mother love. I do not know which thing, or all of them caused it, I only knew I grieved. I thought about the White Deer day and night, and finally I could not go to heal anymore. I lay in one of the wagons, like a panting, frightened rabbit as the sun set on the Illinois prairie. The weather was changing to burning-off-of-the-prairies time, when leaves all fall, and animals could be trapped, yet heat still shimmered off the cracked earth.

"White Deer, I cannot do it. There is too much here for me. How can I live?" I asked.

I rose and took my huge body out of the wagon. Tears filled my eyes, as I passed the pallets of the sick, saw the old men sitting aimlessly on their haunches in the dust. The white men would not even get them tobacco for their pipes.

I went to stand outside the priest's wagon on the edge of the clearing, and, in my desperation cried out in a loud voice, "So this is your world which has meaning. In the beginning God—"

I stopped calling out and put my head in the door of the wagon cover. Father Petit was not there. A faint light flickered within, some sort of red light burning within a lamp. I hauled my bulk into the wagon church and saw at the end the altar he had set up. The light of the autumn sun came in on the crucifix, a large, painted, wooden one. I looked at the dead god, the ghost god.

And I can tell you, oddest of all things in my life, that the eyes of that man on the cross seemed to come alive to me there. I looked into them, and I saw pain, greater pain than I had felt, or could ever feel. I saw the White Deer's suffering and the eyes of Menominee in the cage and yes, the eyes of the white militia youth at Tippecanoe River, all, all blended in the eyes of the man on the cross.

My tears flowed so freely I could not see, but I brushed them aside and looked at the words in English at the bottom of the cross. "Come unto me, all ye that labor and are heavy laden, and I will give you rest."

I sat down, still staring at that crucifix, at those eyes. And then I let go, I just let go, of all of the weight of hatred and pain, as if I were dropping a bag of heavy rags over a cliff. There was silence in that wagon. The rays of the sun faded and peace came down like the small rain, over me. And my heart felt it, trickling in, for many long moments.

"Son of the West Wind," I said. "You were harder to find than I knew. I took my bag to catch you at the four cardinal points of the earth and here you were all the time, before my eyes. I found you through pain."

A voice, was it in my mind? said the words, "All pain ends in me, all love starts in me."

And my needy soul asserted itself. "Very well, the priest has said that if we ask in your name—be that Snow Deer, West Wind or Christ—we will have our needs. So cause a general healing, now if you love us, for too many have died along this Trail of Death."


That very week the weather changed. The cool weather moved briskly in, sweeping out the dust and foulness. My babe was born as cold rain fell, and the old women who helped me in my time of trial were strong and free of fever.

"The dying has stopped and birth begins again," they said to each other.

And later, when Pauk came to me when deciding what the name

of our son should be, I told him, "White Deer," and he smiled for the first time in many weeks.

"And so we bring something of the Twin Lakes with us," he said.

"Little White Deer," I said, and looking at the baby, saw a face that was not mine, or Mother's or Pauk's. It was round and happy, with straight, brown, white man's hair. It was not my father's hair. Was it his McClure father's? "Is there no way to be rid of the white blood in my ancestral line? Will it last a hundred generations?" I asked this little one. I smiled and put my finger inside his little hand. I took him to Father Petit and had him baptized, and I told Pauk I soon would do this for myself, too. He did not seem to object.

I watched to see if Pauk was coming alive again at this birth of a son. Truly my husband did seem to smile now, and at the naming party, where four men of our tribe swore to defend this new man-child, he was proud. At times in the next few days, he stayed with me and Little White Deer in the wagon at night and we talked quietly, remembering the days and games of childhood and our life together. He told me then that I was of his heart, ever had been first in his love, since the time he watched me planting pumpkin seeds in the quiet village of Quash-Quay. I could not see his eyes, but I took his hand in the darkness and loved him even more in sorrow than ever I had in joy.

But during the day, as he rode the trail, Pauk looked behind him often, across the prairie grass, over streams lined with cotton-woods, to the woodlands we had left. I knew his heart was there, in spite of the birth of this son he did love.

We went through western Illinois and came at last to the Grand-father River. We saw for the first time Mississippi, place of maj-esty and deep medicine, draining our lands, spawning our myths, dividing the people of the woodlands from those of the prairies. To cross its depths was to go beyond some point almost as definite as the river by the Hunting Grounds of Heaven.

Ah, would Pauk now have Black Mood? This I asked myself in fear. My new faith gave me strength, but still my mind would picture Black Mood as inky as midnight, as dark as the giant crow's wing.

Our people prepared to cross on the white man's ferry. It took several days; on one of the last I climbed the bluffs behind the river with my baby. I watched the waters below in the river, low and a little murky in this late fall time. "Look, Little White Deer," I said as I nursed, sitting on a carpet of newly fallen leaves under a sycamore tree. "Our people are getting ready to make the great crossing. Even now the first ones go onto the ferries. They will go through Missouri and on to Nebraska Territory, whatever that may be."

I held him up, silly mother that I was, but all either of us could see was the curling smoke of Potawatomi campfires. There was no sound from below. It was as if all those hundreds of people did not exist. A pang of fear gripped me.

So few they were, and a few hundred more waiting across the river. A few who had escaped back home. So many had died, so many dispersed. How fragile we were. And yet, though I could not see them, I could sense their spirit down there. Truly I could feel an energy, rising as the smoke: the spirit of the *Neshnabec*, strong, defiant, unbowed through these awful sufferings.

I gathered strength from this spirit and from the river, greatest of all in the heartlands. "Thus is it ever so, *Manitto Wabo* takes strength from the waters," I whispered. I did think myself as having special powers from the Master of Life. Surely my healing powers had proven it.

But always I had felt power at the rivers, at the Tippecanoe when the white militiaman confessed the sin of his race, at the Wabash and the Illinois.

"Son of Man," I cried aloud, "Tell me of my people!"

And I did hear a voice as the scene dimmed, leaving only the river, a ribbon of Potawatomi silver in my sight. The voice filled my thought and yet was not my thought.

"This great river flows from the heart of the earth; its sources are deep, beyond what you or any other one may know on this earth. The Potawatomi were nurtured, fed by the cleanness, the purity of the deep rivers from the time the Spirit moved on the face of the deep and bore Spirit Woman to form our race. Borne upon the face of the rivers, nurtured by them, they returned good, harming no one, respecting, reverencing the God of nature as they went.

"They are beloved of the Spirit and none can really harm them.

Try as they will to destroy the body of this people, they can never still the spirit. As long as there are waters on this earth, the strong and bold Potawatomi will live. Every brook, every lake, every river of the land sings, and will sing a song of admiration to the Potawatomi, who endure and move on, as rivers move.

"A hundred, a thousand years from today, there will be Potawatomi, rejoicing the earth and all its waters, singing songs of joy and affirmation to the Spirit of All. And the waters will answer back, 'Hail, people of nobility and courage, who could not be broken. As the rivers live, you live and always will.' "

My heart glowed with gladness.

"Son of Man," I cried aloud. "What of your daughter Dawn? And this child White Deer?"

All was still; a sacred moment of *Manitto Wabo*. Then the voice spoke in my mind. "You will not cross the river. But White Deer will cross many waters, bathed in blood."

That was all. The scene returned before my eyes. I picked my way down the trail and found my husband by our wagon. "I have my trail things packed. I do not cross this river. I shall not go further," he said.

Although I was not surprised after what I had just experienced, the true meaning of what he was saying caused me a moment of fear. "Where—"

He interrupted me. "I shall return to Lake Mocksinkickee. Boulder Lake is my home."

"Yet all must go. So the President in Washington says—"

"He cannot make my feet cross this river."

"You may die."

"It is not a life to live in white man's camp in Nebraska Territory. There Indians are kept as white men keep their cattle, in herds. There are others of us back there, hidden in the woods, in spite of what they think. I shall help lead them, as my father did before me. If I live a month, or a week, or a day on the lands where I belong, at least I will have lived a *Neshnabe* man."


I nodded, not saying anything. My baby was beginning to stir in the cradle board on my back.

I looked deeply into my husband's eyes, as I had not for these many moons we had been on the trip. Not a trace of Black Mood was in them, I realized with wonder. And they were not clouded with liquor. I saw nothing in those black eyes but strong manhood. Something had happened when he made up his mind not to cross. Perhaps he had become the wise speaker-chief, like the chief of the Old Ones, that he had always wished to be. Never had I loved him more.

"We go with you," I said.

"So I had hoped," he said, nodding gravely. The baby was now crying; I took him out to nurse and both of us watched his father go to finish plans for leaving, down by the spot where wagons were crossing on more than one ferry.

Ah, I thought with pride, my own husband became one with the *Manitto Wabo* vision I had—Potawatomi manhood. Yet I thought of what my mother would have said, "Hopeless quest he makes—"

With little hope, perhaps, and yet there are times when one man alone who says and stands for the truth becomes truth itself for all who will look and see.

Without that man, the truth will have no witness.

Thus it was for the suffering Son of Man. And thus, in his own small way would be my husband, Paukooshuck, chief of the Potawatomi.

I fixed my travelling pack. I went to the bark bag where I kept the special good things from my life and my mother's life—the French necklace of Brown Squirrel, band chief at Lake of the Boulders, the hair clip of Mulberry Blossom of the Miamis, my grandmother. I lifted out her cross of silver and put it around my neck. My hand paused over the bag of gold pieces—the tainted money Hyacinthe Lasselle had owed my father. I listened to the sounds at the river outside, for a moment, then my fingers closed over the bag. I put it in my pack and went outside, reminding myself that I must see Father Petit before I left.

Pauk was walking towards the river. I could see him threading his way amidst the bustle of neighing horses, children crying, and wagons creaking as wheels went onto the wooden ferry. I saw him approach one of the officers; they walked to a clearing just back of the river to talk, and I put Little White Deer into his cradle pack and hurried down to the clearing.

The officer's voice was raised; he did not see me, though I stood very near. Pauk must have been telling him he was going to leave. It was the officer Pauk had argued with before.

"Had to drag you grunting and kicking from Twin Lakes and watch you make trouble all the way across Illinois—" the officer said. Perhaps he was irritated by the cold wind, by the pitiful crying of the old and sick ones who screamed in fear as they went onto the ferry, or perhaps this officer was just one of the dregs of the Spirit's creation who are lower than beasts. I only know that before I knew it, he was struggling with Pauk and, pulling out a huge knife, he cut him horribly in the neck. My husband spouted blood like a butchered stag; then the officer hit him on the side of the head with the butt of the knife. As I rushed to my husband's side, the officer stalked away as if he did not care what happened next.

The cries of my baby rang in my ears, and blood covered my skirt, but what I said out loud was, "Thank you, Master of Life, he has missed the jugular vein. But all of my skill and Yours will be called for—help me!"

After what seemed forever, doing all the things I knew to do and ripping up my skirt for binding, I did stop the bleeding. No one was there, God be praised, and I pulled Pauk into the woods and made a makeshift camp. Finally I could nurse the screaming baby and rest to collect my thoughts.

The afternoon had worn on, and the final wagons were going onto the ferries. The priest and the officers would be the last to go. Trying to stay out of sight of the soldier who thought he had killed Pauk and might connect me with his crime, I went to the river. Ah, the wagon was there and my friend Father Petit with it.

He was surprised to see me with the shreds of my bloody skirt hanging over my leggings. "I do not have much time," I said to him. "They have all but killed my husband and think him dead.

We will find our way back to Boulder Lake, or we will die. It is in God's hands.''

His mouth dropped, but he closed it decisively. He had seen so much on this trip that nothing surprised him.

"You have won me to your Lord, as you know," I reminded him. "Now I ask one last thing. Pray for me. And tell the solders that we have buried Paukooshuck, and his wife and baby have gone off alone for awhile in the woods to still their grief."

The priest pulled at his chin, considering. "I shall stand surety for you," he said. "One gentle woman and a baby will not cause concern. Even if you should not return—they do not have energy or time to search. Winter is coming fast. There are others who have strayed from the trail, and they plan to round them up later on."

I knelt and he blessed me and made the sign of the cross. I left the wagon just before they came to take it to the ferry. Passing by the edge of the woods, I saw the small group of broken wagons which awaited fixing. One with a broken axle belonged to one of the officers. It was not the unspeakable one who had tried to kill Pauk, but a kind Baptist one—whose wife had given me nappies and a sugar tit for Little White Deer when he was born.

Two bright print dresses were hung over the backboard of the wagon, drying from the wash. She had gone on across and would return for them tomorrow. At that moment, I did something I had never done, I stole one of those gowns. Looking for the one I thought would best fit my thick figure, I picked it up and took a shift as well to replace my bloody skirt, and a bonnet.

Stole—well not really. I flipped a five dollar silver piece into the wagon. There would be no hubbub; anyone could have taken the clothing that day. The money would come in handy to them. I did not have a good reason at that moment for taking the clothing, it just seemed good to do.

We hid in the deep woods beyond the clearing and no one came to search, although I listened for every sound. By morning Pauk was fully conscious, although the baby was fretful.

I brewed herbs and Pauk sat up and drank them. "My head pains awfully," he said.

"The skull was cracked a little," I said. His eyes would not focus right.

"I will be able to see better soon. We are going."

I murmured protest.

"We dare not stay," he sighed. "They may return to do a sweep of the woods. They think me dead, but should they find me alive—"

I knew he was right.

It was a cloudy day and by noon we left, walking on a sort of trail through brush by the side of the road, not daring to show ourselves. That night the moon was half-full and shed light, so we walked our slow, halting way down the road itself. It was easier going.

Thus we did go for several days, and though we made some progress, things worsened for us. We had no extra skins for moccasins, and my feet bled. Pauk had become feverish; I feared gangrene. We had almost no food; I worried that my milk would give out and I could think of little else.

We made camp by a stream and built a leanto; it was spitting cold rain. Soon the snows would come—I knew what I must do.

Next morning, before Pauk and Little White Deer awakened, I went to the stream and washed myself. I shivered as the cold hit my bare skin, but I kept on until the trail dirt was washed away. I looked at myself in a pool of the water. Dark brown-red, slightly curly hair. Skin dark, but not much darker than a poor farmer's wife's skin. I picked up the white woman's dress that I had brought with me and put it on.

It fit better than I had hoped; lack of food on this trail had shrunk my bulk and I was thinner than I had ever been in my life. I went back to camp and found the little Bible Father Petit had given me at my baptism and put it in my bodice. Pauk was awake and looked at me. I gave him a little of the mush I had made on the campfire.

"Our food is almost gone and we are going into winter. You must remember that I am a granddaughter of band chiefs. I shall be as the Old Ones were—the Potawatomi huntresses of the past. What I am hunting for is our lives. I shall do what I must."

He nodded gravely, looking at my strange clothing. "You must take care of Little White Deer for a while," I told my husband. "I have nursed him most of the night, so he will sleep in the warm cradle board, I think. But should he wake, give him some of the mush thinned with water from the stream. Or the sugar tit the white woman gave us.''

He hesitated. Potawatomi men did not take care of babies.

''The Thunder Bird, Wamego, giver of war rules, told our people to be ready to use the unexpected to win. We are in a war to live. We must do what we never expected if we would win.''

Pauk reached out for the baby.


I went into the little village with the last of the rags from my old skirt on my feet and my money purse around my wrist. I had not had to wear one of these flouncing white women's dresses since I had been in the Baptist mission. ''They pick up burrs and cling about your ankles,'' I told myself, annoyed.

A few log cabins lined two or three streets; women leading children hurried in and out of them. No one seemed to notice me and I prayed as never before that they would not. Potawatomi loose after the Federal march west would be objects of fear and hatred.

''Borstein's General Store,'' said a sign outside of one log cabin. I went in and, taking out my money purse and looking as smart and saucy as I could, I said to the clerk, ''I have a few things to pick up. Can you help me, please?''

His eyelids batted once or twice, perhaps because I had on only a thin shawl over my flouncy dress on this cold day. I bent slightly, so he would not see the rags on my feet. ''Do you have ready-to-wear?'' I asked.

''Shore do. A few things, that is.''

''I'll need a warm coat. Tore mine on a tree limb and I just think I'll get a new one.'' I smiled sweetly.

He showed me a dark blue wool cape and I asked the price.

''Three dollars,'' he said.

Was that reasonable? I didn't know. Best look doubtful. ''And a man's greatcoat?'' I asked.

He brought an old, worn one out. ''That will do, for the poor gentleman I have in mind.''

Without much trouble I soon had two pairs of strong leather boots, a small sack of meal, molasses and plenty of jerky. There were lemons in this odd place away from all the world, small and shrivelled, but I bought two for Pauk. I had seen Mrs. McCoy at the mission use them in a hot drink to restore invalids.

"And I'll have twelve of those linen squares." He looked at me oddly.

What was the word in English? Oh, yes. "Baby napkins."

"We don't sell 'em cut up. You'll have t' tear em yourself. But why not try the new soft muslin all the women like so much for baby napkins. I just got a few bolts in," he said.

The few sad linen shreds I had for Little White Deer's bottom were thin and worn. No creek water could wash them clean. I thought perhaps his fretfulness was caused not only by cold and travel but by bottom rash. Perhaps the old ones were right; pouches of deerskin with milkweed fluff in them did not give bottom rash. But Potawatomi had long since stopped using them. Well, after all my people weren't stuck in the past. We had learned to benefit from new things; certainly we had shown that in the last two hundred years. I would try the new, soft cotton napkin material.

A woman had come in. Her skirts were dirty from the slush of the streets and she had almost no teeth. Still, she looked down over her eyeglasses at me.

"Are you a stranger in these yere parts, Ma'm?" she asked. "I don't recollect seein' you roundabouts."

"No, I am a travelling missionary from the Presbyterian Board of Missions."

"Oh? That so?"

"You may know that we have many missions among the Indians, poor creatures. Have for years." I was trying to stay calm and at ease, but it wasn't easy.

"In fact, I am on God's work now." I smiled and flashed my Bible. It was actually true, of course.

"In what way?"

"I am accompanying a poor, sick Indian man back to our mission at Logansport. He was trained by us but went back to his tribe and was taken on one of the marches. We will nurse him back to health in our hospital."

"Oh," she nodded. Her jaws sank in where the teeth were gone. "Waal, that's good o' you."

"Thank you, Spirit of All," I breathed to myself. She believed me, or at least it seemed so. It should not have been hard. There were many people on the roads of Illinois in these days of the marches.

As I paid my bill, I asked if there was a stage station in town and the clerk told me he sold tickets. "Stage east leaves at 4 p.m. this very day, service to Danville and Indianapolis. They could leave you off at Logansport." My heart leapt like a deer's.

I hurried behind the Blue Boar Tavern to put on my cloak and shoes. Then I walked out of that village and went to camp. Little White Deer was asleep; his father slept by his side in the blanket roll. I jostled his shoulder.

"We must hurry," I said. "The stage leaves in three hours. It is taking us to Logansport." Hope lit his eyes, the first I had seen in several days.

"How did you get along? Was he hungry?" I had reached for the baby. I was bursting with milk and needed him to nurse. He began to snuffle greedily even in his sleep.

"I gave him mush with my finger and he ate it," Pauk said. The tone in his voice was midway between scorn and wonder. Mush-feeding was not one of the things Potawatomi warriors counted in their list of medicine skills.

"I think he may have bottom rash." Pauk spoke hesitantly and then turned away. He was unwilling to say more, but I could see a smile play about his lips. "I think I am better," he said, and he added, as if to himself, "A man is not less a man by knowing when to take help."

"Nor woman neither," I said, tearing muslin for my new baby napkins.


I need to make the story short. We boarded the stage and I muffled up Pauk and sat him in the corner where he could sleep in the warmth. I held the baby, also closely muffled so he could not be well seen, and put my cape around us both when I nursed. And I answered questions with a straight face, talking well about services at the mission which did not exist, about sewing classes we had for little Indian girls, and gardening lessons we gave and types of corn seeds and all the things I could remember from my own mission days. I answered the questions about why I had a baby with me on this mission of mercy by saying that I could not leave my own baby at the breast even though my Savior called.

We stayed at the inn in Danville for a week and had our meals in our two rooms (since I was a respectable Presbyterian woman). And Pauk did get better, so that I thought that the skull bone had knit by the time we got back on the stage for Logansport.

I bought two horses, a gun and some supplies and we came at last through snow to Mocksinkickee, Lake of the Boulders. I did not let Pauk see the tears in my eyes when I finally caught sight of its silvery ash trees and gray-green waters, not yet frozen. Potawatomi women do not cry at such things. Probably it was the white blood in me that made me so weak.

"I do not wish to use your money or live with white man's ways any longer," Pauk told me. "We will build our own winter shelter and live as our people have lived. Only, we will buy food. Our lodge will be open to any of our people who are left. These Federal men will not bother us till spring, I think. They are are home by the fires."

"I will keep my happies and sugar tit, though," I said, smiling, as I helped him bend trees to begin the winter shelter there on the south side of the lake.

Pauk killed deer and raccoons and traded venison for supplies to the family who had squatted on the camp of Brown Squirrel and were the only ones on that side of the lake. The settlers left us alone; we stayed and watched our little one grow and finally crawl about the floor of the winter shelter where our ancestors had been for a hundred years. As they did, we waited for spring to come and thaw the lake and bring life to the land again.

Spring did come to that lovely place, as it had in the days of my mother and grandfather. We took Little White Deer out on the point, in front of our winter shelter, and he took steps among the flowers of spring, coming in order as white man calls them: salt and pepper, spring beauties, trilium with delicate red petals, violet. And the strawberry and bramble bloomed, as they had since the first woodland peoples crossed the ice and came to these woodlands, as the Delaware say.

Pauk taught Little White Deer the words of things in Potawatomi, duck, *gishib*; star, *osseo*; smoke, *pukwana*. And I thought this spring was a gift from the Spirit of All to us alone, that we were his beloved children, and that I would capture this Month of the Deer and put it under glass, as white men do butterflies. That way it could never be taken from me and I could look at its beauty always.

A few Potawatomi came out of the woods of Michigan and found us out, and they stayed and ate venison and beans, and we all whispered, "What will they do to us?"

"Where can we stay?"

"Will they take us to Nebraska Territory in cages?"

At the end of Deer Month Pauk walked all around the lake which had been his father, Aubenaubee's, domain but was no longer. He came home with the old dark shadows in his eyes. "The man who is a squatter on the land of Brown Squirrel's camp will buy it soon from the government. He is planting apple trees."

Bigley was the family's name. I liked them. They had given us cornmeal and many apples in return for the game Pauk killed, and they did not turn us in to the Washington city people.

"He put the plow to the land today," Pauk said. "I stood out of sight and watched. He has girdled the trees and now it is bare there, with dead sticks and sad, chopped-off trunks. The ground where he plowed—it showed black spots. Fifty. I counted. Fifty campfires where the Potawatomi lived. Now they will grow apples to make hard cider."

"I know, my husband," I said softly. Then I ventured something I had been thinking about. "We have enough of my father's money to buy a small piece of the land. We could even learn to farm."

"We could even learn to farm." He sounded like an echo, a scornful one. "Their pigs stink of manure," he said. "It flows down the hill into the lake."


Now that we were out of doors we rode our horses about and walked the shores of the lakes of the north. We went to Twin Lakes camp and saw the charred ruins of the church and the houses. Someone had squatted on the land and had built a tavern. Pauk saw Whippoorwill, one of his old friends there.

"You are here?" Pauk asked. "I thought you fled to Michigan, to where three rivers meet."

"Yes," Whippoorwill said. "I helped the white man with some of the traders' accounts and they will let me stay. There are others."

"I would not be surprised if there were," my husband said. "Rats run in packs."

"Do not harden your heart toward us, Paukooshuck. After all, you did sign to sell your land."

"And so I did," Pauk said.

As spring turned to summer and Little White Deer took his first steps, Pauk was often gone at night. The Washington city men had heard there was an Indian at Long Point and come to look. Soon we took to the swamps. There the mosquitoes bit my little son, and I did not see how things would go. We seemed a people without a future, and my proud, strong chief of a husband had no *alanyas*, no young men, to counsel. He often sat by the lake in the early morning, when none of the white settlers could see him.

As summer came in full, Pauk went away for a week to the camps near Logansport, the old dead camps of Winnamac, where some Indians of all tribes, displaced and blown about by the wind, gathered to drink with Miamis, who had not yet gone west as a tribe. Perhaps he thought that he could find some solace, some idea of the future there.

But it was not to be. I looked out the shelter door one morning to see a horse coming our way. It was ridden by Whippoorwill. Behind it, on a sledge, was the body of my husband Paukooshuck, chief of the Potawatomi. He had begun to drink, after all, in the Indian tavern near Winnamac's camps and had been stabbed to death in a fight. Through my anguish I could not help thinking of another tavern and another killing in the night.

We buried Pauk on the Point, where he had loved to watch the waters of the lake lap at the mossy shore. We had the old rites. Whippoorwill, some of the others who had helped the government and been allowed to stay and some of the Miamis from Winnamac's camp, were speakers at the burying.

One of them, The Catfish, was kinsman of my father Asondaki and had seen him fall bravely at Tippecanoe. "Brave was my kinsman Asondaki Alamelonda, to die for the tribes when he did not need to. Brave also Paukooshuck, son of Aubenaubee of the Potawatomi, who came to see his lands through great suffering.

Uncowed, unbeaten, he died, a *Neshnabe* man." So said my kinsman Catfish, Mialanaqua.

We walked to the grave in single file, saying nothing. We threw in moss from the shore, pebbles from the lake he loved. They sang the song asking the spirits to welcome Pauk, telling of our sadness that we would no longer see him. The men covered him with earth and we left. He was buried sitting up, in the old way, as he would have liked. That was for him and the old ways. But I held up Little White Deer and had him throw in a picture of Christ in the garden of sorrows from my little Bible. That was for me and the new ways my son and I would have to live with.

What would Little White Deer and I do? I did not know, but whatever it was it would be here in Indiana on ancestral lands. This much I could do for my husband, chief of the Potawatomi. And it was in my own heart too.

The Catfish, my Miami kinsman, asked me to come with him and his family for a while; this I decided to do. And so, as they loaded the horses with the few things we had, and Little White Deer ran about in the water off the point chasing minnows, I stood watching the lake. A hot wind rippled the ash and willow leaves on that summer evening, blowing forlornly through the abandoned, burned camp of the Potawatomi. The fires were dead and scattered by white man's boots, the winter shelters pushed down and kicked to pieces.

Somewhere nearby, I heard the sound of an axe.

I spoke to them, these white men who had taken from us this Lake Mocksinkickee and I said, "And so you have won. You were the stronger; we the weaker, and the law of Thunderbird tells us that after we have fought and lost, we must make a good peace. This I shall do; may others of the Potawatomi, Shawnee, Delaware and Miami do so too. Many of us have gone now. We leave behind the sacred graves of our ancestors and the memories of two hundred years. Our hand has lain delicately upon these lands and waters; we leave them to you pure, clean and free.

"Some few of our remnant remain in these woodlands, mute witnesses to the memory of love, joy, tears, and proud life lived here by a strong people. We are mute witnesses too, to what has been done on these lands. May none of us forget how the Potawatomi left, not we nor you, even to the hundredth generation.

"There is no price that will redeem what has happened here, on these lands. All the pure, clean waters of the rivers of this state can never wash the stain away.

"Still, we must try.

"See to it that you take what you have bought at such high price and use it well. See that your filthy animals do not befoul this lake, that your greed and search for pleasure do not destroy the purity given by the Master of Life.

"He Who Sees All shall judge between my people and yours. In the meantime, do not forget us Kickapoo, Shawnee, Delaware, Miami, and Potawatomi. We may be absent, but we are not gone. Our presence lives in every stream, in every tree. Be alert, use these lands well. We are watching you."

And then I left.

To the Tune of "Auraleigh," ( or "Love me Tender")

# 1858

## A Shadow Falls Across the Land

A Shadow falls from shore to shore, begun at Kansas
    lands,
It creeps across the Northern hills, and o'er the Southern
    strands.
Shadow dark, civil strife, stay back from my door,
Let us live our days in peace, without the shade of war.

Not a household in the land is spared the shadow's
    course
"The fort's been shelled, march out the guard, go get
    your gun and horse"
Shadow stop, stay your path, fall into the sea—
Let not the shade of battle take my child away from me.

# Chapter Twenty

## The Poore Papers

### The Secret Diary of Harriet Poore Houghton

Today I took my wedding dress out of the trunk and tried it on in front of a looking glass. I saw a different person than the one who had worn all that lace and creamy muslin in the garden wedding at Susan and Thomas's house twenty years ago in Mt. Pleasant.

I twisted and turned, swirling the dress about and saw the bust is tight, the waist three inches short of meeting, even with stays. Carrying four children has done that. I put on a serious look for the mirror and examined the way my face appears today—puffy but I think still pleasant. It is the eyes that are the same. Wide, with a world hidden behind them. And afraid.

This is my diary, my voice, my thoughts, which go unshared still. If I cannot go out of this house to talk to the world, and I do not often share my whole heart with my family (except in monosyllables, poor family), still I can talk to this page, the whole pent-up reservoir of emotions pouring out, never to be read, except after I am gone. I would not mind it then.

> *Give voice to the world behind my frightened eyes, oh*
> > *Lord*
> *I am a bird kept in my own nest, hopping and eating*
> *Not singing.*
> *Within this nest I chirp a little*

*To nestlings some, to mate more*
*But seldom to the world.*

And never, never to Mama.

Goodbye to Mt. Pleasant. 'Twas a sad leave-taking for me. Those tree-lined streets with Mr. Lewis Brooks's fine house in the midst, the Houghton mill up the road and around the corner. And the two graveyards I loved, Brooks and Houghton Cemeteries.

I was told we must go to a new town to be near the Iron Horse. The railroad holds us all in thrall, a paternalistic monster which provides and takes tribute from us. A giant dragon sleeping in a cave. Bring water and food and watch the fire and smoke come from its mouth. So it is with all our towns now in this Old Northwest. We must get our goods east and to Chicago, and we must have our towns now on the railroad.

Soon almost no young men will have the opportunity to ride the Mississippi to New Orleans atop a boatload of hogs. So Thomas Jefferson Brooks says; and he will take his sons and my William and go, so they will know what it was like.

I do not know if I can stand it if William leaves that long. When he goes out of that front gate, I perspire and my heart palpitates. I cannot sleep if he tarries long at church picnics or takes the horse to see his Brooks cousins. Sometimes when he is gone all day, I am physically sick in the weeds in back of the house. It is the same as if I must leave the house myself. I know it is not right, but I cannot be from home.
Since.

The Campbellite Christians are about. Somehow they hold a fascination for me that has the intrigue of the forbidden. They outrage Mama with their talk of abolishing church constitutions and disciplines and depending only on the New Testament. "There should be no organization in a church except what is expressly taught by Christ and his apostles." We should all be disciples of Christ, they say and insist all are equal in the church. All are to be preachers, too! The Disciples of Christ, they are calling themselves and their services are simple and sincere with frequent communion.

But with my infirmity, I do not go to church, and I miss that dearly. Being in a Christian community is not all I miss. I did not go to William's academy graduation, I could not see Hattie at the spelling bee. If William were to be married—what then? I should be torn in half by that.

There does not seem to be a chance of that happening soon. Will's shyness runs parallel to mine and is particularly marked when it comes to young women, though it seems to come more from natural diffidence than from some infirmity of spirit.

Now he goes for most of an autumn on the flatboat to New Orleans. How could I say no? My concern for dear ones is still alive, even though the part of me that should sing and laugh and walk abroad is numb.

Since. It could be the beginning of a poem. Perhaps I could write what wrings my heart.

*Since*—

There it is, the cork. Could I pull it, a torrent might flow.

I must darn socks, wash clothes on the boiler. Tomorrow, tomorrow, can I write it—WILL LEAVES.

# Chapter Twenty-one

# The Account of Thomas Jefferson Brooks
### (Continued)

I think I first felt old when we took the flatboat trip down the Mississippi in 1858. I say we because I took my boys Lewis and Tom and their cousin Will Houghton, Harriet and John's son.

"One last trip," I said to them. "You should see this slice of life before the whole loaf's gone."

Lewis, ever practical, had said, "Father, it could have some educative value." Lewis was a formal sort of young man, married two years at that time. To show you the bolt of cloth he was cut from, I'll tell you a little story. When Lewis married, he decided he could save himself the expense of building a home to "go to housekeeping." He took some log rollers, chains, and a team and brought one of the old log cabins from Hindostan Falls to be the first home for his bride.

"Why would you want to go take one of those old cabins from Hindostan?" I asked Lewis, and he looked at me as if he did not understand the question. It did not bother Lewis that people avoided Hindostan Falls unless they had business at my mill there, that they were never caught after sundown near its moldering cabin ruins and fallen-down fences. If they had to be there, folks would walk over half a mile to avoid that graveyard. To tell the truth, I never went near it either, although I'm not superstitious. That field of mostly unmarked graves had wretched memories for me. Anyway, the people of the area had spun all sorts of tales about Hindostan and believed it had caused a curse to be on our end of the county.

Susan was fearful for Lewis and his new bride Amanda's

health. "Suppose some sort of miasma still lurks in that house. It was, I think, where the apothecary lived. I can't recall whether he fled or died, but there could be miasma still."

"Germs, Mother," Lewis said firmly. "We know now that Hindostan was destroyed by poor sanitation from the river, caused by microbes. Nothing mysterious about that. Time has done its job and I've cleansed the cabin from top to bottom. Doctor Philpot tells me nothing more is needed to make it the ideal honeymoon cot."

Lewis set up his cabin at the new town where we all lived, Loogootee. Strange name, that, for the frame-house village that was built, a few miles above Mt. Pleasant when the railroad came through. Judge Goottee, one of Mt. Pleasant's leading citizens, had helped plan a new town when it became obvious time and the Louisville Limited, were going to pass us by if we didn't do something. The "Lo" came from a Mr. Lowe, another of the town's builders.

I never liked Loogootee, with its raw, flat streets and warehouses. I don't to this day. Mt. Pleasant, the place of new start and salutary air, on the hill amidst the fertile fields of corn and copses of beech and sassafras trees, is the home of my heart. But one must make a living, too. I was also thinking of Lewis's future. When he was sixteen he had said, "I should like to come into the mercantile business with you, Father. Perhaps I could organize the store a bit for you." I didn't want to think of all those organizational skills going to waste in a town wilting on the vine, off the main road.

Lewis spoke like a gentleman. He should have. I had imported from New England the best schoolmarms, one of them my own sister Rebecca. I had paid to have all the children in the area educated in the Mt. Pleasant schoolhouse, in the latest methods of spelling, geography, mathematics. We even taught Latin. People in the state said that eight years at that school was like an academy education.

The Houghtons, Reilleys, Gibsons, children of my partner in the mercantile—all went there together.

We all loved Mt. Pleasant and we all mourned when it died, not in a flash of thunder and lightning, as Hindostan did, but in little weak spurts, like heat lightning seen afar off. First the railroad came in a few miles north, then the judge and some others of us, including Brooks Mercantile, as I have said, moved to the main street in the new town there, Loogootee, then the other stores left. Finally, the church and school closed down to "relocate in the new metropolis of Martin County," as the *Loogootee Trumpet* put it.

The location did not affect me much, one way or another. I was a millionaire, with a fortune made most recently of brokering hogs up and down the Mississippi and to the East. More hogs were grown in Indiana in 1858 than any other state in the Union and I brought a good many of those pork chops to the tables which ate them.

Anyway, looking at prospects for sales that year in the newspaper, I said to my Susan, "I think I should take Lewis and Tom and do the grand flatboat trip to New Orleans."

"New Orleans?" she said, no doubt surprised. "You haven't taken a flatboat for at least five years. You yourself have said the steamboats and the railroad cars are much faster and safer, no comparison. Still, I suppose there's a certain feeling to it all, out there on the river." She smiled and I knew she understood. We would need to be gone longer from her and the family if we took the old-fashioned trip, but she was busy, anyway. The Methodist Church was raising a new, brick structure and was getting ready for its dedication.

"Well, October is late in the year to be taking the trip," I told her, "but it was when I could get away. I just want them to know what it was like, especially when I was their age. Those long stretches of dark trees, the flatboatmen singing, 'Goin' down the river, the OH-HII-OHH,' " I sang a little in my poor bass. Susan patted my hand.

"We can't pole a boat north on the river and then walk the Natchez Trace, of course," Lewis said when I had told him of the plan. "An article I read recently in the Vincennes paper said the Trace was so sunk in several places it was almost impassable. But we can take a steamboat all the way from New Orleans. The expense would be justified."

"I think you're right," I said. Lewis was almost always right. I looked at this oldest boy of mine. Handsomest face God ever gave a man, delicate, wiry physique like mine, well-trimmed mustache, neatly brushed clothes. I admired Lewis, I loved Lewis. I even liked Lewis, most of the time I did.

"Pa, let's see the renowned cities of Memphis and Natchez," Tommy said. His voice had the strong enthusiasm of a twenty-year-old in it. He read a lot, but not deeply, and his vocabulary smacked of *Harper's Magazine.* "Let's inspect the plantations, see the slaves. I want to experience the 'detestable institution' for myself." His eyes, as dark as inkwells, flashed. "And we can eat in the famous hostelries of the South."

Detestable institution. His Grandmother Poore had been at him again. I loved my wife's mother with all my heart, but she was an abolitionist, a thing about as popular in Southern Indiana as a skunk at a quilting bee. She was costing me business because of her unpopular views, although I was ashamed of myself for thinking of it that way.

"I think you might want to lay low with that kind of talk in Martin County, Tom. Now in Ft. Wayne, or even Indianapolis, you might find sympathy for it. But here—too many folks came up from Caintuck or North Carolina. Some of them, or their ancestors, owned slaves and they sympathize with slavery."

"Well, there may be Southern sympathizing, but there's no real disloyalty here to the government," Lewis said proudly. He was president of the Young Americans Debating and Forensics Society, which always honored the Founding Fathers with a fine luncheon under the trees the day before the Fourth of July.

"No, but few would care if states are free or slave, if it comes to that."

"As it has in Kansas," Tom put in, raising his hands in warning.

"Enough of this. I think we have seen the kind of grief this fight over slave and free can bring to a family," Susan said sharply.

We all knew what she meant. Grandmother Poore had been part of some kind of underground railroad system in its early days. She had let the family home be used by a young Quaker family, fine folk really with connections to our McClure friends in Knox County. These folk had kept a station over there.

"You mean Alf and Nancy Jane McClure," Tom said sadly. He had been over to visit them at the home place, had remembered the day six years ago when news came from an old Quaker man in Orange County that a tragic thing had happened. In a cold snap in February, when the Ohio froze, Alfred and Nancy Jane McClure had been helping some fugitive slaves across the river. A wind blew up and the ice broke into pieces and they were—both lost. The slaves had been able to get to shore, but had been captured and taken back to Tennessee.

I still felt outrage and pain about Alfred and Nancy Jane. There they were: he a fine young father of four who had wanted to study law but had never quite found the means to do it, she, a tall forthright young woman, actually his cousin as well as his wife, with beautiful red hair. They left those four young children to fend in the world for themselves. Futile.

These strong political hoo-haws that men (and in this case women) line up for and cheer for and die for—what did they mean? The futility of it all! The whole McClure family was split over slavery, now, and some were dead. I had come to be a disbeliever in political causes.

Susan said, "And I don't see why our boys need to traipse around the South poking their noses about. There's trouble brewing down there, and we're as Yankee as they come."

Well, in spite of Susan's fears, all was put in readiness for the flatboat trip. Will Houghton was included. He left his doting, fluttery mother, who clucked over him but as usual did not voice her fears (at least so I could hear). We left by stage for Alton, Illinois, where the load would be shipped, and travelled the Vincennes road west.

"So, Pa, you used to come along here on horseback in by-gone days when there were Indians? Were they fierce?"

"Not when I saw them." My mind flashed to the Delaware, beaten and bewildered when I first knew them around here. And the brave Potawatomi, now long gone. The Miami, too, had left, except for a few who lived around the Mississinewa River in the central part of Indiana. The name rang in my mind. We were now a state called Indiana which did not have the very people who had given it its name.

We were passing through good Illinois farmland. From the stage we could see farmers getting in dry feed corn with the new reaper machines. They were getting ready to plant winter wheat.

This was flour country, and there would be a boatload of it ready for me assembled by my Illinois partner Seth Turnable when we got to Alton. Flour and a group of the best bred new Poland China hogs (none of your alligator-snout, pioneer monsters for me, please) would be the basis of a good sale in the South.

Alton was one of the pushing-off places for steamboats, barges, and the few freight flatboats still plying the Mississippi. I had shepherded flatboats to New Orleans often from here. Lewis had never made the trip; actually, since he was sixteen he had taken care of the pincushions and cracker barrels while I spent my time on buying and brokering trips.

"Look at the steamboats," he murmured, as the stage deposited us on Main Street near the levee. Lewis pointed to scores of double smokestacks, black and tall, clustering around several ornate decks. They made the steamboats look like giant birthday cakes with huge candles.

These huge stern and side-wheelers dwarfed the smaller barges and our three flatboats, which we found floating easily near the shore, ready to receive their cargo.

"I have never been on a steamboat," Will Houghton said, "or done anything exciting like that." That was an understatement. His mother did not let him out of her sight; I was surprised she had allowed the trip. He was a fine, strong boy with a shock of corn-yellow hair and had been the best scholar at Mt. Pleasant school. Each night of the journey so far he had sat by the light of a lamp with pen and ink, entering his thoughts into a journal.

These boys were part of a passel of over fifty cousins, the progeny of my mother-in-law Hannah Chute Poore and her husband John, whom I never knew. He had died of heart failure after building a log cabin in the woods. But that is another story.

This remarkable lady had just had her likeness, a daguerreotype, done recently, in her best black Sunday dress and a pioneer bonnet. Her grandsons each had one of these likenesses and looked at it from time to time with affection. She still had some of her teeth (more than I could say for myself; I had new false ones) and her good sense at the age of 78.

My partner Seth appeared and took us all for a tour of lower Alton. Tall new warehouses and factories stood on the street, dwarfing the earlier village buildings. We walked past a three story city hall, a firehouse, and a huge, long penitentiary with hundreds of rooms.

You could see the same huge buildings in most cities in the East, and I had spent much time marvelling at new bridges, factories, and mansions in Philadelphia, Pittsburgh, and New York City. America was building herself into a whole new age.

Seth went over details to be ready for setting out tomorrow. "This summer's wheat harvest was good and flour is cheap," he said, showing me figures. "We should do well. But try to move it before you get to New Orleans. The word is, prices are lower there this month."

He tipped his hat, twitched his curling mustache, and went gravely off.

"You boys will have a chance to do some things you have not done," I said to Will, Lewis, and Tom the next morning over breakfast at the Hotel Alton. "I am putting you in charge of securing and loading a whole boatload of hoops."

I told them it would be their job to contract for the hoops, bent saplings which were not meant in this case for ladies' dresses but were used to go around barrel staves. They were still much in demand in the South, particularly at the ports to make the shipping barrels.

"Go around to these shipping offices on the levee. See if anyone there has hoops to contract out. But I suppose you'll have to go into the farm country, too, to see who has been clearing land and to pick up hoops direct from farmers."

"How long do we have?" Lewis wanted to know. His eye was always on the time. I knew it, although he tried not to be obvious about it. Amanda, his pretty wife, was at home and so was the babe. I was a grandfather now! This trip would take a month and a half, and how the baby would grow while Lewis was gone! Still, I did understand. Lewis was not mine anymore. 'Tis true, as my mother used to say, every hour a grown child spends with a parent is an hour away from a spouse.

"Three days, boys," I said, "is all you have. So fly!" Off they went. Lewis decided to buy his hoops in town from the warehouses and brokers. The younger cousins asked about some, and then rented a wagon from the livery and took the road east into the country.

As the wagon disappeared down the dusty street, I went back to the hotel. I was trying to decide whether it was worth my while to spiffy myself up a bit, to change out of the old trousers and worn shirt I had worn to inspect the boats. There was to be a political rally in town, but I had grown cynical about politics, as I have said.

Still, what else was there to do? Two men, one named Stephen Douglas, an Illinois judge, the other Abraham Lincoln, a country lawyer, were to debate in the battle each was waging for the senate. Both were supposed to be crackerjack speakers and had spent the summer on the stump arguing against each other.

This is the first time we had heard of Lincoln. The Republicans had put him up to run against Douglas, a senator all the Northwest knew. In fact, the Vincennes paper had reported only two weeks before this that Lincoln had the effrontery to say "A house divided against itself cannot stand; America cannot exist forever half white and half slave."

"Why not?" the Vincennes paper's Southern sympathizing editors wanted to know.

Lincoln, the article said, believed the states should not even have the right to choose which they wanted. People in Indiana were divided right down the middle about that. Half thought he was right, that slavery wasn't going to work forever, the other thought this Illinois lawyer was the gol-durndest, anti-states right, nigger-loving fool that ever came out of the Northwest Territory.

At the hotel, I bathed in the washbowl and put on a stiffly-starched shirt with an even stiffer collar. If I was going to be tortured, I might as well go it all the way.

The debate was one of those raucous events with men spitting tobacco on the floor and cheering hoarsely. Lately women had been coming to the events, which tended to outrage my old-fashioned sense of decency. Women were intruding their nosy noses into everything these days. My partner had even told me that some woman had come to the Alton prison and found it too full of rats and cockroaches. She went to the Illinois legislature on behalf of the poor prisoners and got them to close the Alton prison down.

Anyway, the crowd quieted down and the debate began. Douglas, a short, serious man, said that he held it the most sacred thing in our nation that no institution should be forced on an unwilling people. "The abolition party really thinks that under the Declaration of Independence the Negro is equal to the white man and that Negro equality is an inalienable right conferred by the Almighty and hence all human laws in violation of it are null and void. I hold that the signers of the Declaration of Independence had no reference to Negroes at all in it when they declared all men are created equal. They did not mean Negroes, nor the savage Indians, nor the Fiji Islanders nor any other barbarous race. They were speaking of white men." If equality isn't a part of our legal system, then each state is free to choose slavery or no slavery, was what he meant.

Lincoln, a tall, cool drink of water with a lean, determined face stood up. He first denied he was an abolitionist and took Douglas to task for always saying so out here on the Illinois stump. "I do not want to interfere in the institution of slavery. Let it stand, but do not extend it into the territories."

Still, he said he did believe the Founding Fathers meant it when they said "*All* men are created equal."

"Slavery in this country is a wrong—moral, social and political wrong, a cancer on the body which should not be allowed to spread. That is the real issue," he said, or words to that effect. "That is the issue that will continue in this country when these poor tongues of Judge Douglas and myself shall be silent. It is the eternal struggle between these two principles—right and wrong throughout the world. The one is the common right of humanity and the other the divine right of kings, which says, 'You work and toil and earn bread, and I'll eat it.' "

After the talk was over, I worked my way through farmers and barbers arguing the points the two men made. I wanted to smoke a cigar, several of them, in fact, which I always hesitate to do when ladies are present in public places, and I had needed to go up the path for about an hour. Another problem with politics is that, like sermonizing, it is always so long-winded.

Well, the boys came back in two days with their hoops.

"The farmers had them all right, although they say folk don't ask much for them anymore,'' Will said. He was full of the doings of the people of the Illinois countryside, talkative and happy, like a dog let out of a kennel, wagging his tale and sniffing everywhere.

I had moved our gear onto the flatboat which would lead the flotilla, stocked the cabinets with bags of meal and flour and put sides of pork and beefsteaks into the cooler, which had some of the last of Alton's river ice from last winter in it. I still marvelled at the new systems which kept ice for almost a year under straw in huge warehouses.

Also stowed in the bow cabin was the crew: two rotund deckhands of about forty, and the helmsman, who would also serve as head hand of the second and third boats while we travelled separately. They had their instructions: cook the old meals, sing the old songs. ''Put the hoops on the third boat; Lewis, you supervise. We start at first light,'' I said heartily. In a few minutes we were slamming our gear onto the bunks in the main cabin.

After the ham and beans, simmered in a little too much grease over the open fireplace, we got ready to turn in. I patched over the hold opening with loosely woven netting to keep out mosquitoes and we lay in the dark, talking.

''I like the lapping of the water, Pa,'' Tom said. ''It sounds comfortable, like rain on the window when you're in bed.''

There was something in his voice that made me know he wanted to go on, to tell me something more. ''Everyone talked of Kansas at the homesteads we visited,'' he finally said.

''Yes?'' I asked.

''Both rich and poor. They can think of nothing else. Different opinions. Either it's black Republicans trying to force states to be free and deny their states rights, or it's Democrats pushing to extend slavery everywhere.''

I grunted without committing myself. I was not going to let myself get riled over these political fracases. I had my share of political solutions to things seeing John Tipton in action. Even Lewis had his share there. He was living in peace in a house in Mt. Pleasant.

''Pa, a small farmer with a poor enough homestead told a story about abolitionists. Guess he hated 'em. Said his brother was one of the rabid, nose-in-the-air abolitionists. The farmer brother decided to make the abolitionist smell his words, so he said. This farmer had a former slave working for him. He called him a greasy, blue-black nigger. He told the Negra to work in the harvest all day and come in to dinner and sit near the abolitionist brother. The Negra did, and the farmer said the black man stank so bad the abolitionist was cured and never said another word about freeing the slaves. Could something like that have really happened?''

Lewis chuckled ruefully. "I don't believe that farmer had that happen," I said. "I read that same story on the front page of the Cincinnati paper when I was there. It's travelling about.''

There was silence, then Lewis said, through the darkness, "Father, this young whelp is reading *Uncle Tom's Cabin.*''

The waves lapped. Lewis went on. "It's an abolitionist tract, written to agitate. It will only cause trouble.''

I sidestepped. "Tommy, I thought your sister Susan gave you *The Angel Visitant,*'' I said, "to read for the improvement of your soul.''

Somewhere a frog croaked. "So she did,'' Tom said with a little laugh. "Guess I'll read them both.'' After another silence his strong, young voice could be heard earnestly saying, "I want to know everything, to try it all, to live. Everything isn't in Loogootee, Indiana!''

"That's how I feel, too,'' Will Houghton chimed in.

"Very well, boys,'' I chuckled. "Cast off your lines, let the river carry you along and investigate every current and backwater.'' After all, that's what the trip was supposed to be about, wasn't it? And they could stand a little toughening anyway.

The next morning I went on deck as morning mists rose from the river. The cliffs of Missouri loomed white, gray, and remote on the other, far side.

The sun would melt off the mist by eight o'clock and the day gave promise of being fine and fair. The bosom of the river beckoned, like a lover. I responded, thrilling as I had at seventeen. The smell of bacon and hot bread drifted up from below.

If my father had been there at Alton that October and asked me whether I believed in Heaven, I would have pointed at the scene around me and nodded my head.

The hands took over the other two boats, and we four relatives manned the main boat. I gave my boys instructions as I had been given them so long ago when Drake and I made our manhood voyages down the river. So long! I looked at my two sons, enough like me forty years ago to give me a shock, and I felt the movement of the years, like the movement of the water under the boat, relentless, cold. I had buried my brother Brookie last year, and Susan and I had lost three of our ten children. Well did I know the slings and arrows of outrageous fortune, the fardels—ah, Drake. How wise you and your friend Hamlet were.

I thought of Father, of my family. Only Lewis, Becky, Lucy and I were left of that row of smirking, healthy brothers and sisters that sat in the pew in Lincoln. Father had seen so little of me and my brothers out here, and I now regretted it. I knew how much children meant, and my own consumed my interest and life in a way I would never have guessed could be possible. Especially Tom.

Of course he was my favorite. I loved to watch him when he wasn't looking, to see his earnestness and concern for all helpless things, his sensitivity. He liked to say he was a man of feeling. I looked at his round, flushed face and I saw—well, I saw Emily.

Twice my heart had been knit to my blood kin in this strong way. I hoped the second attachment would not disappoint me the way the one to Emily had. Anyway, it was too late. My life was wound up with Tommy's. He was warp of the weaving, I was woof. Some have said you should not do that with a child.

So we floated the Mississippi to St. Louis, past breathless hot shoreline, where grapevines hung thickly and fish jumped in the shallows.

Tom read to us from *Uncle Tom's Cabin*. "Listen to this," he cried. "The evil slaveowner of the young mulatto man is going to make him give up his wife Eliza and marry somebody else."

*"But we were married as Christians right here on the planta-tion,"* Eliza says, clinging to their child.

*"Don't you know a slave can't be married? There's no law in this country for that,* her husband says. *I can't hold you for my*

*wife if he chooses to part us.* That's awful. Lewis, don't you think so?"

Tom was sincerely disturbed by what he read, but he also wished to test his older brother.

"Well, yes, who could say otherwise. But it wouldn't be right to force the South into possible war or secession over something like that."

"What makes you say war?" I asked sharply. Not many believed the issues we fought over would go that far.

"Anything is possible, with hotbloods on both sides. I shall be glad to try to sense the climate a little bit down here myself." He looked apprehensive, but the moment soon passed. "How about *The Angel Visitant?*" he asked, slapping his brother on the back.

"Will, you read it to us for a while," Tom suggested. Their cousin picked up the book with a slight smile and obeyed the command.

He thumbed through the pink book, which had a gold rose embossed on its cover. "Let's see, 'Hope Ever,' 'The Absent Mother,' 'The House in Shadow.' "

"These modern writers and poets are always mourning under a weeping willow tree," I mused.

"Here's one," Will cried heartily. 'Home Angels'."

I have the book here now and will copy out part of what he read.

*My baby has not finished yet*
*The third of life's young years;*
*His eyes are blue as violets*
*And bright as evening tears;*
*His hair is golden as the beams*
*That usher in the dawn*
*And softer than the tassels are*
*That plume the growing corn.*

*No fear that we shall entertain*
*An angel unaware*
*That heavenly look upon his face*
*That glory on his hair,*

*Remind us whence the darling's come,*
*And bid us not forget*
*That He who left the child to us*
*Will come to claim him yet.*


He put the book down, and looked out over the river. Then the others took up the book and read more of the sad, sweet poems to each other. Their voices showed they were genuinely saddened by them. They, as all the young people of our day, seemed to like to be sentimental. As for me, I went below to talk to the hands as they fixed our supper. I did not like to think of the things in *The Angel Visitant* and had not walked through a cemetery for many a year. Besides, I smelled fresh cornbread.


We came to Cairo, where we lashed the boats. I shall not tell you all the details of this trip, so like any other on that broad river, of the poling away from sawyers, the taking turns, of the tying up and drifting down in storms, of the watch as steamboats passed for the wake. I gave my young charges the steamboat engineer's book and showed them the serpentine crooks it showed in the river, the letters with neat writing: Helena, Vicksburg, Memphis.

I also gave them my 1816 Cramer's *The Navigator*. They gave it a look or two, without really realizing that whole banks, loops of river bed and villages had disappeared in this half a century. The river had changed, as I had, and these young whelps couldn't appreciate either of those things.

I had hoped the hands would sing, "Floating down the river, the Ohio," but instead they sang "Auraleigh," and camp and minstrel songs.

I told the boys about Mike Fink and his brawling, murdering habits. Will was thoughtful. "That behavior was probably some aberration in his personality caused by social causes or upbringing or heritage. Some of the new social philosophers have some ideas about this."

The others nodded seriously and talked of it, and that was the last I mentioned Mike Fink.

But what I really remember when I think of those young men,

on that sunset flatboat trip on the river is a feeling of awe, at who they were. There they were, willingly taking the helm standing duty with the other men, treating me with fondness and deference, talking of the bright future, laughing their deep, male laughs that resounded over the water.

They were exceedingly fine men, I thought. Bright, strong, honorable. I was aware that for my sons, Susan had to take real credit, and I had something to do with it, too. But beyond that, this new generation had been honed by the times.

The times and circumstances of a man's upbringing shape him as much or more than family. The new social theories were right about that. My own family back in Lincoln had been shaped, warped if you will, by the strange, dark stream of a stagnant and dying Puritanism in New England.

These young men in the Northwest, a whole generation of them, had been influenced by the frontier. All across Indiana and Illinois and Ohio and Michigan, too, were a generation of young men coming to maturity who were some of the finest the world had seen. The woods had formed their young childhood and made them tough and hard-working. The simple schools and simple morals of their times had made them gentlemen. And their neighborhoods and mothers and the peaceful times had made them reverent, decent men.

If they were tested—a shadow fell on my heart as I thought it—they would not be found wanting. Tested. I left off thinking of it, just as I had stopped thinking of *The Angel Visitant*.


We sold our hogs at Natchez for nine cents a pound, not a bad price for the times. We walked about in Natchez-Under-The-Hill, watching gamblers and women with baskets of fruit on their heads. We took tea, and the boys talked loudly about all the Negroes we were seeing. Young dandies with ties and stickpins strutted about, taking liqueurs and watching us out of indolent eyes.

We walked about the town, looking at the stately mansions with balconies and small neat slave houses in back. House servants churned butter and darned socks in rocking chairs outside on the porches.

"Listen to this," Tom cried again. He had brought *Uncle Tom's Cabin* with him, and he hung over the fence of one of the mansions, where two slave women were tending a kitchen garden. They were bent over gathering green beans, and they were close enough to us that we could hear them humming in rich, tremulous tones. Tom was not even aware of his surroundings.

"This Prue, this old slave woman, she tells her story. *A man kept me to breed child' en for market and sold 'em as fast as they got big enough; last of all he sold me to a speculator. But I had one child after I come here and I thought then I'd have it to raise.* But she can't because she gets fever and can't nurse it and the mistress won't buy a bit of milk for the poor little thing—it dies and Prue takes to drink and they whip her to death."

He was almost shouting; his face was flushed. "Do you suppose they do all those things to Negroes back in those little cabins there?" The women had finished picking the beans and had set their baskets down to yawn and stretch. They looked at us curiously, and I pulled at Tom's sleeve to take him and the other two down the street.

That night the boys went to Natchez-Under-the-Hill and had a bit too much absinthe. When they came in about midnight, Tom and Will were bleeding. Their eyes were blacked, their clothing torn.

"Some of the local dandies have been following us around. They took our comments along the street today as an insult to Southern honor," Lewis said. He shrugged. His clothing was rumpled and the buttons torn off his shirt.

"Did you—"

"I acquitted myself well, I think."

"I thought you didn't agree with your brother."

"Well, after all, there is such a thing as Northern honor."

Will was splashing cold water on his eye. I shook my head. What would Harriet Houghton think of her baby boy now? And this angel visitant had been in my care? He seemed proud as a peacock of his wounds, won in the field of honest combat.

Well, I would watch them all a bit more closely, as we approached the great city at the mouth of the Mississippi. True, they did need toughening, but after all, New Orleans was not exactly a camp meeting grounds. Not at all.

### The Poore Papers

To: William Houghton, with Thomas Jefferson Brooks, New Orleans P.O.
From: Harriet Poore Houghton, Mt. Pleasant, Indiana

October 15, 1858

Son William:

Your uncle promised he would pick this up at the post office in New Orleans as soon as you arrive. My fond hope is that you are having some enriching experiences, something I have not been able to take advantage of myself.

Son, you know I did not wish you to go; still, once you were gone I felt I had done the right thing, even though I have worried constantly since you left. I think of you being down there in the swamps. I am afraid of the swamps worse than anything. They remind me of Hindostan, and you know how afraid I am of that place, above all others. But Louisiana is bad for swamps, too. They say the river overruns the very streets of New Orleans. Who knows what foul effluvia and infusoria may be lurking in the mud of the streets?

Take soap and water and wash the frame of the bed you sleep in before you settle in. For your stomach take an apple every day. I well recall my mother settling us down every night around the fireplace and solemnly passing round apples to each of my sisters and me and Alvan. We have never had dyspepsia, not a one of us. Neither does your Grandmother Poore, even at her age.

Your little brother Hilary was kicked in the head by the mule as your father was mounting to ride to Houghton mill. Poor little tyke, he was sent flying into the picket fence and could not be revived for almost two hours. Eventually, though, my shouting and pleading seemed to penetrate the fog in his small brain and he awakened.

"Ma, I dreamt so," he said. "My head is shot quite in two."

I am enclosing the copy of *Plutarch's Lives* that you sent for—it came in from Cincinnati. It pains me to think you say that in a couple of years more you may go to Asbury College. What will we do in the house without your footfall on the stair? I do not dare to think—but 1860 is a long way off.

As if it is not enough to have you wishing to leave, Hattie is now talking of going to the woman's academy. Your cousin Susie Brooks is at the root of all this talk. She will be educated, she says, even if it means leaving all those Brookses to board away in Cincinnati. So now Hattie has this odd bee in her bonnet.

The Campbellite Disciples of Christ have been preaching and many flock to hear them. I asked the preacher to come to our house, and he has visited two nights now. How I love this new style of worship, so simple and sincere. It takes you as you are.

John McClure and his friend and cousin Jacob Joe Scott were in town to pay their respects to your Grandmother Poore. They both have reason to do so. Mother was kind to John McClure's father Alfred back in the days when they ran the Underground Railroad station. It is still operating, more so than ever in these frightening times, but not with our kin, thank God.

Jacob Joe and his cousin are going over to Earlham College to take a look at it. Jacob Joe's father, John Robert, wants his son to go to college, but the boy says the extra religious and mental polish his father wants on him will rub him bare. Still, he has promised his father to see what is over there. He has resisted going to this Friends' College so long and refused to go when his brother Zach went a while back. He says he's as good a Friend as any of them at the college, but he is contented with farming. Still, he does concede that adventure awaits outside in the world, so he is willing to go.

John McClure certainly is not going to Earlham. His aunt has drummed any thought of furthering his education or even learning to spell correctly from his mind. He is along for the buggy ride and the adventure, against his aunt's wishes. Jewell Simpson would be happy if John never spoke to one of his McClure kin in his life again, but he is a man now and resists her wishes when he wants to.

So all of you young men must have your adventures while I have all the adventure I need right here at home.

Your loving mother,
Harriet Poore Houghton

# Chapter Twenty-two

## The McClure Papers

To: Mrs. Catherine McClure Hogue, Vincennes, Indiana
From: John Robert Scott, Old Fort Knox, Vincennes, Indiana
October 25, 1858

Dear Cousin:

I had hoped to see you personally before this time, but my wife's health does not allow me to be away from her much. It seems unjust that a debilitating disease such as this should claim one so good at heart. Each year she loses more of her muscular control. Last year she could not walk, this year she finds trouble even in eating. She holds a fork as a two-year-old child does.

I must think that the complete care of my mother Jenny through so many years when Mother did not have her senses must have weakened my dear wife's constitution. I thought that after Mother died, (has it been ten years now?) Mahalia would regain her strength, but the condition has only worsened.

Someday there will be a special seat near the Throne of Grace for her, I am sure of it. Meanwhile, I try not to take visits that will last more than a day. I know when I come to visit you Hogues, you will want me to go up to the old George McClure place and visit your brothers with you and go about to see your sisters Polly and the rest.

And I, of course, could not resist the opportunity to catch up with family. I do try to keep up with Johnny and Elizabeth and the rest of Uncle Will's family who still live around here, but they now have so many children and grandchildren that it fuddles my head to keep them all straight. Archie McClure and his sons and grandsons, of course, are at Duggerville making money returning runaway slaves, and so the least said of them the better.

Mary and Samuel Emison have remained good friends, that is, they were. Samuel, of course, is gone now. It was a pleasure to see the Emisons and McClures so happily joined through so many years, with so many blessings, and may I say riches, coming to both. Even in this generation our children are friends.

You will want news of my own flock. James, of course is well in Kansas, succeeding as an attorney in that fledgling, troubled state. I pray daily for him; there have been outbreaks of shooting and deaths in the border town where he lives. He does not share my Quaker faith, and so does not seem to mind involving himself in active fighting for the freedom of the state. At least he is on the right side of the cause, but the means—

Our Jacob Joe is ever the fair-haired boy. I know you often hear me describe him in this slightly jocular way. I guess it is because to praise this fine young man in the way he deserves makes him sound dull and prudish, which he is not. Jacob Joe is constantly at his sick mother's side, as he was by Mother Jenny's when she was with us. He shows good signs of becoming an excellent farmer, putting his poor old Hoosier dirt-scratching Papa to shame, but I hope he will wish to go to Earlham soon. You know I believe in a year or so of college, at least, for each man in the gentry. I did not have it myself, but I have contributed to Earlham often to support the idea of a liberal Christian education.

Jacob Joe has given me the satisfaction this past month of going up to look at the college with your grandson John, as I suspect you know. He has just returned to say he enjoyed what he saw there, but that he needs to be a good farmer first. Whatever else life does to him, he says, he will always have the land. He is always reading the journals sent out by the land grant colleges around us, and is insisting on the new system of rotation. He has some of our fields fallow, others in clover and he carefully manures and adds lime as if he were conducting a scientific experiment. He has just talked me into a self-raking reaper which is supposed to be the best in the market and does the work of ten men.

His twin brother Zach—well, what shall I say to you dear cousin, who knows me so well? Zach is no longer outwardly into mischief, constantly disrupting the lives of all around as he did when he was little. No, he now has a little refinement. He did, after all, go to Earlham College for a year (I insisted he go when he was eighteen, thinking something there might rub off on him, but instead they asked him to leave after a drunken brawl which involved about a fourth of the young men in the Freshman Class and which was at his instigation).

He smiles and has a courtesy which attracts both men and women (particularly young ones, I ruefully admit). But he is involved in something very distressing to me. I believe he is organizing lodges to support Democratic politics at its most radical level—retention of slavery no matter what.

You have heard the rumors just last summer of the spread into Indiana of that Cincinnati lodge, the Knights of the Golden Circle. I think it has found attraction because so many of us are the children of the South; you know those in our own family are fearfully split about whether there should be slave states or not.

I fear Zach has something to do with the sudden upspringing of the Knights of the Golden Circle among us. Others of the McClure cousins are involved, along with young men all through these southern Indiana and Illinois counties.

Zach rides about all too often at night and stays away, going into Illinois and even Kentucky on clandestine business. "Politics," he calls it and snarls when I ask for more information. I admit, my dear cousin, that he is out of hand. I have been a poor parent, and add that to the list of my sins. Still, I do not think ultimately we can answer for any other person's actions on this earth, even those of our own children, and the sooner we learn that the more peace we have. I do love him, come what may. He is my own child.

How odd it is that I should begin to re-live the sorrowful things that happened to my own mother and father. You know what they are all too well. You grew up with my brother Ish, never spoken of by my family since we had the news of his death and return of his few things from Texas. You knew the awful things he put upon the family—treason, even murder. Pray God this Zach, who was born within a few years of Ish's death and seems so like him, may not cause the pain Ish did to those around him. Some things are hard to explain, are they not, but there is a just God who rules. That I know without a doubt.

My pen pauses in the cataloguing of the affairs of these children—the descendents of that great old matriarch from Ireland, our grandmother, Jane McClure. Sentimental fool that I am these latter days, I give a nod of deference to that great old thief, TIME. I am greatly aware of him lately. He is a thief, eventually stealing all we have. All the aunts and uncles we knew, and most of the cousins are gone. Still, Time, when he passes has left much behind. There are literally hundreds of descendents now from one strong old woman and her husband who was killed in the French and Indian troubles in Pennsylvania.

And since you are so often kind enough to say you are interested in my opinions, I will give you one.

It is well to honor our ancestors in whatever ways we can. It did not seem important to me ten years ago; now it does. I think one must be fifty before the daguerreotype of life comes into focus.

We talk of family trees, and I think it is well we do so. Those who came before us are the roots of the tree of love in our lives. They give nurturing strength to all the branches of the family, which flourish through the ancestors' hardships, sacrifice, and faith, as well as our own efforts in the present day. The ancestors sent their deep roots far into the earth. We do not, perhaps cannot appreciate these roots while we are young. What are the hidden roots, some of them long dead, to the fair, green branches blowing free at the top of the tree? But when time has matured us into fuller older branches, we can sense and know the nurturing roots beneath us. We are closer to the ancestors as we, too, grow old. At least it was so with me.

I like to go to Upper Indiana Cemetery to stand among those quiet daisies and bending grasses, not because I think anyone I love is there. As a Christian I know they live in the world to come. No, I love to be there because I feel at one with a thousand years of sacrifices, sorrows and triumphs, all the way to Ireland, and beyond that to Scotland and the cold plains of Scandinavia.

The lives that cluster there, someway, reach out and touch me and say, "We mourned and laughed and prayed and loved. We endured life and found it finally deep and full of meaning and so, too, child of our future, can you.'' And if I can take a family child by the hand and show him this, so much the better. The clustering lives there may not call to him or her at that time, but perhaps someday that child will remember and come back and feel the pull of the past touching him or her, also.

We cannot visit Grandfather John's grave; Pa said it was unmarked, in Pennsylvania. I had hoped to make a trip with you when I came to Upper Indiana, to that spot under the old elm tree, where Grandmother Jane rests so peacefully with all of her children and many of her grandchildren.

Jack, Jim—over twenty of our fellow grandchildren are gone. We seem to be part of a dwindling group. Let us go visit Upper Indiana together soon, Cousin, you and I. I want to very much.

I pray we might take with us our cousin Jack's grandchildren. Your grandchildren, too. Uncle Dan'l would have wanted it so. I know it yet gives you pain to think of your dear Nancy Jane's death—so much worse since Alfred also died there on that blustery day on the Ohio River. They died doing what they lived for, but that does not bring them back or ease the pain we feel for promising children who died much too young.

Their children, young John, Mary Jane, Anna and Bob do not know their McClure relatives. Jack's wife Lizzie, before she died, and now his daughter Jewell, have made sure of that. I do not need to write these words; we have talked so often of it and in such sorrow.

I have been with the lawyers in Vincennes and your right to visit the children is secure, much as Lizzie tried to take it from you. I know the law fell down when it gave those orphans to their other grandmother Lizzie McClure and then to Jack's married sister, as narrow-minded a woman as her mother. It would have been easier if we had not had a Southern sympathizing judge who thought that Alfred and Nancy Jane must have been crazed to live and die as members of the Underground Railroad, and if you and your husband John Hogue were not anti-slavery yourselves.

I know you and John Hogue were in the right to go to court to get to see them, even though it seemed that awful court struggle was part of what led to your dear John's death. You were their grandparents. You had some rights to know how they are being reared.

They are being brought up ignorantly! I do not even know if those children know how to read. I cannot forgive Jewell for that, recalling what cultured people Jack and Alfred were. But I can tell you that the legal right is yours, Catherine, now, if only for four times a year. And so I urge you to confirm the visit time, a month in advance, as the court says. The last time you waited a week too late, and they used it as a pretext for not letting us see the children. They are spiteful people; with folk like that you must invoke the very letter of the law. I am happy to represent you in this, since you have no husband now that John Hogue is gone.

I had wanted want to go with you when you make your visit, to see that all is done well under the circumstances for those four orphans, but that is impossible with Mahalia's poor health. You know I feel I have much obligation as well as love. "Quakerism" is the terms of reprobation Lizzie and Jewell Simpson kept using at the trial (when they weren't talking about "drunken atheists," "county disgraces," "free thinkers" "abolitionists," and "nigra lovers.") I guess we McClures have to plead guilty to having all of the above things in some branch or another of the family, but then who doesn't? Well, Lizzie is dead and Jewell can steep in her own spite.

I hope for your continued good health, cousin, and that of your children. Please let me know how the visit went.

Your Cousin<br>John Robert Scott

To: John Robert Scott, Old Fort Knox, Vincennes, Indiana
From: Catherine McClure Hogue, Vincennes, Indiana
November 28, 1858

Dear Cousin:

Well, I have been to beard the lion, as Pa would have said.

Lioness, that is. I have gone to see my grandchildren. I had brother Rob harness the old wagon and drove myself out. They didn't invite me to partake of Sunday dinner, needless to relate, but they did give the poor old lady a glass of lemonade.

'Twas a stuffy day for November, I tell you, late Indian summer and warm. Reminded me of Caintuck at the time of the revival in Ought One. That day the preacher sweated till his fancy shirt stuck to his chest. You weren't born yet but were there in the nest, but it was the revival Pa always used to talk about, up at Cane Ridge. I sang about Jesus and danced in the aisle with Cousins Elizabeth and Mary, being "In the Spirit" as they say. Still am, I guess, although my style is different from the normal. Upper Indiana Church board has had me up more'n once for saying us Presbyterians ought to just admit that everyone can be saved. Stop lettin the Methodists steal our thunder. I said it, and still say it loud and clear.

They had asked that we come at three to the farm to see the children. You know 'tis next to Uncle Dan'l and Jack's back farm. That way makes it easy for Uncle Archibald Simpson, Jewell's husband, to see to the other farm until the children are big enough to take it over. Anyways, we went in and sat on the setee. Horsehair it is, latest New York style, stiff as a stone and slick as ice.

I didn't want to start up all the whole hoo-ha, but I had to know. "Are they—are all of them doing well in school?"

Jewell let out a long sigh, as if I'd asked the wrong question. "They have been going up the road apiece to the old school at the bend of the road, when Archie can spare 'em from the fields and I can spare the girls from the housework. Well, Mary Jane's too old, anyway, to go this year."

Mary Jane is nineteen now, you may recall. Stayed in school a couple of years longer than usual 'cause she had missed so much.

"Is John back in school?" I asked. I knew he had been expelled right after they came to live here for setting a hog loose to tromple up the loft in the school house. I didn't mean to smile when I asked about him, John Robert, honest I didn't.

"No, never has been back. Didn't seem necessary to me," Jewell said high and mighty as Queen Victoria. Jewell was picking at the starch on her dress with her fingernail. Her hair was pulled back tight in a bun. Things were kept spit and polish in that parlor, I tell you.

"I hope you will let Bob and Anna, at least, go eight years and get some learning."

Her mouth was as puckery and tight as a miser's purse. "You McClures always trot out eddication, don't you? I knew your Pa, George, when I was a chile, and he was about as eddicated as they come, talkin' 'bout Cizzero and all them. Didn't do him a plug nickel's worth o' good. His farm never did produce much. Ma always allowed he was all the time in town writin' somethin' for the paper whilst the wheat got moldy. Keep your farm and your farm'll keep you, Ma always said."

"I suppose she did," I said, my temper smoldering like a grass fire.

"Most of the McClures who weren't drunks were snooty. That's what it seemed to me, anyways."

"So you've said." It was, I thought, her mother Lizzie who had testified in court that she didn't intend to have the children brought up to free-thinkin' ways. Said their pa Alfred always was talkin' high falootin' nonsense about "victims of society's ills" when he meant shiftless poor folks, and spoke of "peaceful persuasion" instead of war.

That was what caused all the troubles, Lizzie told the court. Alfred and Nancy Jane wouldn't have died if they'd been back in Knox County taking care of their business instead of cheating other people out of their own property, their legally owned slaves. That's what Lizzie McClure had said. Now Jewell's whiny voice interrupted my woolgathering.

"Your pa was an abolitionist before the word was even invented. I heard he voted to have his own brother called before the elders at Upper Indiana for slavery."

"You disremember, Jewell," I said a little smugly. "It was both of his brothers, Will and John, Pa called out. Not that it made any difference. They went right on holding people in perpetual articles of indenture." I changed the subject. "I've become anti-slavery too. I bet you didn't know I take the Massachusetts' society's paper, did you? But let's not quarrel. Can the children come in?"

And they did, John Robert, and it was a sight to gladden these old eyes. First Mary Jane, homely, round and buck-toothed at nineteen, but as good as gold to me. She came over and kissed me and put a little package in my hand. "I missed your birthday last month, Grandma," she whispered. It was a little pincushion shaped like a heart. She had made it herself.

Anna is still a little girl of twelve with ringlet curls and a distant, distracted manner. Her parents' early death has hurt her and she is cold inside. Her brother Bob is big for his age at thirteen and hearty. He sketches and draws well, they say. It was John that struck me the most after all these months of not seeing him. He has grown into a man now at sixteen. John Robert, he is so like Uncle Dan'l. 'Tis strikin, even eerie. The same slight physique, the same round, handsome-looking face with sharp, squirrel eyes, the same hank of almost black straight hair.

He, of all of them seems the most McClure, the most untouched by the attempt of that finicky, pug-faced woman to turn him into a prig. "Tut, tut Aunt J.," he laughed as his aunt tried to straighten the collar he had put on for the occasion. "You're a-gonna turn me into a giraffe the way you're stretchin' my neck." To his credit, I think he even loves her. But he stays his own man, good-humored, joking, sympathizin and down to earth.

'Tis a Southern-sympathizin household, through and through. "Fine state of affairs we'll all have," Jewell sniffed, "if we get all the niggers on equality with us like Alfred and Nancy Jane wanted."

John laughed and yet he is loyal, patriotic. "The Constitution over all, Grandma, must defend that, hey?" he said and winked at me when his aunt was tirading about "states rights." Sensible, that's what he is, like his mother, my dear Nancy Jane, but without the "book larnin'" she had.

Certainly, though, I sighed to see no trace of the elegant manners, the airy schemes and wispy, wonderful dreams of Jack and Alfred McClure. So Jewell has done her job there.

Jewell and Archibald's son Henderson came in then. He stretched his long legs in front of the horsehair sofa and popped his knuckles as he sat listening to us talk. Henderson Simpson is just John's age and they are as alike as two nuts on a pecan tree. But to me Henderson often seems a bit freer with the young maids at church socials than he should be.

John said he would come to stay with me a bit this summer, said it in spite of his aunt's warnin eye, fixed like an eagle on his. I spect he will.

I hope this letter finds Mahalia in better health and that you will come to see me soon. As for what you said about going to Upper Indiana churchyard, about the ones gone before, I share your idea. I often think, if only I could have Pa here for one hour, to ask him questions, to tell him things I never could say, or even thought of when he was here. But it is not to be.

Your loving cousin,
Catherine Hogue

### The Account of Thomas Jefferson Brooks
### (Continued)

Our flatboat show (and I call it that, because really it was that, a portrayal of a real keelboat trip of forty years before, complete with polemen singing) went into its final stage, or should I say float. We came into the wide Mississippi delta and New Orleans.

And I did feel the years fly away and saw myself that first trip with Drake, sleeping by the market in the open, cooking crabs in a communal pot, watching the floating bordellos of 1818, anchored at the waterfront. There were none of these today, although the city was notorious for hundreds of brothels. As we tied up, boatmen told us stories of places called Lily of the Bayou's, Little Fontainebleu's, and the Black Tulip.

I pretended not to hear Will Houghton ask, in hushed tones, if the Black Tulip was run by a colored woman. "Oh, son, it might be; there ere enough o' them running establishments, but this un' is a dark-browed white lady. But there are also Chinee, Hungarians, and the Queen of Araby." He laughed uproariously.

By evening the boys had walked by the gambling parlors, the drinking dens, the apartments of kept octoroon women in the French Quarter. The Quarter was not just the scene of lurid pleasures, though. It had elegant new apartments and gardens.

Ah, but that had changed since my trips ten years ago. Then, the French Quarter was seedy, overgrown—folk had moved into the new American section and the uptown Garden District.

Now, though, the old district was restored. A Creole woman had come back from living in France and built blockfronts, handsome living quarters of red brick around the central Place d'Armes. She had the square cleaned up and ordered a handsome statue of Andrew Jackson, the savior of New Orleans, to be put up in the square, across from the St. Louis Cathedral. Fashionable folk had returned to live there, and it was a pleasure to stroll in it again.

The city, though, sprawled far beyond what I could imagine even forty years ago. We toured the new district in Lafayette, where wealthy planters of mixed heritage and Americans were building homes.

"They seem like little Greek temples," Will Houghton murmured, staring at the two story mansions, with curl-top pillars and wrought iron balcony railings.

"Somewhere on the edge of this beautiful garden area are the Lily of the Bayou and the Black Tulip," Tom whispered to him. I heard it and it made me anxious. I had wanted to toughen these boys, but how far did we need to go in the name of toughening? In my day it might have been natural—well, that was another thing. These were my own boys!

The boys split up the flatboats for lumber and managed to dispose of the wood for quite a decent price. Meanwhile we had sold the rest of the cargo and sent the crew home with banknotes in their pockets. Now we were on our own for a few days, until it was time for the steamboat to take us up the river.

Something I have to admit is this. We did not sleep in the open and eat from the communal cooking pot. No, although I did whip up my famous chicken ragout in the galley for the boys. These bones, at least needed a soft mattress and hot water. We stayed at the expensive St. Louis Hotel. It had a Papist dome, a grand spiral staircase my young men went up and down as quickly as good taste allowed. We sauntered about the cotton and sugar exchange in the rotunda and listened to finely-dressed men making sales.

Everywhere were slaves, carrying loaded trays on their heads, serving as footmen on carriages, holding up the billowing skirts of young ladies so they would not be soiled by the mud and filth of the wet streets. Tom kept nodding his head and quoting from *Uncle Tom's Cabin*.

On the fourth night at the hotel St. Louis we decided to avoid the ornate dining room and chose to eat at Antoine's. Tom and Will were drinking wine and telling stories from their day seeing the sights.

Will Houghton's fair complexion was heated with wine and the stuffiness of the room. A waiter served potatoes in little bags and fish broiled in butter with almonds. Delicious. I had never had anything like it, before or since. "We went to the oven tombs," Will said.

"Oven tombs?" I asked. I knew what they were very well, but I wanted him to tell me.

"In Louisiana they bury above ground. The coffins would float if you buried them as we do. So they are in houses. There are some down there that have voodoo signs on them."

"Voodoo?" I asked, rhetorically.

"The black arts, Pa," Tom said. "There are red x's for luck on the tombs. Whenever they are wiped off, they reappear, mysteriously."

"That's what Marigny told us."

"Who's that?" I wondered aloud.

"A young gentleman who walks around with fancy trousers and a sword on in broad daylight," Lewis said, slightly amused. "A beaux. We met him when we had coffee in the marketplace and he took us around to tour the spots of interest." Lewis had tagged along with the boys for want of something better to do. I was aware he had been ready to go back to Amanda for three days now. Well, we would soon do it. I had booked passage on the steamboat *Westphalia* tomorrow.

"He took us to a place that chilled my blood," said Tom.

Will nodded gravely and went on. "There is a house, haunted they say. A Madame Lalaurie lived there, a beauty who even entertained Lafayette. But one night at one of her huge suppers, the house caught on fire. The guests, trying to save the servants found a torture chamber upstairs, where helpless slaves were chained and put to the lash and shameful personal things were done to them—"

"Really, Will," I said, looking at the flaming cherries in a chafing dish before us. Somehow I was losing taste for the meal. I was thinking, a little nervously of Harriet Houghton. Her daughters thought babies came out of doctors' satchels. Will himself had turned his head in embarrassment on the trail to Alton when we passed two horses copulating. Harriet had entrusted her baby boy to me for an educational experience. Well, his education was proceeding apace.

"Marigny is taking us to the opera tonight," Tom said. I noted he did not say, "asked if we could go," or "if it suits your plans." Toughening was occurring.

After much discussion Lewis, who was bored with my company by now, decided to accompany his brother and cousin.

Well, the opera would be something for them to see. The last time I was here, it was becoming all the rage and it seemed folks were still flocking to hear effeminate-looking men and masculine-looking women screech and yelp in French or Italian.

All the best society came; marriages were arranged in the boxes at intermission; clever insults were exchanged by the young men. After the last act, there were duels on the outskirts of town, with "matters of honor" being constantly settled. The loser was taken, with his honor, to the oven tombs at one of the cemeteries. So people told me.

I walked back to the St. Louis Hotel. In my room I saw the huge, canopied bed; it looked inviting. My stomach was growling from the oysters, trout and cherries. I lifted the corner of the mosquito netting and climbed up. I would just lie here for a moment and then get up, perhaps take a hand of cards below at the tables.

"Pa—wake up. It's Tom and Will. I don't know what to do." Lewis's voice was urgent. How long had I slept? A grandmother clock in the corner said it was one o'clock in the morning. My God!

I sat up and swung my feet over the bed. "Where are they?"

"Down in the American section. I think Marigny has taken

them to Lily of the Bayou's—or one of those places. I tried to talk them out of it. They had been drinking brandy all night.''

"You stay here, Lewis. Nothing you can do.'' I bolted out into the night.

I flagged a hansom cab. "Lafayette District,'' I said, and then "Lily of the Bayou's.'' If Susan or Harriet knew—

The driver deposited me by a brightly-lit, three-story mansion on the edge of the district. I went to the door and knocked at the huge dog-mouth knocker. A colored man in red livery let me in and a huge-bosomed woman welcomed me. She had ostrich plumes pinned in her hair.

"Skip the polite drivel,'' I commanded. "I am looking for two young men from the country, wearing dark travelling suits. One has almost white hair, the other looks a bit like me and has dark hair.''

Ostrich Plumes looked indifferent, even faintly hostile. She probably did not like people dragging country boys out of her best girls' beds. I reached in my pocket and took out a fifty dollar bill.

She put out her hand, smiling, and I gave it to her.

"Nobody here like that tonight. I would have seen. I am the hostess of the day.''

I came up to her and stood near. Her breath smelled like onions, strong ones. "Be very sure. I will have you beaten if what you say is not true.'' It was an idle threat, but it worked.

"Sir, I swear to God that no one like that is here. Try the Black Tulip. It is, I admit, the premier house in town.''

She told me where it was, three streets down, two across. I thought my heart would burst as I strode, then galloped along the now-deserted streets.

The house was like a plantation house, built eight feet up from the ground, with winding staircases leading up; I took them one at a time. I was exhausted with all this running around. God damn young snorts. Wait until I got my hands on them. I wondered what I would do once I found out they were inside. The door opened. This time an old colored man, with white gloves on, directed me into the parlor.

I explained my mission to him. "I will tell the missus,'' he said.

Cigar smoke wafted around the chandeliers; the sound of a

tinkling piano drifted out from a back room. Couples strolled up the huge winding staircase to the floors above.

In a moment someone appeared in the doorway to the back. It was a handsome, still slender woman who could have been in her late fifties, I thought. She wore a sweeping dress of black velvet and real pearls at her throat. The Black Tulip—

"Your young men are in the back playing the piano. No loss of western virtue has occurred here tonight, at least for them." The voice was pleasant, resonant. She came within ten feet of me. She gasped; she stopped. "Hello, Thomas Jefferson," she said.

It was Emily.


Of course it was. After I recovered from my pained shock, I told myself I should have known. Same large, saucer eyes, same sensitive mouth, same red cheeks (now aided by the cosmetician's art).

After a long moment of looking, she said, "Well, let us go to my private suite and talk. Or don't you want to?"

Of course I did. I walked as if in one of the voodoo trances the boys had been talking about, under the glittering chandelier of the grand salon to a small suite of rooms next to the piano and billiards parlor.

Emily ordered cakes and applejack, and I ate and drank. She did the talking, looking right at me with a frankness and honesty I did not expect.

"I couldn't get in touch with you, although I knew you were looking for me. Then I knew you would think I was dead. It was best that way." I looked at her with exasperated pain in my eyes.

She sighed and went on. "I fled what was death to me in Lincoln. I felt that if I was confined one more day in that house in those gloomy hills and tarns I would poison myself, or waste away on purpose. I know I hurt the children—and you. But that is past. I came down the river on the boats, serving food, and I came at last to New Orleans at the end of the year."

At the end of the year! Then she had been here when I first came on the keelboat! And I did not even know the end of my quest was right here in New Orleans.

"I liked New Orleans, felt as if it were the home for me," she went on. "The heat, the swamps, the strange creatures, the odd smells and foods, were as exotic as I seemed to myself then. I came under the protection of an older man. He set up a house for me and then he died and left me the house."

"And so you fell into this life because you were destitute, an unprotected woman in a bitter world."

She laughed, her laugh ringing through the room, startling and hurting me. "I did something I could make money with and which suited my temperament. Some preachers' children have ardent natures." Her smile faded a bit.

With sincerity and even humor she told me about her business and then, responding to her candor, I told her of my life, of our brothers and sisters: of Rebecca, leader of the literary club of Lincoln, and "Little Lucy," who now had nine grandchildren, and Lewis, a taciturn but successful farmer in Mt. Pleasant.

And of Dan'l, our Brookie, who, using Cleveland as a head-quarters, had taken his giraffe around to modest fame and fortune in five states, and then returned with his young wife and three children and a few of the menagerie animals. He had settled into retirement near us for a few years until apoplexy took him. He was buried in the Brooks cemetery, and the giraffe was lying not far from him, just outside the wrought iron gate. Emily laughed a little and shook her head from time to time as I spoke, leaning a slender arm on the table and looking at me with eyes that still seemed young.

And then there was a time when we stopped talking. The French clock on her mantel said four o'clock in the morning. I put down the glass of applejack I had refilled several times from the decanter and looked at the oriental carpet.

Something impelled me to ask, "How could you do it? How could you bring yourself to leave all we learned behind and do this?" My voice reflected the pain I still felt, in spite of the comfortable conversation we had just shared.

A long sigh escaped her lips. The kerosene lamp was flickering. "It was, is easy. I don't believe in God," she said. "No, I don't believe in God or immortality. And when those go, there is no pain in anything you choose to do. If there is no God, everything is legal, *n'est pas?*"

"I suppose you might look at it that way." I had never heard of such a thing. In all the denying I had done, I had always thought men should do good, and live morally because it made them happier and helped others. But Emily was saying—I didn't want to think about what she was really saying. I took her hand.

"Come away with me, with us, Emily. Come north. You'd like Mount Pleasant, where Lewis has his home." I thought of those quiet streets, the Methodist church. "Well, maybe not Mt. Pleasant, but Loogootee."

"Don't be ridiculous, Tom Jefferson. Can't you see me in the hardware store, or at the ladies' jelly-making bee?" Again, that resonant laugh.

She squeezed my hand. "Thomas, I am content here. If not happy, then content. I shall soon retire and take a place on St. Charles street, and have a garden. There is money enough for the rest of my life."

"If you will not come—" All at once I felt exceedingly sad. Perhaps it was the abundance of applejack.

"It is best if we do not see each other again. Lead your life, let me lead mine. If you think of me, do it with love and as much understanding as you can muster."

I stood and kissed her on the cheek. Through the open door I could see the chandelier; its lights cast hues of the rainbow about the room.

"I can still hear your boys and their French friend. I will give them coffee and see they get home in a cab. They will think all New Orleans madames are as motherly as aunts." She smiled, a little ruefully, I thought.

I nodded and staggered out into the hall, reeling a bit myself. I do not recall how I got back to the hotel, but I did. Somebody must have called a cab for me.

On the steamboat going home, Tom was reading a book he had picked up in a Vieux Carre bookstall. *Philosophies of These Times* it was called. Well, at least that would be better than *Uncle Tom's Cabin*, I thought, nursing my aching head.

"Listen to this book," he said, leaning back on a chair in the grand salon. The Mississippi raced by outside the window, and he cleared his throat and read: *"It is patently obvious, say certain*

*European new-thinkers, that one has but to deny the existence of God for complete freedom of action. If there is no God, and no immortality with its threat of punishment for misdeeds, a man has complete license to do as he wishes. Not even the impact on others need be considered.''* He put the volume into his lap. ''I have not heard of that school of thought. Have you, Father?''

I nodded my aching head. ''I—have heard of it.'' I felt particularly cussed at the moment, and said, ''I do not know if I believe in God, and yet I do not feel I have license to do anything I wish.''

Will and Tom did not look surprised. They knew I did not often favor the Loogootee Methodist Church with my presence. They had observed my custom of reading the *Cincinnati Enquirer* in the kitchen when scriptures were being pondered in the parlor.

Lewis looked at me. There was a sort of simple, direct light in his eye, and I recognized it from seeing it in his mother's eye before. It was the light of conviction. ''It seems to me that knowing one perfectly good man should convince us of the existence of God.''

I looked at these young men, who had broken the flatboats up themselves, who had thought the St. Louis hotel too expensive, who had gone to the whorehouse and played the piano only. And I looked at Lewis, whom I could not understand but could deeply admire. ''Yes, Lewis,'' I said, ''you could be right. Indeed, I believe you must be right.''

Cussedness immediately re-asserted itself, though. ''But immortality, that's a different issue.'' I told them of their ancestor in Massachusetts, the one who preached to the Indians and my own questions at the graves of the Pilgrim Brookses.

''Father, it was not really very reverent of you to shout at peoples' graves,'' Tom said coolley.

''By the way,'' I said, insulted by the condescension in his voice. ''Where were you boys last night till 4 a.m.?''

''Father, I do not wish to be disrespectful, but you also were away from the hotel. Gentlemen do not ask each other questions that will cause discomfort. You can be assured that our actions were above reproach.'' Loftily he returned to his book. Will Houghton stalked away in the other direction.

Cussedness. They had gone beyond toughness into cussedness. When all the sales were touted up and expenses weighed, this trip had cost me $200, but if it bought some cussedness for these perfect young gentlemen, I suppose it was worth it.

Well, to sum up: Lewis returned to his Hindostan-Loogootee log cabin and supervised both the store and his growing family. I made him manager of my mercantile. Thomas found a fine young girl and even though both he and she were young, married her, and within a year presented us with a grandchild, Lewie. Our daughter Emily married Dr. Thomas Campbell. Our other, younger children grew. I looked forward to a rich, rewarding old age among those I loved, living in plenty and peace.

Plenty we had, peace, we could not have. In 1860 the man I had seen in Alton, the tall drink of water from Illinois, Lincoln, won the election for Presidency of the United States. The Southern States, already unsettled over Kansas and the threats of the North, announced that living in the United States with Lincoln as President would be intolerable and that they wished to form their own nation. We waited in Southern Indiana, a-tremble for our sons and our nation, as our President took office and a new, dangerous era to begin.

# Chapter Twenty-three

# The Deposition of Kezegat Dauja, of the Potawatomi
### (Continued)

When I took my son Little White Deer to be raised among the kinsmen of the Miamis in 1839, I remember one thing my own mother, Swiftly Running Feet had told to me. "All of earth's people are on a journey to the stars. Let your child take his own path there. Do not try to force your ways upon him or to make him like yourself. Let him find his own way."

I recall looking at her and saying, "That seems to me wisdom. You have always been so wise, Mother. Why so?"

"The Manittos give wisdom to those who become mothers late in life. It is a compensation for all the years without small ones in the lodge."

But I did not always find I had wisdom, even though I had waited years to be a mother and was determined not to force my way on Little White Deer. True, there are certain things he must learn: the difference between right and wrong, the Catholic way I now loved, the Indian tradition, as his father would have desired.

But what was the Indian way in that day, in 1839? It could not be Potawatomi. I had promised that we would never really leave these northern woodlands in Indiana, and that promise still rang in my heart. But today there were only a handful of us Potawatomi, driftwood on the rivershore, after the flood has left. There was Pokagon, northwest of us, and a few others. How could I teach my son what being a Potawatomi would be like when there weren't any Potawatomi, at least around here?

There were Miami, and they were our kinsmen. I was staying with The Catfish and his family. I learned their language, which was really very much like Potawatomi, over a year's time and it became the language I used to speak to Little White Deer, because it was the language of the lodge.

Cabin, I should say. We lived with Catfish's family in a sturdy cabin by the Mississinewa—Catfish, his son and daughter-in-law, two little ones and White Deer and I. I can see us in there the first winter, before the fireplace, cooking fowl, turning it slowly, laughing, and I can still feel the healing that was going on in my heart among these good people.

And I can see us in summer or two that followed, as I settled like a happy dog into the easy life there, farming with squash and pumpkins and corn and beans the rich bottomlands of the Mississinewa. The Catfish, Mialanaqua, had joined himself to his son's wife's people, the band of Metocina. They were peaceful people. As a point of fact, they were related to me, too, although distantly. The grandfather of Asondaki Alamelonda, my father, was of the Ohio bands and so were these Miami. The bloodlines crossed each other often in me and the child.

While Mialanaqua was there, he taught Little White Deer of ancient ways. He spoke to him of the Miami Old Ones who learned to grow the precious white corn the Miamis were so fond of, of Fire Tiger, who lived in Mississinewa rapids, of rifle-shooting and game-playing.

As moons turned into years, and Catfish found that Little White Deer listened to him, as the boy grew to be a four-and-five-year-old fascinated with woodland ways and the attention of the old man, Mialanaqua began to spend hours of every day with his young relative. He taught him Miami lore in a way the boy could understand. It seemed to be important to this old band chief. On and on it went, stories of Nanabush, tales of why the roses have thorns, names of blacksnake and garter snake and how to make a fire—it was as if the lore of a hundred years or more, going back to the grandfather Rising Star, were being unwound like the cocoon of a butterfly for my son.

But Mialanaqua, The Catfish, died when White Deer was five. The old man, bowed by the troubles of the Miami, took cholera in the epidemic of '43 and '44 and along with his son, died before the white doctor could get to him. The white doctor was busy with his patients in Miamisport. He only saw Indians when he was finished with the innkeepers, farmers, and housewives with hysteria. And he was never done with them, it seemed.

But I tell you, healer that I am, I could not help the Miamis during this time either. This old man and his son were killed not by the cholera, but by the Miami treaty proceedings that were then going on.

Once the Potawatomi had been forced from the lands of the rivers, it was only a matter of time till the brave and kingly Miami should also go. These Miami, who had led the several nations in triumph in the time of George Washington, vanquishers of the proud St. Clair, were now being forced beneath the yoke of the white man. Never has a tribe before or since so destroyed an American army as the Miami did with St. Clair's green troops. Six hundred of the Americans lay dead when the Miami led the united tribal troops. Brown Squirrel my grandfather was there and the shaman, too. Blighted and evil though that Kasgo the shaman was, he was a fine warrior in his youth, so it had been said.

None of that mattered now, however. These proud Miami must bend to the white man's land-lust and the changing times. During this time the Miami promised to send representatives to look at the lands of the West, where the other Indians had gone, so that they could get ready to go too. "Look carefully," I all but screamed when I heard this. "We Potawatomi did the same, and when we got to the good lands to settle, we could stay only a while, because the whites wished us to leave and go elsewhere. The pushing out never seems to end."

When The Catfish returned from small councils and large treaty proceedings, he sat by the fire and did not speak. It was the Black Mood. I above all others should know what that looked like. He broke it in the next few years only to talk to Little White Deer about Miami ways. The rest of the time he sat around, silent.

For many of the Miami it was not thus. Their chief, Little Turtle, had told them long ago that the Bird of Thunder commanded the people to stand bravely, to fight gloriously and after that, if they lost, to seek a good peace. That is what the chiefs Richardville and Godfroy of the Miamis were doing. They were seeking the best "deal" to go West, at least I saw it that way, and I did not disapprove. After all, what had the brave defiance of Menominee and even Paukooshuck wrought? Imperishable glory in song and story of some future Potawatomi, that is all. They were both gone from Indiana with no recompense.

Mialanaqua, The Catfish, was one of the last of the Old Ones of the Miami. His pride was as big as the sun: he had been one of the few of the band to stand with the brothers at Tippecanoe. He had known Tecumseh. Sometimes he broke out of his gloom to talk about the Great One, and when he did, Little White Deer listened.

"Tecumseh's cause was just. That was why some of us defied Little Turtle to go to the Prophet's camp. To stand together, even if we died, to keep some part of our lands—it was a right thing. So I said to Asondaki Alamelonda on the night before the battle''— here he looked at me—"and he put on the paint of war and came with us." I smiled a little in appreciation.

"Fighting in a just cause is the law of the Bird of Thunder from oldest times. My grandfather Rising Star went to the Ohio camps in the first place because he could not stand with the Miami who joined themselves to the British in the Revolution. This was not a just cause. No, those British people across the sea greedily wanted to own these lands. And Rising Star died when he forgot the Bird of Thunder, when he joined a stupid cause and went with the English to kill Kentucky people. We must be ready to fight for a just cause, and for that reason I do not regret that I, all of us, fought at Tippecanoe."

But new times were calling for new voices around the council fire. Francis Godfroy and Richardville were the new leaders. They were "white sharp," their own blood as polluted as my own with white mixture. This gave them a shrewdness that made it possible to get things out of the whites. They went to the treaty talks knowing the Miami would have to leave soon and they acted difficult, holding back, like a bride who will not be wedded.

"We want to cooperate, brothers," these two negotiators said, "but not all of our tribesmen want to go. Not at all. What are your arrangements? Are you going to drag us disgracefully across the country like the Potawatomi? How much will we be getting? What are the payments for going? Possibly some, like us, can stay as a reward for helping you. It will be possible to expedite this matter if we know the answers to these questions."

There were things to settle, many things. Would the land they owned be settled for? At three dollars an acre or less? Would debts the tribe owed be settled by the government? The traders wanted to know that, too, of course.

The white men seemed more eager to settle this time, more nervous. Many people had not liked the way we Potawatomi had been treated and the government had given instructions to be firm but fair. There was going to be a just settlement financially, so they said.

Richardville and Godfroy said it a different way. "The white men have treasure pots as big as fat men's stomachs. Bottomless, in fact. At each annuity, they pay more. We will get the last drop of blood before we go. We look out for our people." They looked out for themselves, too. Take my word for that.

It was the dickering that made The Catfish go into Black Mood. "All our troubles began when we started bargaining with them over double crosses and furs. Now we go out bargaining for blood money. Guilt payment they will make. How many dollars? Which people to stay here and get a few acres. This from the people of Little Turtle."

Finally, in 1840, it was settled. The Miami would go west in five years; the government would pay $500,000 in twenty annuity payments. Some favored people, like the families of Godfroy and Richardville, would not have to go and would receive fine lands.

Cholera, they say and I believe it, is hastened by the Black Mood. There was a piece in the *Miami County Sentinel*, which I had begun reading now, which told of a man in Indianapolis, who died of cholera in less than twenty-four hours. He had been discouraged, the article said. Of course he was outside and exposed. McClure he was by name, perhaps that relative of mine who helped at the disgraceful treaty proceedings of 1826. Be that as it may, it is true that cholera takes those who are low mentally, who have yielded to fear or discouragement. They open their minds and bodies. So it was with my kinsman Mialanaqua, The Catfish, cousin of my father.

And yet I think that what Godfroy and Richardville did to get the best settlement for the Miamis, holding off their time of departure until the whites grew frantic, threatening troops and the cutting off of payments, was good for the tribe. True, like fat robins, these two French-Miami men both lined their own nests with satin ribbons and got permission for their families to stay in Indiana, exempt from migration. Godfroy (his heirs, that is; by this time the old man was dead) received thousands of acres of land for his own in fee simple. As for Richardville, it is said that for a few years he was the richest man in Indiana and the richest Indian in America.

But it was also true that when the Indians went west in 1847, finally, they left with debts paid and went by steamboat instead of with guns at their backs over roads baking in the sun.

Here is how they went. They assembled, 323 of them who were on the lists to go. They got onto the canal boat and went by Wabash and Erie Canal to Ft. Wayne and then south on the Ohio canal to the Ohio River. Here they boarded steamers to go to St. Louis and from there to the Missouri to Kansas, to good, fair lands near rivers.

Little White Deer stood with me as we said goodbye to relations and friends when these voyaging Miamis left. There was sadness and dignity in their faces, resolution and willingness to accept the fate that had been given them, unlike my people, who raised their fists and shook them at the bad magic that had come their way.

Then my son and I returned to the camp of Meshingomesia, who had been allowed to stay. We, too, had been exempted. Because of my help in translating and my father's white connection, which had been documented by the priest in Vincennes, we were given the name McClure and allowed to stay. I did not take it. Too much water had gone over the rapids for me to call myself by a Scotch-Irish name.

Because I had promised to follow the Old Ones' injuction to allow a child to find his own path, I asked Little White Deer what name he wanted. He was an unusally old man for a small boy, and I knew he would understand the choice. He thought a long while. I knew what was going through his mind. He knew the name was white; he often saw white children in town. No gentlemen or ladies they, with their bare feet and gray, worn calico and dark sunbonnets.

Still, they lorded it over the Indian children. ''Wah, wah, Tecumseh,'' they would shout down the streets when we went to buy supplies. They waited on us last at the store and whispered things you couldn't quite hear behind their hands. Mostly, though, they practiced a bad form of race hatred, ignoring us. They just looked through us as if we were panes of glass.

Yet in spite of that, my son said, "I shall be McClure, I think. And I do not want to live on Meshingomesia reservation, Mother. I wish to live in town."

"Why, my son?" I asked, startled. I had been practising my healing out there on the reservation. People paid me and along with the interest from my father's money, which I had put with a decent Christian banker in town, there was enough to live on.

"It is not fun on the reservation. You have taught me to read, and I want to go to school in town."

My mind was numb. School? Into my mind flashed a picture of a young girl scrubbing floors, making buttonholes and practising round, fat, D's until her fingers cramped. Was it something to be desired? A good in life? It did not strike me so.

Could I do my healing in a white man's town? I did not know. Pathway to the stars—it seemed his was a different one from mine. Thus was it ever so, I suppose. We prepared to move into Peru.

What could I do if I did not heal, I asked myself as we put our things into a tiny cabin on the edge of town. Place a notice in the *Miami County Sentinel* saying, "Well-bred *Manitto Wabo* needs suitable employment. Good at boneset. Can furnish madstone." Somehow my talents did not seem very well suited to Peru, Indiana.

Here fate, or was it God, intervened. I spoke to Mr. Gabriel Godfroy, one of the leaders of the Miami who stayed in Indiana, and soon the trustees of the county asked me to open a small school in my home. More than 300 Indians had been left behind in Indiana, and some were in the town. They wished me to teach the Indian children of Godfroy and his relations. Some of these were related to the famous Francis Slocum, the white girl who had grown up among Indians and came to prefer them. These Slocum relatives had also been given land and allowed to stay in Indiana.

The state was planning instruction for the adult Indians in the county as well. Outside in the fields they were trying to teach the Miami to farm. Godfroy himself wished them to learn, and he let tenants come onto the land the government let him have. He wanted these farmers to teach the Indians to guide a plow, use a harrow, make hay that did not mold, ditch the fields.

The Indian children I began to teach told me what their fathers said of this. "Go into the fields each day? Do the women's work? Why my own women will laugh at me. Harness my best pony, the one I traded from Chief Lafontaine himself, to a *plow*? No, I cannot today. I have traps to set, fish to catch with my cousin. Some other time."

So they said, and white men listened to it and thought the Indians lazy. When the tenant farmers Godfroy let onto the land left, they said "These Miami will never learn. Too stupid and too lazy." But I will tell you why the Miami would never learn to farm, if you really want to know. It was because farming was the occupation of the white man and thus a thing of loathing. For years the Indian had hated the plow and the scythe as instruments of destruction that cut into the edge of the very campground itself, and they could not in ten years learn to love the plow. It was a symbol of their degradation.

Still, the county and the government and Godfroy himself tried to teach these Miami Indians to be white. In town I tried to teach their children to be white also. This was not hard. The younger generation needed no instructing, thank you. Look at the things the white man had! Brass buttons and pianos and *Harper's Magazines* with pictures of zebras and buggies and cookstoves and cans to keep blackberries sweet and juicy even in the deep of winter and velvet settees and crazy quilts and chairs of the hair of horses. And ice cream and chocolate candy, especially chocolate candy.

I was to teach "The American Way." I did my best. But, because I was paid to do it and I guess a little bit proud that I, who had hated school, was now a teacher, I threw myself into the American Way and the *McGuffey Reader* they gave me.

I taught about the boy with his hand in the dike, Napoleon, Horatius at the bridge and the Ninety-first psalm. I read to them Portia's speech on mercy in Shakespeare. Meanwhile, out on the reservation a Quaker named Josiah White founded a technical institute to teach manual labor to the Miami, brick-laying and fence making and all the rest. We would teach them to be good citizens in this land where many groups now lived!

We all did our work well. Too well. Little White Deer came to me when he was sixteen and said, "I wish to go to the Sisters of Providence School. I am Catholic; I can now do figures and read the classics in translation. I wish more of an education."

More! I was shocked. "Those Indian institutes teach you to become all white and to ignore your Indian past."

"Well," my son said, "and what is it you have been doing here in Peru?"

And so he went to South Bend to the school and I was sad and happy about it. I continued in my teaching, being paid by the county. I studied the rudiments of geometry and even taught a little of that. But one night, as I was sitting on the bed, I read Chief Logan's farewell, when he chided the whites so eloquently for killing his innocent family.

I said aloud to myself, "Why, this is what we should be studying here at my school. I am not teaching the right things. These children are learning to be white fast enough. What I need to teach them is how to remember they are tribal people.

"Did I not stand at the grave of my husband and promise that our people would never really be gone from these Northlands? That our ways of life and nature should enrich this land forever? And now I talk to them only of Napoleon and George Washington."

Ah, Dawn, you have forgotten who you are.

As I sat on my bed, solemn, lost in thought, it seemed that the Snow Deer's voice echoed in my mind. "The Indians in the West are caged birds, moving about at the white man's command. These around you, free in villages and cities, are broken-hearted and dispirited. Rejected, they draw near to the only humans around them, the whites, who shun them like people with a filthy disease. Sadly they mimic the ways of this larger people, they turn from the past. Soon this Indian people will not even speak the Miami tongue."

I listened to the voice; it flowed through me like cold, refreshing spring water. Always before it had brought promises and commands.

"You are a healer. Now heal these Indian children left in your charge like fish about to die on the shore of time."

The next week I began to teach Indian ways some of the time each day. I clapped and sang songs and did dances. I told Logan's

story and the tales of great chiefs like Little Turtle, legends of both
Miamis and Potawatomi, the tale of Son of the West Wind, the
story of how the corn spirit came to us all. I did cattail mat work
and beadwork and even some quill work.

"It is not much," I said to myself or to the Snow Deer if he
might be around, "but it is something. If I, and a few others like
me, keep the campfire alive, someone else as I pass from the
scene may see the embers glow and blow and fan and keep it yet
alive. This beautiful race who lived in the lands of rivers and
woods must live to tell their stories to all for the time to come.
Here, in this old Northwest, where they lived. We are a trickle in
the stream of time, but we are part of the rich stream from which
all men drink. I shall do the little that I can."


Time passed. Little White Deer stayed at the school. Once or
twice he wrote to me to bring up Indian herbs to cure him; white
man's medicines could not heal him. I took up my herbs and he
got well.

In Peru things went on as usual. The Elks Club met, but not
with us in it. Mrs. Stensdalhl had her English tea party in back of
her picket fence on Sixth Street, but none of us went. Mrs.
Mobley ran off with a horse doctor from Texas who wore flashy
jewelry, leaving her husband and two children, but none of us
knew it until we read it on the front page of the *Miami County
Sentinel*.

We read in the *Miami County Sentinel* that a Southern senator
beat a Northern one senseless in the Senate of the United States
over whether white men could hold black ones slaves. We read of
the bloodshed in Kansas over whether they would become a slave
state or not.

"Do not worry or care about these white men's quarrels. We
have enough problems of our own," the children of chief Godfroy
and Richardville and Frances Slocum said. Miamis did not concern themselves about the politics of the time. They could not
afford to.


Little White Deer returned from the academy, knowing fine

farming skills and algebra and American history. He was ready to be a teacher himself. He read a letter from the *Miami County Sentinel* to me. It was about how the South had decided it would not tolerate Abraham Lincoln as President, that it would form its own nation.

"War is coming," he said.

"We do not care," I told him. I said it because it was in my heart and also because I heard it all around me, from Meshingomesia's reservation and from the Slocum and Godfroy and Richardville relatives and all the rest.

I said further, "Care about the grandsons of the destroyers at Tippecanoe? The people who marched the Potawatomi west and forced the Cherokee out on the Trail of Tears? Who have cheated already on the treaties they signed ten years ago? All are equally bad. Let them slaughter each other." I thought of the militia pushing me into the group, my husband with his neck cut almost through. "Let them rot from shore to shore, over the farmlands they took from us. Over whether they shall deny a whole race its freedom. They denied us freedom in a different way. Let them rot, I say!"

"And so they will, I think," Little White Deer said softly. "It seems a shame."

I was outraged. "Shame! Were not Pickaway and Fallen Timbers shames?"

"A shame, nevertheless, for this land we all must live in, America."

"What did they teach you in that school?"

"To be Indian in my heart, American in my citizenship. Yes, American—I see your anger. Mother, I must live the life God gave me to lead. We all must, in this land, and do it together, too." The lamps in our little house flickered oddly. They needed trimming.

He read more to me each evening while we ate our supper, with the lamps lit and the cloth on our table. He read that efforts to get the Southern states to come back to the council table had failed. He read that General Scott was making preparations to defend Washington city. He read that new President Abraham Lincoln spoke at his inauguration saying he had no designs on slavery where it was already established, but that the Constitution would prevail. Then my son read that the South had a good army already raised, and the *Miami County Sentinel* was urging people to find arms and prepare to defend the nation.

The last time he read was a fair day in April, when trees were putting out light green seeds and dogwood were unfolding their cups in the woodlands. I was weary from talking to the county officers about my school for the next year, weary of hearing the talk of the white man's war on every corner in Peru.

"Sumter, the Northern fort, has been fired on in Charleston Harbor," Little White Deer said.

I sighed but did not answer and got up and left him alone.

When I returned in a while he was still sitting at the table. His face was in shadows.

"Mother, I am going to the war," he said.

"And so you are," I answered, hearing my voice as if it came from a fog. I suddenly felt I needed to sit down.

"Oh, not with the Miami County company that is forming. I have had enough taunting in the streets of this town when I go to get ice cream. No, I shall go to the southern part of the state. To where my grandfather lived and worked. By the White and Wabash rivers, is it not?"

I nodded numbly.

"And his father, Daniel McClure."

I could not even nod at that.

"The cause is just, as my uncle The Catfish once said. You above all should know what the freedom of man is."

"I do."

"I cannot stand by. I do not know why."

Because you are the vision child of the White Deer, whose eyes shone with pain and compassion for all the distressed of the world, you cannot stand by and see a brother in pain, I thought, but I did not say it.

I could not speak, I could not cry.

But I could work. I went to put wood in the cookstove. My son would need meat and bread for the trail.

He wished to leave that very next morning, to take the road south.

When it was time to put out the lights and go to our beds, I took the cross of Mulberry Blossom and put it about his neck.


"My name is Walter McClure. White Deer—Walter—it is close enough," he said, looking gently into my eyes.

And so my son went to war, on the road to Indianapolis and directly south.

But oh, Trail to the Stars, how many bends you have, how much you ask of mothers!

# Chapter Twenty-four

# The McClure Papers

To: John Robert Scott, Old Fort Knox, Vincennes, Indiana
From: Jacob Joe Scott, Richmond, Indiana

April 20, 1861

Dear Pa:

I closed down my little schoolhouse out here in the sleepy hills today and went back to my college, Earlham, where I learned so much in the two years, much of it not in books of Euclidian geometry. It is my pleasure to write to thee to tell of the furor over the start of civil war.

The college is torn with the alarums of battle. Most of my old friends and teachers walk about, reminding each other that our duty as Friends for over 200 years dictates exactly how we should feel about the firing on the Federal fort. The Quakers' call has been for reconciliation since we first set foot on these American shores. We must preach and stand for non-combatancy. Have nothing to do with this system. Do not enlist.

But what if a draft should come? Many will get a paper to exempt them from the war. Or they may be able to "pay out" should a general draft come. " 'Tis a Christian's duty," they say to pay the fine and not go. If they do pay the fine, or get the certificate, they worry about being dragged off and abused, as other Quakers were in the War of 1812. Not many of us think that will happen. These are more enlightened times.

Others say we should not go even that far with a government which forces war on its citizens. We should simply ignore the draft and go to jail.

Then there are the abolitionists among the Friends here. Thee knowest some of them well, Father, since thy days with Simon's Net, though thee hasn't been active in the underground railroad for ten years now. Some arguments, and even faces, thee would recognize.

"Above all else in this war is the duty to free those in bondage. If this is what the conflict is about, we should fight." So say the abolitionist Quakers.

If this is what the conflict is about—Father, what is the conflict about?

Around Vincennes no one talks about freeing the slaves. Preserve the Union is everything. Well and good, I say, but I know as well as I know a crabapple from a rubber ball what the real thorn in the side of America is. No matter what my McClure cousins say, it is that dreaded institution of slavery.

Thee knows I promised my mother on her deathbed that I would not go to war should that dreaded necessity come. But should Abraham Lincoln free those very slaves we speak of, should he risk the ire of the Democrats and free the slaves, I should consider going to war to make the deed stick. There is no indication that things would ever reach that point.

Having given my promise to Mother, I shall wait a year and see how the war goes on. Then I shall decide on the only basis she would have wanted me to—my conscience before God.

I hear my cousins John McClure and Henderson Simpson are preparing to enlist. God speed to them.

Pa, thee has not spoken to me of Zach in any recent letters. It throws a shadow across the page for me to think of him at this moment. While brave boys from our neighborhood are marching to the colors, he is meeting in the Dugger barn, waving those warped crosses, signing articles of hatred, pledging to defy the government—Knights of the Golden Circle. Of Hell, I say.

There is a debate tonight in the assembly hall, ice cream made from ice house ice to follow.

Your son
Jacob Joe McClure

To: Catherine McClure Hogue, Vincennes, Indiana
From: John McClure, Vincennes, Indiana

April 25, 1861

Grandma:

In haste I send this to you. Aunt Jewell has turned green as a gord. Tomorrow we head for Rendeevoo Camp.

Grandmother, we are a gonna see the elephant. And also get JEFF DAVIS'S SCALP. The troops from Martin County, they are a callin them the Martin Guards, are organized, too. They voted in Miz Poore's Grandson, Lewis Brooks as Captain and her other grandson Will Houghton as Lieutenant.

We are G Company of Knox County, for G-Hossaphat G-Go and beat the Rebels black and blue. We will get back in three months, so they say. We are a three months regiment and can come home as soon as that's over or we get to Richmond, which will probably be soon. There are only whinin cowarts and poor white trash among the Rebels.

I know you must a heard of the doins in Vincennes and all the towns in Indiana. The bonfires, the speeches, then everybody and his nephew signs the roll.

I caint get enough of it. After the Vincennes rally where we joined, Henderson and I went down to Evansville. We found the folks there millin about and the Crescent City Band a playin Hail Columbia fit to be tied. We all followed the band into the market house where Mr. Conrad Baker (I think he's some sort of relative o ourn) spoke on "Treason, Heinous vipers nipping at the heels of the Republic." Something like that.

Here comes the good (or bad) part, at least for the McClures.

Zach Scott, Archie McClure III and Calhoun Dugger were in the balcony of the hall and hooted and hollered things like "States rights," and "Don't tread on us," and "Black Republicans," until Mr. Baker had to stop the meeting and have 'em carried out.

After these traitors were booted out, Mr. Conrad Baker made us all stand and he thought up a oath for all to take. We put our hands over our hearts and pledged ourselves to the Constitution, the flag and the United States of America forever. We hip-hip-hoorayed for ten straight minutes. Then The Crescent City Guard come forward and signed their papers right there and then. They are the Evansville company and will be going with us. Think! All from southern Indiana going together.

You and Uncle John Robert are always talking about the Revolutionary soldiers—your Pa's. You took us to see Upper Indiana where they are all buried, Great-grandpas Dan'l and George and all the Emisons and Bairds and Mr. Samuel Thompson, who all fought with Clark. Now, jest think, I and Tommy Thompson and Ralph Emison and some of the Baird relations, and lots of us McClure cousins are all a going together to this war, like the grandfathers did.

Grandma—we leave day after tomorrow for Terre Haute where the Governor will tell us how many companies he needs to go right away to Virginia. Seems like Washington city is in danger. We are just the boys to save it—the Young Americans from the old Beech Woods! So we call ourselves.

Point is I don't have time to say goodbye to you, Grandma. Could you come in tomorrow to see our train off at 10 o'clock? Please Grandma. Try and be there. You are all I have. Don't tell Aunt Jewell I said so.

We are goin for GLORY!

Your grandson
John McClure

To: John McClure
From: Catherine McClure Hogue
(never sent)

April 25, 1861


Dear Grandson John:

NO, no, I will NOT come to see you go off for what is going to be the end of the world for me. I am reading all about it today in the *Vincennes Western Sun*—Mrs. Stafford sewing the flag, Baptist Women's Club making donuts, everyone carrying old muskets.

I've been through it all before, for the good God's sake! I'm an old woman, seventy-four years old. When the troops came back from the Revolution, I wasn't born, but I can remember all the talk about Clark's army. They chewed over it all till the moon went down, talking all about the huzza-ing and back-slapping around the Ohio River campfires and the way the Indians ran as they shot into the woods. But then there would be a silence and their eyes would cloud while the fire hissed and popped and one of them would say, "McMurtry had his thigh bone smashed in the Ohio and they had to drag him onto shore. He screamed awful—"

Or—"After the Battle we put the dead in the Indian cabins and burnt the cabins over them. The smell—" "Clark's cousin was an Indian captive and tried to get away but he was shot."

"So many died of infected wounds in that heat. I can still hear them crying like babies on the litters, out of their heads. Nothing we could do."

Glory, you say!

Now and then, in our house in the still of the night my pa would raise the hair on our heads shouting in a banshee voice, "My God they are coming from the woods. Re-load! Re-load!"

I myself stood with my girl cousins as our boys went to Tippecanoe. Tall and handsome, they were as they left that bright September day when the world was in its childhood. Then I watched them trickle back in, walking on crutches, the blood soaking the stumps of amputated limbs. One boy I had taught in school who had an awful wound threw up right at the side of the road, then fainted.

Burrill Stonecipher of the Parke Dragoons took to the woods

after that. He never would come in. Built him a shack and made his son Tyge go out with him, snow and sleet and all. He had a stove out there. Only explanation he gave was "Life ain't the same after a war."

Glory, is it?

I could go on. The miserable skeletons who found the way back from Canada after Tecumseh was killed—a woman I saw screaming, "My baby, my child," over a new grave with a flag on it in Upper Indiana Cemetery, the Delaware going west on their ponies as silent as a ghost-train.

And I have not even felt war first hand.

Till now. Blood of my blood, John McClure, I lost my own daughter, Nancy Jane, in the early part of this war against owning men. She died a victim of the war that is coming, as sure as the first man to be killed for Lincoln.

She never saw you grow up to be a fine young man. I have had to fight for you myself, and now I am to lose you.

You go to throw yourself upon this bloody altar we seem to keep rearing to some horrid god. I need you, John, for the years I have of life. So few, so few.

No! No! My heart cries and hurts as if someone is wringing it out like a dishrag. The only glory here is the glory of ghastly wounds, fractured lives and weeping women. And an early grave with the rest of the kinfolk up the road there at the cemetery.

And if that is glory, I say the word is a mockery.

Grandma Catherine


Letter actually sent to: John McClure, Vincennes, Indiana
From Catherine McClure Hogue, Vincennes, Indiana
April 25, 1861


Dear Grandson:

Yes, I will be there. I enclose a copy of *Pilgrim's Progress* which came over from Ireland and ended up in our attic along with Grandmother Jane's dusty old wool wheel. Take the book with you on your progress through an unknown land. Since I may not get to tell you at the station, and your aunt will give you plenty of Christian advice, I send some practical words of wisdom with you given me by my father and all my McClure uncles. "Do the best you can and things will generally turn out better than you think."

Grandmother Catherine

## The Poore Papers
## The Secret Diary of Harriet Poore Houghton
## (Continued)

April 25, 1861
My worst fears are realized. This letter has come:
On Recruiting duty for the Martin Guards

Mother:

I shall be leaving tomorrow night. C Company of Martin County has almost 100 men.

My dearest Mother, I wish to be part of the Campbellite Disciples of Christ church before I go on this lonely journey to I know not where. I ask you to come be with me when I am baptized. We will be immersed tomorrow at 5 p.m. in White River at Hindostan. Then I go to join the regiment. I pray you will be with me on this most important day of my life.

Your son,<br>Will Houghton

My God. I am torn like a silk scarf in a strong wind. My mouth is dry. I cannot speak. My secret: I wish to be baptized, too, to become a Campbellite Christian with my son. There, I have said it. Somehow it gives me strength.

But how to execute this so-yearned-for deed? I cannot leave this yard. To Hindostan Falls! That place of rotting cabin beams and blackened fireplace hearths, of overgrown paths and iron rusting in weeds. Not even the farm people go to the mill there happily. The very stones seem to moan the awful tales of the past.

It so much reminds me of shed, a path through swampy land in another time.

And yet even there I would go to be with my son, to go in the baptizing waters myself. To be clean.

Somehow, I know not how—

For several days now, as this war hysteria rages and I must face Will's leaving, I have felt my own release is near, just beyond this window, just as you feel the fresh air rise to meet you and dark seem to retreat just before dawn, even though the sky is yet black. I cannot almost touch freedom. My poem has lain unfinished these months. If I can finish it—I will put pen to paper and see.

I will call it July, 1828

*Since—*
*That day, I have not gone out.*
*Since—*

*Raw summer tempest wind buffets*
*Harsh and bare, the cider mill among the oaks.*
*Unfinished. On the floor odd machinery, huge wood*
*screws flung like cast-off toys on the dirt. Sister plays*
*outside, unknowing.*
*The Indian stands tall, his eyes glazed*
*The fire in them a flash.*
*Memories of other fires crowd on the child.*
*Kind man and woman, second mother, father really*
*Told tales of gods and heroes, nature's kin*
*Drums beat, skies opened, Nature's secrets poured out*
*before her eyes*
*As firelight licked the corners of the Indian hut.*

*And other fires: the fires of Mama's hearth*
*The night before, the apples, the Indian's jesting bright,*
    *yet just a little off*
*Played on an out-of-tune piano.*
*The light now in that cider shack is not as those before*
*For it is frightened and frightening.*
*In the Indian's eyes desperation, rage*
*At manhood defiled. Madness—*


I cannot go on. I cannot look further within that darkened glass. But William, my son, will you give yourself to God, leave for war without me? My love for you is strong. Stronger than fear. Stronger than the past. I must go on.


*His mad eyes fall on the child. His face is hard, tortured.*
*Sister flees. He wails unearthly wails.*
*All Indian graves are opened East to West and spirits cry.*
*The child slinks to the corner, covering small, new breasts*
    *with her arms.*
*His eyes fix on her but do not see.*
*The wind screams wild, branches claw at clapboards. He*
    *runs outside the door,*
*Uncovers his manhood, rips out a knife, rumples the*
    *child's dress,*
*The child cries out, no sound escapes. Log walls close*
    *in—*
*He drops the knife, takes up a strap and mounts the cider*
    *barrel*
*Walls push close with cruel arms, flail at the child*
*Wind shieks high a chant of death.*
*Death.*

No more. It is out.


All that is behind the frightened eyes in the mirror can come forth into the light of day. 1 p.m. I have asked my dear husband

John to walk out the gate with me. To the corner. He has done so. I thought I would faint and my knees did buckle, but I got there. Then I wanted to go one more block, to the store. 2 p.m. I have asked John to harness the buggy. We have to go now to Hindostan Falls.

## The Account of Thomas Jefferson Brooks
## (Continued)

I saw some of the oddest things I ever saw the day before the Martin County Boys went to the War of the Rebellion. Down by the river, at the ghost town of my youth, Hindostan Falls, the Reverend Pomeroy was dipping people into White River. My sister-in-law, her hand held by my wife Susan, went down to the waters. Walking into the shallow edge, struggling with mud and sand, Harriet Houghton gave her hand to the Reverend and he swooped her backwards. She came up a dripping and happy Cambellite Christian, Disciples of Christ persuasion.

Then her son Will Houghton, who is the new lieutenant of C company where so many of the Mt. Pleasant and Loogootee boys will serve, was also dunked. He came up shaking like a wet dog. His mother clasped him to her heart and cried in the loudest voice I've ever heard her use, "You have given yourself to the Lord. I give you to your country." I heard the minister say it was time that we had the baptising at Hindostan Falls, that we should stop thinking of it as a ghost town and let its memories and people rest. He said Hindostan was clean now and all of us and our sons and the strength of our state were living testaments that the town had not lived and died in vain.

Susan says Harriet has left her house now, through a miracle. Maybe it was a miracle, but I always believed, myself, that Harriet would come out of that house if there was something she wanted to do badly enough outside.

I saw many other odd things those next few days, as the Civil War smoldered into flame. Indiana was preparing in force to send Lincoln help. I saw a band lead men down the street into a recruiting office. I saw a young sluggard who could never have been driven to a plow, strutting about in his father's old Mexican War uniform, followed by a group of adoring females. I saw a train roll into Loogootee puffing out U.S.A. in telegraphic signals.

I saw an Indian who had hitched rides on wagons all the way from Peru come into town to join the Union Army. His name, of all things, was Walter McClure, and he came to help free the slaves, he said. Well if he did he was about the only one. Lewis gladly signed him into C company.

I saw bonfires and bombast and exhilaration and shouting and orating and in all of it hardly an ounce of common sense. Even Lewis was carried away by it all and began marching and drilling everyone from eight to eighty in Loogootee's main street to form a home guard, in case of Rebel attack, I suppose within the night.

The next morning we went by train to Vincennes, all of us, Susan, my children and their spouses and Grandmother Poore, John Houghton and Will, carrying little Hilary on his shoulders. Harriet did not go; yesterday at Hindostan Falls had been enough for her and she was on the setee with a cold compress on her forehead.

Tom and his wife and baby Lewie came too. Tom stood silently in Vincennes as the Martin County men hurried from the train to Main Street, where there was to be a southern Indiana sendoff for this first regiment from our territory to go to the Civil War. Oddly, across from us Mrs. Catherine Hogue stood next to that sour crabapple of a woman Jewell Simpson, the two of them still not speaking, although they elbowed each other to catch a glimpse of the McClure boy, John.

All the men from three counties stood silently, in ranks, with the old guns they had brought from home. A Mrs. Carrie Stallard gave them a flag sewed by the women of Vincennes. She read a speech:

"We believe the bravest and best blood will be poured out in defense of the flag under which our fathers, with George Washington as their leader, fought and won such glorious victories. Our heavenly Father was with them; he will be with you. Death to the traitors that would dare to trail that flag through the dust of shame!"

I looked about and saw all the faces, quiet, intent. Then I turned to look at Tom. There were tears forming in his eyes.

"Father, I should be with them."

"No," I said too quickly, feeling again the sudden fear that had clutched me when Lewis said he would go. "Little Lew is sickly and your wife not strong. You cannot leave. We all know that."

"I cannot bear thinking about my brother. Thinking he may be in danger, when I am here safe at home, not knowing if he is dead when I am alive and well."

"Lewis is strong. He will survive."

"How do you know?" he demanded.

Right away I said, "The Brookses are too cussed to die in a war." I had answered casually, but it was a good question, because ultimately this was not a matter of hoopla and marching bands, and home in three months with battle ribbons on the chest. I knew different. My own father had witnessed the first battle of the Revolutionary War as a boy of twelve, and he had dragged himself home, an emaciated, worn-out man from one of the final battles. Wars had ways of eating up the good years of man's life.

Suddenly I felt the shadow of the burial pits of Concord falling over this bright day. As Mrs. Carrie Stallard carried on her speech, as the congressman spoke and presented his cheese and bread for the trip north, as young men I knew and loved sweated in the early May heat, and licked their lips and shifted their weight from foot to foot, I suddenly stood again at those graves of the Pilgrim Brookses.

Truly, oddly, it was as if I was there and I seemed to hear Father speaking of life and death. I saw myself kicking at the bones, hating the death that stole them off after their sacrifices to live free. But then I raised my eyes and saw something else that was there too in that long-ago scene. I saw the house in back of the cairns when I visited at a later time, owned by some Brooks even to this day. Some of the family had survived, several in fact, to build that house. Not all had died in the awful times. Weren't we here too?

I had always looked at the death grounds, the cemeteries when I should have been looking at the living that was going on around me. Now we would all have to cling to survival, Susan, I, Lewis, Tom, should he go as he wanted to (God, prevent it!). Survival, through Yankee sharpness, cussedness, whatever it took was what was called for. The Brookses had done it before, they could do it again. And as for the question of immortality, which Father and I had so earnestly wrestled with there in New England, it would have to wait. It was living for my sons I had to be concerned about today.

If God willed. The words came into my mind without my calling them forth. I stood stock still, realizing the terrible stakes in this game we were all so willingly undertaking, and for the first time in my life, I prayed.

"God, if you are there, help my boys survive this war. And help the land I love survive, too. Someway, God of my fathers. The land we all love must survive."

## The Poore Papers

## Hannah Poore's Journal

April 26, 1861

This day I did watch go to the wars those I much love, Grandsons Lewis and Will and friend John McClure and many others I have known and cared about from the time they were children. And though they did not then think of me, other things being on their minds, I did think of them and all the young men like them across the land, and this is the letter I wrote in my mind:

Dear Abraham Lincoln:

I was born in the year the War for Independence drew to a close. My childhood in the little New England town where I grew up was bright with the promises that war had won, the dream my own kinsmen died to win: individual opportunity in a land of freedom, newly united as a nation.

My husband felt the promise of the dream and together with our children we left the land of our fathers since the 1630's. We came to seek the dream anew in the Northwest.

Tens of thousands of us, your own ancestors also, poured in, a tide of hope. We grubbed and coaxed and forced the dream from these virgin fields and forests. My husband died, but we, a generation of pioneers, went on singing our glad, exultant song:

"It works. The dream of opportunity in a free land works. I can send my children to school, I built a church here. I can grow and sell my crops and build a good house! No one tells me what to do. The dream of freedom works!"

The old Northwest, these middle states! What greatness now springs from this middle west as these our children reap the harvest we have sown, in character, industry, and fine true hearts. Finally, from the soil of this Northwest has risen a race of young men as giants of the earth. Nurtured by peace they are, and their small schools and decent communities, formed by hard work and simple values and the love of God and their parents' pride of effort. And instructed by the land, the brown rich, rejuvenating soil of this heartland.

Mrs. Stallard at the Vincennes station said these young men were the bravest and best, and well she spoke, I think. I am moved by them, by the homes they leave. Across all this heartland tonight they rise, a solid tribute to the dream of freedom in one, united nation that the Revolution bought. The dream, struggled for in so many ways by all of us before them, is tested! These young men will not let it die. Never, I think, has such a sacrifice been made on such an altar.

Value it, Mr. President. Take care of these boys, Abraham Lincoln.